by Jason Finigan

THE MIXED-ENASSI NOVELS
Destiny's Edge
The Enemy Within

THE ENEMY WITHIN

JASON FINIGAN

Peregrine
A Peregrine Book

THE ENEMY WITHIN

Cover art by Jana Pivkova.

Edited by Darryl Roberts.

ISBN: 978-0-9866951-5-5

ONE

"Captain Cael, please report to the bridge."

Captain Cael Navek, of the Caitaran Explorer ship Cetani, put the data pad he was reading down and pressed the intercom switch on his desk.

"This is Cael, what's the problem, Commander?"

"Sir, we're receiving a transmission from the probe located on E4Y-307, as well as an emergency transponder signal," Diela Kital, his first officer, informed him.

"E4Y-307," Cael echoed thoughtfully. "Isn't that the world Captain Kel and his team were sent to investigate?"

"That's correct, sir. The Lekur's last transmission had them entering the sector, but we've heard nothing from them since. High command has listed the Lekur as officially missing."

"Very well. I assume the transmission is encrypted?"

"Yes, sir."

Cael sighed and stood up from behind his desk.

"Have communications begin work on decrypting the message right away, Commander. I'm on my way."

1

"Aye, Captain," Diela said before the intercom went dead.

"What the hell have you gotten yourself into this time, Kel?" Cael muttered to himself as he reached for his uniform jacket hanging from the back of his chair.

Stepping out from his ready-room and onto the Cetani's bridge, Cael made his way down from the command dais to the communications centre where Diela was hovering behind the young lieutenant manning the com.

"What have you got for me, Diela?" he asked.

"It's definitely a message from Captain Kel, sir," she answered, straightening her posture and turning to meet him. "We've only managed to decrypt a portion of the message so far though."

"Enough to determine what the hell happened to them and why it's taken them so long to report in?"

"Yes, sir," Diela nodded, "Apparently, the Lekur was shot down while entering orbit around the planet."

"Shot down!" Cael echoed loudly, his tail beginning to flick from side to side slowly with alarm. "By whom?"

"By a race called the T'kri, sir. Captain Kel and the surviving members of his crew are in hiding with second group of aliens, and they're requesting our immediate assistance."

"Natives?" Cael asked.

"No, sir, they're apparently colonists, a species new to us called humans."

"Tell me about these T'kri," Cael prompted.

"They're a reptilian race, violent, and apparently sexless, neither male nor female. They have a pretty substantial presence on Alessi—"

"Alessi?" echoed Cael, interrupting her in mid report.

"Sorry, sir, that's the name the colonists have given the

planet."

"I see," Cael said, and indicated for her to continue.

"The T'kri have one major base, Ru'kayesh, and several domed garrisons, one in each of the six colony towns."

"Has Kel provided us with the locations of these installations?"

"He has, sir," Diela confirmed.

"What about these colonists, what are they like?"

"They're like us, in that they're an upright, bilateral species, but they have little to no fur except on their heads. Kel reports that one of them is even a telepath."

Cael's eyes narrowed slightly at this.

"So they have telepaths," he said.

"Apparently so, sir. It seems that one of Kel's crew, a telepath by the name of Kiyel, has formed a telepathic bond with one of the male colonists."

Cael frowned, his ears flicking briefly.

"Anything else?" he asked.

"Not yet, sir," she said, shaking her head. "We'll know more once we've decrypted the rest of the message."

"Very well. Get me a secure line to the Taigana, and then patch it through to my ready-room; I want to speak with Admiral Chuul right away," Cael ordered.

"Aye, sir."

No sooner had Cael returned to his ready-room and sat down than the com screen on his desk began signalling an incoming message. Activating the unit, he watched as the Alliance insignia disappeared from the screen and was replaced by a severe-looking and dishevelled Caitaran female in her nightclothes.

"Admiral," Cael said, his ears dipping slightly, out of respect for the other's superior rank.

"You'd better have a very good reason for contacting me this early in the morning, Captain," Admiral Chuul said sternly.

"I'm sorry for waking you, Admiral, but I thought you should know that we've just received a message from Captain Kel of the Lekur," Cael said. "He reports that they were shot down in an unprovoked attack by a race called the T'kri just as they were entering orbit around E4Y-307. He's requesting immediate assistance."

"They were what?" Chuul exclaimed loudly as she almost shot up from the chair she was sitting in, an alarmed look crossing her face.

"My crew is still in the process of decrypting the message, so we should have more information about Kel's situation soon."

"You were right to contact me, Captain. How long do you estimate it'll take before your crew has finished decrypting the message?"

"We should have it ready within the hour, Admiral."

"Excellent," Chuul said, nodding her head slightly in approval. "Contact me as soon as it's done. In the meantime, recall any remaining survey teams you still have out there and set a course for the planet immediately. The Taigana will rendezvous with you there to deal with these T'kri. Chuul out."

Jev and Kiyel sat battered and exhausted under the naturally-formed vine shelter deep within the forest; the same shelter they had used before to evade detection by the T'kri. Hours earlier, after having successfully sent a message to the Cetani, a Caitaran Explorer-class starship that was waiting for them in deep space, they, along with Mikkel, Jev's brother, Janice, a former member of the rebels, and what remained of the Caitaran crew of the scout ship Lekur, were forced to flee the burning wreckage of the T'kri shuttle which they had stolen while fleeing the T'kri.

Jev's head had just fallen onto Kiyel's shoulder when all of a sudden, a long, piercing scream rang out in their minds, causing them both to cry out in pain and sit up with a start. Instinctively they pressed their hands up tightly against their ears in an effort to block out the sound. But it didn't do any good and the horrible screaming continued.

Upon hearing Jev's and Kiyel's sudden cries and completely oblivious to the screams that now assailed the two telepaths, the others leaped to their feet with alarm.

"Oh God, we've got to go," Jev cried out, his eyes widening with horror just as some of the most disturbing images he had ever seen began flooding his mind, and he quickly, but unsteadily, rose to his feet.

"What?" a startled and confused Captain Kel asked. "Go where?"

"Clearhaven, Captain. We need to get to Clearhaven right away!" Jev said, visibly straining against the scream and the images that still continued to assail his mind. He was almost in tears.

"What is it, Jev, what do the two of you see?" Tiela asked, concerned by the level of panic that was being conveyed through Jev's strained voice.

"I... I can't..." Jev said, shaking his head as strained tears began rolling down his cheeks, his voice taut with pain. "Kiyel and I have to get to Clearhaven, right now. There's so little time."

"Kiyel?" Kel asked, confused and uncertain.

"Captain, if what we're seeing is happening now, then we may already be too late to save him," Kiyel answered.

"Too late to save who?" Kel asked, his confusion quickly

beginning to give way to frustration, and it showed by the way his tail was flicking back and forth behind him.

"Sir, please, Jev and I really do need to go, now! We'll rendezvous with you later, back at the caves," Kiyel pleaded.

Kel saw the desperate urgency that was in Kiyel's eyes, and he reluctantly nodded his head.

"Very well, Kiyel," he said. "I don't like this one bit, however, and Jev doesn't look to be in any condition to be travelling right now."

"We'll manage, Captain. We have to," Kiyel said, as he and Jev quickly dropped to all fours.

Then, without another word, they sped off into the forest.

Jev could feel the adrenaline pumping through his system, filling him with energy he desperately needed, as he and Kiyel raced through the forest. The scream they both had heard and felt only a few minutes earlier had suddenly stopped, as had the images, but the pull on them from Clearhaven continued to grow steadily stronger. It made them push themselves harder, to run even faster.

We have to get there, Kiyel, Jev sent, leaping over a fallen log.

We will, Jev. I just can't believe what we saw, Kiyel told him.

I can't either, even though I know human history and what some people are capable of.

Seconds later, they erupted from the edge of the forest and sped across the open field towards Clearhaven. It took them only seconds to reach the town.

Their sudden appearance in the crowded streets predictably caused the townsfolk to quickly scatter into their homes and businesses, some of them screaming in terror. There was nothing Jev or Kiyel could do to avoid this though, and paid them no mind as they instead continued making their way through the streets, in a desperate effort to reach the source of the scream they had heard.

Suddenly, Jev skidded to a halt before one of Clearhaven's pre-manufactured homes which was in a rather obscure part of town, away from the main streets.

This is it, he sent.

Are you certain? Kiyel asked.

Definitely, I can feel him inside. Something isn't quite right, though.

Standing up, Jev threw himself against the flimsy wooden door, breaking the latch and causing the door to fly open on its hinges. Together he and Kiyel then stormed into the home and quickly scanned the room.

I can hear something in the back room, Kiyel sent as he got to his feet.

Quickly, but quietly, they made their way to the back of the home until they stood before another closed door at the end of a short hall. On the other side of that door they could hear the unmistakable wailing cry of a child and the sound of someone repeatedly being slapped.

They burst through the door into the next room, practically disintegrating the door into tiny fragments, as they did so, and they suddenly came face to face with a scene that made Jev's stomach lurch with disgust, for on a bed along the far wall of the room, lay a small naked and bleeding boy that could not have been more than three years old, by Jev's estimation, who was broadcasting his intense pain and fear as he wailed and struggled beneath a dirty, naked and somewhat obese man straddling the boy's torso.

The scene in front of them left no doubt in either of their minds that this man had been brutally raping the child. Staring at the man with disgust and revulsion, a fiery rage quickly built up within them both, as they seized his mind, discovering that he was, in fact, the child's own father, and learned all the unimaginable horrors that he had done to his son. With tails lashing violently from side to side, and with teeth bared in a deep-throated growl, they slowly began advancing toward him.

The man screamed and fouled himself, while staring in sheer terror at the two angry Caitarans now bearing down on him. Then, faster than either Jev or Kiyel thought possible, the man climbed off his son and started backing away from the bed. It was then that Jev clearly saw that the man's son was actually tied down to the bed by his wrists. That fact was not lost on Kiyel, who, with a vicious, angry snarl, launched himself at the man and slammed him viciously up against the wall. The man's terrified screams echoed throughout the room as he quickly found himself being lifted up off the ground by sharp claws, embedded in his neck.

Get that filthy piece of garbage out of here, Kiyel. I'll see to the child, Jev sent.

I'll show this... 'person'... the error of his ways, Enassi, he sent, sneering contemptuously at the man, and none too gently, carried the still screaming and struggling man out of the room.

Jev cautiously made his way towards the side of the bed and looked down at the child, whose wide, frightened eyes followed his every move. But as soon as Jev reached down to undo the ropes that held the boy in place, the boy began to cry out in absolute terror, and struggled against them with all the strength he had in him. Jev tried calming him by sending soothing and reassuring thoughts, but the boy seemed unreachable, having gone feral with fear, and losing all contact with reality. Jev knew he had to act quickly, realizing that the boy's struggles would undoubtedly make his injuries even worse, so he extended his claws and quickly began slashing through the ropes, tearing them to tiny threads. As soon as the final rope had been cut though, the boy scrambled to get up off the bed and away from Jev. Jev's Caitaran instincts were quicker, however, and he quickly gathered up the kicking and screaming child into his arms, holding the boy firmly, but gently, against his chest. Jev jumped and gasped, as the youngster barely missed his most private parts, and he lifted the child up a little higher to avoid another such incident. Their struggle continued for several minutes more, until, finally, the boy's strength and stamina began to wane. Jev tried talking softly to the boy, doing his best to assure him that he was no longer in danger, but to little effect. Then he had an idea.

It's okay, little one, Jev sent soothingly to the boy, who suddenly stopped struggling altogether and looked up at him in awe. *No one's going to hurt you, I promise.*

Just then, Kiyel came back into the room, causing the little boy to jump in Jev's arms again. Kiyel's expression was grim.

Jev looked up at him. The father is he—

He's dead. I couldn't allow him to live; not after what he did to his own son, Kiyel sent. "How is the boy?" he asked aloud in Caitaran.

"He's hurt pretty badly, I'm afraid, Kiyel, and absolutely terrified," Jev replied. "Kiyel, he has a talent. That's what I sensed outside. It was his screams that we heard out in the forest."

"I know, I could feel it, too."

The boy, whose curiosity was apparently stronger than his fear, gently reached up with his hand to touch the side of Jev's face, and felt the soft, silky hair that covered it.

"Kitty!" the boy exclaimed suddenly.

"We can't stay here long, Enassi." Kiyel said. "The townsfolk have already seen us, and they're sure to investigate."

"What about the boy?" Jev asked.

"We can't leave him here with the colonists," Kiyel answered, shaking his head. "They're completely ill-equipped to deal with his talent and to heal his injuries. He'll have to come with us. There's simply no other choice."

"Big kitty," the boy said, with barely the beginnings of a smile forming on his lips.

"Yes, big kitty," Jev repeated in English, looking back at the boy.

"Daddy hurt me," the boy said.

"We know, little one. That's why we came here. He won't hurt you ever again. I promise," Jev answered.

"Kitties don't talk," the boy said softly.

"We do; we're a special kind of kitties," Jev replied, smiling at him, and being careful that none of his teeth were showing. The last thing he wanted to do was frighten the child any more than he already was. "What's your name?" he asked.

"Aiden."

"I'm Jev and that over there is Kiyel. We're going to get you out of here and get you all fixed up so you don't hurt any more, okay?"

Aiden nodded his head weakly.

"But what about my daddy?" he asked.

"Your dad won't be hurting you, or anyone else, ever again."

"Oh," Aiden said, almost in a whisper.

All of a sudden Jev felt him go slack in his arms. The boy's eyes had closed, and his breathing quickened, as did his heart rate.

"Jev, he's going into shock. He needs medical attention right away!" Kiyel said with alarm.

"But Tiela's much too far away," Jev answered, looking back up at Kiyel, with panic in his eyes.

"There's always Doc O'Riley," Kiyel suggested.

"You're right!" Jev said. "And his home isn't too far from here."

"Then let's get going. We can't wait any longer."

"Grab me that blanket over there, will you, Kiyel? We'll need it to keep him warm."

Kiyel did as Jev asked, quickly retrieving the blanket and wrapping both Jev and the boy up, before they all left the room, and then the home, together.

"Janette, I think we've got another problem," Tanis said, suddenly walking into her office and causing Janette to jump in her chair, with a start.

"Dammit, Tanis, don't scare me like that!" she gulped.

"Sorry, Janette, but there's something I definitely think you need to hear."

"Is it about that explosion we saw earlier?" she asked, peering over Tanis' shoulder and seeing a young man standing in the doorway.

"No," Tanis said, and he beckoned the young man to enter the office. "I've just been given some rather interesting news by Paul Goodman here, and I thought you should hear it directly from him," he said.

"Very well, Mr. Goodman, what is it that you have to report?" Janette asked.

Paul regarded her nervously for a moment before answering.

"First Councillor Pelletier, just a little while ago, me and several other townsfolk witnessed two forest cats, larger than any we've ever seen before, and wearing some kind of cloth, run straight into town."

"Hold on a minute, are you absolutely certain about this?" she asked incredulously.

"Yes, ma'am, I am," Paul answered.

"Incredible! That's now the second time a forest cat has been seen wandering into a town," she said, and looked over at Tanis.

"The one in Hillsforde," Tanis nodded.

"I wouldn't know anything about that, First Councillor," Paul said, "but I do know the cats were seen headed for a house at the far end of town, the one belonging to Luke Mills and his son, Aiden. It was almost as though they knew exactly where to go. A short time later, screams were heard from inside, and then the same two cats came running out of the house with what appeared to be a child wrapped up in a blanket."

Janette raised an eyebrow.

"Mr. Goodman, I'll grant you that it's plausible to think that two forest cats might suddenly attack one of our people. They are wild animals, after all, and known to be fiercely territorial. I'll even entertain the possibility that they'd suddenly wander into town in broad daylight where they could be seen by dozens of townsfolk. But to suggest that they'd actually have the wherewithal to actually kidnap a child is frankly just too incredible to be believed," she said.

"I know. I could barely believe it myself. Nevertheless, that's what happened. What was even more incredible, though, was that this time the cats weren't running on all fours like you'd expect. Instead, they were running on their hind legs."

"What?!" Janette exclaimed, jumping out of her seat.

"Tanis, did anyone go inside the house to check it out?" She asked.

"Yes. Two of our townsfolk found an adult male with his throat literally ripped open like he was mauled by a large animal. There was blood everywhere. In one of the back rooms was a bed with freshly cut ropes attached to it. There were some blood stains on the sheets as well. They were pretty shaken up by what they found in there."

"My God!" Janette exclaimed. "Who do we have in security?"

"Right now there's no one. Most of them are out investigating that explosion, and won't be back until tomorrow. The ones we have left are actually with Doctor Sam O'Riley, in Hillsforde, recovering from wounds they suffered at the hands of the T'kri."

"Great, just great," Janette said, with a sigh, as she sat back down in her chair.

"Umm, well. There was one other thing that I did notice," Paul said, speaking up.

"There's more?" Janette asked, looking up at him.

"I can't be certain," he said, "but I think they might have been heading towards Hillsforde, since that's the road they took when they left."

"Tanis I want you to get on the com to Doctor O'Riley, right away. If any of our security personal is able, I want them to attempt to capture those cats," she ordered. "Thank you, Mr. Goodman. Now, if the two of you will excuse me, I have some calls, of my own, to make."

"Right away, Janette," Tanis said, and with Paul, turned and left the room, closing the door after them.

* * *

Together Jev and Kiyel ran along the path Jev knew would take them to the town of Hillsforde and Doc O'Riley's house. On more than one occasion, they were forced to run past groups of colonists travelling along the same path, all of whom scattered in fear upon seeing them. They didn't stop, though, and kept on running, ignoring the colonists.

Already, Jev saw that Aiden's face was becoming paler, and his breathing had grown laboured as he took in only short, ragged breaths. Seeing this made Jev push himself harder, and he began to run faster, until finally, they crested the hill overlooking the town of Hillsforde, where they allowed themselves a moment to catch their breaths.

"We're just about there, Kiyel," Jev said. "I can just make out Sam's house."

"You know he's not exactly going to be thrilled to see us when we get there; not with us looking the way we do," Kiyel told him.

"I guess we're just going to have to risk using another illusion, then."

"Are you sure you're strong enough for that, though?" Kiyel asked.

"For this little guy, I must be," Jev answered.

"Tiela's really going to kill us," Kiyel muttered.

Jev just smiled a lopsided grin at him as they started down the hill.

It took them only a few minutes longer to reach Sam's home. It was a rather large house, being three stories tall, and located on the outskirts of town. Jev knew, from the times he visited the house in the past, that most of the space inside was actually reserved for patients recovering from injuries or illnesses, who were treated on the second and third floors. Sam, for the most part, lived on the main floor, but he did have a small office on the second floor which he used occasionally to sleep in when he had to be close to a patient.

"Are you ready, Enassi?" Kiyel asked, almost in a whispered voice when they approached the door.

"As ready as I'll ever be," Jev said.

He then closed his eyes and began carefully forming in his mind the image of himself as he appeared when he and Kiyel had first left Hillsforde. He felt the familiar tingling sensation, as Kiyel began sharing his energy with him through their link, giving him the extra strength and stamina he needed to complete the illusion. With the image fixed firmly in his mind, he sought out the minds of those within the home and began planting it deep into their sub-consciousness, thereby ensuring that they would see only his human self when they looked at him.

Opening his eyes again, he nodded his head to Kiyel, who quickly removed his uniform and tossed it behind some bushes next to the door before reverting back to his four-legged posture. Once again he looked just like the forest cat that Jev thought he had rescued on that fateful night.

Taking a deep breath, Jev then knocked briskly on the door.

They could hear footsteps inside, approaching the door, and moments later the lock disengaged and the door opened a notch. From the crack in the open door, Jev could see Sam's weary face peering out at him. Sam's expression went from curiosity, to wonder, to recognition to outright joy.

"Jev?" Sam said, suddenly throwing the door open wide. "Oh my God, lad, you're alive! I was afraid you'd died with your father, when the inn burned down! How... where've you been?"

"Hi, Doc," Jev said, with a genuinely happy smile. "Yeah, at the time the fire started, I'd gone out for a walk with Kiyel."

Sam looked down to see Kiyel standing there beside Jev.

"He's still with you then? Amazing," he said, obviously surprised to see him.

"Yeah, Doc, listen, can we please come inside, we've kind of got an emergency, here," Jev said, indicating the unconscious Aiden in his arms.

For the first time, Sam's eyes were drawn to the child in Jev's arms, and he frowned deeply.

"Of course," he said, as he stepped back, his tone suddenly serious. "You'd better come in."

TWO

Once they stepped inside, and stood in the main foyer, Sam closed the door behind them and gently and carefully retrieved Aiden from Jev's arms then led them through his living room down a hallway to a small examination room at the back of the house. It was sparsely furnished room, in which there was only a single exam table, and several cupboards, filled with medical supplies, above a long counter spanning the width of the room, at the end of which was a small round sink.

Sam gently placed Aiden down upon the exam table, and then began removing the blanket from the boy's bruised and battered body, which they all quickly saw was now covered in blood and sweat.

"Jesus!" Sam exclaimed loudly, gasping in shock at what he saw. "What the hell happened to him?" He looked up at Jev, who stood opposite the table next to Kiyel.

"It's a long story, Doc, and I promise, I'll explain it all to you later," Jev said. "But right now he needs your help. I'm afraid he's lost a lot of blood, and he's in shock. Is there anything you can do for him?"

"I don't know," Sam said, while he began going over the many cuts and bruises that covered Aiden's frail little body. "I need you to get me some towels and some warm water to clean off all this blood so I can see where he's hurt. You know where everything is. And get that cat out of the room, I don't want him anywhere near the child," he said.

"Kiyel isn't going to harm him, Doc," Jev said, as he reached into a cupboard and grabbed the towels. "In fact, he helped save Aiden's life."

"I wish I had your confidence in him, lad; he's still a wild animal, after all," Sam replied.

"He's no more a wild animal than I am," Jev said.

"That's what I mean," looking over at Jev, a wry grin stretching across his face.

"Very funny," Jev said, handing Sam the towels and walking over to the sink.

"Do you realize that I got a call from Tanis, Janette's personal assistant, about this boy?"

"No, I didn't. But I can't say that I'm surprised. Just be glad you didn't go into that home and see what we saw," Jev said, grabbing the large pot sitting on the shelf above the sink and filling it up with warm water, then bringing it over to Sam, who began cleaning the blood off Aiden's nude body.

As Sam worked, he began to get a better idea of the extent of Aiden's injuries, the most serious of which appeared to be centred mainly on his posterior. As he carefully lifted Aiden's legs, and saw the fresh blood slowly seeping out from his horribly raw and inflamed anus, he was forced to fight back a sudden urge to throw up. He took in several deep breaths until his stomach had finally calmed down.

Looking at the wound again, he knew that he needed to work quickly, as the boy was loosing too much blood.

"Jev, I need you to run and grab me two units of plasma from the duty nurse upstairs. Tell her to give you a vial of antibiotics, also, and hurry!" he ordered.

Without hesitation, Jev did as Sam instructed and quickly hurried out of the room, returning several minutes later with two plastic IV bags and a small glass bottle.

Sam, who, in the mean time, had begun working on Aiden's injuries, saw Jev return, and indicated for him to put the plasma and the antibiotics on the counter behind him.

"Your nurse asked if you needed her help," Jev said, as he put them down.

"I assume by her absence that you told her I didn't?" Sam asked.

"I didn't think she'd appreciate seeing Kiyel here," Jev told him as he looked down at Kiyel. In his mind, he could hear Kiyel laughing.

With a smile and a shake of his head, Sam readied an IV for Aiden after getting out an angiocatheter and a sealed packet of IV tubing from a drawer below the counter behind him, and then had Jev help him gently turn the boy over onto his side. From one of the upper cabinets, Sam readied a mild sedative which he promptly injected into a vein in Aiden's arm, with a syringe.

"Alright, Jev, I need to have both you and Kiyel step outside, while I get to work."

"But—"

"But nothing, Jev," Sam said, cutting him off in mid-sentence. "The risk of infection to Aiden is too great for either of you to be in here while I work."

Nodding his head reluctantly to Kiyel, they walked out of the room together. Jev looked back at Aiden on the table one last time before sighing and closing the door behind them.

Waiting out in the hall, for Sam to complete the operation on Aiden, was sheer agony for Jev. He began pacing back and forth. At least twice, he found himself reaching for the door handle, to see what was taking so long, but then he remembered Sam's warning about the risk of infection, and he thought better of it, and instead he continued to pace the hall. Kiyel, meanwhile, lay quietly by the door to the exam room, his tail flicking occasionally while he waited with Jev for word on Aiden's condition.

After about two hours, Sam still had not finished with Aiden. Jev was beginning to get more and more worried, when all of a sudden, the door finally opened, and an exhausted looking Sam stepped out of the room and into the hallway.

"Well, that's as good as I can do for him right now I'm afraid," Sam said.

"Will he be okay?" Jev asked.

"That's yet to be seen. I've managed to stitch up the tear in his rectum and stop the bleeding, but it was torn up pretty badly. I can't guarantee that an infection hasn't already set in. Even though I've given him a strong dose of antibiotics, it might not be enough."

From beside him, Jev could hear Kiyel sigh with relief.

"Now," Sam continued, "while Aiden is resting and his body is recovering from the surgery, let's go into the living room, so you can tell me exactly what happened to this boy and who the sorry son of a bitch is that raped him."

"Okay," Jev said, cringing slightly at the sudden wave of

anger he felt coming from Sam.

Sam led Jev down the hall, Kiyel dutifully following them, and back to the living room where he indicated for Jev to sit on the couch, while he sat in the chair opposite him.

"Alright, Jev, let's hear it. How was it that you two happened to be at that house, and ended up taking Aiden from there when you did?" Sam asked.

"Well, when Kiyel and I were in Clearhaven, we were passing though a somewhat uninhabited area of town, when we heard a child's screams; or rather, Kiyel did, as his hearing is pretty sensitive. We ran to the home where he'd heard the screams—and by this time, I was able to hear them as well—and since we were the only ones in the area, I kicked in the front door and we entered the home. That's when we found Aiden. He was tied down to his father's bed, with his father straddling his chest. Both of them were naked, and it became pretty obvious what his so called father was doing to him. I guess, if you've spoken with Tanis, you already know what they ended up finding in the house after Kiyel and I left with Aiden." Jev said.

"Yes. He told me that they found what was left of a man's body, his throat shredded, and the room covered in blood. They also found the bed with some cut ropes, and blood on the sheets."

"It was Kiyel, actually, who did that to Aiden's father. I helped Aiden by cutting the ropes that held him to the bed."

"Tanis told me that the place looked like a bloodbath had taken place in there," Sam said shaking his head in disbelief.

"We just wish we could have done more to him. If you ask me, he should have been made to suffer as Aiden did. I just can't believe he did that to his own little boy," Jev said. He suddenly lost what little control he had left over his emotions and began to cry.

Sam got up from his chair to console him.

"It's okay, Jev. He's gone and Aiden is safe now. You did the right thing. You and Kiyel both did real good," he said.

Jev could only nod as Sam held him comfortingly.

"I need to ask you something though. When you were at that house, did you happen to see two forest cats, there?"

"I knew you were going to ask me about that," Jev said, sitting up straight when he managed to get his sobbing under control.

"I take it you did, then," Sam said, returning to his chair.

"Not exactly. You see, the two forest cats... well, one of them was Kiyel," Jev said.

"I gathered that. And the other cat? Does Kiyel have a mate who came into town with him?" Sam asked.

That question actually made Jev laugh a little, and he looked over at Kiyel, who was sitting on the floor beside him, patiently looking up at him with a bemused expression on his face. His head was cocked slightly to one side, which made Jev laugh even harder.

Sam looked at him with a serious expression.

"I'm glad you find this so amusing," he said, clearly confused. It was not the reaction he had expected.

"I'm sorry, Doc, it's just that when you asked me that, I couldn't help myself," Jev said, quickly sobering up. "You might as well come have a seat, Kiyel."

Sam watched with shocked amazement as Kiyel suddenly stood up; not on four legs as he expected he would, but rather on two, and then took a seat next to Jev.

"Jev, what the hell is going on, here?" Sam asked, his voice filled with apprehension.

"You see, Doc, Kiyel isn't native to this planet," Jev answered.

"He's an alien?" Sam said, in a shocked whisper, and looking uneasily at Kiyel.

"Yes, I am. To your world, at least," Kiyel replied for himself, completely startling Sam, whose eyes suddenly opened wide with alarm.

"Jesus!" Sam exclaimed.

"It's okay, Doc," Jev hurriedly said, trying to reassure him. "He's not going to hurt you."

"Like he didn't hurt Aiden's father, you mean?"

"That bastard was going to kill his own son!" Jev said heatedly. "Kiyel did what he had to in order to save Aiden. And believe me, if I'd had the strength, I would have done exactly the same thing."

Seeing the surprised look on Sam's face, Jev forced himself to take a deep, calming breath.

"I'm sorry, Doc, I shouldn't have yelled at you like that."

"No, it's me who's sorry, Jev," Sam said. "Had I seen that bastard raping his son as you two did, I'd probably want to tear him to pieces, myself."

Jev nodded his head appreciatively, and smiled as he pictured Sam doing just that.

"So, Kiyel, I guess what I'd really like to know now, is how you came to be on Alessi in the first place," Sam said.

"About a decade ago my people sent a probe to this planet, to determine its suitability for colonization. The problem was, for reasons that we weren't able to fathom at the time, the probe suddenly stopped transmitting its data. So my team was sent here to investigate. The T'kri spotted our ship, and shot it down. Seven of us managed to survive the crash. The others made their way into the forest and took refuge within some caves. I had been injured though, and wasn't able to follow, so instead, I made my way here, and that's when Jev found me outside by the inn."

"Then that metal fragment..." Sam said, his voice trailing off.

"Was actually a piece of wreckage from our ship, yes," Kiyel answered. "The reason I was able to find Jev when I did was because I'm a telepath."

"I figured you were at least empathic, since Jev was able to sense your feelings," Sam said.

"Then it shouldn't come as a surprise to you to learn that Jev also is a telepath."

"As incredible as that sounds, it would actually make sense, now that I think about it," Sam admitted.

"Well it's true, Doc. In the weeks I've known him, Kiyel has taught me things that I'd only dreamed were possible. But not only that, I found that the more time we spent together, the closer to him I was beginning to feel, and before I knew it, a bond had formed between us; first emotional, and then telepathic."

"Wait a minute, you're saying..." Sam tried again.

"That I'm gay and that Kiyel and I are mates? Yes," Jev answered.

"Now that's something I didn't see coming," Sam said. "But then you always were able to surprise me," he added with the slightest hint of a smile. "There is one thing that I still don't quite understand, though. Tanis told me that there were two cats, so if one of them was Kiyel, where did the other one come from? Did another of his crew join you?"

"Actually, the other cat was me," Jev answered.

"Excuse me?" Sam said, genuinely confused.

"Doc, you know about werewolves right?"

"Of course I do, but what do they have to do with anything?" Sam asked.

"Well, just like werewolves undergo a transformation, so have I; in part because of the link I share with Kiyel, but mostly because of latent abilities that I never knew I even had."

As soon as Jev told him that, he reached into Sam's mind, and carefully removed the image that he had planted in there earlier, allowing Sam, for the first time, to see him as he truly was.

"Jesus!" Sam exclaimed again, jumping out of his chair in sudden shock. "Jev?"

"Yeah, it's me, Doc. I'm the first Caitaran hybrid in existence."

"But that's... that's just not possible!"

"It is for one who has telekinetic and telepathic abilities," Kiyel told him, "which Jev apparently has. Had I not seen it with my own eyes, I wouldn't have believed it possible either. My people have never before encountered another species that could change as Jev has."

"This is just too incredible," Sam said, stumbling slightly as he sat back down.

"I know," Jev said, "and I really do apologize for dumping this on you all at once. If we had more time, I'd explain it further. But Kiyel and I really have to get going, and we need to take Aiden with us. Tiela, the ship's chief medical officer, will probably be able to do more for him there."

"Does this Tiela of yours have the necessary equipment to help Aiden's body fight off infections, Kiyel?" Sam asked.

"Yes, and also to speed up the healing process," Kiyel replied. "We also know, from examining Jev before he changed, that the chemistry of our two species is very similar."

"But because of Aiden's young age, his system will react differently to treatment," Sam pointed out. "I want him to have the best chance of recovering, so I'd better come along with you, just in case he doesn't react well to your meds."

"You really want to come with us?" Jev was actually a bit surprised. "But what about your other patients?" Jev asked.

"Jev, there are several people here who are fully qualified to handle any emergency that might come up. I may be the colony's top doc, but I'm certainly not the only one. I never did like being in charge of everything, anyway. Too much paperwork," Sam said, with a wry grin.

"And you know something," he continued, "this new look of yours actually suits you nicely. I definitely want to look you over, though."

"Oh god not you too!" Jev said, rolling his eyes at Sam. "I swear examinations must be a hobby or something to you medical people."

"You know me better than that, Jev," Sam said sternly. "Just because you've changed species, doesn't mean I'm no longer your doctor. And besides which, legally, I'm now your guardian as well."

"What are you talking about?" Jev asked, suddenly taken aback by that unexpected piece of information.

"In your father's will, should anything happen to him, he named me your guardian."

"You... you're not kidding, are you?" a bewildered Jev asked.

"Would I say it, if I didn't mean it?" Sam asked in return.

"No, I don't suppose you would," Jev answered, with a huge smile on his face. "It actually kind of makes sense, though. Dad always treated you more like family than just the family's physician."

"So you don't have any problems with me being your legal guardian, then?" Sam asked.

"You know I've always looked up to you, Doc. So, no, I

don't have any problems with it at all. In fact, I'd be really honoured to have you for a guardian," Jev said.

"Thank you, Jev," Sam said, and he smiled.

"Since you'll be coming with us," Kiyel said, "it would probably be a good idea if you pack a few things for yourself before we leave."

"Yes, I'll definitely need to gather some supplies for myself, and for Aiden. Just give me a few moments, and I'll be right back," Sam said, before hurrying back into the exam room.

While he was in the exam room, he carefully removed the catheter from Aiden's arm, and put an adhesive strip over the tiny wound, which dripped a bit of blood. Aiden was still asleep, which was a good thing. He needed to rest, to help his injuries heal faster. Sam then left to get the things he would need for the journey.

"Alright, we're all set, I think," Sam said, as he looked into the living room, slinging a pack over his shoulder.

"I'll go get Aiden," Jev said, as he walked back to the room where Aiden lay. Carefully picking him up, Jev grabbed the blankets and made sure they were wrapped securely around the frail boy, and carried him over to the living room, where Kiyel and Sam were waiting for him by the front door.

"Report, Commander!" Captain Harris barked, looking up from his desk at his first-officer standing smartly at attention before him.

"Sir, they've just been sighted," Gregori answered.

"It's about bloody time," Captain Harris said, putting the report he had held in his hands down. "Where are they?"

"Near Doc O'Riley's clinic."

"Are you sure it's them?"

"Yes, Sir. They were two large forest cats, walking upright, and one of them was carrying what looked like a small child in his arms. Doc O'Riley was with them, also."

"Damn it!" Captain Harris cursed, "If they keep this up we won't have a colony left to defend!" he said. "Very well, Commander. Do we know where they were headed?"

"They were last seen crossing the valley, sir, making their way towards the forest."

"Who do we have in that area?"

"Just Michaels and Simms, sir," Gregori answered.

"Raise them on the com, and get them to that location," Harris ordered. "Then get another team ready to join them. This time we'll make sure they won't get away from us."

"Aye, sir," Gregori said, saluting before he left the Captain's office.

Captain Harris leaned back in his chair to reflect on the events of the past several hours.

Having gone to the crashed T'kri shuttle in search of Mikkel and Janice, and unable to find any sign of them—or the Caitarans they were with—in the immediate vicinity, he ordered his team to return to base while he traveled alone to Clearhaven in the hopes that some of the townsfolk may have seen something.

It was there, while he roamed the streets that he learned the T'kri had completely pulled out of Clearhaven—a fact which surprised even him—and it was also there that he learned of the sudden appears of two forest cats in the middle of town.

Immediately he knew the cats had to have been Caitaran, especially when he heard that they later left running on their hind legs with what appeared to be a child.

As quickly as he could, he contacted the rebel base, and arranged for a pick up. He knew from talking to several individuals that the cats were headed towards Hillsforde, and he needed to act fast if he was to have a chance at intercepting them and hold them for questioning.

One way or another, he was going make Mikkel pay for his betrayal, and for taking Janice away from him. And those two Caitarans were going to lead him straight to him.

After leaving Sam's clinic, and heading up the hill that would lead them away from Hillsforde, Jev and the others quickly traversed the open valley until finally they disappeared into the surrounding forest. It had taken them some time to get there, though. At least twice, they were forced to leave the path and seek shelter behind some bushes or large boulders to avoid being seen by any traveling colonists. Unlike when Jev and Kiyel raced from Clearhaven to Hillsforde in an effort to save Aiden's life, this time they could not afford to be seen and possibly be followed, by either T'kri or rebel patrols.

They were now several hours into the forest, and well on their way to the caves, where Kel and the others waited for them. Kiyel looked behind him to check on Jev and Aiden, and he smiled. Aiden, who was still under the effects of the sedative Sam had given him, slept in Jev's arms while instinctively gripping him tightly—just as a Caitaran cub would—with his hands. He had many fond memories of the times he sat, watching his mother with his younger brother, Kehlan, who held onto her with his little hands while he slept in her arms.

But Kiyel's reverie was abruptly ended when he witnessed Sam, who had been following behind Jev, stumble, and only just manage to maintain his footing.

"Are you okay, Doc?" Jev asked, turning quickly, hearing Sam falter.

"Yeah, I'm alright. Just not used to all this hiking, is all. I haven't done anything like this since I was a lad in med school!" Sam said, as he stopped for a moment to catch his breath.

"We can't rest yet, though," Kiyel said, as he scanned the area around them, and not feeling at all at ease where they were, "it's not safe. We need to get deeper into the woods," Kiyel said.

"Just give me a few, to catch my breath, Kiyel. I'll be fine in a second," Sam said, while leaning up against a tree.

"I can't sense that there's anyone following us, Enassi," Jev said, reaching out with his mind into the forest. "We did a pretty good job of avoiding anyone on the path when we left."

"No, you're right. But I'll still be more at ease once we're deeper in the woods and farther away from Hillsforde."

"Let's just be glad that Aiden is sleeping through all this," Jev said, looking down at the child wrapped up in blankets in his arms.

"All the more reason we get him to see Tiela as soon as possible," Kiyel said. "If he wakes up, and is still in pain, his cries could alert either the T'kri or the rebels as to our whereabouts.

"Alright, I'm ready," Sam said, standing next to them.

"We should be able to reach the caves in a few hours," Kiyel assured him.

"Are you going to be able to make it, Doc?" Jev asked.

"Boy, I've been walking farther than this since before you were born. I'll make it. I'm just not used to it. With the two of you around, though, I'm betting that I'll be doing a lot more walking in the near future."

"You're probably right," Kiyel agreed, giving him a toothless grin.

"Alright, Kiyel, let's get going," Sam said, shaking his head, but with a smile.

* * *

"Tanis, what's the status on the teams that went out to investigate the explosion?" Janette asked, walking out of her office to the desk where Tanis sat.

Tanis looked at his watch briefly before answering.

"They arrived twenty minutes ago, Janette," he said.

"Have they made a report yet?"

"Not yet. I'm expecting it to be delivered within the next few minutes."

"When the team leader gets here, have him join me in my office will you?" Janette asked.

"Of course. Did you need me to be present as well?" Tanis asked.

"I always need you, Tanis. I don't think I'd be able to do this job half as well without you here to help me," Janette said, and sighed wearily.

"I've always liked doing this sort of work," Tanis admitted, practically glowing from the compliment she gave him. "Even on Earth before we left."

"It shows," she replied, smiling at him. "Just send the team leader in when he gets here."

"I will," Tanis told her before she returned to her office, and not even bothering to close the door behind her.

Kiyel's ears pricked up and he stopped in his tracks as he suddenly felt a presence heading toward them.

"We've got a problem," he said, turning to Jev and Sam.

"What is it?" Jev asked.

"There's a number of people rapidly headed our way," Kiyel told him.

Jev opened up his mind, and just at the edge of his senses, he saw them.

"Damn!" he cursed softly.

"What? What's going on?" Sam's breathless voice asked behind them.

"We need to move, and quickly. We're being tracked by rebels," Jev said.

"What, you're sure it's the rebels and not T'kri?" Sam asked, nervously looking around him in a vain attempt to see what it was that Jev and Kiyel were talking about.

"You can't see them," Kiyel told him. "They're about two kilometres to the north of our position, close to where the crash site is."

"It's definitely the rebels," Jev said. "Captain Harris is with them, and he's really pissed,"

"Pissed?" Kiyel asked, not familiar with the word.

"Mad, upset and definitely infuriated; all of it directed toward us. Somehow he knows we're out here, and he's coming for us," Jev explained.

"So what do we do now?" Sam asked.

"We can't allow them to delay us," Jev said resolutely. "Aiden needs help from Tiela, and we're definitely in no shape to fight them off ourselves."

"Agreed," Kiyel said. As he began looking around them, his eyes suddenly settled on a familiar vine structure a few yards away from them, and he began to smile. "Follow me. I've got an idea."

THREE

When the door to her office opened, its hinges creaking slightly, Janette turned from the window to see Tanis, and another man she didn't recognize, walk purposefully into the room. The man appeared to be in his early thirties with dark brown hair that contrasted rather strikingly with his steel gray eyes. She decided that he looked rather handsome. A thin smile stretched across her face as she started back to her desk.

"I take it you're the one who was responsible for the team that investigated the explosion?" she asked.

"Yes, Ma'am," he answered, returning her smile, "I'm Cam Shepard."

Janette took the proffered hand and shook it warmly.

"I wish we could have met under better circumstances, Mr. Shepard, but thank you for coming nevertheless," she said.

"It's no problem, Ma'am."

"Then, if you would be so kind as to take a seat, we can

33

get started with your report," she said.

Nodding his head in agreement, Cam sat down in one of the chairs in front of her desk, and then politely waited for her sit down in her chair before proceeding.

"First Councillor Pelletier, when my team arrived at the site of the explosion, we found the remains of a downed T'kri shuttle. This was determined by the recovery of what I can describe only as a black-box from the charred remains of the craft."

"How do you know it was a black-box? It could just as easily be another component of the ship itself, such as a device meant to regulate the air circulation within the craft," Janette interrupted.

"No, ma'am, it's definitely the ship's black-box," Cam said, shaking his head. "For one thing, it was located in a very hard to reach area near the cockpit. It also was heavily shielded and was the least damaged object we found. Shielding of that type—on human vessels at least—would indicate some sort of recording device, like a ship's black-box."

"Very well, please continue," Janette said, accepting his reasoning with a nod.

"On the off chance that there might have been colonists on board, my team meticulously went through the wreckage to look for survivors. Considering how extensive the damage was, however, it was extremely unlikely that anyone could have survived, but I still had to be certain."

"Of course," Janette said.

"As expected we didn't find any survivors, but we did discover skeletal remains in the passenger compartment. There was something odd about them, however."

Janette looked quizzically at him, her head cocked on one side.

"In what way?" she asked.

"Well, you might think me crazy, but the skull almost looked as though it belonged to one of the forest cats."

"A forest cat?" Janette echoed, gasping in shock.

"Yes. I know it's impossible, but that's what it looked like. Of course it could just have been that the heat was so great that somehow the skull became deformed. I highly doubt it, though. Bone simply doesn't react to heat like that. Mostly it just disintegrates."

Janette leaned forward in her chair.

"Mr. Shepard, earlier today, roughly an hour after the explosion, several of our citizens witnessed two large forest cats leave the forest and enter Clearhaven. They went straight for a house where a man lived alone with his four-year-old son. When they came out, both of them were running on just two legs, like a human."

"You're kidding!" an incredulous Cam exclaimed loudly.

"Until now, I didn't give those reports much thought. But after hearing your report, I'm beginning wonder if we should seriously consider the possibility that there's another alien species here on Alessi."

"Another alien species..." Cam echoed, his voice trailing off as he struggled to absorb this new information.

"If this is indeed another alien race," Janette continued, "it would explain a whole lot of things that have been happening these last few days. If you recall, about a month ago, sometime at night, there was a large explosion up in the hills near Hillsforde. At the same time there was a dramatic increase of activity around the T'kri base, and squads of T'kri soldiers going from home to home in search of something. In fact, those searches were still continuing, right up until the sudden, unexplained T'kri withdrawal from our towns. And now, just a few weeks later, a ship explodes just outside the forest near Clearhaven, the same one you were sent to investigate, and inside the wreckage there's a skeleton of an unknown species inside. I'd say it's a safe bet that we're dealing with another alien race. Things are beginning to make more sense to me."

"I'm sorry, Ma'am. I don't follow you," Cam said.

"Think about it, Mr. Shepard," Janette said. "Imagine you're an alien race looking to colonize a new world. You come across this world and decide to investigate. But then you get shot down by the T'kri. You, and the rest of your crew, who have somehow survived, manage to capture a T'kri vessel in an attempt to escape, only to be shot down once again by the T'kri."

"That sounds plausible, ma'am," Cam said, absently scratching the back of his head.

"It's the only theory that fits the evidence we have. The only question I have now is, are these aliens potential allies?" Janette asked.

"I think it's worth finding out," Cam said.

"Is it? Suppose these new aliens are the ones the T'kri have been at war with? Suppose they're even more ruthless than the T'kri. If that were the case, we'd end up swapping one occupying force for another."

"I guess I can see your point," Cam said. "There's something else that happened while we were out there that you should know about, First Councillor."

"And what's that?" Janette asked.

"Well, we managed to gather up the skeleton, but before we could take it to Doc O'Riley to see if he could tell us anything about them, Captain Harris and his rebels showed up."

"Oh, great!" Janette exclaimed, sighing loudly.

"Don't worry," Cam said, with the faintest hint of a

smile. "We managed to leave with the remains, even though the Captain was definitely not too keen on letting us have them. It was only because of an approaching T'kri shuttle that he let us go."

"How interesting. Before you came here, Captain Harris actually paid me a little visit. He certainly never mentioned anything to me about any remains on the shuttle. In fact, he wasn't forthcoming with any information at all, and was more interested in learning what I knew. It was a very unproductive meeting, to say the least."

"Ma'am," Tanis interjected. "I've told you this before, and I know you've always dismissed it, but I seriously think you should consider that Captain Harris is planning a coup of some sort to replace you."

"I've never dismissed it, Tanis. I just wanted to give our rebel leader the chance to prove you wrong. He hasn't done that, I'm afraid. Instead, he's done just the opposite."

"If there's anything I and my team can do, you only have but to ask, First Councillor," Cam said, standing up.

"Thank you Mr. Shepard. I might have to take you up on that offer. An armed rebellion against the colony itself isn't something that I'm prepared to let happen," Janette said.

"Corporal Davis, what's the hold up?" Captain Harris demanded, walking up along side the Corporal who looked to be intently scanning the surrounding bush.

"I think they're onto us," Corporal Davis replied quietly.

"How can you tell?"

"Because they're no longer making any noise."

"And that means..." Captain Harris said impatiently.

"That they've gone stealthy to attempt to throw us off

their trail."

"Can you still track them?"

"Yes, but it will be slow going. We'll need to be careful in case they've set up some kind of ambush," the Corporal replied.

"They don't have time for an ambush, Corporal. They've got a young child with them, who they kidnapped after murdering the boy's father. God only knows what they intend to do with the child," Captain Harris explained. He knew it was full of crock, but if it got the Corporal to refocus his efforts on finding them, then so be it.

"Follow me, sir, and try to move quietly," Corporal Davis finally said, as he began to move forward again.

So close now, Jev. Soon I'll have you, and I'll make you lead me to your brother, and justice will be served. There is no room in this colony for traitors, Captain Harris thought to himself. The sneer on his face was the only indication of the vengeful thoughts now coursing through his brain.

"They're getting awfully close, Kiyel," Jev whispered from his perched position in the tree, its heavy foliage providing them with the perfect cover from the approaching rebels.

"We just need to let them get a little closer..." Kiyel said, his voice trailing off as he gauged the rebels' movements through the forest.

"I hope I have the strength for this," Jev commented quietly.

Kiyel looked over at him, and smiled.

"You do," he assured him. "I used to play this trick on some of the younger students at school back home. It's no more difficult than breathing."

"Sounds a lot like throwing a rock from where you're at in order to misdirect the person tracking you," Sam mumbled from beside Jev.

"The principle's the same," Kiyel said with a shrug of his shoulders, "but instead of using a rock, we'll be creating false images and sounds in our followers' minds. Then when it's safe, we'll quickly make our way back towards the caves," Kiyel explained.

"This should be fun to watch," Sam said.

"Quiet now, here they come," Kiyel said in a whispered voice, his ears and head swivelling round toward the approaching rebels.

I'm ready, Jev sent as he gripped Jordan more tightly against his chest.

Soon the rebels came into view, cautiously making their way towards them, and although their passage through the forest was quiet by human standards, it was easily heard by the sensitive ears of the Caitarans. As soon as the rebels were only a few short yards away from them, Jev and Kiyel quickly sent their combined thoughts out to them, touching each of the rebels' minds.

Jev almost laughed out loud as he realized just how right Kiyel was, that tricking the rebels would be a relatively effortless task. He watched with amusement as the one who was leading them suddenly stopped in his tracks and signalled to rest to do the same. Soon they shouted out in alarm as Kiyel began projecting into their minds the images of several squads of T'kri soldiers suddenly advancing on their position, blasters in hand and firing at them indiscriminately.

Almost as one, the rebels began returning the T'kri's fire. Their Captain began barking orders in a desperate effort to get them to form ranks, but it was for naught, as even more T'kri soldiers quickly began to appear, filing out of shuttles that had landed in the nearby clearing. Upon seeing this new wave of T'kri solders, the rebels scattered. There was no longer any semblance of order in the ranks, as every rebel, overwhelmed by the appearance of so many T'kri, fled into the forest and ran for their lives. Before long, not a single rebel remained and the forest was quiet once again.

Only when Kiyel was no longer able to sense the rebels nearby did he allow himself to relax, sighing heavily as he leaned back against the trunk of the tree, utterly exhausted. The effort had cost him more of his energy than he thought it would, a fact which he could only attribute to his lack of sleep and proper food, not to mention all that had been required of both him and Jev these past few days. Jev, on the other hand, showed no signs of being exhausted.

"Oh my God, did you see them run?" Jev asked gleefully.

"I did, indeed, Lad," a completely bewildered Sam answered, almost in a whisper.

Despite his weariness, Kiyel couldn't help but smile at Jev's excitement.

"That should give us enough time to get to the cave with Aiden," he said.

Jev, feeling Kiyel's exhaustion, turned to him.

"Are you alright, Kiyel?" he asked, his excitement quickly giving way to concern for his Enassi.

"I'll be fine," Kiyel assured him with a tired smile. "We've really been doing too much lately. I'm afraid we won't be much use to the others if we keep going like this."

"We're almost to the caves, now, though, so we should be able to get some rest once we're there. Knowing Tiela, she'll make sure of it," Jev said.

"Of that I have no doubt," Kiyel said.

"So what now?" Sam asked.

"Now we get down from this tree and hurry to the caves, before the rebels realize they've been tricked and try to pick up our trail again," Kiyel said.

"I'll go first," Sam offered.

With Jev and Kiyel watching, he carefully climbed down from the tree, until he was once again on the ground.

"You go next, Jev," Kiyel told him. "Do you want me to take Aiden?"

It was then that Jev suddenly realized that Aiden continued to maintain a death grip on his fur, even though he was still unconscious. He smiled at Kiyel and shook his head.

"I don't think this little guy wants to let go," he said. "I should be able to manage okay."

"I'll follow right after you, just in case," Kiyel nodded.

Holding onto Aiden tightly against his chest, Jev began the slow climb down from the tree. Although he only had the use of one arm, he found the descent relatively easy, jumping the last couple feet to the ground. It was then that he finally began feel how tired he was, the adrenaline that had been coursing through his system wearing off, and he stumbled slightly. Sam, who had been watching him closely, was there, and caught Jev before he could fall.

"I'm okay, Doc. Thanks," Jev said, indicating to Sam that he could let him go once he steadied himself, which Sam did, though with some reluctance.

Kiyel leaped to the ground and rushed over to Jev's side.

"Guess I'm more tired than I thought," Jev said, his ears dipping with embarrassment as he looked up at him.

"Will you be able to make it?" Kiyel asked, his tail flicking with concern.

Jev nodded his head and smiled at him reassuringly.

"Then let's get going before the rebels realize they've been tricked and come back," Sam said urgently.

After checking to make sure he had Aiden firmly secured in his arms, Jev indicated that he was ready and together they then slipped quietly into the brush.

It was mid-afternoon by the time they reached the path that would lead them to the caves, and both Jev and Kiyel were utterly exhausted. Jev had almost lost his footing twice, and Sam began to worry that the two of them would end up collapsing from exhaustion before they could reach their destination.

Fortunately though, Jev's and Kiyel's strength held out until they were within sight of the mouth of the cave. But that was as far as the two of them could go. Sam watched helplessly as they both suddenly began to collapse against a large rock, Aiden still held tightly in Jev's arms.

"Oh that's just great!" Sam muttered to himself.

Kneeling next to them, he quickly discovered that they were both only semi-conscious, and in no condition to travel any further. A sudden gust of wind drew his attention away from the pair, and he looked up into the sky where he saw the sky beginning to grow dark as storm clouds began to roll in. *This is not good,* he worriedly thought to himself

All of a sudden he sensed that he was no longer alone. He stood up to see two large Caitarans, who had somehow managed to sneak up on him without making a sound, approach and carefully lift Jev and Kiyel up into their arms. Sam could only look in astonishment as Jev, Aiden and Kiyel were swiftly carried into the caves, leaving him standing where he was in complete bewilderment.

"I presume you're a friend of Jev's and Kiyel's," a deep voice suddenly said from behind him, speaking in heavily accented English.

The suddenness of the unfamiliar voice startled Sam. He spun around to find himself staring up at the imposing figure of an obviously older Caitaran male, and he backed away slightly.

"Um, sorry, what?" Sam stammered.

"Since you've arrived with Jev and Kiyel, I presume that you're a friend of theirs," the Caitaran repeated.

"Uh, yeah, sorry. My name's Sam O'Riley," Sam said.

"Jev has told us of you," the Caitaran said, his ears flicking in recognition. "Please, come inside, there's a storm approaching and we don't want to be caught out in it," the Caitaran said.

"No, you're right," Sam agreed. "I'm sorry, but, who are you?"

"My name is Kel, commanding officer of the Caitaran scout ship Lekur," the Caitaran said, before turning and starting towards the cave, obviously expecting Sam to follow.

Once inside, Sam saw Jev and Kiyel lying down and being made comfortable near a fire in the center of what was the largest cave he had ever seen. Aiden, he could see, was still wrapped up in his blankets, but was now lying next to Jev, who was closest to the fire.

"Captain, that child needs medical attention right away," Sam told Kel.

"Tiela!" Kel called out, getting the attention of the smaller, white and grey-furred Caitaran who had just thrown a blanket over Kiyel.

"Yes?"

"I'm told the child with Jev is in immediate need of medical attention," Kel told her.

"Right away, Captain," she acknowledged, and quickly, but carefully, scooped up Aiden in her arms.

Kel then turned to Sam.

"Go tell Tiela what's needed for the child. We'll watch over Jev and Kiyel."

"Right," Sam said, and he hurried over to Tiela who had already carried Aiden to a large flat rock in the corner of the cave.

Noticing Sam hurrying towards her, she looked up at him.

"I'm Tiela," she said, as she began removing the blanket from Aiden after gently laying him down on the rock.

"You're the medic Kiyel told me about?" Sam asked her.

"Wow, I'm famous," she said sarcastically, but then offered him a friendly smile. "I'm the Lekur's physician, yes," she told him, pointedly informing him of her proper position.

"Gotcha," Sam said, accepting the rebuke. "I'm Sam O'Riley. I used to be Jev's doctor before he became, well, different."

"So you're a physician also then?"

"Yes," Sam told her.

"Can you tell me what's wrong with the child?"

"His name is Aiden. He's four years of age. When Jev and Kiyel brought him to me, he was in severe shock due to significant blood loss from a wound inside his rectum, the result of his being sexually assaulted by his father."

"What?!" Tiela exclaimed loudly, her enraged voice echoing throughout the cave. "I hope the father has been attended to," she practically spat out. Her ears were laid flat against her skull and her tail was flicking jerkily, showing her deep distress.

"Yes. From what I've been told, Kiyel took care of him personally."

"Good," Tiela said, and she tried to force herself to calm

down.

"I repaired the damage as best I could with the limited equipment I had to work with. Kiyel mentioned you have technology and medicines that can do more for this boy though," Sam said.

"I'll see what I can do," Tiela said.

Sam watched as she reached for what he assumed to be a scanner of sorts and began to examine Aiden's little body. From where he stood, he could see the image of Aiden's anatomy displayed on the scanner's screen. The more he looked at it, though, the more he felt as though he was going to be sick to his stomach. No matter how much damage to the human body he'd seen, it still affected him greatly when he saw that it was a child who was injured. And for one so young to have to go through what this little one did, it was almost too much for him to bear.

"You managed to suture most of the damaged area," Tiela finally announced, turning off the device. "However, there's still a sizable tear in his lower colon."

"Damn!" Sam cursed.

"Considering the level of technology you had available to you, it's a wonder you were able to repair as much as you did," Tiela told him in an effort to calm him, somewhat, though she herself was on the verge of tears, as well.

"Is there anything you can do?" Sam asked.

Tiela nodded her head.

"The scans I took of Jev before he changed revealed that human physiology is somewhat similar to our own, so the drugs I have won't harm him. I'll have to monitor the dosage, however, since this child is much younger than Jev. As for the damaged section of his colon, I'll have to dissolve the sutures you used. Then, I'll use this tool here to encourage the body to heal the wound more quickly than it normally would," she said, holding up another device.

"What should I do?" Sam asked.

"For now, just wait. I'll need your input with regard to normal body functions of a child of his age, and how we can expect him to react."

"I can do that," Sam said, glad that there was at least something he could do to help.

"This may take some time," she warned him, to which he nodded his head in understanding.

Sam watched every move she made. He could tell when the sutures were dissolved, as she said she'd do, as Aiden's breathing began to become more laboured, and his skin was already beginning to turn pale. He was just about to warn her, but stopped when she began to use that second device over top of the affected area. Her face was as intense as he'd seen any physician during an operation. There was no mistaking her desire to do all she could to help Aiden. He could even see her fear of doing something to make things even worse. Eventually, he could see that Aiden's breathing returned to normal, and his skin began to return to its normal pink tone.

Tiela moved the device away from Aiden's abdomen, and moved it over to where the wounds on his wrists were. Before his very eyes, Sam watched as the deep bruising began to diminish, and finally fade away as though the child had never been injured. She repeated the process by his ankles, which were just as swollen and inflamed as his wrists had been. They too began to heal before his eyes.

"I wish you were here a long time ago, when this invasion started," Sam said, in obvious awe.

"I'm sure you've seen your share of misery and death," Tiela said in a compassionate tone.

"More than I care to, ever again," Sam said, with a shake

of his head.

"The child will recover. The re-generator was able to close the wounds, but they're not completely healed. It'll still be several days before he recovers completely, unless I can get him aboard our ship sooner.

"I thought your ship crashed," Sam asked, confused.

"I'm speaking of the Cetani, which is the ship from which our scout ship was launched," Tiela explained.

"Ah, okay. A mother ship in other words," Sam said.

"Yes, I guess you could call it that," Tiela said with a bemused grin.

"So what about Aiden, just how much healing does he need to do before he's one hundred percent?"

"Not all that much actually. It's more that his body needs to reinforce the tissues around the wounds. His wrists and ankles are completely healed. There was just too much damage for the re-generator to heal his internal wounds completely, but it's enough that the bleeding has stopped. When it heals fully, it'll be as though he had never been injured."

"What about the stretched tissue around the sphincter muscles and the possibility of infection?" Sam asked.

"The tissue should return to normal. I can deal with any infection by giving him a broad spectrum antibiotic. I'm just not certain what dosage I should administer."

"You said our physiology is practically identical?" Sam asked.

"Almost."

"Then why don't we start with what would be appropriate for a child of his age, size and weight if he was Caitaran," Sam suggested.

"I'll administer half that amount, considering our species has more muscle mass than yours. If he doesn't react badly to that, I'll begin increase the dosage gradually," Tiela said, after considering everything she had learned of the child's physiology.

"Sounds like a plan to me, doc," Sam said.

"How do the two of you feel?" Kel asked as he approached Jev and Kiyel, who were sitting up next to the fire, still wrapped in the blankets Tiela had given them. In his hands, he carried two hot, steaming, mugs of k'yarri, which he offered to them both.

"Exhausted," Jev answered wearily.

He gratefully accepted the mug Kel held out to him and took a tentative sip, sighing appreciatively as he felt the warming effects of k'yarri spread throughout his body.

Kiyel simply nodded his head as he, too, accepted the mug offered to him by Kel.

"I asked Taaj to prepare you both something to eat," Kel told them. "It should help you regain some of your strength."

"Thank you, Captain," Kiyel said.

"While he's doing that, I'd like to know what happened to cause the both of you to rush off like you did."

Jev took a long sip from his k'yarri before answering.

"The reason is over there, Captain," he said, pointing to where Sam and Tiela were hovering over Aiden, who lay on the blanketed rock that served as Tiela's exam table.

"The child?" Kel asked.

"The child is a sensitive, Captain," Kiyel told him, "but his talent is wild. Jev and I had to leave you and the others because we both received a very powerful psychic scream from someone in great pain."

"That scream, sir, came from Aiden," Jev finished.

"You said the child's talent is wild. Does he present a

danger?" Kel asked Kiyel, his ears flicking with concern.

"I don't believe so, sir," Kiyel said, and shook his head. "Aiden's talent is wild because it was awakened prematurely, the result of him suffering a great trauma. Jev and I should be able to control his talent for now, so it doesn't affect anyone else. But he'll need proper training to learn to control it himself."

"What was the cause of his trauma?"

"It was his father," Jev said, his ears flattening against his skull in distress as he recalled the events in Clearhaven. "He was being raped by his father."

"He was what?!" Kel yelled, tail lashing from side to side, his ears so flat against his skull they were almost impossible to see. "Where is he?" he demanded to know, his words taut with anger and spoken through tightly clenched teeth.

"Dead," Kiyel answered.

"How?"

"I took care of it," Kiyel said, averting his gaze.

Recognizing Kiyel's unwillingness to discuss the child's father's death further, Kel grudgingly allowed the matter drop. His tail, however, continued to flick behind him.

"Do you know how Aiden is doing, Captain?" Jev asked, quickly changing the subject.

"Tiela assures me that he's doing fine," Kel said, moderating his tone, "thanks in part, she says, to your physician's valuable knowledge of human physiology."

"See, I told you the two of them together could do it," Kiyel said, and he pulled Jev into a comforting embrace.

"Yeah," Jev said with a relieved smile on his face, and he allowed himself to relax in Kiyel's arms.

FOUR

"We're approaching the Alessi system now, Captain," the young ensign stationed at the con called out.

"Very well, Ensign," Cael answered, his ears pricked forward. He stood up from his command chair and stepped down from the dais to the con station. "Reduce speed to one quarter sub-light. Take us in nice and slow."

"Aye, Captain," the ensign replied, her fingers expertly working the console in front of her. The steady thrum of the Cetani's powerful engines began to diminish as the ship shifted to sub-light drive with an almost imperceptible shudder.

"Tactical, give me a passive sensor sweep of the planet. I want to know the instant there's any reaction to our presence down there," Cael ordered.

"Don't worry, Captain," his tactical officer said from his station beside the con, "if so much as a joule is used down there, we'll know about it."

Cael acknowledged his tactical officer with a flick of his ears as he stared at the star-filled view-screen in front of him. He watched as the planet, an insignificant-looking blue-white disc in the center of the view-screen, slowly grow larger as the massive ship crept steadily toward it.

"Captain, I'm receiving IFF codes from the Taigana and the Ikuta," reported his com officer. "They've assumed a geosynchronous orbit on the far side of the planet's moon."

"Plot a course to rendezvous with the Taigana, Ensign," Cael ordered to the con.

"Aye, Captain," the ensign answered. "Course plotted and laid in. ETA to intercept is in fifteen minutes, sir."

"Thank you, Ensign." Cael then turned to his com officer. "Hail the Taigana, Lieutenant."

"Sir, the Taigana is hailing us," his com officer said.

"On screen."

A Second later the star field and planet on the forward view screen were replaced with the image of the Caitaran Fleet Commander, dressed sharply in her duty uniform and standing on the bridge of the Taigana.

"Admiral," Cael said, with an acknowledging flick of his ears.

"I see you didn't waste any time in getting here, Captain," Chuul said, with the faintest hint of a smile.

"Kel is a friend," Cael answered succinctly, as though no further explanation was required.

"Of course," Chuul said. The smile then vanished from her face. "We've studied Captain Kel's report."

"I'm guessing from the Ikuta's presence you've already decided on a course of action against these T'kri he speaks of?"

"Indeed we have, Captain," Chuul confirmed. "As soon as you've rendezvoused with the Taigana and the Ikuta, I want you to join me here for a tactical briefing. You'll be given your new orders then. Inform your CAG officer that upon your arrival, his assault craft and crew are to transfer temporarily to the Taigana. They'll be joining the task force which I've put together to deal with these T'kri."

"Understood, Admiral," Cael said. "We should make the rendezvous in fifteen minutes."

"I'll wait for you then, Captain. Chuul out."

Aiden stared up at Jev in wonder as he sat on his lap, his little hands touching Jev's face. He giggled when Jev's nose and long whiskers twitched. The wounds he had suffered were almost completely healed now thanks to the combined efforts of Tiela and Sam, and he was adjusting amazingly well to the presence of the other Caitarans. It was the humans' presence that Aiden shied away from—much to Jev's sorrow—hiding behind Jev or Kiyel whenever Mikkel, Sam or Emily came near. Tiela had told him Aiden's uneasiness around humans was due to the trauma he suffered but assured Jev that he was young and would grow out of it eventually with their help. It was just going to take some time and patience on their part.

Of all the Caitarans, Jev thought Jaffay would have been the least likely to have anything to do with Aiden. To his utter astonishment though, Jaffay took to the boy almost immediately, and though hesitant at first, he soon was running about the cave on all fours with Aiden riding on his back, laughing with glee. Tiela had to remind Jaffay a number of times to be mindful of Aiden's still healing wounds, though she, too, couldn't resist a smile upon seeing how happy Aiden was. While Jev was also nervous, he could see that Jaffay took special care to be very gentle with him. He seemed to know exactly when Aiden had

had enough.

They were now two days in the caves since finding the probe and sending a message to the Cetani, and still they waited for its arrival. As the hours passed, Jev was keenly aware of the growing tensions within the cave. He was especially aware of Kel's growing concern that they would again be discovered by the T'kri should they stay in the caves for much longer. To mitigate that possibility, Kel had ordered Jaffay to ensure that there were at least two people standing watch by the mouth of the cave at all times; partly to ensure they had ample warning should the T'kri eventually find them, but also to keep an eye out for the Cetani's arrival.

Jev brought himself back to the present and looked down at Aiden, only to discover that the boy had fallen asleep in his arms.

"He's finally asleep, is he?" Kiyel said as he approached and sat down beside them by the fire.

Jev looked up at Kiyel who handed him a steaming mug of k'yarri.

"It's been a long day for him," he said.

Kiyel gently brushed Aiden's cheek with a finger, eliciting a low, tired groan from the boy, who shifted slightly in Jev's arms.

"Tiela says it'll probably be a day or so before his injuries are completely healed," he said.

"Any word on the Cetani?" Jev asked hopefully.

"Not yet, I'm afraid," Kiyel said with a long sigh. "Jaffay just relieved me from watch a few minutes ago."

"It's a wonder he still has any energy left after playing with Aiden all morning."

"He enjoys being with him, much more than he lets on."

Jev smiled at him.

"Been reading him have you?"

"I didn't have to," Kiyel said with a small smile of his own, "not with how strongly he's been projecting his feelings."

"I wonder if Aiden can feel it."

"It's possible," Kiyel answered, his tone turning serious. "His talent was awakened prematurely, so he may not even be consciously aware of it. He needs to be taught to develop and control his talent. For that we'll need to take him to the Telepath Guild on Caitar."

"I'm not so sure the colony council will be thrilled with the idea," Jev said.

"Probably not," Kiyel conceded. "However, once the Cetani arrives and our diplomats establish contact with the Alessians, our telepaths should be able to impress upon them the need for Aiden to receive formal training on Caitar."

"I sure hope so."

Movement by the mouth of the cave suddenly caught their attention. They looked over and saw Jaffay skid to a stop just a few yards inside the cave, his eyes wide with excitement and his tail flicking wildly behind him.

Something's up, Kiyel sent.

Holding onto Aiden, Jev quickly rose to his feet with Kiyel.

"I think you all need to come out and take a look at this," Jaffay announced, getting the attention of the others in the cave.

Kel and Tiela, who had been engrossed in a lengthy, but quiet, conversation with Sam at the back of the cave, hurried towards him.

"Report, Jaffay," he ordered.

But Jaffay just shook his head.

"It's easier if you come see for yourself, sir," he said, then turned and hurried back out of the cave.

"What's going on?" Sam asked, joining Jev and Kiyel.

"I don't know," Jev answered, watching as Kel, Tiela and the rest of the crew quickly filled out of the cave, "but we'd better find out. Come on."

Hurrying outside they found the others standing out in the open, staring up into the sky in silence, not moving, as though each of them had been frozen in time and space. From above there was an almost deafening sound of airborne craft. Jev looked up, and gasped audibly, for it was then that he saw a massive formation of ship flying high above them. There were so many of them they filled the sky, almost blotting out the sun.

The noise of the ships had wakened Aiden, who put his hands to his ears in an effort to block the sudden sound. But instead of being frightened, like Jev thought he would be, Aiden was staring up at the ships flying overhead with a curiosity that only a child could have.

Kel, seeing Jev and Kiyel emerge from the cave, turned to meet them.

"Kiyel, can you confirm—"

But Kiyel was already way ahead of him, pre-emptively scanning the ships that flew overhead.

"They're Caitaran, sir," he said. His tail began flicking behind him with excitement as a huge grin stretched across his face.

"My god, there must be hundreds of them," Mikkel said in awe, finding his voice.

"At least," Kel said, "and more than the Cetani is capable of carrying alone."

"She's not alone then," Jaffay said.

"No, there's definitely a carrier up there," Kel said.

"I'll bet my tail it's the Taigana," Jaffay said with a scowl, his tone contemptuous. "Chuul always was an ambitious female. She probably wants to claim for herself the credit for eliminating the T'kri."

Kel regarded his tactical officer wryly.

"Maybe so," he said, "but you have to admit, she knows how to make an entrance."

Jaffay just snorted derisively and watched as a group of ships broke away from the rest and fly off towards the T'kri's base.

"Damn," Janice swore when she realized where the ships were headed, "they're headed straight for Ru'kayesh!" She then turned to face Kel. "What the heck did you put in that message you sent, Captain?"

"Just the location of every T'kri installation on Alessi as provided by your former commanding officer," Kel answered, with a smug grin.

"Well it seems they got the message alright," Mikkel said. "It looks like the other group is headed for Clearhaven."

Moments later they heard the unmistakable sound of weapons fire and distant explosions. The fight for Alessi had begun.

"Look!" Taaj said suddenly, pointing. "One of them is breaking away from the others."

As one, they all looked to where Taaj was pointing and saw that there was indeed a ship breaking formation. What's more, it seemed to be headed in their direction.

"That's not an assault craft," Kel observed as the ship drew closer, his ears flicking in recognition, "that's one of our shuttles."

"Well, no matter what it is, there's no place for it to land around here. There's too much brush. It has to be headed for a clearing nearby," Mikkel said.

"Then that's where we're headed as well," Kel decided.

"We'll have to cut our way through the forest," Mikkel said. "It'll take us too long to go around."

"Cut through the forest, with what?" Jev asked.

He watched curiously as Mikkel walked over to his bag, which was resting against a nearby rock. From his bag he pulled out a small machete. Jev instantly recognized it as being one of the tools the colonist regularly used to clear away brush on their farms.

"With this," Mikkel said, brandishing the blade in front of him.

"Let's get going then," Kel ordered, nodding his head and indicating for Mikkel to take point.

With Mikkel expertly using his machete to clear away the brush blocking their path, it didn't take them long to reach the clearing. Already they could hear the shuttle's thrusters slowing its descent, and by the time they breached the tree line, the shuttle had landed.

Jev had never before seen a ship quite like the Caitaran shuttle. Its sleek design was in complete contrast to the T'kri shuttles, which were quite bulky. Compared to the T'kri shuttles, the Caitaran shuttle was also much larger, and it looked capable of carrying at least twenty people inside its hull.

Kel led them toward the shuttle just as the shuttle's ramp began to lower. From inside the shuttle emerges a tall, dark-furred Caitaran male, dressed sharply in a military uniform. Right away Jev could tell that this was a high-ranked officer. His suspicions were confirmed when he saw Kiyel and the other Caitarans come instantly to attention. At Kiyel's gentle urging, he did the same.

Joining the officer were two others; a Caitaran male, dressed in an elegant, flowing robe that made Jev think the wearer belonged to some religious order, and a short, bird-like alien, covered in brown and white feathers, with two, large, yellowish eyes, and dressed in loose, drab-coloured clothing.

She's a Brekari, Kiyel sent in a bemused tone, feeling Jev's interest in the new arrivals.

Really? Jev sent, surprised. *From what you've told me of them, somehow I imagined they'd be taller.*

So did I before finally meeting one in person, Kiyel sent with a wry grin.

What about the other two? Jev asked.

The one in front I think is Captain Cael, Kiyel sent, indicating the Caitaran in uniform. *He's the Cetani's commanding officer.*

And the one in the robes?

That's Guild Elder Veir Onawi, the Telepath Guild's liaison with the Cetani.

You've met him? Jev asked, his eyes narrowing as he regarded the Caitaran.

Only briefly, Kiyel sent, feeling Jev's sudden uneasiness. *We met when I first reported for duty.*

Does he know you joined the military under an assumed name? Jev asked.

He knows my entire family, Kiyel admitted, his ears flattening backward slightly. *Don't worry though,* he quickly added, reassuringly, *he's sympathetic to my situation and he's agreed to keep the knowledge of who I am hidden.*

As the three new arrivals stepped off the ramp and began making their way towards them, their strides sharp and deliberate, Kel stepped forward to greet them.

"Hello, Kel," Cael said as he warmly shook Kel's outstretched hand.

"It's damn good to see you, Cael," Kel said with a relieved smile.

"I'm sure," Cael replied with a bemused grin. "Why is it every time you manage to get yourself into trouble, I'm the one who has to come save your tail?" Cael asked with feigned annoyance.

"Just lucky I guess," Kel replied wryly. "What are you doing here, though? I thought you'd be up there coordinating the strikes against the T'kri."

"Admiral Chuul decided she wanted to reserve that honour for herself. Instead, I was put in charge of the diplomatic mission."

"That definitely sounds like Chuul," Kel said with a soft chuckle.

"Excuse me, Captain, but time is of the essence here," the Brekari behind him said in a high-pitched, almost sing-song voice that somehow perfectly articulated the guttural hisses and growls of the Caitaran language, surprising Jev yet again.

"You're quite right, Ambassador," Cael acknowledged with a flick of his ears. "Kel, this is Ambassador D'lin. She's here to help with the negotiations with the colonists for the Alliance."

"Ambassador," Kel said, greeting her with a nod of his head.

"It's good to meet you, Kel," D'lin said. Her gaze suddenly fell upon Mikkel, Janice and Sam, who were standing together. "Are those the humans you spoke of in your report?" she asked.

"They are," Kel confirmed.

"Fascinating," D'lin said, clearly intrigued. "I would very much like to speak with them."

"I would be happy to introduce you to them, Ambassador, but you should know they don't speak Caitaran," Kel told her.

"They don't speak Caitaran?" D'lin echoed, looking surprised. "Then how do you communicate with them?" she asked, her head cocked to one side slightly.

"We were able to learn their language, thanks to our two telepaths, Kiyel and Jev," Kel said, looking over at them.

"Hello, Kiyel," Veir said, moving to stand before him.

"Elder Veir," Kiyel said, acknowledging the other with a flick of his ears. "It's good to see you again." He placed the palm of his hand lightly on Veir's chest, greeting the other in the manner that Jev reconized was customary for telepaths.

"I am glad to see that you are well," Veir replied, returning Kiyel's greeting. "I'd feared the worst when I read the reports of the Lekur's disappearance. You can imagine how relieved I was when I heard that you were well. I was surprised, however, to learn that you'd formed an Enassi link," he said, and looked at Jev quizzically.

"No more so than I was, Elder," Kiyel said. "This is Jev, my Enassi."

As soon as Kiyel introduced him, Jev felt Veir's mind gently probing the edges of his. He watched with some amusement as Veir's eyes suddenly opened wide with shock when he felt Jev's and Kiyel's link.

"I don't understand," Veir said, looking at Kiyel with a perplexed expression on his face, his tail flicking behind him. "The report said that your Enassi was human."

"And when Jev and I first met, he was," Kiyel said.

Veir's and Cael's ears pricked forward in surprise at this, and both of them stared at Jev in disbelief.

"This wasn't in your report," Cael said quietly to Kel, his tail flicking slightly.

"There wasn't time," Kel replied apologetically. "The T'kri could have shown up at any moment and we had to get that report out fast," he explained.

"Please take my hand and open your mind to me," Veir said, stretching his hand out to Jev. "I need to see for myself."

Kiyel? Jev sent nervously.

It's alright, Jev, Kiyel sent, reassuringly.

As soon as their hands joined, Jev cautiously began to lower his barriers, believing that Veir would try to force his way in. But Jev was surprised when instead he patiently waited for Jev to lower each barrier before gently proceeding deeper into his mind. And then, after only a few seconds, Jev felt Veir carefully withdraw.

Bewildered with astonishment, Veir slowly turned to Cael.

"It's true," he said, in an almost whispered voice. "I don't know how it's possible, Captain, but somehow it's true. He's a hybrid of our two species; human and Caitaran."

"I could have told you that," Tiela said, rolling her eyes at the Elder.

"There's something else you should know," Kiyel said, getting their attention once more. He then looked down at Aiden. "We've discovered that this child has a talent. His name is Aiden."

"Another human telepath?" Cael asked, his eyes narrowing slightly.

"We don't know yet," Kiyel said, his tail flicking. "His talent was awakened prematurely. He needs to be tested by the Telepath Guild."

"Can the humans not see to his testing?" Veir asked.

"No, Elder. To the humans, telepathy is a fringe phenomenon. They're highly sceptical of its existence," Kiyel explained.

"If, as you say, the humans deny the existence of

telepathy, they'll insist that the child remain with them," D'lin said.

"He can't stay here, though," Jev said. "He's terrified of humans because of what happened to him."

"It also seems that he's grown quite attached to us," Kiyel added.

"So I see," Veir said, looking down at Aiden, who was shyly peering out from behind Jev's leg, which he hugged tightly.

"We can deal with the child's disposition later. For now though, it's imperative that we contact the leaders of the colony right away," D'lin said.

"In that case, we should get in touch with First Councillor Janette Pelletier. She's the leader of the colony," Jev said.

"You know this First Councillor Janette Pelletier?" D'lin asked.

"The council would sometimes meet secretly at my father's inn, so I would see her then," Jev explained.

"Excellent," D'lin said. "Would you be willing to contact her for us, then?"

"Excuse me, Ambassador," Kiyel interjected, "but when she last saw Jev, he was human, like her. There's no way she'd recognize him now, and she certainly wouldn't trust him."

"Mikkel could probably do it, though," Jev said thoughtfully. "He's had just as much contact with the First Councillor as I have."

"You've already asked him if he has?" Cael asked.

"I didn't have to, sir. He's my brother," Jev explained.

"I see," Cael said, his ears flicking with surprise.

Upon hearing his name, Mikkel quickly made his way to his brother's side.

"What is it, Jev?" he asked.

"They need someone to contact the council for them. They asked me to do it, but..." Jev said, pointedly looking down at himself.

"I get it," Mikkel said, giving Jev an understanding grin.

"I thought maybe you could do it instead."

"Of course," Mikkel said.

Jev smiled at him in thanks and then turned back to Cael. "My brother says he'll do it," Jev told him, reverting back to Caitaran.

Cael acknowledged this with a flick of his ears. "Do you know if the colonists are capable of receiving communications through a video terminal?" he asked.

"Yes they are, sir," Jev nodded. "Every building in the colony is equipped with a video terminal. But the system isn't set up to connect to a terminal outside the network. The T'kri made sure of that."

A wry grin then formed on Cael's face. "Since it appears that the T'kri are somewhat busy at the moment, I'm sure we won't have too much trouble hacking into the system without them noticing." he said.

"No, I suppose not," Jev said.

Right then and there he decided he liked this new captain.

When the first ships appeared in the sky over Clearhaven, Janette knew there was going to be trouble. From her office window, she watched with guarded anticipation as the column of ships flew over the town and head straight for the T'kri garrison on the coast. In the streets below, the people of Clearhaven began gathering outside, looking up with cautious curiosity, and murmuring nervously amongst themselves.

Then, without warning, an explosion suddenly erupted within the garrison. Its deafening sound shook the building, and caused her to instinctively shield her eyes from the blast. Within seconds of the first explosion, Janette watched in shock as a number of T'kri shuttles lifted off in a frantic effort to escape the attacking ships. The swift and merciless manner in which they struck, however, rendered escape by the T'kri impossible, and within seconds, every T'kri shuttle was destroyed.

With the T'kri shuttles destroyed, the attacking ships quickly turned their energy weapons on the garrison itself.

A gleeful grin began to form on Janette's face as she realized she was witnessing the destruction of the T'kri. Even as she silently cheered the attackers on, however, a nagging thought at the back of her mind began to form. What was going to happen once the attackers were finished with the T'kri? Was the colony next?

Suddenly the door to her office slammed open, causing her to jump with a start.

"Janette, there's a call coming in for you," Tanis said urgently as he raced into her office.

She spun around and gave him an incredulous look.

"You've got to be kidding me, Tanis!" she exclaimed with disbelief. "Do you see those ships out there? Do you hear the explosions?" she asked, emphatically waving her hands towards the window.

"Yes, but I definitely think you need to take this call, Ma'am," Tanis insisted forcefully.

"Very well, Tanis," she said reluctantly. "But in the mean time, you'd better round up as many security personnel as you can and get those people outside off the streets and back into their homes."

"Right away, Janette," Tanis said, and hurried out of her office.

With a long sigh, she made her way back to her desk and sat down, then activated her com terminal. Immediately she recognized the face that appeared on her screen.

"This really isn't a good time for a chat, Mikkel," Janette said, flinching as the sound of another explosion outside shook the building.

"This isn't a social call, First Councillor," Mikkel's image said, "I'm sorry for contacting you like this, but I thought you'd like to know who it is that's attacking the T'kri."

"You know who they are?" she asked, incredulous, her eyes opening wide.

"Of course," Mikkel said, with a sly grin. "I'm with their leaders right now."

"Well then, tell them to break off their attack. We're getting hammered over here!"

"I'm afraid that's impossible, First Councillor," Mikkel said with a shake of his head. "The ships that are attacking the T'kri belong to an alien race called the Caitarans."

"So there is another race on Alessi," Janette said, leaning back in her chair.

"A couple of months ago, the T'kri shot down a scout ship belonging to the Caitarans. The crew has been in hiding here on the planet ever since. By shooting down their ship, though, the Caitarans now consider themselves to be at war with the T'kri."

"Are the rebels—?"

"The rebels have their own agenda, First Councillor," Mikkel said with a frown, abruptly cutting her off in mid-sentence. "I left them so that I could help the Caitarans."

"Given everything we've been through with the T'kri

though, do you really trust these aliens?" she asked.

"Yes, First Councillor, I do. And what's more, so does my brother," Mikkel said.

"Your brother! You mean he's alive?"

"Yeah, he's alive. Thankfully he wasn't at the inn when the fire started," Mikkel said, with a wide grin.

"Thank heavens for that."

"First Councillor, the Caitarans have asked me to convey to you their request to meet with the council."

"I see," she said, her brow furrowing slightly as she leaned forward in her chair again. "And where exactly do they want to meet?"

"If you are agreeable, I'd like to suggest the public square in Clearhaven, outside the Council Hall."

"That's right in the middle of town, Mikkel," she said with some trepidation.

"I can understand your hesitation, First Councillor," Mikkel said. "And to be perfectly honest with you, when I was first introduced to the Caitarans, I had my reservations about them as well. However, they've proven themselves to be honourable people. They truly wish to help us."

"Very well, Mikkel," she said with a reluctant sigh. "I'll defer to your judgment in this. Tell the Caitarans I look forward to meeting them."

"Thank you, First Councillor. They'll be happy to hear that. Mikkel out," he said, reaching forward to close the channel.

As the screen went blank Janette got up from her chair and made her way back to the window. There she watched as the attacking ships continued their devastating bombardment of the T'kri garrison, sending thick, black, billowy smoke up into the sky as flames consumed the garrison.

I hope to God you're right, Mikkel, Janette thought to

herself.

FIVE

A gentle tug on his tunic drew Jev's attention to Aiden who stood beside him.

"Do we get to fly in that?" Aiden asked, looking in awe at the shuttle.

"Yes, we do," Jev replied.

"Cool," Aiden said.

Jev smiled as he felt the sudden burst of excitement from Aiden.

"Kiyel, Jev," Kel called out as he started making his way towards them from where he had been talking to Cael and Ambassador D'lin, next to the shuttle. "Captain Cael has offered to help us pack up the equipment in the cave before we leave. While we're gone, I'd like for the two of you to wait here for us on the shuttle with Aiden."

"Are you sure you don't need our help as well, Captain?" Jev asked.

"I think we'll be able to manage, Jev," Kel said, his ears flicked appreciatively. "Besides," he added, "I believe you'll have more important matters to attend to while we're gone."

"I don't quite follow," Jev said, looking at Kel quizzically.

"If I heard correctly, didn't Mikkel inform the First Councillor that you were still alive?" Kel asked.

"Yes, he did," Jev answered.

"Then don't you think it would be prudent for you to do something about your appearance?" Kel asked. "The last time she saw you, you were human after all."

Jev nodded his head in understanding.

"The two of you get on board and do what you have to. We'll be back shortly," Kel said with a grin, patting Jev's shoulder.

"Aye, sir," Jev said, acknowledging Kel's order with a flick of his ears.

"You realize, this presents us with a bit of a problem," Kiyel said as soon as Kel left to round up the rest of the crew.

"I know," Jev said with a sigh. "We won't be able to maintain the illusion and help Aiden control his talent at the same time."

"Elder Veir should be able to help us. He's already on the shuttle," Kiyel said.

"Then what are we standing out here for?" Jev asked.

Together they hurried on board the shuttle, where they found Veir sitting alone in the passenger compartment. Jev guided Aiden over to an empty seat across from Veir, and then strapped him in.

"Elder," Kiyel said, acknowledging the other with a flick of his ears as he sat down with Jev.

"Kiyel," Veir answered, looking up at him. "Have the others left for the cave yet?" he asked.

"Yes, they're gone," Kiyel answered.

"There's something troubling you," Veir said, looking genuinely concerned. "What is it?"

"We need to ask if you can help us with something," Jev said, his tone hopeful.

"If it is within my power," Veir said, leaning forward in his seat, his ears pricked with interest.

"Since realizing Aiden's talent woke prematurely, Kiyel and I have been using our abilities to help Aiden maintain control of his talent so he doesn't begin randomly broadcasting his thoughts and feelings."

"That was a very sensible thing to do," Veir said, nodding his head in approval.

"Yes, but we're about to fly to Clearhaven. When we get there we may no longer be able to help him," Kiyel continued.

"Why's that?" Veir asked, looking at Kiyel, confused.

"Because once we land to meet the council, it's going to take most of our concentration to hide Jev's true form from them."

Veir's eyes opened wide with shocked amazement. "You're talking about changing how people perceive you!" he exclaimed. "But that's never been done before. Not even by other Enassi!"

"Jev and I have done it twice now," Kiyel said.

"But unfortunately it takes so much out of us that we have almost no strength left to do anything else," Jev added. "That's why we need your help. We'd like you to help Aiden maintain control of his talent while we concentrate on our illusion. At least until we can get the First Councillor to accept me as I am now."

"So why is it so necessary that you do this in the first place?" Veir asked.

"She's just been told by my brother that I'm still alive.

She's going to expect me to appear as I use to."

"Kiyel, we're going to have a long talk about all of this once we get back to the Cetani," Veir said.

Kiyel grinned slightly at him before turning his attention to Jev.

"Are you ready?" he asked.

"Let's do it," Jev said, with a reluctant nod of his head.

Veir sat and watched in stunned silence as Jev's body began to shimmer and change before his eyes. His Caitaran features began to wash away like sand being swept away by the tide, revealing human features underneath. Jev's transformation only took seconds, but when it was finally complete, Veir found himself staring at a young human with light-coloured hair and piercing blue eyes.

"Incredible!" Veir said, staring at Jev with amazed astonishment.

A sudden cry of fright beside Jev caused him to look over, where he saw Aiden shrinking away from him in fear.

Inwardly cursing himself for forgetting Aiden's fear of humans, Jev acted quickly, reaching out with his mind in an attempt to reassure the frightened child.

Hey, its okay, he sent soothingly. *It's just me, Jev.*

Jev's assurance seemed to work as Aiden began to calm down somewhat. However, he continued to remain hesitant about getting too close to him.

"Go ahead, Aiden, touch his face," Kiyel suggested, smiling assuredly at him and nodding his head to let him know it was alright.

Looking at Kiyel and then back at Jev, Aiden tentatively reached out with his hand to Jev's face. His eyes then opened wide with shock and he quickly drew his hand back when his fingers touched fur.

You see? Jev sent.

"How come you don't look like a cat anymore?" Aiden asked as he brought his hand up to touch Jev's face again. This time he did so out of curiosity rather than fear.

"This is a disguise for when we get to Clearhaven," Jev explained.

Suddenly, one of the pilots came running into the passenger compartment, his face filled with concern. "I heard a yell. Is everything alright in here?" he asked, his eyes taking in the scene before him. His gaze quickly settled on Jev. "Who in the name of Dahel are you?" he demanded, advancing toward him, his tail flicking jerkily.

Jev recoiled back in shock from the intensity of the pilot's sudden, and unexpected, reaction.

Veir quickly stood up and approached the pilot, preventing him from coming any closer.

"Everything's alright, Ensign," he assured him. "Return to your cockpit. I can handle things here."

"Very well, Elder," the pilot said reluctantly, taking one last long look at Jev before turning to head back down the corridor to the front of the shuttle.

"I didn't like the way his mind felt," Jev whispered to Kiyel, in shock. "It felt too much like Gaev's did."

"I felt it, too," Kiyel said, his eyes narrowing slightly. "It was the same kind of xenophobia, only not as intense."

"You could feel that from him?" Veir asked in surprise as he returned to his chair.

"Yes," Jev answered quietly, staring after the pilot as a shiver of discomfort ran down his spine.

It took Kel and the others a little over an hour to pack up the equipment in the cave and return to the shuttle. As soon as the equipment was stowed on board, Cael ordered the shuttle pilot to lift off.

Throughout the cabin, the muted whine of the shuttle's engines could be heard as they fired up. Moments later the shuttled lurched as it slowly began its ascent. Underneath them, they both heard and felt the landing struts retract back into the hull.

Once again Aiden's excitement rose, his face practically pressed up against the glass of the view port, as he watched, the shuttle steadily rose into the air.

Within seconds the shuttle cleared the treetops. After angling the nose of the shuttle towards Clearhaven, the pilot pushed on the throttles causing the shuttle to surge forward. They were finally on their way.

At no time during the flight did Aiden's eyes stray from the scenery below as he looked out the view port, filled with excitement. It was all Jev could do to keep the wonder-struck boy in his seat. Clearly the shuttle's straps were not designed with four year old children in mind.

Just then the shuttle's intercom crackled to life, followed by the pilot informing them that they were about to land.

As the shuttle began to slowly make its descent, circling around as it did, Jev could see from his view port a growing mass of people gathering near the town square below. Only the barricades, hastily erected by the town's security forces, prevented the townsfolk from entering the square.

Then, with a slight bounce, the shuttle touched down, landing in the center of the square. The whine of the shuttle's engines began to lessen as the pilot shut them down.

"Alright, people, listen up," Cael said, getting everyone's attention as he stood up in the middle of the aisle. "Before we go out there to meet this colony's leaders, I want to remind each of you that this is a diplomatic mission. As such, Ambassador D'lin has asked that all weapons remain on the shuttle."

"No weapons, Captain?" Jaffay repeated, looking incredulously at Cael, his ears flicking with alarm.

"That's correct, Lieutenant," Cael said, in a tone that brook no argument. "The colonists on this world have been kept as virtual slaves to the T'kri for the past several years. The last thing we need is for them to get the impression that we will do the same."

"I understand the reasoning, Cael," Kel said, "but surly it would be prudent for us to at least bring along an armed escort once we leave the shuttle."

"Prudent, maybe, Kel, but Ambassador D'lin is in command of this mission once we're outside, and these are her instructions."

"Understood, Captain," Kel said. It was clear, however, that he wasn't the least bit happy about it.

"Jev," Cael said, turning his attention to him. "Since you and your brother are both familiar with the colony's leaders, can the two of you make the introductions for us?"

"Yes, sir," Jev said. He then turned to his brother behind him and relayed the Captain's instructions.

"And, Kiyel, until a permanent diplomatic team is assigned to this world, I'd like for you to serve as interpreter for us," Cael said.

"Aye, sir," Kiyel said.

"As soon as I release the airlock, only Ambassador D'lin, Captain Kel, Jev, Mikkel, Kiyel, and I will meet with the colony's council..." Cael continued.

"Captain," Tiela interrupted, "with your permission, I'd like to join you as well."

"For what reason, physician Tiela?" Cael asked, his ears pricking with interest.

"Maintaining this illusion is causing a great deal of strain on Jev and Kiyel. I feel I should be nearby in case they require medical assistance."

"Very well," Cael said, before turning to the rest of the crew. "The rest of you are to wait here until you hear from us."

After receiving several nods of acknowledgment, Cael pressed the intercom switch on the panel on the wall beside him.

"Ensign, we're ready. Lower the ramp," he ordered.

"Aye, sir," the pilot's voice said from the intercom.

From the rear of the shuttle, and on the other side of the airlock, came the hiss of hydraulics as the rear hatch opened and the ramp began to lower. When it was down and locked, as indicated on the display panel next to the door, Cael opened the airlock door and indicated for Mikkel to begin leading them outside.

As they started down the ramp, Kel quickly became keenly aware of the growing number of townsfolk who were gathering behind the barricades.

"Kiyel, can you get a sense of the mood of these people?" he asked quietly, his tone uneasy.

"They're curious about us, Captain," Kiyel said, "and understandably cautious. But I don't detect any malice directed towards us."

"Just the same, keep an eye out for any change in their demeanour," Kel instructed.

"Of course, sir," Kiyel agreed.

Mikkel led them to where Janette and the council were waiting for them in front of the council building. It was the largest building in the town square, with three levels instead of the normal two and almost twice as wide. Adorning its roof were several large solar panels. Other than its size, however, it was practically indistinguishable from any other pre-fabricated building in Clearhaven.

"Hello, Mikkel," Janette said, greeting him has they neared.

"First Councillor," Mikkel said, shaking her proffered hand.

"So these are the Caitarans you spoke of are they?" she asked, glancing over his shoulder nervously.

"I'd like you to meet Captain Kel, commanding officer of the Caitaran scout ship Lekur, the ship I told you about that was shot down by the T'kri, two months ago," Mikkel said, indicating for Kel to join him.

"It's both an honour and a pleasure to meet you, First Councillor," Kel said in heavily accented English, offering his hand to her.

"I didn't know you could speak our language," a startled Janette said, tentatively shaking his hand.

Kel grinned at her reaction.

"We're fortunate to have a gifted pair of telepaths who have imprinted us with your language," he said.

"Telepaths?" Janette echoed, looking at him somewhat sceptically.

"I understand that it isn't a gift readily accepted by your people."

"I'm afraid you're right."

"In our society, Telepaths are highly regarded individuals. A good number of them are employed by the courts as Truth seers. Others are trained as diplomats and work with the Brekari, and a few even join the military where they're assigned to advisory positions."

"I see," Janette said, clearly impressed. "Now I wish we

did have telepaths in this colony. They would have been a great asset to us during the occupation."

"Indeed," Kel said, with a slight nod of his head. "As for your colony not having telepaths though, I personally know of one who is in fact a very gifted telepath."

"You do? Who?" Janette asked.

Instead of answering, however, Kel simply stepped aside and motioned for Jev to step forward.

"Jev!" Janette exclaimed happily, quickly pulling him into a tight embrace."

"Hello, First Councillor," Jev said, blushing slightly from embarrassment at her sudden display of affection.

"You have no idea how relieved I was to hear that you were alive," she said.

"I have a pretty good idea. I was there when Mikkel called you up on the com."

"You were?" Janette asked, finally letting him go. "I didn't see you."

"You wouldn't have recognized me," Jev said, grinning slightly. "I've changed quite a bit since we last saw each other."

"I don't understand," Janette said, eying him up and down and looking quite perplexed. "You don't look any different to me."

"That's because I've been using my abilities to hide my true appearance from you," Jev explained. "I'm going to drop the illusion now so you can see me as I really am," he said.

When Janette tentatively nodded her head, Jev finally allowed his control over the illusion to relax. Gradually his human features began to fade away, revealing to Janette and the assembled council members his true appearance. A collective gasp rose up from the council members, who had taken a step back. Although Janette had not moved, Jev could see her eyes opening wide as the last of his illusion disappeared and a light-coloured Caitaran now stood before her.

"It can't be," Janette said in awe.

"That's what I first thought when he showed me how he'd changed," Mikkel said.

"You knew about this and you didn't tell me?" she asked, turning on him.

"Would you have believed me if I did?" Mikkel asked with a small shrug of his shoulders.

"No, probably not," Janette conceded reluctantly. "But still..." she said, eying Jev warily.

"I know this is difficult for you to accept, First Councillor," Jev said, "but just imagine how difficult it was for me to come to terms with the fact that I'd suddenly changed to become a Caitaran hybrid and that I was no longer human."

Janette drew back involuntarily from the forcefulness of Jev's admonishment. "I'm sorry, Jev. I meant no insult to you," she said.

Jev could feel Kiyel's comforting hand on his shoulder and he forced himself to relax.

"I almost died because of this change," Jev finished, quietly.

"You're okay now, though, right?" she asked, genuinely concerned upon hearing this.

"Yeah," Jev said, with a slight nod of his head.

"How... why did this happen?" Janette asked.

"We don't really know," Kiyel said from behind Jev, startling Janette again as a second Caitaran began speaking to her in English.

"First Councillor, this is Kiyel," Mikkel said, introducing him to her. "He's a telepath and one of the survivors of the ship that was shot down."

"He's also my life-mate," Jev said proudly, a thin smile stretching across his face as he glanced up lovingly at Kiyel.

"Oh my!" Janette exclaimed, gasping in astonishment. "When did this happen?" she asked.

"Shortly after we met," Jev told her. "I'd always known that I was gay, First Councillor. I just never thought I'd find myself falling in love with someone like Kiyel."

"No, I suppose you didn't," Janette said, with a wry grin.

"You should know that besides being life-mates, Jev and I also share a very special telepathic bond which among our people is known as an Enassi link," Kiyel said.

"In what way is this link of yours special?" Janette asked, intrigued.

"Enassi links among telepaths are very rare. It's a total blending of mind and body. And it's indissoluble, except by death. Through this link Jev and I are constantly aware of each others experiences and feelings. Our minds are never alone."

"Never alone?" Janette echoed in surprise, "But then how do the two of you maintain your individuality?"

"We have our own thoughts, of course, though sometimes even those are shared," Kiyel answered, with a grin.

"That's incredible," Janette said, amazed. "I've enough trouble managing my own thoughts and emotions as it is. I couldn't begin to imagine what it'd be like to have someone else constantly in my head like that."

Kiyel barked out a laugh.

"I assure you, First Councillor, for us, life would be quite unbearable without the link."

"Forgive me, First Councillor," Mikkel interjected, getting her attention. "But perhaps we could finish this conversation some other time so that I can finish with the introductions and we can all get inside?" Mikkel suggested.

"Of course, Mikkel," Janette said apologetically, indicating for him to proceed.

"This is Captain Cael, the commanding officer of the Caitaran explorer ship Cetani; Ambassador D'lin, who is here to represent the Alliance during this meeting; and Tiela, the medical officer from the ship that was shot down," Mikkel said, pointing to each in turn. "You should know that neither Ambassador D'lin nor Captain Cael have learned English yet, First Councillor," he added.

"Then how will we be able to talk to each other?" she asked him.

"That's my job, First Councillor," Kiyel told her. "I have been asked by Captain Cael to act as an interpreter until a telepath from the Cetani, who'll eventually be assigned to be your permanent interpreter, can be imprinted with the knowledge of your language."

With a nod of her head, Janette then turned her attention back to Kel.

"Is this everyone from your shuttle, Captain?" she asked.

"No, some of our people have remained on board. Since their presence wasn't deemed necessary for this meeting they are taking the opportunity to get some much needed rest."

"In that case, why don't you let your people to make use of our inn where they can freshen up and get some refreshments and get something to eat if they'd like," Janette suggested, pointing to the tall wooden building across the courtyard.

"Thank you, First Councillor. That's most kind of you," Kel said, clearly impressed by her unexpected, but very welcome, invitation.

"Not at all, it's the least we can do for all the help you've given us ridding this planet of the T'kri."

"Believe me, First Councillor, that was a pleasure," Kel

said, with a toothless grin.

"Now, allow me introduce you to the members of the Alessian council," Janette said, turning her attention to the councillors standing behind her. "To my right is my aide and good friend, Tanis Rowe. Beside him is Councillor Erica Hayes, and next to her is Councillor Jeff Steiner. To my left is my head of security, Cam Shepard. Beside him is Councillor Bob Shuler, and next to him is Sam Hunt," she said, pointing to each in turn.

"Councillors," Kel said, bowing respectfully to each of them.

Just then there was a commotion by one of the barricades. They all turned their heads where they saw three men pushing their way through and heading towards them.

"Oh, God, what's he doing here?" Mikkel asked, with a low moan as he recognized the familiar face of the rebel leader.

"It's nice to see you again too, Mikkel!" Johnathan retorted sarcastically, with a scowl.

He was flanked on either side by his second in command, Gregori, and another officer, who Mikkel didn't recognize.

"First Councillor, I demand the right to be included in these talks," Johnathan said, his tone serious.

"And just what gives you any right to come barging in, uninvited and making demands, Captain?" Mikkel spat.

"I am the commander of Alessi's military forces," Johnathan said, as though that was reason enough.

"You're not the commander of anything," Mikkel countered indignantly. "As far as I'm concerned, you forfeited that position when you abandoned Kel and his crew up in the mountains to deal with the T'kri alone."

"I made a decision to strategically withdraw from a bad situation," Johnathan said, dismissing Mikkel's criticism with a wave of his hand.

"No you didn't, you ran away like the coward you are," Mikkel said, with a contemptuous growl.

"Alright that's enough!" Janette yelled, glaring at both of them until they both looked away from each other. "Mikkel, Captain Harris is correct when he says he has the right to request being present during these negotiations."

Johnathan grinned smugly at Mikkel. However his grin quickly disappeared when Janette angrily turned on him.

"As for you, Captain," she continued. "Contrary to what you may believe, you have no right to make demands of anyone. There are some in this colony who wouldn't mind it one bit if I tossed your rebel butt in jail, and right now I'm more than just a little tempted to do just that. Do I make myself clear?"

"Yes, First Councillor," Johnathan said, grudgingly accepting the rebuke.

She's one formidable female, Kiyel sent to Jev, clearly impressed.

You have no idea, Jev replied. *It's one of the reasons why she so easily defeated her opponent during the elections.*

Who was her opponent?

Captain Harris, Jev answered wryly.

"Well then, now that that's all taken care of, shall we head inside?" Janette asked Kel, partly turning to the council building behind her.

"Agreed," Kel nodded.

Having never been inside the Council Chambers before, Jev was completely unprepared for the sight that was to greet them as they walked through the chamber doors. On the outside, the council building was as plain and featureless as any other building in Clearhaven. But the inside was an entirely different matter altogether. The walls of the council chambers were covered in dark wood paneling with meticulously crafted ornate trim. Along the far wall were three very large windows covered by white sheer curtains. Underneath the windows was a raised dais on which sat a number of wood desks, which had the same wood paneling and ornate trim as was on the walls, all laid out in a semi-circle. Centered in front of the dais was a beautifully crafted wood table, stained in a deep red colour, with intricately carved edges, and around it were twelve chairs, each of them meticulously crafted to match the table. Hanging from the chamber's tall ceilings were several large domed lights.

"Impressive craftsmanship," Kel said in awe, his deep voice echoing throughout the council chambers.

"It took a team of artisans and contractors from the surrounding towns almost two years to complete the work in this room," Janette said, grinning at him with gratitude. "Of course, this was before the T'kri arrived."

"Of course," Kel said.

Janette led them to the table, and indicated for each of them to take a seat.

As soon as everyone was settled in at the table, D'lin carefully rose from her chair.

"Ladies and Gentlemen of the council of Alessi," she began through Kiyel, bowing respectfully to the councillors. "I bring you greetings from the Alliance. It is a great honour for us to be here with you, and it is my hope that before we are done here today, the beginnings of a lasting friendship between us will emerge."

Janette then rose from her seat.

"On behalf of the citizens of Alessi, and all of us here on the council, I welcome you to Alessi, Ambassador," she said.

"Thank you, First Councillor," D'lin said, and waited until Janette sat back down before continuing. "Before we begin, I think it necessary that Captain Kel briefly describe to you the events that led up to us meeting here today."

Kel rose from his chair and bowed his head respectfully at Janette and the council.

"Approximately ten of our years ago," he said, speaking in heavily accented English, "Caitaran High Command launched a survey probe to this world. Its function was to gather data to determine this planet's suitability for colonization. Roughly two months ago, that probe stopped transmitting its data."

"Your people have had a probe on Alessi all this time? Why is it we've never discovered it?" Janette asked.

"First Councillor, the probe landed high up in the mountains; near the T'kri base you call Ru'kayesh, in an area not easily accessible. It had also, at some point, been covered by a landslide which we now believe was caused by the T'kri."

"I see," Janette said, nodding her head. "Please continue, Captain,"

"When the probe stopped transmitting, my team was sent to investigate. Upon our arrival, however, we were detected by the T'kri and shot down in an unprovoked attack.

"Then the reports we received of an explosion up near Greymarsh was in fact your ship crashing," Bob said.

"Yes," Kel confirmed, acknowledging him with a flick of his ears.

"If I could interrupt here for just a moment," Johnathan said, rising up from his chair.

With a nod of her head, Janette indicated for him to proceed.

"Given this new information, I have to recommend we thank these aliens for their efforts in ridding Alessi of the T'kri, and then send them on their way."

"I think you'd better explain yourself, Captain," Janette said, her eyes narrowing ever so slightly.

"We've always known that the T'kri were at war with another race. But until now, we didn't know with whom. During the Caitaran's attack, we managed to capture and interrogate several T'kri. What we've learned has convinced me that any agreement with these aliens would be a dangerous mistake; one that could destroy this colony."

"What have you learned, Captain?" Janette asked as she leaned forward in her chair.

"Based on the T'kri's description of their enemy, we've determined that this race could only be the Caitarans."

"No, that's not possible!" Jev yelled angrily, leaping up from his seat.

"Jev, please sit down," Janette said.

"But it's not true," Jev said, turning to glare at the rebel leader with contempt. "There's no way the Caitarans could be at war with the T'kri as Captain Harris suggests."

"Oh really, Jev?" Johnathan asked calmly, but with a wry grin, when Jev reluctantly sat back down. "Isn't it possible that you've allowed your feelings for the Caitarans to blind you to the possibility that they just might not be who they claim to be?"

"You're forgetting something, Captain," Jev said. "I'm a telepath. But more than that, I'm Kiyel's Enassi. You've seen that fact for yourself, and you know what it means. Through this link, I've gained all of his memories and knowledge. I can assure you that at no point in their history have the Caitarans ever encountered, or even heard of, the T'kri."

"With all due respect, Captain Harris," Cael said through Kiyel, "Jev's recollection of our people's history is quite correct. Neither Alien Affairs nor Caitaran High Command have any records of any encounter with the T'kri until our scout ship was shot down by them on this world."

"Captain, during your interrogations, did the T'kri reveal

the name of species they are at war with?" Janette asked.

"Indeed they did," Johnathan answered, turning to face her. "They called themselves the Chemians."

"They're called what?" Cael exclaimed loudly with alarm when Kiyel translated this, his tail flicking erratically behind him.

"You've heard that name before?" Janette asked, surprised by his sudden outburst.

"All Caitarans know that name, First Councillor, and what it represents," Cael said with a scowl. "Just a little over a thousand of our years ago, an extremely xenophobic, and violent, religious sect was banished from our world for attempting to overthrow the government. They called themselves the Chemians, after their leader, Rul Chemia. Their goal was to rid Caitar of all alien influences which they believed was undermining the purity of the Caitaran way of life."

"Were there any indications that telepaths were a part of this group?" Jev asked Cael, leaning forward in his seat.

"The Chemians hated telepaths almost as much as they hated aliens, Jev. But that didn't stop them from kidnapping telepaths and forcing them to assist in their cause."

Jev nodded his head.

"Then that would explain the reaction of the T'kri officer we captured and attempted to question. It was terrified of our presence; of Caitarans. Until now, we didn't know why."

"You and Kiyel both fought with the T'kri, personally?" Cael asked, his ears pricked up in astonishment.

"Yes, we did, and killed several of them as well."

"But how is that even possible?" D'lin asked, looking quite bewildered. "You're both telepaths."

"Yes, Ambassador, but while Caitaran telepaths are incapable of fighting, because they would feel the pain they inflicted, human telepaths apparently don't have that limitation, At least, not that I've seen," Kel said.

"And because Kiyel and I are Enassi-linked," Jev continued, "he's picked up that trait from me, which means he's capable of fighting as well."

"Incredible," Cael said.

SIX

When Jev walked into the inn after having left the council chambers almost two hours later, he found Jaffay, Izha and Taaj sitting at a table in the corner by the fireplace.

Joining them, he sat down and ordered a cup of coffee from the innkeeper.

"The meeting's not over already, is it?" Jaffay asked.

"For now," Jev said, letting out a long and weary sigh.

"I take it diplomacy's not your thing," Izha said, with a wry grin.

"Gods no," Jev said, almost laughing. "I was glad when Cael asked for an adjournment so he could consult with his superiors. Tiela suggested I take a break also. So here I am."

"It's no wonder, what with all that you and Kiyel have been doing lately," Jaffay said.

Jev's coffee arrived and he took a tentative sip from the steaming cup.

"Thank you," he said, looking up at the innkeeper with

an appreciative grin.

"Don't mention it," the innkeeper said, before turning to return to the bar.

"Speaking of Kiyel, why didn't he leave with you?" Taaj asked.

"He's still needed to act as an interpreter for Ambassador D'lin," Jev said.

"Well, I for one, don't envy him the job," Taaj said.

Jev grinned at him appreciatively.

"Believe me; Kiyel is just as anxious to get out of there as I was."

"It's not fair that you and Kiyel really haven't had time alone to just enjoy each others company," Taaj said.

"We're hoping to get some time off after these talks are done and we're on board the Cetani."

"Fat chance of that happening," Jaffay snorted derisively, his nose crinkling slightly. "I wouldn't be the least bit surprised if Admiral Chuul orders a full inquiry into what happened here. And I bet you she'll have more than just a few questions for the two of you."

"Don't worry, Tiela already has that covered," Jev said.

"Has she, now?" Jaffay asked, his ears pricking with interest.

"Just before I left, she informed Kiyel and me that after we get on board the Cetani, she's taking us off active duty and ordering that we not be disturbed until she's certain there aren't any complications with our link or my transformation."

"She's a crafty old medic, that one," Jaffay said, with a boisterous laugh.

Jev drank the last of his coffee and indicated for the innkeeper to bring him another.

"So, what was it that made Cael ask for a recess?" Izha

asked.

"It was something the rebel leader said, actually," Jev replied, nodding his thanks to the innkeeper who placed a fresh cup of coffee before him and took away his empty cup. "Amazingly enough, his team recently managed to capture and interrogate several T'kri. From them they learned that the race the T'kri are at war with is called the Chemians."

Jaffay suddenly sputtered and coughed into his drink then looked up at Jev in disbelief.

"You're kidding me, right?"

"I'm afraid not. Cael just finished explaining to us who the Chemians are, and how they came to be banished from Caitar."

"They're a dark part of our history that we're not particularly proud of," Jaffay said, his ears twitching slightly with embarrassment.

"It would certainly explain why the T'kri reacted to us the way they did," Izha observed.

"That it would," Jaffay said dryly.

Just then they heard footsteps coming down the stairs by the bar. Jev turned in his seat to see Janice making her way towards them.

"I see they finally let you out of there," she said, smiling at him as she pulled up a chair from an adjacent table and sat down next to him.

"Tiela said I needed to get some rest," Jev said. "How's Aiden doing?" he asked.

"He's fine. He's upstairs sleeping like a baby. Doc O'Riley and Elder Veir are watching over him right now," Janice assured him.

"He actually let you and Doc put him to bed?" Jev asked, his ears pricking in surprise

"Actually, I was the one who put him to bed, Jev," Jaffay told him.

Jev nodded his head appreciatively at him.

It was at that moment that the front door suddenly swung open, causing such a noise as to draw everyone's attention to the front of the inn where they saw Janette enter and purposefully make her way towards them.

"Jev, I'd like to have a word with you," she said. From the tone in her voice and the expression on her face, Jev could tell she wasn't happy.

"What's wrong?" he asked.

"Why didn't you tell me you had a child with you, a human child?"

Jev's tail began to flick nervously behind him.

"It wasn't necessary, First Councillor. You already knew," he answered.

"How did you know that?" she asked, stopping in her tracks and staring at him in shock.

"I am a telepath, remember?" Jev said, grinning wryly at her. "The moment you saw us coming down the shuttle's ramp, Kiyel and I were both easily able to pick up your realization that we were the ones who took Aiden from his home," he explained.

"So then, which one of you was responsible for killing Luke Mills?" Janette asked.

"Kiyel was," Jev answered truthfully. He was no longer smiling. "And before you ask, yes, it was necessary," Jev quickly added.

"How in the world can you think ripping a man to pieces is necessary, Jev?" Janette asked incredulously.

"Leave the lad alone, Janette." As one, they all turned to see Sam and Elder Veir coming down the stairs. "You have no cause to be barking at Jev like that," Sam said.

"Sam!" Janette exclaimed, surprised to see him. "What are you doing here?"

"My job," Sam told her curtly. "Jev, Aiden is beginning to wake up," he said in a gentler voice as he looked at him. "Why don't you go on up there and see him. I'll take care of things down here."

Jev acknowledged Sam with a grateful flick of his ears, and relieved to have a reason to be someplace else, rose from his chair and hurried up the stairs.

"You knew?" Janette asked Sam after Jev had left, looking at him incredulously. "You knew that these people had Luke Mills' child and you didn't report it?"

Turning back to her, Sam folded his arms across his chest.

"Of course I knew, Janette. It was your aide, after all, who informed me that Jev and Kiyel were headed toward my clinic."

"But they killed the boy's father, Sam," Janette said incredulously. "And quite brutally I might add."

"I know what they did, Janette. And had I been there, I probably would have done the same," Sam replied.

Janette gasped in shock.

"How can you say such a thing?"

"Because, First Councillor, it took me several hours to repair the numerous injuries Aiden's so-called father inflicted upon him, that's why," Sam spat with disgust.

"What injuries?" Janette asked, becoming concerned.

Sam shook his head.

"I think it'd be better if I let Jev explain what happened, when he comes back down," he said, sitting down in the chair that Jev had just vacated. "I think he'll be able to show you more effectively than I could tell it," he finished, tapping the side of his temple with his finger.

As if on cue, Jev's footsteps could be heard coming down the stairs. He wasn't alone, however. With him, holding his hand and trying to rub the sleep out of his eyes, was a very groggy-looking Aiden.

"He said he was thirsty," Jev said, answering Sam's unspoken question.

"He can have juice or water, Jev," Sam cautioned him. "No milk until I'm certain his system can handle it."

Nodding his head, Jev led Aiden over to the bar. As soon as Aiden saw the innkeeper though, he quickly hid behind Jev's legs.

"I'm sorry about that," Jev said, his ears dipped slightly at the innkeeper's startled reaction. "He's terrified of other people."

"What happened to him?" the innkeeper asked, her eyes opening wide.

"It's a long story," Jev said, with a long deep sigh.

"Isn't it always?" she asked, shaking her head sadly.

"What would you like, Aiden, juice or water?" Jev asked, turning slightly to look down at him.

"Juice, please," Aiden said, timidly poking his head out from behind Jev's legs.

The innkeeper smiled kindly at Aiden then turned and took from the cooler behind her a glass pitcher filled with apple juice and began pouring the contents into a tall glass which she then set on the bar top.

"Thank you," Jev said, taking the glass and handing it to Aiden who smiled up at him appreciatively.

He then led Aiden to the table where the others sat. As soon as Aiden saw that Janette, Sam, and Janice were at the table, though, he could feel Aiden's grip tighten in fear.

It's alright, Aiden, Jev sent to him soothingly. *They're not going to hurt you.*

"You promise?" Aiden asked, looking up at him with concern, but loosening his grip slightly.

"I promise," Jev said aloud, with a reassuring smile. "Why don't you go sit with Jaffay and drink your juice."

Aiden's face brightened immediately at this.

"Okay," he said.

Jev watched with amazed amusement as Aiden then strolled up to a surprised Jaffay and somehow managed to climb up onto his lap without spilling a drop of his juice.

"I just finished suggesting to Janette that you could show her what happened when the two of you entered Aiden's home, Jev," Sam said, getting his attention. "That way she can see for herself that it was necessary for you and Kiyel to do what you did."

Before Jev could respond to Sam's suggestion, however, the door suddenly slammed open, drawing their attention once more to the front of the inn where they saw a concerned-looking Kiyel enter and head directly toward Jev. Following right behind him, and looking equally concerned, were Kel, Tiela and Mikkel.

Jaffay quickly stood up from his chair, lifting Aiden in his arms as he did. "Captain, what's wrong?" he asked.

"I don't know, Jaffay. Kiyel all of a sudden announced that he had to get over here right away."

"Are you alright, Jev?" Kiyel asked as soon as he reached the table, his tail lashing from side to side.

"I am, now that you're here," Jev answered with a relieved smile. He welcomed Kiyel's warm embrace and rubbed his nose to Kiyel's affectionately. "We just had a bit of a disagreement is all."

"It's more than just a disagreement, Jev. A man has been murdered!" Janette said incredulously.

Kiyel let go of Jev and glared at her, his ears flattening against his skull in anger. "I know precisely what has been going on here, First Councillor," he said, the forcefulness of his rebuke causing her to shrink back from him in fear.

"There is a way we can resolve this, Kiyel," Jev said.

Kiyel took in a deep breath and forced himself to relax as he turned back to his Enassi. "You mean show her our memories of what we found in Aiden's home?" he asked.

"You can actually do that?" Janette asked in awe.

Kiyel and Jev both nodded their heads in assent.

"It's one of the reasons why telepaths are so highly regarded by our courts, First Councillor," Kel told her.

"If you're willing to do this, you would see and hear everything that we did as though you were actually there," Kiyel explained.

"What do I have to do?" Janette asked.

"Just grab a hold of my hands and open your mind to me," Jev told her.

Janette hesitated only slightly before doing as Jev instructed, holding her hands out to him, which he then took a hold of and gripped tightly in his before gently sending a probe deep into her mind. The suddenness of Jev's intrusion into her mind caused Janette to take in a sharp breath and try to pull away from him. But, his grip on her hands was firm and he refused to let go.

Feeling her discomfort, and not wishing to prolong the experience any longer than necessary, Jev quickly located the area in her mind that he was looking for, then began sending his memories to her; showing her the moment when he and Kiyel heard Aiden's cries in the forest, and the horrifying scene that confronted them when they burst into Aiden's home.

It took him several minutes to complete the transfer, but once done, he gently withdrew from her mind. Kiyel comfortingly held him as he began to tremble slightly from having to relive the memories.

"Oh God, I think I'm going to be sick!" Janette exclaimed, bending over slightly as she struggled to recover from the experience.

"Now do you see why we had to do what we did?" Kiyel asked.

"Yes," she answered in a shaky, almost whispered voice. There were tears in her eyes. "How could he do such a thing, especially to his own son?" she asked.

"I don't think anyone could really know for sure. It was obvious he was sick, but even so, he couldn't be permitted to harm anyone else."

"No, of course you're right," she said, wiping away her tears. She then looked at Jev. "I'm terribly sorry for doubting you, Jev," she said sincerely. "I've known you long enough that I should have trusted you."

"It's alright, First Councillor," Jev answered, accepting her apology.

"There is one thing I don't understand though. Just a little while ago Aiden asked you a question, as though he was responding to something you'd said, but you didn't say anything. How's that possible?"

"That's another thing we need to discuss with you," Kiyel told her. "Aiden is a lot like us."

"You mean he's also a telepath?" Janette asked, glancing over at Aiden who was still nursing his drink.

"We're not sure. Because of the trauma he suffered at the hands of his father, his talent was awakened much earlier than it normally would. Right now, Aiden doesn't have any control over his abilities, so Kiyel and I—and now Elder Veir—have been using our abilities to suppress his talents."

"But why would you need to do that?" Janette asked, confused.

"If we didn't, he would broadcast wildly and begin affecting the moods and thoughts of others around him. What's worse, he wouldn't even be aware that he's doing it," Kiyel explained.

"That's why," Jev said, and knowing she wasn't going to like what he was going to suggest, took a deep breath, "Aiden needs to come with us when we leave."

"No, absolutely not!" Janette said, emphatically shaking her head. "Regardless of what problems he might have, he's a part of this colony and we'll take care of him."

"I'm afraid that won't be possible," Kiyel said.

"Why's that?" Janette asked, turning on him.

"Because the more Aiden's talent grows stronger—and it will—the more he'll begin to affect the people around him. Aiden needs very specific training to teach him to control his talent, and of course, how to use it properly. Your people, while fully capable of taking care of a normal child his age, are ill-equipped to train a telepath."

"Couldn't you train him here?" she asked.

Kiyel again shook his head.

"He's too terrified of humans. It would make teaching him very difficult, if not impossible."

"I have a suggestion," Sam said, drawing everyone's attention to him. "What if I were to adopt Aiden and go with him, Janette?"

"Out of the question!" Janette protested, both surprised and alarmed at his suggestion.

"Why the hell not?" Sam asked. "Just think about this rationally for a second, Janette. Who on Kiyel's home world knows anything about raising a human child, or treating him medically if he were to get sick or injured? And besides which, while Aiden may not trust me yet, he does know me."

"Alright, you do have a point there," Janette conceded reluctantly. "But what about your patients at the clinic, Sam? We need you here."

Sam shook his head.

"You and I both know that there are other perfectly qualified doctors who work at the clinic now besides me Janette," he reminded her. "And even more can be trained."

"You're really going to come with us to Caitar?" Jev asked excitedly.

"Truthfully, I was never cut out to be a colonist, Jev. I only signed up because I desperately wanted to get away from Earth and all her problems."

"I'm not going to win this, am I?" Janette asked with a weary sigh.

"Nope," Sam said with a wry grin.

"Don't feel too bad, First Councillor," Jev told her, shaking his head with amusement. "My dad wasn't able to win an argument against him either."

"Alright, I'll agree to this, but only on one condition," Janette decided.

"And what might that be?" Sam asked, his tone turning serious once more.

"That this is what Aiden wants," she told him.

"How about it Aiden?" Jev asked as he turned to him. By this time Aiden had finished his juice and was now resting comfortably in Jaffay's arms. "Would you like it if Doc O'Riley were to become your new dad?"

"Why can't you or Kiyel be my daddy?" Aiden asked hopefully.

Jev shook his head sadly. "I wish we could, but neither of us is really old enough. I'm only sixteen years old," he said. Aiden's face fell. "But do you know what we would be if Doc O'Riley was your new dad?" Jev quickly added.

"No, what?" Aiden asked, his voice trembling slightly.

"We'd be brothers."

"Really?" Aiden's eyes opened wide with surprise. "You'd really be my brother?" he asked, suddenly becoming excited.

"Yes I would," Jev answered with a smile.

"And Kiyel, too?"

"And Kiyel, too," Jev assured him, his ears flicking in assent.

Aiden suddenly hopped off Jaffay's lap and ran to Jev, wrapping his arms around his neck happily as Jev picked him up.

"I'd say that's a yes," Taaj said, grinning.

"I'll have the papers ready for you to sign by the time you leave tomorrow, Sam," Janette told him, sighing with resignation. Despite her misgivings though, she couldn't help but smile at Aiden's enthusiasm.

"Thank you, Janette," Sam said.

"I'm still thirsty," Aiden said quietly into Jev's ear.

"Doc, is Aiden allowed to have some more juice?" Jev asked, looking at him.

"Just a little bit, Jev. I'll get it for him," Sam said, nodding his head in assent as he got up from his chair.

"Thanks, Doc," Jev said, setting Aiden down. "Go ahead and sit back down with Jaffay. Doc will bring you your juice in a minute."

"Okay," Aiden said happily, already hurrying over to Jaffay who lifted him up onto his lap.

"Well, now that that's taken care of, First Councillor, if it's alright with you, may I have a moment alone with my team?" Kel asked.

"Of course, Captain. I'll leave you to it, then," Janette said before turning to Jev. "You take care of yourself up there, alright?" she told him.

"I will," Jev promised.

Then nodding her head to the others at the table, she turned and left the inn.

"So, what's up, Captain?" Izha asked.

"Tomorrow morning, a shuttle from the Taigana will be coming to take us back to the Cetani. Kiyel, a telepath from Alien Affairs will be on board. She'll be taking over as an interpreter for the remainder of these talks. Captain Cael would like you to imprint the colonists' language on her when she gets here."

"Aye, Captain," Kiyel said, acknowledging his order with a flick of his ears.

"Before the shuttle arrives, we need to unload all our gear from Captain Cael's shuttle, and prepare to load it onto the one arriving. And lastly, when we're on board the Cetani, we have been instructed by Admiral Chuul to attend a debriefing."

"Captain, you'd better inform the Admiral that Jev and Kiyel will not be at that debriefing. Until such time as I'm satisfied there are no lasting side-effects to Jev's transformation, and that their link is stable, I'm taking them off active duty," Tiela interjected.

"She's not going to be very happy about that, Tiela," Kel said with a frown, his tail flicking jerkily. "I'm afraid she's going to insist that they be there."

"She can insist all she wants. But until I've certified them fit to return to duty, neither she, or any of her staff, are to come anywhere near them."

"And if she tries to push the issue?"

Tiela grinned at him wickedly.

"Then I'll introduce her to my mother," she said.

"I feel sorry for the Admiral already," Kel said with a light chuckle, which earned him a quick, but playful elbow to the ribs from her.

"As for you two," he continued, turning his attention to Mikkel and Janice, "you have a choice to make. Cael has granted you permission to come with us when we leave, in which case you'll officially become permanent members of our armed forces. Of course, if you decide to come, you'll have to undergo extensive training, which is quite gruelling even by Caitaran standards. Or, if you wish, you can remain here on Alessi."

Mikkel and Janice looked at each other for a moment before nodding their heads together in silent agreement.

"Captain, if it's all the same to you, now that the T'kri threat has been abated, we'd like to stay and help rebuild the colony," Janice said.

"I had a feeling you might," Kel said with an understanding grin.

"You're not coming with us?" Jev asked, looking at Mikkel. Tears began to form in his eyes which then rolled down his furred cheek as he suddenly realized he would soon be saying goodbye to his brother.

"I have to stay, Jev," Mikkel said, reaching up to rub his tears away. "They need me here. And besides, someone needs to keep an eye on Captain Harris."

"But I need you, too," Jev said, with a sob.

"You know I'll always be here for you, Jev," Mikkel

promised, pulling him into a tight hug. "We'll see each other again soon. I promise. Once things get settled here, I'll come and visit."

"We both will," Janice added, and offered him a reassuring smile.

"Alright, people" Kel continued after Jev and Mikkel finally separated from each other, once again getting his crew's attention. "We have a busy day ahead of us tomorrow. So I suggest that you all take this time to freshen up a bit and get some much deserved rest. The First Councillor has made arrangements with the innkeeper to provide us with rooms to sleep in for the night—and showers."

Jev's ears pricked up at this last bit of news, as did every Caitaran at the table. The prospect of finally being able to have a shower gave him much relief as his fur had long ago lost its sheen and his skin underneath was beginning to feel very dry and itchy. He knew that the others had to be feeling just as uncomfortable.

"A shower," Tiela whispered dreamily, her tail flicking anxiously behind her. "It's been so long since I've had one that I'd almost forgotten what one was."

There were several heads nodding in agreement at this.

"What do you think, Kiyel? Care to join me upstairs?" Jev asked, looking at his Enassi with a mischievous grin.

"I think I'd like that," Kiyel answered enthusiastically.

"Oh will you two please get a room," Tiela said, rolling her eyes at them with mock indignation, which caused everyone at the table to erupt in laughter.

"We definitely plan to, Tiela," Jev said, once he managed to get his laughter under control, "one with a nice, soft bed to sleep in rather than a cold, hard floor like in the cave."

"I'm all for that," Izha said, her nose crinkling slightly as she remembered their time in the cave.

"I'll have Taaj bring you up some fresh uniforms from the shuttle when you're done," Kel told them.

"Thanks, Captain," Kiyel said with an appreciative flick of his ears.

"Come on, Kiyel," Jev said gleefully as he grabbed a hold of his hand, and then began leading him up the stairs.

SEVEN

The next morning, Kiyel was roused from his sleep by a soft, but persistent, knock on the door. Dragging himself out of bed, he stumbled to the door and opened it slowly. Standing in the hallway outside his and Jev's room in the inn, and wearing a wry expression, was Tiela.

"Tiela, what's wrong?" He asked while trying to rub the sleep from his eyes.

"Oh nothing," she said with a bemused grin. "We were just wondering when the two of you were planning on waking up is all. The shuttle carrying the telepath from Alien Affairs is on its way."

Kiyel's ears dipped slightly and a stream of low curses left his lips as it suddenly dawned on him that he and Jev had slept in.

"I'm sorry, Tiela. We'll be down in a minute," he said.

With an understanding nod of her head, she left and started back down the stairs.

Kiyel closed the door and made his way back to the bed

where he gently shook Jev awake.

"Let me sleep for just a few more minutes, Kiyel," Jev mumbled sleepily into his pillow.

"Sorry, Jev, the shuttle's on its way. We need to get up."

Groaning wearily, Jev grudgingly turned onto his side, facing Kiyel, and slowly opened his eyes, blinking them a few times in an effort to clear away the last remnants of sleep.

"Already?" he asked with a tired yawn. "What time is it anyway?"

"It's late. We slept in."

Jev's eyes suddenly widened with alarm and he abruptly sat up, now very much wide awake.

"Damn!" he swore, throwing the blankets off him as he stood up from the bed.

After they both quickly got into their uniforms, they hurried out of the room and down the stairs, where they sped past a startled innkeeper, and out into the courtyard. There, they rushed over to the rest of the crew who they saw were unloading their gear from the shuttle—all of them, that is, except for Tiela, who was watching over Aiden, who was doing a great deal of watching himself. He was fascinated, as only a child could be, by everything going on around him. The only ones not present, that Jev could see, were Sam, Mikkel, and Janice, which he found very odd. He had very little time to contemplate their whereabouts, however, since Kel noticed them and waved them over to help unload the rest of the gear.

When the last crate was finally unloaded and placed with the rest, movement out of the corner of Kiyel's eye caught his attention. He looked up and saw Janice and Mikkel storming away from the Council building in a huff.

"That unbelievable son of a bitch!" Janice exclaimed angrily as she and Mikkel neared the shuttle.

"Is something the matter, Janice?" Izha asked, looking at her with concern. She, like the rest of the crew, was startled by the vehemence in Janice's voice.

"I'll say! That bastard of a rebel leader actually had the unmitigated gall to proposition me!"

"You declined his advances, of course," Jaffay said, ears and tail flicking in disgust.

"You're damn right I did," she answered, and then grinned at him wickedly, "with my knee to his groin."

As one, they turned to look toward the Council building where a small gathering had formed near the entrance. Jev was just able to make out the prone figure of Captain Harris through the throng of people, and saw that the rebel leader was lying motionless on the ground in a fetal position. He cringed visibly and shook his head.

"I guess I should go see if he's alright," Kel said with a reluctant sigh.

Jev was about to suggest to Kel that he needn't bother, that the rebel leader got what he deserved, when the loud roar of a ship's engines suddenly filled the air. He looked up to see the shuttle they had been waiting for rapidly making its descent toward them.

At that moment it suddenly hit him that for the second time in his young life, he was about to leave a world behind for another, and he looked at Kiyel nervously.

Feeling his nervousness, Kiyel put a comforting hand on his shoulder.

Don't worry, Jev, he sent reassuringly, *I know you'll like Caitar.*

I'm sure I will, Kiyel, Jev sent with an appreciative grin. *I guess I'm just a little anxious about leaving. There's a part of me that's really going to miss this world.*

I know exactly how you feel. Alessi is a beautiful world, and what the colonists here have been able to accomplish, despite all that the T'kri have done to them, is truly remarkable. But I do miss my home world. I will be glad to step foot on her again.

Nodding his head, Jev watched with Kiyel as the shuttle began to slow its descent, its landing struts lowered, and was deftly maneuvered to land opposite them in the square. As soon as it had landed, and its engines shut down, Kel ordered Taaj, Izha, and Jaffay to begin loading their gear.

From where they stood, Jev and Kiyel watched as a single female Caitaran emerge from the shuttle and begin walking down the ramp. She was dressed in loose-fitting, brightly-coloured clothing which covered most of her light-brown and grey pelt. Right away Jev knew that she was the telepath they were expecting.

Stepping off the ramp, she quickly made her way towards them until she was standing before Kiyel. Reaching up with her hand, she then placed her palm against his chest in the customary greeting for telepaths.

"Greetings, Kiyel. I am Eliya," she said with a friendly smile, her voice soft and gentle.

"Well met, Eliya," Kiyel said, similarly returning her greeting. "This is my Enassi, Jev."

"Ah, so this is the one I have heard so much about," she said, turning her gaze on him. "It's an honor to finally meet you."

As she did with Kiyel, she placed the palm of her hand on Jev's chest in greeting.

"Thanks, I think," Jev said, ears dipping in acute embarrassment as he returned her greeting.

This caused a bemused Eliya to laugh.

"Don't worry; I've heard only good things."

"That's a relief," Jev said with a shy grin. "I was beginning to worry."

"I've been instructed by Ambassador D'lin to see you about getting a language imprint done," Eliya continued, looking back at Kiyel.

Kiyel flicked his ears in acknowledgment.

"I'm ready when you are, Eliya," he said.

"Then let's get this over with," Eliya said, signifying her readiness to proceed with a nod of her head.

The transfer took only a few short minutes, but when done, and Kiyel withdrew from her mind, she looked at him with a puzzled expression.

"That's some talent you have there, Kiyel," she said, absently rubbing her temple. "I don't think I've ever encountered an Enassi pair as completely connected as you two are."

"Our link is unique. We won't know to what extent until we reach Caitar and the Telepath guild has a chance to evaluate us."

"Well, I wish the both of you the best of luck and a pleasant journey home," Eliya said. "By the way, you wouldn't happen to know where I might find Ambassador D'lin do you."

"We haven't seen her, but she's probably on board Captain Cael's shuttle," Jev told her.

"Thank you," she said with an appreciative flick of her ears before turning from them and heading up the shuttle's ramp.

At the same time she disappeared into the shuttle, Cael came down the ramp and beckoned Kel over to join him.

"Is your crew ready to go, Kel?" he asked.

"Just about, sir," Kel answered. "We're just waiting on Doctor Sam O'Riley."

"Then let's get your crew on board. You leave within the hour. Admiral Chuul will be waiting for you once you've docked with the Cetani."

"Aye sir," Kel said, ears giving a little flick of acknowledgment before he turned to Jev and Kiyel. "I suggest that the two of you collect Aiden and get yourselves on board."

"Where is Doc, Captain?" Jev asked.

"I saw him heading out of Clearhaven earlier this morning. He was in quite a hurry," Kel said.

"I wonder where he could have gone to," Jev said, wrinkling his nose in thought.

"Don't worry," Kel assured him, "I'm sure he'll be back soon. He has to, now that he has a child to look after."

"I'd like to say goodbye to my brother, if I may, Captain," Jev requested.

Kel nodded his head in assent and Jev left with Kiyel to where his brother and Janice were helping Izha with some of the gear.

"Mikkel," Jev said, getting his attention.

Mikkel turned, his smile turning to a frown when he saw the suddenly sad expression on Jev's face.

"It's time for you to go, isn't it?" he asked.

"Cael just gave us the order," Jev confirmed.

"I'm going to miss you little brother," he said solemnly, drawing Jev into a tight hug.

"I'm going to miss you too."

"You be sure to take care of yourself up there. And I promise, once things get settled here, Janice and I will come and visit," Mikkel assured him, reluctantly releasing him from his embrace.

"Don't take too long."

"We'll be there before you know it."

After giving Mikkel and Janice a final hug, Jev said goodbye to them, and then he and Kiyel made their way to where Tiela was standing, holding a smiling Aiden's hand.

"Are you ready for another ride in the shuttle, Aiden?" Jev asked.

"Uh huh," Aiden said, looking up at him with wide-eyed excitement.

Jev smiled as he picked Aiden up into him arms and together with Kiyel boarded the shuttle, quickly getting themselves settled into seats at the rear of the cabin. Aiden, of course, wanted to sit in the seat next to the view port.

Not minutes after they sat down, several colonists walked in and sat down in seats opposite them. There was a mix of males and females, but mostly males. A few noticed Jev and Kiyel and gave them cursory glances before sitting down. Most, however, ignored them. Jev could sense no open hostility directed towards them, still he watched them nervously.

"What are they doing here?" Jev asked Kiyel in Caitaran. He kept his voice low so as not to draw any more attention to them.

"It was Ambassador D'lin's idea," Kiyel answered, leaning over slightly. "She suggested to the First Councilor that her people should have the opportunity to view Caitaran society first hand to allay their fears of us."

"But why pick these people? They're all rebels."

Kiyel smiled at him wryly as he glanced over at the humans.

"I wouldn't at all be surprised if this bunch saw an opportunity to get away from Captain Harris, and volunteered."

A light chuckle escaped Jev's lips despite his nervousness.

After what seemed like hours, but was really only

minutes, Tiela and the others finally began filing into the cabin. Each of them quickly sat down and began conversing amongst themselves. Their mood was jovial, and Jev could feel their excitement, as they were finally about to return to the Cetani.

Rather than sitting with the others, Tiela sat down in the seats facing Jev and Kiyel, folding her legs underneath her and draping her tail across her lap as she got settled in.

"How are the two of your doing?" she asked.

"A little tired, I guess," Jev told her, with a slight shrug of his shoulders. "Certainly not as tired as we have been these past few days."

"I really owe you both an apology," Tiela said sheepishly.

"What the heavens for, Tiela?" Kiyel asked, his head cocked to one side as he regarded her with a perplexed expression.

"The two of you have been doing so much recently and I knew how exhausted you both were when I woke you up this morning."

"It couldn't be helped, Tiela," Kiyel said, dismissing her worry with a wave of his hand. "You did what you had to."

Just then, Sam entered the cabin, and upon seeing Jev and Kiyel, quickly sat down across from them in the seat next to Tiela. In his hand, Jev saw he held a somewhat large leather bag, which Sam then promptly placed on the empty seat beside him. Jev could see Sam's chest heaving as he struggled to catch his breath.

"We were beginning to worry that you weren't going to make it, Doc," Kiyel said with a relieved smile.

"To be perfectly honest with you, Kiyel, I didn't think I would either," Sam admitted, wiping away the beads of sweat that had accumulated over his brow. "I had to get a few things from the clinic, and then rush back to get the adoption papers completed. It took as long as it did only because Janette wasn't awake yet when I got back."

Their conversation was abruptly interrupted when the intercom above them crackled, followed by the pilot's voice informing them that they would be taking off in a few moments. Almost immediately afterward, the shuttle's engines roared to life.

"Well," Jev said, reaching over to hold Kiyel's hand, looking at him with a nervous smile. "Here we go."

The shuttle set down on the deck of the hanger bay with a dull thump. The entire trip from the surface of Alessi had lasted only minutes, during which time Jev had been captivated by the breathtaking view outside the shuttle.

Like all of Alessi's colonists, Jev had never before seen Alessi from space. He had been asleep in his cryo-tube during the journey from Earth. It was only when the colony ship had landed in what was now Clearhaven that he, along with the rest of the colonists, woke up. Many had been lost during the crossing, including his mother.

The intercom above them crackled to life once again as the pilot informed them that the shuttle was secure and that they could now disembark.

Aiden, who amazingly enough had begun to doze off during the flight, awoke with a start.

"Are we there yet?" he asked, yawning deeply.

His question made Jev chuckle lightly, as it was an oft-repeated refrain asked by antsy kids since time immemorial.

"Yes, we're here," he said.

"Cool!" Aiden exclaimed with delight, turning to look

out the view port at the hanger.

As Jev began unbuckling Aiden from his seat, he turned his head to look at Kiyel.

"So what happens now?" he asked.

"Now we get the two of you settled into your new quarters, and then tomorrow I want to see you both in the medical bay for some tests," Tiela answered for Kiyel as she rose from her seat.

Kiyel looked at her quizzically, his head cocked slightly to one side in confusion.

"What's wrong with the quarters I was assigned?" he asked, "It's more than large enough to accommodate Jev and me comfortably."

"But you didn't have an Enassi then, and your old quarters doesn't have sufficient shielding for Enassi-linked telepaths. As I understand it, Enassi pairings can be quite... intense... or so I've been told," she said with a knowing grin.

"I'd forgotten about that," Kiyel said quietly, cringing slightly as his ears dipped in acute embarrassment.

Tiela laughed at his embarrassment.

"Don't worry about it, Kiyel. Before we left, I arranged for Ardem and Sanaa, an Enassi couple here on the Cetani, to meet you. They'll take you to your new quarters and help you get settled in," she assured him.

"Thank you, Tiela," Kiyel said.

They were the last ones off the shuttle, following after Kel and the rest of the crew, who were themselves guiding their human passengers out of the shuttle. Jev stopped at the bottom of the ramp, hesitating for a moment as he took in their surroundings. The hanger bay was bustling with activity as flight support crew hurried to carry out their assigned duties. Jev could feel Kiyel place a steadying hand on his shoulder, reassured him through their link, and together they continued forward, following the others.

They were headed for the far end of the hanger bay where a group of Caitarans stood, waiting for them. Among them was an older female wearing a uniform much like the one worn by Captain Cael, only more elaborate. Jev did not have to ask who she was, for she had an air of authority about her that it could only be Admiral Chuul, the one Captain Cael had indicated would be waiting for them. Jev was also able to sense right away that two of the Caitarans, a much younger pair, were telepaths.

"Welcome home, Captain Kel," Chuul said in greeting as soon as they approached.

"Thank you, Admiral," Kel answered, acknowledging her with a respectful flick of his ears. "It's very much a relief to be back."

"So these are the human colonists I've heard so much about," Chuul said, indicating the group of humans who were huddled together and looking more than just a little out of place amongst the Caitarans.

"Indeed they are," Kel said. "I understand from Captain Cael that you wish to debrief us right away, so may I suggest we get them squared away in guest quarters until someone is assigned to show them around?"

"An excellent suggestion, Captain," Chuul said with a nod of her head. "Ensign Leit here has been assigned to see to their needs for now."

Kel turned to Izha and directed her to have the humans follow the ensign.

"At some point, we'll need a member of the Diplomatic Guild imprinted with the Alessian language, who will then be responsible for them," Kel said to Chuul as soon as the humans and the Ensign had left the hanger bay."

"Of course," Chuul said. "Well, shall we head to the briefing room then?"

"Just a moment, Admiral," Tiela interjected suddenly. "I'm afraid I have to insist that Jev and Kiyel be excused from the debriefing, at least for now."

Chuul turned to her, the set of her ears showing her displeasure.

"Captain Cael warned me that you would. Surely, Commander Tiela, whatever your concerns are, they can be dealt with after the debriefing."

But Tiela shook her head.

"As their doctor, I have to insist that both of them be given time to recuperate. They're both of them only recently linked and they have been under a great deal of stress, far more than is normal for telepaths their age. Especially Jev."

"Just as stubborn, like your mother," Chuul said with a frown, her tail lashing from side to side in agitation.

"Thank you, Admiral, she'll be pleased to know that you remember her," Tiela replied, grinning mischievously. "She, of course, remembers you quite well."

"And I suppose it was you then who asked Eskad and Sanaa to be here," Chuul said, pointing to the telepath pair. "They wouldn't explain to me why they were here other than to say they were here for Kiyel and Jev."

"That's right, Admiral. I asked them to meet us to help Kiyel and Jev get settled in, and to watch over them for me."

"I see," Chuul said.

"Believe me, Admiral," Eskad said, getting her attention, "we were just as surprised to receive Tiela's call. Kiyel is listed as a grade three telepath. It's unusual for a telepath at that level to form an Enassi link."

"But not unheard of," Sanaa quickly added.

"Very well, Physician," Chuul said with grudging reluctance. "But I expect to be constantly updated on their status. The moment you deem them fit for duty, they are to immediately report to me."

"Of course, Admiral," Tiela agreed.

"The rest of you, follow me," Chuul said.

Turning, she led the group out of the hanger bay, leaving Jev and Kiyel, along with Sam and Aiden, behind with Eskad and Sanaa.

"Well met, Kiyel, and welcome home," Sanaa said.

Both she and Ardem placed their hands on his chest in the traditional telepath greeting.

"Thank you, Sanaa," Kiyel said, returning their greetings.

"And this must be your, Enassi," Eskad said, as he and Sanaa both greeted Jev similarly.

"This is Jev," Kiyel said, introducing him to the pair.

"I didn't think there were other Caitarans on this world," Sanaa said.

"There wasn't, until Kiyel and the crew of the Lekur were shot down," Jev told her.

"I don't understand," Eskad said, looking at Jev quizzically, his ears pricked forward.

"It's a rather long story," Jev said. "There's something I'd like to know first, though."

"Of course," Eskad said, indicating for him to continue.

"Do you think it's possible that we could get something to eat? We were in such a rush getting ready to leave this morning that we haven't had a bite to eat since waking up."

Ardem let out a laugh, and nodded his head.

"I think that can be arranged," Eskad said.

* * *

Having powered down the engines, Hraka exited the shuttle, stopping at the bottom of the ramp when he saw Jev and Kiyel leaving the hanger bay with a pair of Caitarans he didn't recognize. Following after them were two of the humans he recognized from the shuttle.

"Was that him?" he heard a voice suddenly ask.

Hraka turned to find a young technician finish securing a fuel line to the shuttle's undercarriage while staring after the departing group. Recognizing him, Hraka nodded his head.

"That is the abomination, yes," Hraka said, his nose crinkling in disgust.

"He doesn't look all that dissimilar from us."

"No, he doesn't," Hraka agreed. "And that's what makes him so dangerous."

"So you still intend to go through with this plan of yours then?"

"To protect the purity of our race, I am." Hraka's eyes narrowed slightly as he regarded the technician carefully. "You're not having second thoughts about this are you, Tiimo?" he asked.

"No, of course not," Tiimo hastily answered.

"What about Daac and Ghien, are they here yet?"

"They arrived about an hour ago," Tiimo confirmed. "They're waiting for us in the crew lounge on E deck."

"When does your duty shift end?"

"I just have to finish refueling this shuttle."

"Good," Hraka said, and for the first time smiled. It was not a pleasant smile.

Leaving Tiimo to finish, Hraka exited the hanger bay and made his way through the busy corridor until he reached the elevator. When the lift reached E deck, and the doors opened, he immediately headed for the crew lounge. Stepping through the doors, he quickly spotted the two individuals he was looking for seated at a table at in the far corner, away from prying eyes and ears, and he made his way to them.

"Hraka," a dark-furred male greeted him, acknowledging his presence with a flick of his ears.

"Daac, Ghien," Hraka said, nodding to each in turn at the table as he sat down in an empty chair.

"Is it true then, what they're saying, that there's a hybrid on board?" Ghien asked.

"It is. I saw him for myself on the shuttle," Hraka answered.

"What does he look like, this hybrid?" Daac asked, leaning forward in his chair.

"He's like us in many ways, except he's shorter than most males and he has light-coloured fur, just like a female."

"I understand he's a telepath as well," Ghien said

"Our ancestors warned us that this day would come," Hraka said, his eyes narrowing in thought. "And a day would come when a Caitaran not born of Caitar would walk among us, and he would be the harbinger of death to our people."

"You quote from Chemia's prophesy. Do you think that this hybrid is the one he spoke of?" Ghien asked.

"I do," Hraka answered. "This is why the abomination must be destroyed, along with all who would support him."

Daac and Ghien both nodded their heads in agreement just as the lounge doors opened to admit Tiimo into the room.

EIGHT

After leaving the hanger, Ardem and Sanaa led Jev, Kiyel, Sam, and Aiden through the busy corridors of the ship to an elevator, where they stopped and waited for it to return to their level.

Aiden, who was increasingly becoming nervous with so many Caitarans giving them curious looks, gripped Jev's hand tightly in his and moved behind him to try to avoid their stares. Jev saw his discomfort and smiled down at him reassuringly, while at the same time giving his hand a gentle squeeze.

Just then the lift door finally slid open. They stood back to allow a group of Caitarans to exit the lift, then piled in themselves. When the door closed, and Ardem touched his hand to the panel by the door, Jev felt the lift lurch slightly as it began to ascend.

"No elevator music?" Jev commented wryly in English as he turned his head to look back at Kiyel.

This caused Sam to chuckle lightly, while a bemused Kiyel just shook his head.

Moments later, the lift deposited them onto a relatively empty corridor several decks up from where they started.

The stark contrast between the two corridors immediately caught Jev's attention. Where the first was filled with so many Caitarans it was almost impossible for them to move, this one was almost completely devoid of life, except for the occasional Caitaran who passed by them.

Sensing Jev's confused astonishment, Kiyel leaned down to speak to him.

"We just came from the lower decks, where our ground troops and pilots live and work. The upper decks, like this one, are where the officers and those responsible for running the Cetani live," he explained.

"Is that why it was so crowded down there and not here?" Jev asked.

"We probably just came aboard during shift change," Ardem answered.

"There's over four hundred crew on board, Jev. Most of them occupy the lower decks," Sanaa added.

"That many?" Jev asked, his eyes widening with surprise. "Wow!"

Ardem and Sanaa both laughed at his reaction.

"You'll get used to it soon enough, Enassi," Kiyel said.

Jev felt a gentle tug on his sleeve and he looked down to see Aiden looking up at him with a hopeful expression.

"Are we getting something to eat now?" Aiden asked.

They suddenly stopped and turned to stare at Aiden with a mix of surprise and amazement on each of their faces. It wasn't what he said that made them stop so suddenly, but rather it was how he said it, for somehow he spoke to them in perfect Caitaran.

Aiden seemed to wilt under their gaze.

"Did I say something wrong?" he asked timidly, again speaking Caitaran.

Jev was the first to recover, and he knelt down to his level.

"No, of course not, Aiden," he assured him. "But how did you learn to speak like us?"

"I don't know," Aiden answered, relaxing visibly when he realized he wasn't in trouble. "I just do."

"This is incredible," an astonished Kiyel said.

"I take it this child has never spoken our language before, Kiyel?" Sanaa asked.

"No, never," Kiyel said.

"Aiden, you can understand everything that we're saying?" Jev asked.

"Some of it," Aiden answered, nodding his head, and smiling proudly at him. "I couldn't before, but I can now."

Jev smiled at him and stood back up.

"So we can see, cub," Kiyel said.

"Hey, I'm not a cub," Aiden protested, looking up at Kiyel seriously, "I'm a boy."

"You know something, you'll always be a cub to us," Kiyel said with a smile.

At this everyone burst into laughter, except Sam, who was looking more than just a little perplexed.

"Would someone mind explaining to me what's going on? I can't understand a thing you're all saying."

"Sorry, Doc," Jev said in English as he quickly got his laughter under control. "It's just that somehow Aiden is beginning to learn how to understand and speak Caitaran."

"Did either you or Kiyel teach it to him?" Sam asked.

"No, and that's just it, he seems to be picking it up on his own."

"It's very unusual," Kiyel added, absently scratching behind his ear.

Sam's brow furrowed in thought as he looked at Kiyel.

"Correct me if I'm wrong, Kiyel, but didn't it take you only a few days to learn English?"

"That's true. But I'm a fully trained telepath. Aiden isn't."

"Plus there's the fact that Kiyel and I are using our abilities to suppress Aiden's talent," Jev reminded him.

Sanaa's ears pricked up at this when Kiyel finished translating everything that had been said, and she looked at Jev with surprise.

"Are you saying the child is a telepath?" she asked.

"We don't know yet. His talent was wakened prematurely," Jev said, reverting to Caitaran.

"So he's here to be tested," Ardem said.

"That's right," Jev confirmed.

"Well, however he's doing it, we're not going to get any answers standing out here in the corridor," Kiyel said.

They reached their destination a short time later, walking through the doors that slid open form them. On the other side was a spacious, comfortably-lit room with a number of round tables scattered throughout. Circling each of these tables were four large, extremely comfortable-looking, chairs. Beside the entrance, where they had just come in, was a long bar, behind which stood a Caitaran who was busy preparing food and some drinks for a pair of Caitarans seated on stools at the bar.

The most striking feature, however, and the one that caught Jev's eye the most, were the four large windows at the opposite end of the room. Outside was the breathtaking view of Alessi below them.

For a few moments he just stood there, looking at the

scene before him in awe. It was not until he received a gentle nudge from Kiyel that he allowed himself to be led by Ardem and Sanaa to a pair of empty tables near the windows.

"Impressive, isn't it?" Sanaa asked Jev as they sat down. "No matter how many times I come to this lounge and look out that window it still manages to leave me breathless."

"It's beautiful," Jev said, reluctantly tearing his gaze away from the view.

"So what would you like to eat?" Ardem asked.

"I don't really know," Jev said. "I've never actually eaten Caitaran food before."

"What, never?" Ardem asked, looking at Jev in astonishment.

"Jev wasn't born Caitaran, Ardem. He was born human, just like Sam and Aiden here," Kiyel told him.

"Wasn't born Caitaran..." Ardem echoed incredulously, his voice trailing off as he stared at Jev.

"It's a long story," Jev said.

"Well, we've plenty of time," Sanaa said.

But before Jev could respond, one of the lounge's wait staff approached their table.

"Is there something I can get for you?" the tall, dark-furred Caitaran male asked.

Looking up at him, Sanaa began by ordering a round of k'yarri for herself, Ardem, Jev, Kiyel, and also Sam, who indicated he was interested in trying a cup after Kiyel explained that it was similar to Alessian coffee, only sweeter and not as strong.

"And for the little one?" the waiter asked.

"Some nanaya juice if you have any," Kiyel ordered.

Sanaa then ordered a simple first meal for each of them, after which the waiter left to get their order.

"Kiyel, what's nanaya juice?" Jev asked, speaking in English for Sam's benefit.

"It's a sweet-tasting drink made from a fruit grown on Brekar that's very rich in vitamins," Kiyel explained.

Sam nodded his head.

"That's just what he needs," he said.

Shortly afterward, the waiter returned to their table with their drinks, which he placed in front of them before leaving again.

Curiously eyeing his drink, Aiden lifted up the glass and took a tentative sip from it. As soon as the greenish liquid hit his taste buds, his face quickly lit up with pleasure and he began drinking in earnest.

"I think he likes it," Ardem said with a little chuckle.

"What was your first clue?" Kiyel asked.

By the time Aiden had finished his drink, the waiter was back with their food, which Jev eyed hungrily as a plate was placed before him.

On it were some strips of cooked meat and a variety of vegetables and fruit that looked very appealing, even though he couldn't identify any of it. The smell alone made his mouth begin to water.

Aiden, in the meantime, was staring at the food on his plate with an uncertain expression.

"What's this?" he asked, pointing to a round, reddish fruit.

"It's fruit. Try some, it's really good," Kiyel assured him as put a piece of meat in his mouth, closing his eyes as he savoured the flavor.

Seeing the expressions of contentment on both Jev's and Kiyel's faces, he did as Kiyel suggested, tentatively putting a piece of fruit in his mouth. To his pleasant surprise, it was very tasty, and like Kiyel and Jev, quickly began enthusiastically attacking the food on his plate.

"So tell us, how is it possible that you could be born human, but look like one of us?" Sanaa asked.

"That's part of the reason why Tiela wants to see Kiyel and me in the medical bay tomorrow," Jev said, after swallowing a piece of meat. "About a week ago we were attacked by the T'kri in the cave we were hiding in. During the attack I somehow began to change, though I don't remember it happening."

"We believe that Jev is not only a telepath but also a telekinetic, and it's this talent that allowed him to change," Kiyel said.

"But how could that cause such a change to occur?" a confused looking Sanaa asked.

"I wish we could tell you," Jev said, his ears dipping apologetically. "At the time, Kiyel suggested that I instinctively altered my DNA in response to the threat, and that because I'm still going through puberty my body was amiable to the change."

"We won't know for certain exactly how Jev did what he did until Tiela has had a chance to take a look at him," Kiyel added.

"It sounds almost too incredible to be believed," Ardem said in awe.

"He's not entirely Caitaran though," Kiyel continued. "Some of his human DNA is still present, as is evidenced by the colouring of his fur, which is the same colour hair he had when he was human. Also, Tiela has said that his vision is slightly better than our own, in that he can see colours more vividly."

"In other words, you're a hybrid," Sanaa said to Jev, leaning back in her chair, and nodding her head in understanding.

"So it would seem," Jev said before returning his attention to the food on his plate.

An hour later, Jev was working on his second helping. From the very first bite he took, he was impressed with how good it tasted. Somehow the flavours seemed more real than any of the food he'd eaten on Alessi.

The others watched with amusement as he took bite after bite, until finally everything on his plate had disappeared. Jev, oblivious to their stares, closed his eyes and leaned back in his chair, rubbing his stomach as he savored the experience.

"When you said you were hungry, you weren't kidding," Sanaa said, looking at Jev with a wide grin on her face.

Jev suddenly opened his eyes and stared at her, his ears dipping slightly from embarrassment. He was saved from further embarrassment, however, when the lounge doors opened and Kel and Tiela walked in.

"Well it didn't take you two very long to find the lounge," Tiela said to Kiyel as she and Kel pulled up a couple more chairs to sit with them.

"How was the debriefing with Chuul?" Jev asked.

"About as well as could be expected, considering," Kel said with a slight shrug.

Jev got the distinct impression that Kel didn't want to talk about the debriefing, so he let the matter drop.

"Did the two of you get settled into your new quarters yet?" Tiela asked, quickly changing the subject.

"Actually, we came here first. We were in such a rush this morning that we didn't have a chance to grab something to eat before we left," Kiyel said.

"That'll teach you to sleep in," Kel said.

"Something interesting happened along the way, though," Kiyel said, "Aiden has begun speaking our language."

"He has?" Tiela said, her ears pricking up with interest as she turned her attention to Aiden.

"How?" Kel asked.

"We don't know," Kiyel said, with a shake of his head, "though it's likely because of his talent."

"I thought you and Jev were preventing Aiden from using his talent," Kel said, looking at them with a confused expression.

"We are, Captain, but only to a certain degree. We can't block his talent completely. Neither of us has that kind of ability. We can only ensure that he doesn't affect others by sending wildly."

"It's amazing what the mind is capable of, given the right motivation," Tiela said, chuckling lightly.

"In his case, it was food," Jev said, smiling at Aiden.

"We'll know more once he gets tested by the Telepath Guild," Kiyel said.

"Speaking of being tested," Tiela said, reverting to English and looking at Sam, "would you care to join me tomorrow when we do Jev's and Kiyel's scans?"

Sam, who up to this point had been simply observing the conversation, and not understanding a single word of it, looked at her with a surprised expression.

"Thank you, I would," he said. "I had actually planned at some point to ask you if I could anyway."

"I figured as much," she said with a knowing grin. "Given your knowledge of human physiology, Admiral Chuul has given me permission to train you to work in our medical bay."

"She wasn't really too keen on the idea at first. Not until, that is, she was told that not only are you a physician, but you're also Jev's legal guardian," Kel said.

"How's he going to work with you when he can't read or speak Caitaran, Tiela?" Kiyel asked.

"He will if you do a language transfer, like you did for us."

"Captain?" Kiyel asked, seeking Kel's permission.

Kel flicked his ears in assent.

A few minutes later, Sam was rubbing the sides of his temple, nursing a small headache.

"I'm sorry if I caused you any discomfort," Kiyel said, flattening his ears backward in apology.

"No, that's quite alright, Kiyel," Sam assured him.

His eyes then suddenly flew open and he looked at Kiyel in shocked bewilderment as he realized Kiyel spoke to him in his native language, and that he had understood him.

"Now you know how I felt when I first realized that I could understand the Captain back on Alessi," Jev said with a knowing grin.

"This is going to take some getting used to," Sam said.

"We haven't been properly introduced. I'm Sanaa, and this is my Enassi and life-mate Ardem," Sanaa said to Sam.

Sam nodded in greeting to each of them.

"It's a pleasure to meet you. My name is Sam," he said, trying out his Caitaran, though he struggled to form the words.

"Don't worry, Sam, you'll get accustomed to our language soon enough," Tiela said with a sympathetic grin. "Right now, however, the four of you need to get settled in to your new quarters. Tomorrow is going to be a busy day for all of us."

"Have Doc and Aiden been assigned quarters yet?" Kiyel asked.

"Yes, they have," Tiela said, and then smiled at him. "In fact, they'll be sharing yours."

Jev looked at her, cocking his head on one side, ears turning in her direction.

"Just how large are our quarters, Tiela?" he asked.

"Large enough, Jev," she laughed.

"Enassi quarters are some of the largest on the Cetani," Ardem interjected helpfully. "They're equipped with a bedroom and an office that can be converted into another bedroom, which yours already has, a sitting room, personal facilities, and a small alcove in which you can prepare drinks and small meals for yourselves."

"That's pretty impressive," Sam said.

"Only the Ambassador Suites, one deck up, where visiting dignitaries reside, are larger, and those include a full kitchen," Ardem added.

"I can't wait to see them," Jev said, clearly impressed.

"Well then, if you're finished, we should get going," Ardem said, pushing back his chair as he stood up.

"I'll stop by later to see how you're settling in," Tiela promised.

"You're not coming?" Kiyel asked, his ears flicking in surprise.

"After being subjected to Chuul's debriefing, Kel and I decided we needed something strong to drink," she said.

"Perhaps several drinks," Kel added dryly.

Jev smiled and chuckled lightly as he and the others then rose from their chairs.

"I guess we'll see you later then," he said.

After leaving the lounge, Ardem and Sanaa once again began leading them through the seemingly endless corridors of the ship. This time, however, they remained on the same level.

Before long, they stopped at a door at the end of a long, empty corridor, which had just closed behind a Caitaran male.

He was about Jev's height and sported a grey and black pelt, which Jev found intriguing as it wasn't a colour he'd seen on any other Caitaran. He was also fascinated by his blue eyes, which again was unusual for a Caitaran.

"You must be Kiyel and Jev," the Caitaran said, curiously eyeing them both.

A look of surprise crossed Jev's face when the Caitaran place his hand on each of their chests, a gesture which he now recognized to be the traditional telepath greeting.

"You're not a telepath are you?" he asked as he and Kiyel returned the Caitaran's greeting.

The Caitaran shook his head.

"No, but I grew up around telepaths," he said. "My name is Riyad. I was asked by the Telepath Guild to help get your quarters ready."

"I guess that's how you knew who we were," Jev said.

Riyad smiled at him with wry amusement.

"There isn't a telepath on board who doesn't know who you are, Jev. The two of you have become quite the source of conversation," he said.

"Ah," Jev said, ears twitching faintly with embarrassment.

"If you've finished embarrassing our friends, Riyad, perhaps you could allow them to see their quarters now?" Sanaa suggested, lightly admonishing Riyad, but inwardly smiling at Jev's reaction, which she found somewhat endearing.

"You're right, Sanaa," Riyad said, quickly sobering up, his ears flattening briefly against his skull.

"Jev, go ahead and place the palm of your hand there," Sanaa said, indicating the flat, hand-sized panel located on the bulkhead beside the door.

As soon as Jev did as he was instructed, the panel lit up

and he heard a low chirp from the computer.

"What just happened?" Jev asked.

"The security system is now scanning your DNA and recording that information in a secure database. Like Ambassador's quarters, Enassi quarters feature a system that's keyed to an individual's unique DNA. Only those who's DNA has been recorded in the system will be able to open the door from the outside," Riyad said.

"So what's to stop someone from just breaking the door down or prying it open?"

"Well for one thing, the doors on the Cetani are constructed of a lightweight, composite material that's actually stronger than three inch thick steel. Also, when closed, the doors are magnetically sealed. It's virtually impossible for anyone to break into the room," Riyad explained.

"In other words, we will be the only ones able to open the door," Sam said, speaking slowly so as to ensure he was understood.

"And security and medical personnel, who can override the lock in emergencies," Riyad said, somewhat taken aback that Sam had spoken to him in Caitaran, albeit with a heavy accent.

"That makes sense," Sam nodded.

With a final chirp, the panel turned dark again and Jev removed his hand from it.

Riyad then motioned for Kiyel, Sam, and then Aiden to each in turn place their palms on the panel, recording their DNA into the system along with Jev's.

"Alright, everything's set," Riyad said after he tapped a few final commands into the panel.

"Thank you, Riyad," Kiyel said, ears giving a tiny flick of appreciation.

With a nod and an acknowledging grin, Riyad turned and

started down the corridor towards the lift, which he then disappeared into.

"Well, Jev, care to do the honours?" Kiyel asked.

An eager grin formed on Jev's face as he placed his palm on the panel, causing it to light up once again. Upon confirming his identity, a low chirp sounded, after which the door to their quarters slid open.

The first thing Jev noticed after they stepped through the door was that other than the light from the corridor and from the star field outside the large windows across from them, they were standing in almost total darkness. It was only due to his Caitaran eyes that he was even able to see. Sam, however, not being Caitarans, wasn't so lucky, and ended up tripping on the leg of a stool near the door as he entered, causing Jev to cringe slightly, but then being forced to stifle a laugh when a series of choice words came out of Sam's mouth.

Movement by the door caught Jev's attention and he turned just in time to see Kiyel touch an illuminated button on the panel beside the door causing the lights to come on.

By the time Jev's eyes had adjusted to the warm, yellowish lights he was already impressed. Their quarters was indeed everything Ardem and Sanaa had told them it was, and more.

They were standing on a slightly raised dais which almost completely encircled a large sitting area with two oversized sofas and a low table in the middle. At the far end were two large windows which presented them with a magnificent view of Alessi below and the stars beyond. On their left was a small bar, in front of which were several tall stools, one of which Sam had already bumped into. On their right were three doors leading to what Jev assumed were their bedrooms and the washroom.

"Well, what do you think?" Sanaa asked, her voice suddenly breaking the stunned silence.

"It's incredible," Sam said, while still taking everything in.

A huge grin appeared on Aiden's face as he practically leapt down from the dais to the sitting area below, where he scrambled up onto one of the sofas.

"We honestly weren't expecting this," Kiyel said, smiling with amusement at Aiden who happily stretched out on the sofa.

"The doors leading to your bedrooms are just over there," Ardem said, nodding to the two doors closest to the windows. "Your personal belongings should already have been brought up and put into your rooms."

"And through the last door is your personal facilities, where you can freshen up and take care of your personal needs," Sanaa said.

"We humans call it a washroom," Sam said.

"An apt description for it," Sanaa said with a wry grin.

"Well, I guess we'll leave you now, so you can get settled in," Ardem said as he touched the panel by the door to the quarters, which then opened. "If you need anything at all, our quarters are right next to yours."

"Thank you, Ardem, Sanaa," Kiyel said, ears and tail flicking appreciatively.

With a nod, Ardem and Sanaa then stepped out into the corridor, and the door closed.

"Well, shall we check out our room?" Kiyel suggested to Jev.

Jev grinned enthusiastically at Kiyel in response, and grabbed his hand as he led him to the door nearest the window.

Sam starred after them with a light chuckle, and shaking his head slowly as they quickly disappeared through the door.

NINE

When Tiela later dropped by Jev and Kiyel's quarters as she promised she would, Jev wasn't in the least bit surprised to see that Kel was with her as well. It occurred to him then that lately; wherever Tiela went Kel was constantly at her side, following her around like a kitten would follow its mother. So when he saw the two of them standing outside their door together, he had to suppress the grin that threatened to form on his face. Better than ever now, he was able to feel the connection that was growing between them. If they weren't already a couple, he knew they soon would be.

Stepping aside to let them in, Jev noticed that Tiela held in her hands several data pads which she promptly offered to Sam upon seeing him.

"These are for you, Sam. They contain all the information you'll need on Caitaran anatomy and physiology," she said.

After scanning over them briefly, Sam nodded with

appreciation.

"Thanks, these will help," he said.

"So how are you two liking your new quarters, Kiyel?" Tiela asked.

"Honestly it's more than Jev and I expected, Tiela," Kiyel admitted.

Kel slowly nodded as he looked around and took everything in, having never before seen Enassi quarters.

"Excellent," she said with a grin. "In that case what do the four of you say to joining us for an early third meal?" she said.

"Sounds good to me, I'm starving," Jev said, his tail beginning to flick in anticipation.

"You're always hungry," Kiyel said, with an amused chuckle.

"Well I am a growing boy."

In more ways than one, Enassi, Kiyel sent with a mischievous grin.

Kiyel! Jev protested, his ears flattening against his skull in acute embarrassment.

Luckily for him though, neither Tiela nor Kel noticed, or if they did, they chose not to say anything.

"By the way, where's Aiden?" Kel asked, suddenly noticing his absence.

"Oh, he's taking a nap. What with all the excitement he's had today he was pretty tired," Sam answered. "I'll go wake him and see if he's hungry."

"No, wait, you don't..." Tiela started, but Sam had already left, quickly disappearing into the room he shared with Aiden.

Moments later, when he re-emerged, he was carrying a

very groggy looking Aiden in his arms.

"Did you get a good sleep, Aiden?" Jev asked.

"Uh huh," Aiden nodded.

"I'm impressed," Tiela said, looking at Sam and Aiden in surprised wonder. "How in Dahel's name did you get him to let you carry him, Sam?"

"Honestly, Tiela, I don't really know," Sam said, clearly as surprised as she was, but also beaming with pride at his adopted son. "I just went in to wake him and he suddenly reached up to me as though wanting to be picked up. So I did."

"Maybe Aiden's finally realized that Sam wouldn't hurt him," Jev said.

"Well, whatever the reason, it's certainly a good sign," Tiela said.

Aiden began to squirm slightly in Sam's arms, wanting to be let down, which Sam did.

"Well, shall we get going then?" Kel asked.

Minutes later, after they left the quarters, they arrived back at the lounge and stepped inside.

They weren't in the lounge for more than a half hour, and already enjoying their meal, when the lounge doors suddenly opened to admit a young and very nervous looking female yeoman. Out of the corner of his eye, Jev saw her begin scanning the room until her gaze finally fell on them, at which point she then began to make her way to their table.

"Are you Kiyel, sir?" she asked with timid apprehension, which Jev found rather odd.

Surprised that she was looking for him, Kiyel looked up at her and nodded.

"There's a call for you from home world, sir," she continued.

"A call, for me?" Kiyel asked, his ears pricking up with

curiosity.

"Yes, sir. I'm told it's your father."

Kiyel frowned slightly, his nose wrinkling.

"Damn!" he muttered quietly. He slowly rose from his chair, his tail flicking jerkily behind him, showing his distress.

We both knew this time would come, Enassi, Jev sent.

I would have preferred to tell him about us later though, when we were on Caitar.

Do you want me to come with you?

No, this is something I should do myself, Kiyel sent.

Jev nodded in understanding as Kiyel apologetically excused himself from the table and then left with the yeoman out of the lounge.

"Jev, what was all that about?" a confused Tiela asked when the lounge doors closed behind them.

Everyone at the table stared expectantly at him, but Jev just shook his head, his ears dipping slightly apologetically.

"I'm sorry, Tiela. I really can't say. I made a promise to Kiyel that I wouldn't."

Kel leaned back in his chair, his eyes narrowing as he stared at Jev intensely.

"This ship is under a strict communications blackout, except for command level channels, until the T'kri threat on Alessi has been dealt with and diplomatic relations with the colonists has been firmly established. For Kiyel to be receiving a communication of any kind indicates that he must have some pretty high level connections. It would appear there's more to our Kiyel than we previously believed."

Again Jev said nothing, even though each of them at the table continued to stare expectantly at him.

Kiyel followed the young yeoman down the corridor to the communications office located on the same level where he was ushered inside and shown into a small room. There the yeoman had him sit down in the chair before a console, above which was a view screen that displayed the Alliance's insignia. Reaching past Kiyel, she activated the unit for him.

"I'll be waiting for you outside, sir, if you need anything," she said, bowing respectfully before leaving the room so he could take the call in private.

The insignia on the screen faded away and was replaced with the image of his father who was wearing a severe expression.

"Kiyel, what in Dahel's name are you doing out there?" his father asked without even so much as a hello.

"It's nice to see you, too, father," Kiyel said.

"Don't be evasive, Kiyel! I know something is wrong. I could feel your distress from here on Caitar. Now what's going on?"

"Father, you may be the most powerful telepath on Caitar, but there is no way you could have possibly picked up my mental state from that far away."

"Alright, call it father's intuition then," his father said with a dismissive wave of his hand. But then his expression and tone softened. "Your mother and I have been worried about you."

"As you can see, father, I'm perfectly fine."

"That's not good enough, Kiyel. We know that the ship you were assigned was shot down and that you were injured. Other than assuring us that you survived, however, that damned Admiral Chuul is refusing to discuss your situation with us."

"That sounds like something she would do," Kiyel said

dryly.

"It took me calling in a few favours just to be allowed to make this call," his father continued. "Now what's going on?"

Kiyel let out a long sigh, resigning himself to the fact that he wasn't going to be able to avoid telling his father any longer.

"I was injured in the crash. But I'm all right now."

His father's expression softened further and became full of concern.

"What happened?"

"The captain ordered a retreat into the forest nearby to avoid being discovered, but I was too weak from the injuries I sustained to follow. I was forced instead to make my way to a small settlement belonging to the colonists where, near death, I collapsed in the snow. Almost immediately after, I was discovered by one of the colonists who took me inside a dwelling where my wounds were treated."

There was an uncomfortable silence as his father sat staring at him through the terminal.

"That was a risky thing you did, Kiyel," his father gently admonished. "For all you knew the colonists could have been the ones who shot down your ship."

"Except I knew they weren't, father, because my mind touched the mind of one who possessed a talent."

His father leaned forward in his chair, ears pricking with surprised interest.

"Wait, they're a race with telepaths?" he asked.

"Didn't Ambassador D'lin tell you that in her reports?" Kiyel asked, his head cocked on one side and looking quizzically at his father.

"There's been no mention of there being telepaths among

the humans at all."

"More interference from Admiral Chuul I'll bet," Kiyel muttered derisively.

"You've bonded with one of these human telepaths haven't you, Kiyel?" his father suddenly asked, the realization hitting him.

"I have, father. He's my Enassi. His name is Jev. It was he who found me and saved me."

"I should have realized it sooner. The feel of your mind is so different now. There's an almost alien quality to it."

"Father, I need to know if you will accept him. I left Caitar because I wanted an ordinary life, not one tied to duty and tradition, like you and mother. That hasn't changed. So if you won't, there's really little point in us returning to Caitar."

His father leaned back in his chair and shrugged his shoulders, though the set of his ears showed he wasn't at all pleased with the situation.

"He's your Enassi, Kiyel. I can't say it's what I'd wished for you, but whether he's human or Caitaran makes no difference. The bond is undeniable. He will be welcome here."

"Thank you, father."

"Don't thank me just yet. There is still your mother to consider," his father said with a slight frown. "At any rate, I would appreciate it if from now on I'm sent the full reports on all matters concerning you and your Enassi. I know you enlisted in the forces under an assumed name, but unless it's cleared by you, I assume Admiral Chuul will continue to frustrate my efforts."

"I'll see that it's done."

"The Cetani is scheduled to leave for Caitar tomorrow at mid-day. Your mother will be joining you shortly before its departure to represent Alien Affairs. I would come myself, but at the moment I'm up to my ears in this Caitaran/Alessian treaty. I will, however, look forward to meeting your Enassi when you return. Take care of yourself, Kiyel."

"And you as well, father," Kiyel said as the screen went black and the insignia returned.

Only when Kiyel was certain that the connection was closed did he finally allow himself to relax, a relieved grin stretching across his face.

Jev was enjoying his second cup of k'yarri and listening to the quiet conversation around the table when he glanced over at the lounge doors as they opened to admit the same group of humans that had been with them on the shuttle. Leading them was the ensign who had been assigned to them.

While the ensign led the group to an empty table in a far corner of the lounge, one of the humans, a tall, lanky man with curly brown hair and dark blue eyes stopped suddenly and looked over at them, a look of surprised recognition flashing across face.

"Is something the matter, Jev?" Tiela asked him.

"I think that man over there knows Doc," Jev said.

"Really?" Sam asked. He looked passed Jev to see the man slowly starting towards them.

"Are you Doctor Sam O'Riley?" the man asked when he finally reached their table.

"Yes, I am. Is there something I can do for you?"

"My name's Shawn Dedrick. You treated my daughter a couple of weeks ago after she was roughed up by a T'kri patrol."

Sam's brow furrowed in thought for a moment, a frown on his lips, as he tried to remember the girl.

"Her name wouldn't happen to be Tanya would it?" he asked.

Shawn nodded, a grateful grin stretching across his slightly unkempt face.

"I never got the chance to before, but I'd like to thank you for everything you did for her." He reached across the table to Sam, offering his hand, which Sam gladly shook.

"You're very welcome, Shawn. She's doing well I take it?"

"Much better now, thanks," Shawn nodded. "She's begun apprenticing with the proprietor of the bakery in Clearhaven."

"That's good to hear," Sam said.

"If you don't mind me saying though, I was a little surprised to see you on board. I thought I saw you on the shuttle on the way up, but I wasn't sure until now. You're the last person I'd have expected to see willingly get on board an alien vessel."

"Normally you'd be right," Sam answered with a slight chuckle. "But the truth is I'm here because of little Aiden here, and Jev."

"Wait, do you mean Mikkel's little brother?" Shawn asked. "I thought Jev and their father both died in the fire."

"Luckily I wasn't there," Jev said, startling Shawn, who suddenly stepped back from him when he saw not the Caitaran he expected, but Jev as he looked when he was human.

"Shawn, this is Jev," Sam said.

"What the...? How'd you do that?" Shawn asked, eyeing Jev warily.

"I'm a telepath," Jev said succinctly, allowing his illusion to fade to reveal his true self.

Seeing his sudden weariness, Tiela offered him her cup

of k'yarri, which he gratefully accepted and quickly drank.

"But you're a Caitaran. There's no way you could be Jev," a clearly flustered Shawn said.

"He used to be human though, just like you, Sam and Aiden are," Tiela quickly interjected. "How and why his transformation occurred is something we're trying to figure out."

"Needless to say a lot has happened since my dad died in the fire," Jev said.

"Right, well, I think I really should be getting back to the others now," Shawn said, his tone anxious. "Thanks again for everything you did for my Tanya, Doc."

Before Sam could respond, however, Shawn turned and hurriedly returned to the group of humans he had come in with.

"He was afraid of me," Jev said quietly.

"Can you really blame him?" Kel asked.

Jev involuntarily flinched at the rebuke, his ears twitching slightly.

"No, I guess not," he answered.

But then suddenly a wide grin appeared on his face as he looked up across the lounge to the lounge doors once again, his tail tip flicking with pleasure.

"Now what?" Tiela asked.

"It's Kiyel," Jev answered. "He got the answer he was hoping for. He's on his way back now."

"What answer would that be?" Kel asked.

Jev was about to answer when the lounge doors suddenly opened to admit a rather cheerful looking Kiyel, who quickly made his way to their table.

I missed you, Enassi, Jev sent as Kiyel leaned down to rub his nose to his affectionately.

Kiyel let out a light chuckle as he retook his seat next to

Jev.

I was only gone for a few minutes, he sent.

"Well, Kiyel, don't you think it's about time you levelled with us?" Kel asked.

"I beg your pardon, sir?" Kiyel asked, looking at him quizzically, the smile on his face quickly disappearing.

"A third grade telepath with your rank would never be permitted to receive a personal communique during a communications blackout. After everything we've been through I think we deserve to know what's going on."

"You're right, sir, you do have a right to know," Kiyel said with a sigh, his ears dipping apologetically. "But I don't think we should discuss it here. It's too public."

"Then why don't we continue this conversation in our quarters," Sam suggested helpfully.

Kiyel nodded in agreement.

Unbeknownst to them, however, as they got up to leave, a lone Caitaran male who was seated in a relatively dark and empty corner of the lounge was watching them closely. He continued to watch them until they exited the lounge, at which point he got up himself and followed them out.

Upon arriving a few minutes later at Jev and Kiyel's quarters, Tiela immediately went to the food prep station to prepare some k'yarri for them, as well as a glass of nanaya juice for Aiden, while the others went to the sitting area.

"Alright, Kiyel, out with it," Kel impatiently said, sitting opposite him, "what's going on?"

"Sir, you were right about me not being a third grade telepath," Kiyel began. "I'm actually a first grade telepath. And although you all know me as Kiyel Lhevi, that isn't my full name, it's actually Kiyel Lhevic."

"So you're a pride leader's son then," Kel said, recognizing the name, his nose twitching slightly.

"But why the deception, Kiyel? Why join the Forces under an assumed name?" Tiela asked when she joined them. She sat down next to Kel and placed their drinks in front of them on the low table that was there.

"Because I'd had enough of the life my mother and father wanted for me, Tiela," Kiyel told her, his voice tight. He reached out to draw Jev closer to him. "I wanted to live a normal life, not one tied to duty and tradition like my parents are. They enjoy that sort of life. I never have. It would probably surprise you to know I'm betrothed to a female, chosen for me as my life-mate by my parents and hers when we were born. I want nothing to do with her, and they know it. Nevertheless, they continued to insist that I go through with the bonding. So one night about a year ago, I left and joined the Forces."

"Kiyel told me about all this shortly after I learned he wasn't an Alessian mountain cat. Elder Veir is the only other one who knows who Kiyel really is," Jev said.

"That would make sense, since the Elder would know your family," Kel nodded.

"Luckily, the Elder sympathized with my situation and agreed to help keep my true identity hidden."

"Well, since your father called you here, he obviously managed to figure out where you'd disappeared to," Kel said.

"Does he know that you nearly died down there?" Tiela asked.

"He does now, but only because I told him. Admiral Chuul has been frustrating his efforts to learn more about what happened to us," Kiyel said.

"That sounds like Chuul alright," Kel muttered derisively, his ears dipping slightly.

"My father has asked that he be provided regular updates on Jev's and my status, so it'll be necessary that I reveal my true identity to the admiral."

"I'd give anything to be there to see her reaction when you tell her!" Kel said with a little bark of a laugh.

Jev grinned. He understood Kel's feelings toward the Admiral, since he shared them as well.

"Well we can worry about that later. Right now I think we should probably get some sleep so we can be ready for our appointment with you tomorrow, Tiela," he suggested.

"You're quite right, Jev. It is getting pretty late," Tiela nodded, getting to her feet and waiting for the others to join her. "But tell me, Kiyel, is everything all right between you and your father now?" she asked as they started for the door together.

"Yes, I think so. It's just my mother I have to worry about. She's on route to the Cetani as we speak."

"To see you?" Sam asked.

"Not specifically, no, although I have no doubt that's the very first thing she'll want to do when she gets here," he answered with a faint grin. "She's been asked by our government to assist with the negotiations with the Alessian government."

"No doubt," Kel echoed, mimicking Kiyel's grin.

Kiyel touched his hand to the panel beside the door which then promptly slid open.

"Well, I guess I'll see the both of you tomorrow," Tiela said, stepping out into the corridor with Kel.

"Good night, Tiela, Captain," Jev said with a slight flick of his ears, before touching the panel to shut the door behind them.

Sam then looked down at Aiden, who had been holding his hand the entire time they were standing there.

"All right, you. It's time for bed," he said.

"But I'm not tired!" Aiden whined defiantly, even though it was plainly obvious he was having difficulties keeping his eyes open.

The three of them laughed as Sam began ushering the sleepy child towards his bedroom.

* * *

Having finished third meal, Hraka decided to return to the solitude of his quarters where he could think. He was lying on his bunk in his quarters, slowly nursing a hot cup of k'yarri, when the door suddenly sounded, abruptly pulling him away from his thoughts. At first he was inclined not to answer it, but then the door sounded again, more insistent this time. Annoyed, he rose from his bunk, made his way to the door and activated the intercom.

"Yeah, who is it?" he growled.

"It's me, Vrash, Hraka," came the answer.

The door slid open, admitting an excited older male Caitaran with a graying pelt.

"It's late, Vrash," Hraka hissed with a scowl as he closed the door, the set of his ears showing his displeasure. "What do you want?"

"I saw him, the abomination, in the upper deck lounge."

"You disturbed me for that? I've already seen him, in the hangar bay," Hraka replied, his tone impatient.

"Not like this you haven't," Vrash said, his tail flicking excitedly behind him. "He changed."

Hraka's ears pricked up with curious interest.

"What do you mean, he changed?" he asked.

"One minute he was Caitaran, the next he looked like the furless aliens from the planet."

At this Hraka's brow furrowed, his scowl deepening even further.

"Is the abomination still there?" he asked.

"No, he and his Enassi and some of the crew from the Lekur left to go to their quarters."

"You followed them?" Hraka asked, eying him incredulously.

"Don't worry, I wasn't seen."

"They're telepaths, Vrash. They didn't need to see you to know they were being followed," Hraka said, his tail twitching angrily.

"They would have reacted to my presence if they did. And they didn't."

"Even so, you better be more careful in the future," Hraka said in a tone that brook no argument. "If our plans are to succeed, we must remain hidden and act covertly for the time being. Later, when the time is right, we can reveal ourselves." His lips then curled back in a wicked grin. "By that point it'll be too late for anyone to stop us."

TEN

A loud reverberating buzzing noise dragged Jev rudely from the depths of sleep. A yellow light on the panel on his nightstand flashed incessantly, in time with the buzzing.

With a tired groan, he reached over and touched the panel, which immediately stopped the assault on his ears. But unfortunately for him the alarm had already done its job. He was awake.

He was, however, in no hurry to get out from under the cozy, warm blankets, which he pulled up tighter against his body.

The shifting of the sheets beside him told him that the alarm had woken Kiyel as well.

"I hate alarm clocks," Jev complained.

"You hate that they were invented, or that they make such an annoying noise?" Kiyel asked as he turned over to face him.

"Both," Jev replied, his nose twitching with obvious displeasure.

"Come on," Kiyel said with a slight chuckle. He sat up and threw off the blankets. "We'd better get up."

Reluctantly, Jev did the same.

About a half hour later, after showering and putting on fresh uniforms, they left their room and were surprised to see that Sam was already awake and preparing for them what smelled like k'yarri in the tiny alcove that served as their quarters' galley.

"Doc? What are you doing up so early?" Jev asked, just managing to stifle a yawn.

"Good morning, Jev, Kiyel," Sam said, handing them each a mug. "I've always been an early riser. It's a habit of mine, I'm afraid."

"And I thought we woke up early," Jev muttered to Kiyel quietly. He took a sip of his k'yarri, pausing for a moment so that he could savor the taste and to allow the warmth of the k'yarri to spread throughout his body. "This is really good, Doc," he said, pleasantly surprised.

"I'm glad you like it. Tiela told me how to prepare it yesterday."

"Well, that would explain it then," Kiyel said, taking another sip as they went to the sitting area.

"Is Aiden still asleep?" Jev asked once they were comfortably seated.

"Yes, thankfully," Sam nodded.

"But I thought you were going to have Aiden checked out this morning to make sure his wounds were properly healed," Kiyel said, looking quizzically at Sam.

"Sometimes, Kiyel, the body can be the best physician,

and getting plenty of rest can be the best medicine. Don't worry, though. I've already gotten in touch with Sanaa, and she and Ardem have agreed to come by shortly, to look after Aiden while we're gone. When Aiden wakes up, they'll bring him along."

As if on cue, the door suddenly sounded, whereupon Sam got up to answer it. After verifying the identity of their visitors, he opened the door to let Sanaa and Ardem in.

"Is that fresh k'yarri I smell?" Sanaa asked, her nose twitching eagerly as she sniffed the air.

"Help yourself to some, I made lots," Sam said, chuckling a little at her reaction.

After getting their k'yarri, Sanaa and Ardem followed Sam to the seating area where they sat down.

"Thanks for agreeing to look after Aiden for us on such short notice," Kiyel said.

"Oh, it's no trouble at all, Kiyel," Sanaa said, with a wave of her arm.

"The truth is, the both of us are very fascinated with Aiden," Ardem added. "He is so unlike our young, and yet there's much about him that is similar."

"I think that's probably a trait that all children share, no matter the species," Sam said, with a bemused grin.

"You're hoping to have children yourselves one day, aren't you?" Jev said. It was more a statement than a question.

"How did you know?" Ardem asked, looking genuinely surprised.

"Ardem, Jev's talent is extremely sensitive. There isn't a whole lot that escapes his notice. Your desire for young was strong enough for us to easily pick it up," Kiyel explained.

"No wonder then that the Telepath Guild is so anxious to have you tested, Jev," Sanaa said.

"Believe me, the feeling isn't mutual," Jev said, with a long drawn out sigh. "I feel like I've been examined and poked and prodded enough as it is, already."

"Speaking of which," Sam interjected, "we might as well get going. I'm sure Tiela is just as anxious to get these tests over with as you are, Jev."

"I doubt it," Jev muttered to himself, but grudgingly rose from his seat with the others.

Cheer up, Jev, it's almost over, Kiyel sent reassuringly

Don't you ever get tired of it, though, Kiyel?

All the time, Kiyel answered, and Jev could feel his annoyance. *It's just that because of my upbringing I've learned to be patient.*

Maybe they should be poked and prodded, and see how they like it, Jev sent, half in jest.

Kiyel just chuckled lightly as they reached the door to their quarters.

Sam pressed his hand to the panel and the doors slid open. The three of them then stepped out into the corridor.

"We'll be by later with Aiden, once he wakes up," Sanaa told them.

"Thanks again, Sanaa," Kiyel said.

Sanaa's ears gave a little flick in acknowledgment and the door slid closed again, leaving them standing alone in the corridor.

"Come on, let's get this over with," Sam said.

As they started down the corridor, though, Jev began feeling a little uneasy. There was something unsettling in the air, but for some reason, he was unable to localize its source. The corridors were slightly crowded with the ship's crew as they carried out their assigned duties, the odd few giving them curious glances as they passed, but there was nothing readily apparent to suggest that anything was out of the ordinary. He tried to dismiss his anxiety as being attributable to his unfamiliarity with the ship. But, still, the feeling of wrongness persisted.

What's wrong, Enassi? Kiyel asked, picking up on Jev's uneasiness.

I'm sure it's nothing, but for some reason, something just doesn't feel right somehow, Jev answered, his ears twitching nervously.

They were almost at the medical bay when, all of a sudden, Jev stopped short. The uneasiness he felt earlier suddenly intensified sharply. He began to sense that something was now horribly, dangerously wrong, and he whirled about in fear.

"Kiyel, look out!" he screamed, throwing his body at his alarmed Enassi, knocking him to the floor and out of harm's way.

Right as he did, a blinding red beam lanced out towards them, accompanied by the all too familiar whine of a powerful energy weapon being fired. The shot, which had been aimed at Kiyel, hit Jev instead, sending him hurtling against the bulkhead where he landed in a crumpled heap, unconscious and bleeding heavily from his arm.

Alarms suddenly sounded in the corridor as Kiyel scrambled to his feet and rushed to Jev's side. He knelt down and pulled Jev to him, cradling his head carefully in his lap. As he did, though, he began to feel wetness on his uniform spread, as Jev's blood began seeping from a gash in the back of his head, where it had hit the edge of the bulkhead.

"Damn," Sam swore, kneeling down beside Jev. He ripped a sleeve off his shirt which he then tightly tied around Jev's arm, in an effort to staunch the flow of blood. "Press your hand down on that wound, lad, to help stop the bleeding," he instructed Kiyel.

Kiyel did as he was told and looked up at Sam with fear in his eyes. Tears rolled down his cheeks, both from the extreme pain he felt from Jev, and because he was suddenly very afraid for his Enassi's life. Already he could feel Jev growing weaker from the loss of blood.

"Help him, Sam," he cried fearfully.

"Medic," Sam called out, looking up at the alarmed crowd that had gathered. "We need a medic, here, now!"

Movement out of the corner of Kiyel's eye caught his attention and he looked over just in time to see a pair of feet disappearing down an adjacent corridor.

"Somebody get that son of a bitch!" Kiyel yelled, seething with sudden fury as he pointed in the direction of the fleeing shooter.

He was only peripherally aware of three members of the ship's security personnel arriving, though, who then quickly took off after the shooter, as his attention returned to his Enassi, whom he held even more tightly.

Meanwhile, Tiela, who heard the commotion and then the sudden blaring of alarms in the corridor, poked her head out of the medical bay and saw the horrifying sight of Jev bleeding badly from his wounds, on the ground with Kiyel and Sam tending to him, along with a large gathering of confused and alarmed Caitarans standing around them. Springing into action, she quickly grabbed her medical kit and called for her staff to follow her.

"Move aside," she barked sharply when they reached the crowd, forcefully pushing her way through to get to Jev instead of waiting for people to move.

She cringed involuntarily when she finally reached him,

seeing just how bad his injuries were. Her training kicked in right away, however, as she knelt down and began to work to stabilize him.

"He's got a lacerated artery in his arm and a severe concussion," she said, speaking to Sam as she studied the display on her diagnostic scanner. "The artery is half cauterized; I can't close it here. We need to get him to the medical bay, now!"

She quickly cut away the cloth Sam had tied around Jev's arm, which was already soaked with his blood, and carefully, but firmly, applied a pressure bandage to the wound, which she taped tightly.

"Tiela, he's fading fast," Kiyel said, his voice taut with fear.

She looked at him with concern, for she could tell also that Kiyel was beginning to fade with his Enassi.

"He's not going to die, Kiyel," she promised firmly. "And neither are you."

With the help of her team, Jev was carefully loaded on a stretcher which Tiela's team had brought. Together they carried Jev to the medical bay with Kiyel and Sam following closely behind.

No sooner had they brought Jev into the Medical bay, though, than a crying Aiden suddenly came running in. Close on his heels were Sanaa and Ardem who were chasing after him, and who looked slightly out of breath.

"What the...?!" a startled Tiela exclaimed as Aiden made a beeline right for Jev, only to finally be caught by Kiyel.

"Sorry, Tiela," Sanaa said. "He woke up screaming that Jev had been hurt and needed help. He ran out of the quarters before we could catch him."

"By the Gods!" Ardem and Sanaa both exclaimed when they saw Jev lying on the table and covered in blood.

"Kiyel, keep him away from Jev so Sam and I can treat his wounds!" Tiela ordered.

"No, I can help!" Aiden cried.

Before anyone could stop him, Aiden twisted out of Kiyel's grasp and reached out past Tiela to touch Jev's arm. Tiela was just about to pull him away when she suddenly saw something remarkable happen. Jev's wound, which had been bleeding profusely, was slowly beginning to heal before her eyes. She couldn't explain it, and neither could anyone else, as they all stared with wondrous shock at what was happening.

"Kiyel?" Tiela said, with an astonished look, her tail swinging erratically.

"I don't understand it, Tiela," Kiyel said. He not only could see Jev's wound healing, but he could also feel it. "The energies coming out of his hand are incredible."

When Aiden finally let go, what remained of the wound was now just a reddish patch of fresh skin. There wasn't any sign of the wound anymore, not even a scar. Only by the fact that the fur was missing could anyone tell that there had been a wound there at all.

"He's a healer!" Sanaa said, almost in a whisper.

Before they could ask Aiden what he'd done, however, he stumbled and lost consciousness. Luckily, Kiyel was there to catch him before he fell.

"Bring him to the other table, Kiyel," Tiela told him.

Even as light as Aiden was, Kiyel grunted slightly as he picked him up and gently placed him on the table. He then moved out of the way so that Sam and Tiela could check on him.

After a few tense moments, Sam nodded to Tiela before turning back to them.

"It's okay," he said, with a relieved expression. "He's just exhausted. He needs to get some rest is all."

The doors to the medical bay opened again unexpectedly, causing Kiyel to jump with a start. He turned and was relieved to see that it was just one of the ship's security personnel entering the medical bay to take up a position by the door.

Tiela, who had also heard security's arrival, looked up from where she was now preparing an intravenous line for Jev, and frowned.

"Just stay over there for now, so I can attend to my patients," she said curtly to the officer.

"I assure you, physician Tiela, I have no intention of interfering," the officer said.

"You need to move back also, Kiyel, so I can get to Jev," Tiela said, her tone softening significantly. She knew exactly what his response would be, though.

"I'm not leaving him, Tiela," Kiyel said, refusing to budge from Jev's side. "He needs me."

"Would you mind at least moving to the other side of him?" she asked, as she tried to position her equipment near Jev.

Kiyel's ears flicked in assent as he made his way slowly, and with some difficulty, around the table, keeping a hand on Jev as he did.

Tiela saw that Kiyel was having difficulty moving around the table and she frowned. Although Jev had been healed by Aiden, Kiyel didn't appear to be getting any stronger. In fact, he seemed even weaker than before.

"Sanaa, please get a chair and put it over on Jev's other side so Kiyel can sit with him. And also, would you get Kiyel some k'yarri from the galley? It'll help alleviate some of the weakness they both feel," Tiela said, as she began inserting the intravenous line into Jev's arm.

Moments later, Sanaa returned with the chair and the k'yarri, which Kiyel accepted gratefully.

While Tiela worked on Jev, Kiyel's attention shifted to the security officer.

"Has the individual responsible for doing this to my Enassi been found yet?" he asked, his tail flicking as he sat down.

"Not yet, sir," the officer answered from the door. "I was instructed by my superiors to remain here in case the assailant decided to finish what he started."

As unlikely a scenario as that seemed to Kiyel, he was, nevertheless, glad to have security personnel present, just the same.

Meanwhile, Sam was closely watching Tiela as she began to connect Jev's intravenous line to an odd looking piece of equipment on a cart that she had positioned next to him.

"What exactly is that device, Tiela?" he asked.

"It's a blood infuser. It'll help Jev replenish most of the blood he lost," she explained, glancing over at Sam as she pressed a sequence of buttons on the device.

"Aren't you concerned about matching his blood type though?" Sam asked.

Tiela shook her head and smiled faintly at him.

"Not with this device. The infuser analyses the patient's blood chemistry and injects the correct intravenous solution which will stimulate his body's natural ability to produce blood. This way, we can greatly reduce, or even eliminate entirely, the need for donated blood."

"When will we know if Jev will be all right, Tiela?" Kiyel asked.

"His breathing is already starting to return to normal, as

is his heart rate. There doesn't appear to be any infection, partially thanks to the blaster cauterizing the tissue in his arm, but also thanks to Aiden's remarkable healing ability. I will, of course, continue monitoring him, just in case. So I think we should know within a few hours."

"So all we can do now is wait," Kiyel said, with a resigned sigh.

"Pretty much," Tiela answered.

Tiela's eyes narrowed slightly as she studied the results displayed on her scanner and tapped a few more commands into the device. It was several hours since Jev had been brought into the medical bay. Sanaa and Ardem had long since left, promising to return later to check on Jev who was finally resting peacefully with Kiyel keeping watch over him, and she was taking the opportunity to go over some of his scans.

"That's odd," she said.

"What is?" Sam asked, peering over his shoulder at her.

"I just compared the scans I took of Jev—before his change—to Aiden's, and there's something here on Jev's scans that doesn't make any sense."

"Well, Jev is a teenager and Aiden is just a small boy," Sam said, moving to stand next to her.

"That wouldn't explain this. Take a look for yourself," she said, handing him the scanner.

Sam took one look at the scanner's display and his eyes opened wide with surprised shock.

"Well, I'll be!" he exclaimed as he suddenly recognized what had Tiela so perplexed.

"You know what this is?" Tiela asked, her clawed finger

tapping at the anomaly in the scan.

"Yes, I do," Sam confirmed. "It's almost too impossible to believe, but there's no denying what these scans are telling us."

"Then this isn't normal for human development?"

"Heaven's, no!" Sam said incredulously. "However, it does explain a few things."

"Such as?"

"Several months ago, Jev came to me complaining of severe cramping. I prescribed to him some pain medication, figuring it was just a case of acute indigestion. But he came back again the following month with the exact same symptoms, and the following month after that. And, now, I know why."

"So if it wasn't indigestion, then what was it?" Tiela asked.

"Jev has both male and female reproductive organs," he explained, handing her back the scanner. "He's what we call intersexed or hermaphroditic."

"Are you trying to tell me that Jev is actually both male and female?" she asked, her tail giving an involuntary twitch.

"No, not exactly. Jev is definitely male, and he identifies as such. However, he just happens to have female reproductive organs as well."

"This is completely unheard of in Caitaran physiology," Tiela said, once again studying the scans.

"It's a rare phenomenon, I agree, even for humans. But if you look closely, you can clearly see a fully developed uterus, ovaries, and even a birth canal," Sam said, pointing to each of the organs in the scan.

"But there's no vaginal opening. Where there should be one, there's only fatty tissue and skin," she observed.

"Exactly," Sam nodded. "Which would explain why

Jev's cramps were so severe before I treated him. At the end of his cycle, the menstrual discharge had nowhere to go."

"So why then, in the two months he's been with us, hasn't he complained of having these cramps, or showed any signs that his menstrual cycle was beginning?" Tiela asked.

"I'm guessing it's probably because of the stress he's been under, especially with this change of his. It has thrown his system completely off," Sam said.

"I wonder..." Tiela said, her voice trailing off as she quickly moved to her desk in the adjacent room and tapped a few commands into the console there.

"What are you doing now?" a confused Sam asked as he joined her.

"I'm calling up the scans I just took of Jev while we were treating him. I want to confirm the anomaly is still present."

"It is, look," Sam said, as the results of the scan were displayed.

"When I initially took this scan, I just assumed they were remnants of his normal human physiology," Tiela said, her ears folding back against her skull in embarrassment. She sat down and stared at the screen. "Not knowing about your biology, it wasn't something that I even remotely thought of, much less looked for."

"Don't be so hard on yourself, lass," Sam said, giving her a reassuring smile. "No one could have expected this. Hell, I didn't, and I've been his doctor for years."

Tiela grinned at him in thanks.

"So what do we do now?" she asked.

"Do? What do you mean? We tell him of course. We tell both of them."

"But with this change in his physiology, we don't even

know if he would be capable of carrying young, or even if he and Kiyel are compatible."

"All the more reason to tell them, I think," Sam said. "Besides, they're telepaths. They're bound to figure it out on their own anyway," he quickly added.

"You're right of course," Tiela said, stiffly getting back to her feet. "I think we'd better go see if he's awake yet."

* * *

Jev lay unconscious on the examination table in the medical bay, propped up by several pillows. They had been provided for him by Kiyel who sat in a chair beside him.

Just as he began waking up, slowly opening his eyes and blinking them repeatedly to clear away the fuzziness, Sanaa and Ardem walked in.

Jev's stirring alerted Kiyel to his returning to consciousness.

"Thank the gods you're awake," Kiyel said, relief and pleasure plainly evident in his voice.

"What happened?" Jev asked groggily.

"You were shot," Kiyel said, holding Jev's hand in his.

As soon as Kiyel said this, the memories of the event came flooding back to Jev in a rush.

"Why does this keep happening to us, Kiyel?" he asked, tears of pain and frustration beginning to fill his eyes. "Why won't they just leave us alone?"

Kiyel had no answer for him, though. He could only sit there, holding his Enassi to give him comfort, and to reassure him through their link that everything was going to be alright.

It was then that Tiela and Sam emerged from her office. At once they saw that Jev was awake as they'd hoped. What they didn't expect to see, though, was that he was leaning into Kiyel and sobbing openly.

Kiyel saw them as they approached and shook his head, answering their unspoken question.

When Jev's sobs soon lessened, and finally stopped altogether, he opened his eyes and saw that Tiela and Sam were in the room with them.

"You gave us quite the scare, lad," Sam said.

"Do you remember anything that happened, Jev?" Tiela asked.

Jev slowly nodded and wiped the remaining tears from his face.

"I remember feeling that something wasn't quite right when we left our quarters, and then a sudden feeling of danger around Kiyel. I haven't felt anything that unsettling since..." Jev said, his voice trailing as realization suddenly hit him like a cold shower.

"The pilot!" Kiyel exclaimed, finishing Jev's train of thought. He then captured the security officer's attention. "Inform your chief that he needs to search for the pilot who brought us from our encampment to the main town on the planet below. He may be involved in the attack."

"Right away, sir," the officer said, and began speaking into his communicator.

"What's all this about, Jev?" Sanaa asked, looking confused.

"When we were back on Alessi, and while the rest of our team was gathering our gear from the cave, we had a very unpleasant run in with the shuttle's pilot. He exhibited very strong feelings of xenophobia, all of which were directed at the two of us," Jev explained.

"It was the same type of xenophobia that we'd felt before in Gaev, our first officer," Kiyel finished.

"I just don't know why I had such trouble picking up on his emotions in the corridor," Jev said. "Usually I can sense strong emotions right away. But this time, it was like I had to fight my way through a dense fog."

"I'm almost afraid to suggest this, but it's possible your attacker carried with him a modified psychic damper. If he did, I'm surprised you were able to sense anything at all," Sanaa said.

"I told you Jev's talents were especially strong," Kiyel reminded them.

"What's a psychic damper?" Sam asked.

"Psychic dampers are installed throughout the ship in quarters where telepaths reside. Especially strong dampers are installed in Enassi quarters due to the increased intensity of emotions that can be released during a pairing," Ardem explained.

"You mean when you have sex," Sam nodded.

"These dampers work by creating a sort of white noise effect that surrounds telepaths, to ensure that their thoughts and emotions don't bleed out and start affecting the rest of the crew. A modified damper works in reverse, preventing a telepath from picking up the thoughts and feelings of others. It would be like causing someone who can see to suddenly become blind."

"It's for this reason modified dampers are illegal," Sanaa added.

"Somehow, I don't think whether they're legal or not has any meaning for the bastard who shot Jev," Sam said.

"What else do you remember about what happened, Jev?" Tiela asked, prompting him to continue.

"Not much, I'm afraid. There was a flash of red light, a sudden pain in my arm and then I guess I must have blacked out," he said.

"Well, the shot that was apparently intended for Kiyel hit you instead when you knocked him out of the way," Sam told him.

Jev glanced down at his arm, seeing the dressing and the intravenous line sticking out of it.

"It cut open an artery in your arm, and the force of it threw you against the bulkhead, which is how you ended up with a pretty nasty gash in your scalp and a severe concussion," Sam continued.

"I guess I have you and Tiela to thank for fixing me up, again," Jev said, managing a weak smile.

"Actually," Sam said, absently rubbing the back of his head, "we did very little except to stop the bleeding and bring you into the medical bay. The one who actually saved your life was Aiden. He's sleeping right over there."

Surprised, Jev looked over at the adjacent table where Aiden lay still asleep. Filled with concern for him, he attempted to get off the table, but was hit with a sudden wave of dizziness accompanied by a sharp pain in his head.
Kiyel, feeling Jev's discomfort moved to steady him and to help him lie back down.

"Easy, Jev. You're in no condition to be moving about right now," he said.

"Don't worry, I'm not going anywhere," Jev assured him, gritting his teeth as he fought back against the pain. "But how did Aiden save me. We left him sleeping in our quarters."

"We don't really know," Tiela admitted. "Somehow, he was able to sense that you were in trouble and rushed out of your quarters and came right here. Before we knew it, he was putting his hands on you and somehow his doing so caused your wounds to begin to heal."

"You mean he somehow healed me just by putting his hands on me?" Jev asked, his eyes opening wide with shock.

"That's it exactly, lad," Sam confirmed. "It's the darnedest thing I ever saw. Sanaa, I remember, called him a healer."

A healer is a telepath with a special talent for being able to heal the injured and cure the sick. It is an extremely rare phenomena and one that is highly regarded in our society, almost revered, Kiyel explained through their link.

If he is one, then he really needs to get tested by the guild, now more than ever, Jev sent.

I thought you hated tests, though, Kiyel said playfully.

His attempt at humour was rewarded with a playful punch in the arm from Jev.

"Unfortunately," Sam continued, unaware of the conversation Jev and Kiyel were having, "healing you took a lot out of Aiden. He's been sleeping ever since, and we've been monitoring him constantly. Tiela has been giving him nutritional supplements to help him recover his strength."

"Incredible," Jev said.

"Not as incredible as what we are about to tell you next," Tiela said.

"There's more?" Kiyel asked. He was just as surprised as Jev to hear this.

"Yes, but it has nothing to do with the attack on you today," she said.

ELEVEN

Captain Cael sat behind his desk in his personal quarters, staring at his terminal, when the door sounded, as he had been expecting.

"Come in," he called out, in a loud voice, looking up from the terminal.

The doors slid open to admit a rather imposing looking grey and black pelted Caitaran male with unusually blue eyes and dressed in traditional telepath clothes. Though Cael knew full well the figure that now stood in front of him was not officially a member of the Telepath Guild.

A scowl formed on his face as he regarded his guest. He did not invite him to sit down.

"You screwed up, Riyad," he said, the set of his ears showing his displeasure.

If the male took umbrage to Cael's curtness, it didn't show.

"In what way have I failed, Captain?" Riyad asked. His tone was even, though Cael could detect a hint of amusement in his voice.

"You know damn well how!" Cael exclaimed angrily. "Do you see this on my screen?" he asked, turning the terminal's monitor to face Riyad.

Riyad scanned the report that was on the screen briefly and shrugged his shoulders, indifferent to its contents.

"It's a report of an attack on our new Enassi pair. You were hired specifically to protect them."

"I know exactly what I was hired to do, Captain," Riyad said, his tone remaining even though his tail began to flick, betraying his growing impatience.

"Then how do you explain the fact that they were attacked, and that one of them now lies in the medical bay with a life-threatening injury?" Cael demanded to know.

"Captain, as a military man, you, more than anyone, should know that it is impossible to defend against all threats, no matter how well prepared you are. This was an unplanned, spur of the moment, attack that I had knowledge of."

"Are you inferring that you know who was responsible for this attack?"

"It's more accurate to say that I've become aware of a small group on board this ship who would wish to see harm come to them."

"Then why haven't you taken action to stop this group?" Cael asked, incredulous of what he was being told.

"Oh I have, Captain," Riyad said, a rather unpleasant grin stretching across his face. "Believe me, I have."

"I think you'd better explain."

"Not yet. But I promise you this; by the end of the day the one who was responsible for this attack will be either dead, or in custody."

"I would prefer the individual responsible be taken alive, Riyad. I want no more bloodshed on board my ship," Cael cautioned him.

"That may not be up to me, but I will do what I can," Riyad answered, with an acknowledging flick of his ears. "In the meantime, I suggest you make arrangements to have Kiyel and Jev assigned to ambassador quarters, where security is tighter, and where I can keep a closer eye on them."

"How do you plan to do that, exactly?" he asked.

"You're going to assign me to them as their adjutant."

"They're telepaths, Riyad. They won't like the intrusion on their privacy," Cael said, leaning back in his chair.

"No, I don't expect they will. But for their own sake, it's necessary," Riyad said.

Cael dipped his head slightly in agreement, knowing full well that Riyad was right.

"Now if you'll excuse me, Captain, I have a shooter to aprehend."

A short time later, after Riyad had left his quarters, Cael sat alone to gather his thoughts, until eventually he came to a decision. With a heavy sigh, he activated the intercom, and called for his first officer to join him. They had a lot to do.

"I still can't believe it, Kiyel," Jev said.

He and Kiyel were sitting in their quarters alone after Tiela had discharged Jev from the medical bay. She insisted that he get some rest, though, after what he and Kiyel had been told before they left, he didn't see how that was going to happen any time soon. So much was going through his mind.

"Neither can I," Kiyel answered, still bewildered. "If

Tiela hadn't told us the results of the scan, I don't think I could have believed it possible."

"But scans don't lie."

"No, they don't."

A sudden, frightening thought came to Jev, causing him to avert his gaze, fear welling up inside him.

"No, don't even think that," Kiyel told him firmly. He put a finger under his chin and tipped his face up to get him to meet his eyes "This doesn't change anything between us, especially not how I feel about you."

"But how can you still love me, Kiyel, knowing what I am?" Tears were beginning to roll down Jev's cheek.

"Enassi, I love you because you are who you are. Nothing could ever change that," Kiyel answered, pulling Jev to him and putting his arms around him in a loving embrace. "If anything, what we've just learned makes me love you even more."

"How?" Jev asked, looking up into Kiyel's eyes.

"Because, the one thing I've always wanted was to have a child of my own with the one I love."

"You would really want to start a family with me?" Jev asked, hope flickering in his eyes.

"More than anything, my love," Kiyel answered without hesitation. "The gods willing, someday I do."

The sound of the door to their quarters sliding open drew Kiyel's attention there for a moment, where he saw Sam walk in.

The smile on Sam's face quickly faded and turned to one of concern when he saw the state Jev was in.

"Kiyel, what's going on?" he asked.

Kiyel looked into Jev's eyes, a silent question passing between them, to which Jev slowly nodded his agreement.

"Jev was concerned that my feelings for him would

change because we discovered he's intersexed," Kiyel explained.

"And have they?" Sam asked, his tone serious.

Kiyel knew, without even having to read Sam's mind, that this wasn't an accusation, but rather the concern of a guardian for his charge's wellbeing, so he didn't take offense.

"I love him more now than ever before, so yes, in that sense, my feelings for him have changed,"

"Why is that?" Sam asked.

Kiyel could not only sense Sam's relief, he could also hear it in his voice, which was now inquisitive.

"For a long time, I've wanted a family of my own. Since I could never love, or be intimate with, a female, I had given up hope that I would one day ever have a child. But after what you and Tiela told us in the medical bay, there's the possibility that that might change."

"Well, Tiela has completed analyzing all the data she gathered from you both. So she'll be here in a few minutes," Sam said. "Rather than asking you to return to the medical bay, we decided it would be better to tell you the results here."

"Good, because I don't want to go back there anytime soon," Jev said, his ears dipping noticeably as he recalled the harrowing events that led to him almost losing his life.

"I quite understand, Jev, and to be honest, I'd feel a lot better if you didn't," Sam said.

The doors to their quarters opened again, admitting Tiela and a jubilant-looking Aiden into the room. As soon as Aiden saw Jev sitting with Kiyel, he bounded down to the sitting area, and almost leapt up onto Jev's lap. Jev could feel Aiden's overwhelming sense of relief that he was alright.

Thank you for saving me, little one, Jev sent to him, causing Aiden to blush slightly.

You're welcome, Aiden sent, startling Jev, as it was the

first time Aiden had ever spoken to him in his mind.

Kiyel looked over sharply at Aiden, equally surprised.

Jev was surprised further when he began to feel an energy flow from Aiden as the boy settled onto his lap to cuddle with him. It felt very warm and comforting for some reason. Suddenly he felt as though a great weight had been lifted from his shoulders. His sullen mood was suddenly lifted and replaced with a feeling of peace that he hadn't felt in a long time.

Kiyel noticed the change in his Enassi right away, then he too felt the energies coming from Aiden.

Is this what they call an empath? Kiyel wondered.

Although the question wasn't directed at Jev, he heard it nevertheless.

I think so, he sent.

"How are you doing, Jev?" Tiela asked when she sat down next to Sam.

"Actually, not too bad," he answered, directing his attention away from Aiden. "My arm is still a little tender, though."

"That's to be expected," Tiela nodded. "Well, shall we get this over with then?"

She reached into her medical kit, which she'd brought with her, and withdrew a medical diagnostic scanner. This one was slightly different, however, in that it looked larger. She placed it on the table before them, where it began to emit a soft humming sound when Tiela activated it. All of a sudden, a three dimensional holographic image appeared a few inches above the scanner. The image was remarkably sharp, so much so that Jev had no difficulties seeing that the image being displayed was of him. That his name was printed clearly at the bottom helped as well. Beside his image was a model of his DNA.

"This is a three dimensional representation of the scan I

took of you, Jev, when you were brought into the medical bay. Everything appears normal, except for the wounds which you suffered, which are highlighted in blue. Now watch what happens when I switch to the internal scan."

With her clawed finger, she entered a few commands into the scanner's control panel, causing the image to instantly switch to a view of Jev's internal organs. In school he'd learned all about human anatomy in health class, including seeing pictures in the e-text books of both males and females, so he was quite fascinated to see how remarkably similar his internal organs looked even after he'd changed. He could clearly see where the differences were, however, such as his heart being slightly smaller than a normal human's would, and having a larger liver. But what intrigued him most was the small organ in his pelvic region, which also appeared to be highlighted in blue, the same as his wounds. The organ itself looked vaguely familiar to him, as did its position within his body.

"Tiela is that what I think it is?" he asked as he pointed to the organ, awed by what he was seeing.

"Yes, Jev, that is your uterus," Tiela nodded.

Jev continued to stare at the image. It was one thing to be told about the results of his scans by Tiela and Sam back in the medical bay, but to be shown them like this was something else entirely.

"Have you been able to determine if Jev is capable of conceiving a child?" Kiyel asked anxiously.

"He is, and he isn't," Tiela answered, which earned her equally confused looks from him and Jev. "Jev is capable of conceiving a child, but not with a human and not with a Caitaran. Since Jev is a hybrid of our two species, part human and part Caitaran, neither one could conceive a child with Jev. Only another hybrid could do that," she elaborated.

"There are no other hybrids, though, Tiela. You know that. Jev is the only one," Kiyel reminded her.

"Except that he's not," Tiela said. She pressed a few more commands into the scanner and the image of Jev was replaced by of two sets of DNA. "Thanks to the scan we took of you, Kiyel, we now know that when Jev established the gestalt link and became what he is now, your DNA was altered along with his."

She changed the display again, the image now showing the two sets of DNA overlaid on top of each other, and Kiyel could clearly see that he and Jev in fact shared some of the same DNA.

"I did that?" Jev asked, in a soft voice, his tail flicking jerkily, showing his growing distress.

"It would appear so," Sam nodded.

Jev dipped his head, flattening his ears backward in apology.

I'm so sorry, Kiyel. I didn't mean for that to happen, he sent.

I'm not, Kiyel sent back, causing Jev to look back up at him in surprise. *It's made us who we are, and I will never be sorry for that.*

Jev smiled at him sheepishly, and leaned into him, basking in his warmth and his love.

"So what exactly does all of this mean for us?" Kiyel asked Sam and Tiela.

"It means that you and Jev are compatible and can have children, Kiyel. But it also means, as a consequence of these changes to your DNA, that you cannot have children with anyone other than Jev," Sam said.

Upon hearing this, an unexpected grin began to stretch across Kiyel's face. That grin quickly grew until finally he burst out in sudden laughter.

Sam and Tiela both looked at Kiyel with almost identical lost expressions on their faces. They had no idea what Kiyel found so amusing.

But Jev knew, and he couldn't resist a grin of his own.

"Up till now, we didn't know what we were going to do about the female back on Caitar that Kiyel is betrothed to. The reason he was betrothed to this particular female was to ensure the continuation of his family's bloodline, and also to ensure that his offspring would be telepaths," Jev explained.

Sam nodded slowly in understanding.

"So, if Kiyel is no longer able to have children with the female..."

"Then my father will have no choice but to dissolve the betrothal," Kiyel finished for Sam, as he managed to get his laughter under control.

"Wait a moment," Jev said, and he reached for the scanner to bring back his scan. Almost intuitively, but with a little help from Tiela, he focused the scan on a particular region and zoomed in on it. "Just how am I supposed to get pregnant if there's no way for sperm to meet my egg?" he asked, pointing to the display showing he had no vaginal opening.

"You don't miss much do you, lad?" Sam asked, with a bemused grin. "If this is something you really want, Tiela and I could operate to create an opening in your perineum where your vaginal opening should be."

Jev's ears flicked briefly with embarrassment as he contemplated his next question.

"Would it look and feel like female's parts?"

Tiela, knowing how embarrassing it was for Jev to even be asking this, chose her response carefully.

"It will look and function as a Caitaran female's does in

every way. It will mostly be hidden, though, as you will still have your male parts."

Jev nodded, the smile that began to form on his face showing that he was both pleased and relieved to hear this.

"One last thing, do you remember several months back when you came to me complaining of really painful cramps?" Sam asked.

"How could I not?," Jev asked, cringing slightly at the memory of the pain he experienced.

"The reason your cramps were so severe was because your menstrual discharge had nowhere to go. If you decide to go ahead with this operation, any cramps you may have won't be anywhere near as intense as they were before."

"That's good to know," Jev said, clearly relieved.

"Why didn't Jev suffer these cramps while he was with us?" Kiyel asked.

"Most likely because his transformation threw his entire cycle off," Sam explained. "We suspect that once his system has a chance to adjust, it'll return to normal."

"This really is a lot to take in," Jev said, absently scratching a spot behind his ear as he tried to absorb everything that he and Kiyel had been told.

"The two of you have some pretty big decisions to make," Sam said. "I'm sure they won't be easy ones, but whatever you both decide, just know that we'll support you completely."

"Thanks, Doc," Kiyel said, giving an appreciative flick of his ears.

"It looks to me like someone has already decided he's had enough for one night," Tiela said.

Jev followed her gaze and saw that Aiden had fallen asleep in his arms.

"Perhaps it's time we did the same," Kiyel suggested.

With Tiela and Sam both nodding in agreement, they said their goodnights. After Sam then led Tiela to the door to their quarters to see her out, carefully, so as not to disturb him, Jev stood up and carried Aiden to his room with Kiyel.

Hraka moved swiftly through the corridors in an effort to stay ahead of the security teams that were still searching for him, but not so quickly as to draw attention to himself from the regular crew he passed, and give himself away. Although he couldn't see them, he could hear the security teams' footsteps running through the corridors.

Except to hide from an approaching security team, the only time he risked stopping was to dispose of the modified psychic damper by throwing it into a nearby incinerator. He'd worn it to prevent the abomination and his Enassi from detecting his presence. Unfortunately, to his utter disappointment, it had only been partially effective, as the abomination had somehow sensed him just as he was about to strike.

His intended target had been the abomination's Enassi, knowing that if one were to die, the other would likely die as well. But the abomination managed to knock his Enassi out of the way. Before fleeing, howerever, he saw that his shot did strike the abomination. He could only hope that he was injured sufficiently enough to result in both their deaths.

He doubted it, though.

The footsteps of his pursuers seemed to diminish, and finally died off completely as he turned down another corridor. He didn't dare let down his guard just yet, though. He made several more turns down adjoining corridors until he finally reached his quarters, where he'd been headed all along.

Pressing his hand to the panel, the doors slid open and he silently stepped inside the darkened quarters, closing the doors behind him.

No sooner had the doors slid shut, however, when, all of a sudden, the lights in his quarters flickered to life. He whirled about, only to be confronted by a grey and black pelted Caitaran male with strangely coloured blue eyes, who was sitting at his desk with a blaster in his hand, pointed right at him.

"Hello, Hraka," the male said, showing his teeth in an unpleasant grin as he stood up. "We've been waiting for you."

That's when the doors to his quarters opened once again. Standing outside, with their blasters drawn and pointed at him, were three security officers.

"You didn't think you'd get away with it, did you?" the male asked, holding his hand out.

Hraka, knowing he was defeated, handed his blaster to the male.

"Damn you. Who in Rul's name are you?" he growled.

The male moved closer until they were almost nose to nose.

"Someone you'll wish you never met, Hraka," the male said in a chillingly even voice.

For the first time in his life, as he stared into the face of this strange Caitaran, Hraka was suddenly afraid.

When Jev woke up the next morning after getting a good night's sleep, he felt well rested and full of energy. And he was also in a surprisingly good mood, in part, he thought, because of the news Sam and Tiela had given him and Kiyel before they retired for the night, although he was almost certain Aiden somehow had something to do with how good he felt.

Movement beside him in the bed drew his attention to Kiyel, who was still fast asleep.

Since they had nothing pressing to do today, owing to the fact Tiela still hadn't cleared them for active duty, Jev felt no need to get out of bed. Instead he turned over and cuddled close to Kiyel.

Through the link they shared, he could sense Kiyel beginning to wake.

Feeling a little mischievous, Jev gently began nibbling and licking at Kiyel's neck, just below the jawline where he knew Kiyel was the most sensitive. This caused Kiyel to be roused quickly. Jev could both hear and feel him begin to softly pur in response.

That feels so nice, Kiyel sent to him, moaning softly with pleasure.

Kiyel rolled over onto his back then, and pulling Jev on top of him, rubbed his nose to Jev's affectionately.

Good morning, Enassi, Jev sent.

They stared into each other's eyes lovingly for a moment before their noses touched again, this time with more passion. Jev felt the tip of Kiyel's tongue touching his lips and he opened them in invitation.

For what seemed an eternity they lay together in a passionate embrace as they shared their first real intimate kiss together since leaving Alessi.

"Ouch!" Jev exclaimed suddenly, cringing as he felt the twinge in his arm.

Kiyel immediately loosened his grip on Jev, ears dipping apologetically.

"Sorry," Kiyel said.

"It's okay," Jev replied, with a reassuring smile.

However, the mood was unfortunately already broken.

Jev lay back down beside Kiyel, resting his head on Kiyel's chest and draping an arm over him.

I could lie with you forever like this, he sent.

So could I, Kiyel agreed.

With his ear to Kiyel's chest, Jev listened to his heartbeat, which was strong and steady.

Just like Kiyel, he thought.

"You're the one who's strong," Kiyel said aloud, hearing Jev's thoughts. "I don't think I've ever thanked you properly for saving my life in the corridor. I wouldn't be here now if you hadn't sensed our attacker."

Jev's ears dropped noticeably with acute embarrassment from Kiyel's praise.

"I love you too much to see you get hurt, Kiyel. I would do anything to make sure you don't," he said.

Kiyel touched a finger to Jev's nose.

"Just make sure you don't scare me like that again," he warned.

Jev could hear the fear in his voice. He knew exactly how scared Kiyel had been of losing him.

I promise, he sent.

"Care to join me for a shower?" Kiyel asked. "Then I can brush your fur afterward as thanks for that wonderful wake up you gave me."

"I'd love to," Jev answered, his ears pricking up with excitement.

They ended up spending a leisurely amount of time in the shower before finally getting out and drying themselves off. But once back in their bedroom, they didn't waste any time picking out the clothes they wanted to wear from the closet. Since they were off duty, they both decided against wearing their uniforms.

Caitaran civilian clothing, Jev noted when he opened the

closet door and glanced over the contents inside, was rather drab in appearance, with very little variety of colours. As Kiyel explained it to him, though, the colours Caitarans wore denoted the guild they belonged to and couldn't be worn by anyone other than members of that particular guild. Because they belonged to the Telepath Guild, they were entitled to wear the colour purple.

Jev chose for himself a light-coloured , loose-fitting overtunic, which folded across at his chest and split at his hips, and a contrasting purple undertunic. The pants he chose were a darker shade than his overtunic, but made of the same material, and ended just past his knees. To complete his ensemble, he selected a purple-coloured cloth belt to secure the overtunic at his waist. Looking over at Kiyel, he saw that he had chosen similar clothes, except that his overtunic also had embroidered purple trim in an intricate pattern. On the shoulders of both their overtunics were tabs similar to the ones on their uniforms indicating they were an Enassi pair.

After he finished laying his clothes out on the bed, he glanced up to see Kiyel opening the drawer in the table beside his side of the bed, from which he took a long bristled brush, and then sat down on the bed, patting it gently beside him.

"I think I promised you a brushing," Kiyel said.

Jev, smiling with eager anticipation, quickly put down the undertunic he was about to put on and almost jumped to sit beside Kiyel, turning his back towards him. Almost immediately after Kiyel started brushing his fur, he began purring loudly with pleasure.

This feels amazing, Enassi. Please don't stop, he sent, instinctively leaning forward more to give Kiyel more access. His tail was swaying from the immense pleasure he was feeling.

Kiyel chuckled lightly as he continued brushing the fur, moving the brush down his Enassi's back all the way to the base of his tail. While he did, he was amazed at how quickly Jev's fur had grown since the transformation, especially the fur on his head, which was now quite long. He decided he liked it this way, and it made brushing it that much more pleasurable, for the both of them.

Suddenly, they were interrupted by the sound of the door outside, and they both froze. They stared at each other for a quick moment before leaping off the bed to get dressed.

"Who in the world could that be?" Jev asked irritably, while pulling on his pants.

"I don't know," Kiyel said, with a low growl. "But whoever it is has a really lousy sense of timing!"

Jev couldn't agree more. They finished dressing and hurried out of the room.

At once, they saw Sam, still dressed in his night clothes, was already at the door and speaking to someone on the intercom. Standing beside him was a wary-looking Aiden.

"Sam, it's me, Ryiad. I'm here with ship's security. May we come in?" the voice over the intercom asked.

Sam, who saw Jev and Kiyel leaving their room, looked at Kiyel uncertainly.

Kiyel, however, nodded for Sam to open the door.

When the door slid open, Jev smiled with relief when he recognized Riyad's familiar figure standing at the threshold. Behind him stood two security officers.

Riyad held his hand up to Kiyel's chest in the traditional telepath greeting, which Kiyel returned before inviting them in. Only one security officer followed Riyad into their quarters, though. The other remained outside.

Although slightly afraid, Aiden looked out from behind Sam's leg at Riyad, and stared at him closely.

With a warm grin, Riyad knelt down to his level.

"Hello, Aiden. Do you remember me?" he asked in a soft, friendly voice.

It took him a few seconds, but eventually Aiden smiled at him and stepped out from behind Sam. He reached out with his arms, as though wanting to be picked up.

"It's okay, Riyad," Jev assured him, seeing Riyad's surprised reaction. "He does this when he sees someone he likes."

Nodding, Riyad lifted Aiden into his arms, who then put his arms around Riyad's neck and settled comfortably against his chest.

"It's strange, I can almost feel him in my mind, and I'm not even a telepath," Riyad said.

"We think he may be an empath," Jev told him. "He can sense and even affect the emotions in others."

"It turns out he's also a remarkable healer," Kiyel added.

"Really," Riyad said, his ears pricking up with acute interest.

"So what brings you back to our quarters, Riyad?" Kiyel asked.

"Actually, there are three reasons," Riyad said. "First, to let you know that your attacker has been found and captured, and that a hearing to determine whether a general court-martial is to be convened is scheduled for mid-day tomorrow."

"Well that's a relief," Sam said.

"Secondly, the captain believes that there may be others, associates of your attacker, who also wish to see the two of you dead," Riyad continued. "For your own protection, then, he's re-assigning you to Ambassadorial quarters on the upper level—at least temporarily. I'm here to facilitate that move."

"And the third?" Kiyel asked, his tail already flicking with obvious displeasure. He didn't like where this was headed.

"To maintain appearances while you're quartered on the Ambassadorial level, I've been assigned to you to act as your adjutant," Riyad said.

"No, absolutely not," Kiyel declared.

"Why not, Kiyel?" Sam asked, taken aback by Kiyel's forceful reaction.

"Doc, I spent almost my whole life trying to get away from that type of lifestyle. I refuse to be forced back into it just because some lunatics have decided to make things difficult for us," Kiyel said.

"I understand how you feel. I would probably feel the same way if I was in your situation," Riyad said.

Kiyel turned on Riyad and frowned, his nose wrinkling.

"And what exactly do you know of my situation?" he asked.

"I told you I grew up in the Telepath Guild, so I know your family, of course," Riyad said, the slightest hint of a grin tugging at the corners of his mouth. "It really wasn't all that difficult to see through the alias you chose for yourself."

"No, I guess it wasn't," Kiyel admitted, ears twitching faintly with embarrassment. "I guess I should be thanking you, then, for not giving me away."

"It was my pleasure, my Lord," Riyad said, bowing his head.

Kiyel's tail gave an involuntary flick.

"Please don't call me that," he said.

"But protocol dictates that I address you by your title, sir."

"In public, that may, unfortunately, be true," Kiyel accepted, albeit grudgingly. "But while we're in present company, I'd prefer it if we kept things informal."

Riyad's ears flicked assent.

"As you wish, Kiyel," he said.

We might as well get used to it, Kiyel, Jev sent, feeling his Enassi's discomfort. *Once the Admiral is made aware of who you really are, it'll be unavoidable I think. And then there's the imminent arrival of your mother to consider.*

It doesn't mean I have to like it, though, Kiyel sent defiantly.

No, and neither do I. But it's possible that we can use your position to our advantage, like getting some privacy so we can finally be alone together.

Kiyel, at first, gave him a surprised look, but then a small mischievous grin spread across his face.

I hadn't thought of that, he sent.

Still grinning, he turned back to Riyad.

"All right, Riyad, let's get on with this move, then."

TWELVE

The day of the hearing came much sooner than Jev and Kiyel would have liked. In fact, they both would have preferred that it hadn't come at all.

They had, after all, only managed to get a few hours sleep after spending most of the previous day moving and getting settled into their new quarters, which, despite the considerable help from Riyad, Sam and even Aiden, was still exhausting work.

With the scheduled start of the hearing set to begin very shortly, they barely had enough time to shower, get into clean uniforms and grab a quick first meal before they had to make their way to the judicial wing of the ship. But, upon arriving at the courtroom where the hearing was to take place, they instead were directed to one of the anterooms adjacent to the courtroom and told to wait until they were called to testify before the tribunal.

The anteroom, Jev saw, was little more than a walk-in

closet. It was just large enough to accommodate the large, very uncomfortable looking, wooden bench set against a side wall, and a small table on the opposite side of the room. On a metal tray on the table was a glass pitcher of ice water and two empty plastic cups, presumably placed there in case they grew thirsty while they waited. The anteroom was not very inviting, and certainly not designed for comfort—the complete opposite of what their new quarters were like.

Although Jev, like Kiyel, did not like the fact they had to change quarters in the first place, he had to admit their new quarters were far more luxurious than he expected. Besides featuring a full sized galley in which they could now prepare and enjoy a private meal if they wished—something Jev was relishing the thought of taking advantage of—their new quarters also boasted a significantly larger and more comfortable lounge, enough bedrooms that Aiden no longer had to share a room with Sam, and even a communications console beside the galley. Kiyel and Jev even had their own private personal which was adjacent to their bedroom.

The door to the anteroom slid open, abruptly drawing Jev back to the present, and a female yeoman, dressed in the formal robes of an officer of the court, entered.

"Sirs, your presence is now requested by the tribunal," she said, her ears dipping respectfully.

And not a moment too soon. Jev was only too glad to finally be out of that uncomfortable room.

They were led into the courtroom, which, they were surprised to see, was filled almost to capacity with spectators, most of whom Jev had never laid eyes on. He did see, however, that Kel and the surviving crew of the *Lekur* were there, as was Admiral Chuul, who, much to his surprise, was sitting at the back of the room, flanked on either side by her adjutants. Seeing her in the courtroom gave Jev an idea, which Kiyel quickly picked up. They both instantly recognized the opportunity her presence gave them to put a sudden end to her interfering with their lives.

At the far end, situated on a raised dais, was a large, rectangular table, behind which sat the three presiding officers. In front of the presiding officers, on either side of the room, were the tables for the Prosecution and the Defense.

Jev and Kiyel were both led over to the prosecuting side, where Jev was asked to take a seat next to the Prosecuting Officer. Kiyel, though, was directed to sit in the chair to the left of the presiding officers, set there for the witness.

The officer, who was chairing the tribunal, a tall, imposing Caitaran male with graying fur, and to Jev's surprise, wearing spectacles, looked over at Kiyel from his terminal, his ears giving a little flick of acknowledgment as Kiyel sat down.

"Please state your full name and rank, for the records," the Chair directed.

"I am Kiyel Lhevic, heir to the Lhevic Pride and telepath first grade," he said without hesitation, using a strong, clear voice, and sitting up straight in his chair, looking every bit the heir of a pride leader that he was.

Hraka, sitting at the defense table, turned his ears and head sharply toward Kiyel, as did the officer conducting his defense, while a surprised murmur began echoing throughout the courtroom. It took the Chair several taps of the gavel to restore order and bring silence to the courtroom once again.

Jev glanced back to where Admiral Chuul was sitting, a satisfied grin stretching across his face when he saw her shocked reaction, which quickly turned to anger. From the witness chair, Kiyel was also watching her, and in Jev's mind he could hear Kiyel's amused laughter as the admiral abruptly stood up and stormed out of the courtroom, leaving her surprised adjutants to scramble after her.

"My Lord, I must protest," objected Hraka's attorney, who shot up from his chair, drawing Jev's attention back to the front of the courtroom. "At no time were we told of the alleged victim's identity."

"Your objection is overruled, councillor. The witness has properly identified himself satisfying your client's right to face his accuser," the Chair said, forcing Hraka's attorney, who was clearly displeased, to sit back down. "However, this tribunal would be interested in learning the witness's reasons for joining the forces under a false name," the Chair added, looking again at Kiyel, the set of his ears showing his displeasure.

Kiyel's ears dipped slightly in apology.

"My Lord, in an attempt to escape what I perceived to be an intolerable domestic situation, I decided to join the forces. I had to use an alias to avoid drawing attention to myself and to avoid scrutiny by my parents, who no doubt would have interfered. I ask the tribunal's forgiveness for my transgression," he said.

The Chair nodded absently as he considered Kiyel's response. And for just an instant, Jev thought he saw a grin tug at the corner of his lips, as though, incredibly, he not only sympathized with Kiyel's predicament, but agreed with his decision as well.

"Let the witness's permanent record be amended accordingly to reflect his actual identity and status," the Chair said into the court recorder on his terminal. "You may proceed, councillor," he then told the prosecuting officer.

Over the next several hours, the prosecution presented its case. After Kiyel, and then Jev, finished testifying, the prosecuting officer called several witnesses, most of whom were present when Jev and Kiyel were attacked in the corridor. But some, including Tiela, testified on the events that occurred afterward. They were both relieved and thankful that Tiela had omitted Aiden's miraculous healing of Jev from her testimony. None of them wanted Aiden to be exposed to further scrutiny than he already was.

When it was finally the defense's turn to present its case, Jev was surprised when the officer conducting Hraka's defense requested, and was granted, a short recess to confer with his client. The exchange between them was quiet, but tense. It was also short. The officer rose from his seat, almost reluctantly it seemed to Jev, to address the Tribunal.

"My Lord, the defense rests," he said, tail flicking jerkily behind him.

The Chair looked over at the defence table, peering over his spectacles as he regarded the officer conducting Hraka's defence carefully, ears pricked up with surprise.

"Are we to understand that your client does not wish to offer a defence, councillor?" he asked.

"Not at this time, my Lord."

Jev sighed deeply, as did Kiyel, the look of surprise clearly showing on their faces, as the officer of the court, the same yeoman who had escorted them into the courtroom, ordered the defendant to stand and face the Tribunal. Hraka did so, defiantly.

"After careful consideration of the testimony given and the facts presented, it is this tribunal's decision that Lieutenant Hraka Zerid, charged with the willful attempted assassination of a Guild official and attempted first-degree murder during a time of war, be remanded into custody until such time as a general court martial is convened. This tribunal stands adjourned."

As soon as the Tribunal's decision was pronounced the

guards surrounding Hraka moved in and placed shackles on his wrists and ankles before leading him out of the room.

Kiyel stared after them, his hand clenched in a fist on the table in front of him.

"Come on, let's get out of here," he said quietly to Jev.

As he and Jev stood up to leave the courtroom, they approached Kel and the rest of their former crew, who were huddled together discussing the results of the hearing.

"Captain, thanks for being here," Kiyel said, ears flicking in acknowledgment. "We really appreciate the support."

"It was the least we could do, Kiyel," Kel said.

"It seems as though you got your wish after all, Captain," Jev said, his lips curling up in a toothless grin.

"What wish might that be, Jev?"

"You did mention to us, before, your desire to be in the room when Kiyel revealed who he was to the admiral."

Kel laughed, for he also had seen the admiral sitting at the back of the courtroom and witnessed her abrupt departure.

"So I did," he said.

"We were about to head to the lounge to grab a bite to eat and something to drink. Would you care to join us?" Jaffay asked.

"Thank you, Jaffay," Kiyel said. "But I think right now, Jev and I would like to spend some time alone for a while."

"Of course, Kiyel," Kel said, his ears giving a flick of understanding.

Jev and Kiyel said their goodbyes to the others, thanking them once again, and then left the courtroom. Almost immediately they were flanked by two security officer escorts, which they only fleetingly acknowledged.

Let's go try out the Ambassador's lounge, Kiyel suggested.

Good idea, I'm famished, Jev agreed.

Almost as if on cue, Jev's stomach suddenly growled noisily as they entered the lift, eliciting a light chuckle from Kiyel in response.

Cael sat in his command chair on the bridge of the Cetani, staring at the planet Alessi on the forward viewscreen in front of him, his mind deep in thought over the recent events involving Kiyel and his new hybrid Enassi. He'd been monitoring their attacker's hearing and was intrigued to learn that all this time he had an heir to a telepath clan on board.

The sound of the lift doors opening behind him drew his attention away from the viewscreen, his head and ears swiveling to see who had entered the bridge. He expected one of the bridge crew, but was surprised to see Admiral Chuul unexpectedly storming onto the bridge. She did not look pleased, and he had a pretty good idea why. He stood up sharply to face her, coming to attention as he did.

"Captain Cael, I want to see you in your ready room, now!" she barked, continuing to his ready room before he even had a chance to respond.

With a low sigh, his ears dipping slightly at the dressing down he knew he was likely in store for, he proceeded to follow the admiral into his ready room.

The doors closed behind him, and the admiral, who had taken a seat in Cael's chair, looked up at him with a deep frown on her face, her ears folded back against her skull in anger.

"Why the hell was I not informed about the true identity of one of our new Enassi pair?" she asked, not even offering to let him sit down, and getting straight to the point.

Cael's tail flicked involuntarily as he stood at attention

before her.

"Admiral, I am just as surprised as you at this turn of events. Like you, I was not made aware of Kiyel's true heritage until the hearing," he informed her.

And it was the truth. He had his suspicions all along, though, especially since Kiyel had somehow managed to receive a personal communique during a communications blackout. But there was no way he could have known that Kiyel was the heir to the most powerful telepath family on Caitar. His records had been sealed by the Telepath Guild.

"Well, someone on this ship knew," Chuul fumed.

"I would guess it would have to be Elder Veir, or someone on his staff," Cael said.

"Damn telepaths," Chuul growled, her ears and tail flicking displeasure.

Before Cael was able to respond, the door sounded.

Annoyed, Chuul looked past Cael to the door.

"What is it?" she curtly said.

The door slid open to admit Cael's first officer. In her hand was a piece of paper.

"I'm sorry for interrupting, Admiral," Diela said, ears giving an apologetic flick, before turning her attention to Cael. "An urgent message for you was just handed to me from one of Elder Veir's aides, Captain."

"Give it here, Commander," Chuul ordered, holding out her hand.

After a moment's hesitation, Diela handed the message to her, which Chuul then quickly read. Her ears pricked up suddenly and she practically leapt to her feet.

"Captain, we'll have to discuss this another time," she said, and promptly left the room.

A bewildered Cael turned to Diela, his brow narrowing

in puzzlement.

"What was all that about, Commander?" he asked.

"I'm not really sure, Captain. Something about a new Enassi pairing, I think."

Cael's ears pricked up with sudden interest.

"Another Enassi pairing?" he echoed. "It's not Kiyel and his hybrid Enassi?"

"No, I don't think so, sir."

"Diela, get me a priority communications channel with the Telepath Guild on Caitar and pipe it through to my ready room. I want to speak with Leader Sahl."

"Right away, Captain," Diela said, with an acknowledging flick of her ears.

When she had left, Cael sat down at his desk, activated his terminal and waited for the connection he'd requested. But as he did, a troubling question suddenly entered his thoughts.

What in Dahel's name is going on with the telepaths?

The doors to the Ambassador's lounge slid open. Tiela, out of breath, rushed in and briefly scanned the room until she found the two people she was looking for. They were seated at a table near one of the large windows on the far side of the lounge, engaged in quiet conversation. Neither of them were aware of her presence until she suddenly appeared at their table.

"Tiela, is something the matter?" Kiyel asked, looking up and noticing her harried state.

"It's happened again, Kiyel," Tiela replied, her ears and tail flicking in excitement.

"Slow down, Tiela, what's happened again?"

"There's been another pairing."

Jev looked at her with startled amazement, his ears

pricking up sharply, as he immediately caught on to what she was referring to.

"You mean another human has formed an Enassi link with a Caitaran telepath?" he asked.

Tiela nodded, grabbing a chair to sit down between them. A server approached their table but she waved him off.

"I just received word from Elder Veir a few moments ago. They'll be by the medical bay later for an evaluation as soon as Veir has finished interviewing them," she said.

"Who's the human?" Jev asked.

"As I understand it, a young woman from the group that came up with us on the shuttle," Tiela answered.

"It was bound to happen," Kiyel nodded, wrinkling his nose in thought. "I wouldn't be surprised if more Alessi humans are discovered to have a talent."

"The human race is notorious for rejecting what they don't understand. At first, even I didn't believe that telepathy existed, either," Jev reminded him.

"It didn't take much to convince you, though, if you recall," Kiyel said, with a wide grin.

Jev's ears twitched faintly with embarrassment, though he also smiled.

"Tiela, would it be possible for Jev and me to be there when this new Enassi pair comes to see you?," Kiyel asked.

"That is why I came to see you, actually."

"Well then, what are we sitting around here for? Let's go," Jev suggested.

As they were all in agreement, they stood up from the table, leaving the remainder of their k'yarri behind, and left the lounge.

They had to take a nearby lift to get to the medical bay, which was two levels down from the ambassadorial level. It deposited them into an eerily familiar corridor, only feet from the medical bay. Jev recognized it as the same corridor that he and Kiyel had been attacked in. The memory of that event caused his tail to flick jerkily, showing his discomfort.

They can't harm you, now, Enassi, Kiyel sent, putting his arm protectively around Jev as they entered the medical bay.

I know, Jev sent, and smiled weakly up at him. *I just don't think I'll get over what happened to us.*

They were met in the reception area by an orderly, who talked briefly with Tiela. She flicked her ears in assent and then dismissed him.

"They're already here," she said, looking back at Jev and Kiyel.

"That was quick," Kiyel said, mildly surprised.

She led them into her office where Jev saw a dark-pelted Caitaran male was sitting next to a young human female at Tiela's desk.

Upon their entry, the two stood and faced them.

"Are you Kiyel?" the male asked, holding his hand up to Kiyel's chest in the traditional telepath greeting, which Kiyel returned.

"I am, and this is my Enassi, Jev," Kiyel said.

The male greeted Jev similarly.

"I am Imas, and this is my Enassi, Eileen," he said.

Eileen, Jev saw, was a tall, slender, woman, with long, dark-brown coloured hair and light-brown eyes. She was still wearing the garb typically worn by the women of Alessi, and despite her apparent frailty, Jev sensed she had a very strong personality. It was no wonder to him, then, that she should be a telepath and that she would form an Enassi Link with a Caitaran telepath. Though he couldn't fathom why he hadn't sensed her talent on the shuttle.

Jev smiled, and held his hand out to her.

"Hello, Eileen, I'm Jev," he said, with a warm smile.

His actions actually surprised her, as she was expecting to be greeted as all the telepaths on board had greeted her. She was not expecting a Caitaran to greet her in such a human way.

"Your name sounds familiar somehow," Eileen said, her brow scrunching up in thought as she shook his hand.

"My father was Lars Bjorn, proprietor of the Cask's Head Inn in Hillsforde," Jev told her. "I'm sure you were briefed about me and Kiyel before getting on the shuttle."

Eileen's eyes opened wide with shock as she realized the truth of what he said. And then, with some trepidation, she reached up to touch the fur on his face.

Jev could feel her hesitantly reaching out with her mind to his as well, so he lowered his shields to share his memories with her.

Is this what'll eventually happen to me? she thought.

Because they were at that moment linked, Jev was able to hear her thoughts, and he could also feel the growing fear that was welling up inside her mind. He knew that he had to act quickly to assuage her fears.

My transformation was possible only because I am both telekinetic and telepathic. They think the attack on me by the T'kri is what precipitated the change. And because I'm sixteen and still going through puberty, my body was amenable to the change, he sent.

Eileen seemed to accept Jev's explanation, but he could tell there was still some doubt in her mind.

"I'm sorry about your father," Eileen said aloud at last as she withdrew from his mind.

"Thanks," Jev managed to say to her, though his voice was now taut with pain.

Although it had been several months since that terrible day, the memory of his father's death in the fire still caused him to tear up. Kiyel, feeling Jev's distress, pulled him close to comfort him.

"I'm sorry, I shouldn't have said anything," Eileen quickly said, both seeing the pain in Jev's eyes and feeling it also.

"It's alright," he said, a single tear rolling down his cheek. "So much has happened since then that I haven't really had a chance to think about it much."

Eileen nodded in understanding.

"So when did the two of you first discover that you were Enassi linked?" Tiela asked.

"Actually, we hadn't formally met until we literally bumped into each other in the corridor outside the crew lounge," Imas said, thankful for the change of subject.

Eileen's face flushed slightly from the memory.

"I was so fascinated with the ship and everything around me that I'm afraid I wasn't paying much attention to where I was going until I suddenly collided with him. It almost knocking me down on my butt," she said, with a little grin. "When we bumped into each other, though, I felt the strangest shock, like a really strong static discharge."

"I felt it also. I didn't think anything of it until later when I was in my quarters. I was trying to get to sleep when, all of a sudden, I began receiving thoughts and feelings that were completely alien to me. I've spent enough time at the Telepath Guild to recognize right away that they could only have come from the human that I bumped into earlier. At the same time I also began to feel a powerful need to be with her. So I left immediately for the humans' quarters," Imas said.

"Right before Imas came looking for me, I was

experiencing the most horrible headache ever. It didn't help when someone was incessantly sounding the door. When I opened the door to tell whoever it was to go away, I lost my balance and stumbled. Imas caught me before I could fall. But all of a sudden, my headache was gone, and in my mind, just for a second, I thought I heard the word Enassi being spoken to me. Looking back on it, I now know it was Imas whose voice I heard."

"And up to this point neither of you had ever met except for that brief encounter in the corridor?" Tiela asked, fascinated by their story.

Imas and Eileen both nodded their assent.

"What surprised me the most, physician, was when I suddenly realized that I could actually understand everything he was saying to me. Speaking your language, though, took a little more work," Eileen said with a mirthful grin.

"It actually took a bit of convincing before she would even accept that she was a telepath, but once she did, she accepted the link between us was real and we've been together ever since," Imas said.

"You, too?" Kiyel laughed.

Seeing their confused faces, Jev decided to explain.

"Just before coming here to see you, we were actually discussing the lack of belief amongst humans in telepathy and other psychic phenomena," he said.

"Well, I for one am surprised that Elder Veir let you both go so soon. I expected he'd want to talk to you for a lot longer than he actually did," Tiela said.

"That was my expectation as well," Imas said. "But then Admiral Chuul, who'd somehow gotten word that Eileen and I were Enassi-linked, barged in demanding that she debrief us immediately."

Kiyel and Jev both frowned, their tails flicking almost in sync.

"We know all about the Admiral's interest in us," Jev said derisively.

"And it looks like she's interested in you, now, since she can't get to us," Kiyel added.

"Well, Elder Veir didn't take too kindly to being ordered to hand over a couple of his telepaths. He told the admiral that he was sending us directly to physician Tiela for a physical evaluation, with a recommendation that I be taken off duty."

A smile quickly formed on Jev's face, his tail flicking with amusement.

"I'm sure she didn't like that!" he said.

"Not in the least. Elder Veir had to threaten to contact the Warrior's Guild on Caitar and make an official complaint about her behaviour, before she backed down."

"Did he send the complaint anyway?" Jev asked.

"Of course, and I think he also forwarded a copy to your father, Kiyel," Imas said, with a satisfying grin.

At this, they all began to laugh, drawing several curious glances from the orderlies in the next room.

"I guess we should get started on your evaluations, then," Tiela said, once she managed to get her laughter under control.

She walked to her desk and turned on her terminal, activating the communications circuit.

Riyad's face soon appeared on the screen.

"Yes, physician?" he asked.

"Riyad, is Sam there with you?"

"Did you wish to speak with him?"

"No, that's alright. But could you ask him to join me in the medical bay?" she asked. "I would like his help with a couple of evaluations."

"He'll join you momentarily, physician," Riyad said, nodding to someone off screen, indicating that Sam had heard Tiela's request and was on his way.

"Thank you, Riyad," Tiela said, before she closed the connection.

THIRTEEN

J ev and Kiyel walked to Tiela's office where she was seated at her desk going over Imas and Eileen's test results on her terminal. She was so focused on her terminal that she didn't see them at the door.

Jev gently tapped the door frame to get her attention.

"Tiela, do you have a moment?" he asked.

"Jev, Kiyel, what can I do for you?" Tiela asked, switching off her terminal and inviting them in and to take a seat.

"Before you came to get us, Kiyel and I were discussing the operation you could do for me. I'd like to go ahead with it," he said.

"I thought that might be your decision," Tiela said with a knowing grin.

"When do you think it could be done?" Kiyel asked.

Tiela pondered the question for a moment, wrinkling her nose in thought.

"I would need to get in touch with a colleague of mine first, His specialty is reconstructive surgery. Provided he agrees to do it, I think it could be done within the next couple of days, if you'd like."

"Thank you, Tiela," Jev said, smiling. "That would be great."

She switched back on her terminal, but when they didn't get up to leave, she regarded them quizzically, ears pricking up with curious interest.

"Was there something else?" she asked.

"Well, yes, as a matter of fact, there is," Kiyel admitted, somewhat hesitantly. "When the *Cetani* returns to Caitar, we'll have to appear at the Telepath Guild to be tested. We were wondering if you would consider coming with us, as our physician."

"What about Sam? I thought he was going with you?" Tiela asked.

"He is. He's family. But he doesn't have your experience with Caitaran physiology. And no other physician on Caitar is familiar with our unique needs, and you are. We need you."

"I don't mind telling you that this is quite an honour you're offering me," Tiela said, clearly bewildered.

"With everything we've been through, Tiela, there's no one we trust more to be our physician," Jev said.

"Thank you, Jev. That means a lot to me," Tiela said, her ears dipping slightly from his praise. "It is a big decision, though, so I hope you won't be offended when I ask if I can take some time to think it over."

"Of course not," Kiyel said, with an understanding flick of his ears. He and Jev then stood up. "You know where to reach us once you've made your decision."

Tiela nodded, and stood with them.

"I'll also get in touch with you, Jev, when I hear if my colleague is available to assist with the operation," she said.

"Thanks, Tiela," Jev said.

They left the medical bay and were immediately joined by a security detail to escort them back to their quarters.

Jev was glad for their presence, as they made him feel more at ease as they moved about the corridors, but at the same time he was disturbed that their presence was even necessary. Hraka's associates were still on the loose, and until they were captured they had to always be on their guard.

Just then, a sudden, terrifying realization came to him.

Kiyel, we need to see if Imas and Eileen can be assigned a security detail. If Hraka's associates can't get to us, then they may try to go after them, he sent.

I was thinking the same thing, Kiyel admitted.

Do you think Riyad will be able to arrange it?

I'll check with him and see. I also have to talk to my father. He'll want to know about this new pairing, Kiyel sent.

When they reached their quarters, Riyad was seated at the desk in the reception area. He looked up from his terminal, acknowledging their entrance with a flick of his ears.

"Riyad, I need a favour from you if I may," Kiyel said.

"Of course, anything."

"I need you to arrange a meeting between me and Captain Cael if that's possible."

"It will be done, Kiyel," Riyad nodded.

"Also, is our communications terminal programmed to contact Amuro estate back home?"

"It is. Do you wish me to establish the link for you?"

"No, that's alright. I can do that. Just get me that meeting with the Captain."

Riyad nodded his assent and activated a channel to the

Cetani's bridge through his terminal while Jev and Kiyel continued into their quarters.

Jev had to smile when he saw Sam and Aiden in the lounge playing an improvised game of checkers.

"Welcome back, you two," Sam said when he saw them come in.

Aiden, happy to see them came rushing up to them and proceeded to give them both hugs. He lifted his arms up to Jev, who smiled and lifted the youngster up into his arms.

"Doc, we'll be with you shortly. I need to speak with my father first," Kiyel said.

"Not a problem, Kiyel. You take care of what you need to," Sam said, and he went to the galley to get himself something to drink.

"Did you want me to give you some privacy while you make the call?" Jev asked.

Kiyel shook his head.

"He'll see you eventually, anyway. Now is as good a time as any," he said.

With Aiden still in his arms, Jev followed Kiyel to the communications console and watched while Kiyel activated the unit. Then, when the Caitaran Forces insignia appeared on the screen in front of him, Kiyel entered a few more commands into the terminal. After a few seconds, the insignia disappeared and was replaced with an image of a very young Caitaran male, who couldn't have been more than ten or eleven years old, and who bore a striking resemblance to Kiyel. Jev suddenly realized that this was Kiyel's younger brother.

From Kiyel's reaction to seeing his brother, it was obvious that he wasn't expecting his brother to answer the call.

"Kehlan, what are you doing home? I thought you were still at the Guild."

"Hi, Kiyel. I was, but father told me I could continue my studies here," his brother answered.

Jev could instantly feel that Kehlan was happy to see his brother, and relieved as well.

"Father said you got hurt," Kehlan continued, his voice filled with concern.

"I did, but I'm alright now," Kiyel assured him.

"Father also said you have an Enassi now. Is he cute?" Kehlan asked, grinning mischievously.

Kiyel's ears dipped sharply with acute embarrassment.

"You little yuta," he said.

Kehlan just laughed, and even Jev had to choke back a snicker, but failed miserably. This earned him a playful elbow to his arm from Kiyel.

"Oh, he's there with you now?" Kehlan asked. "Let me see."

Jev stepped closer to Kiyel so that he was in frame.

"Hello, Kehlan," he said.

"Kehlan, this is Jev, my Enassi," Kiyel said.

"Hi, Jev," Kehlan said, his ears flicking in greeting. "Is that one of the Terrans father was talking about that you're holding?" he asked, seeing Aiden in Jev's arms.

"This is Aiden," Jev nodded, "and he's also an empath."

"You'll get to meet them both soon enough, Kehlan," Kiyel interjected. "Is father there? I need to speak with him."

"Just a second," Kehlan nodded.

He got up from his chair and disappeared from view. A few moments later, a taller, much older, Caitaran male appeared and sat down in the vacated chair.

"Hello, Kiyel," the Caitaran said.

"Hello, father," Kiyel answered back.

His father's eyes shifted slightly to Kiyel's left where Jev stood.

"Who is that standing with you, Kiyel?" he asked.

"He is my Enassi, father. This is Jev, the one I told you about," Kiyel confirmed. "Jev this is my father, Sahl."

"It's an honour to meet you, sir," Jev said, his ears giving a flick of acknowledgment.

Sahl regarded him with a quizzical look, and Jev immediately could tell why. Kiyel's father had been expecting Jev to look human.

"I am one of the colonists, or was until recently," Jev explained. "A couple weeks ago, while hiding out in some caves, we were attacked by the T'kri. Their attack triggered latent telekinetic abilities I never knew I had. A gestalt link was established, and it somehow changed me, making me what I am now—part human and part Caitaran."

"I can request that Tiela, the physician who has been treating us, send you our records, father," Kiyel offered.

"Please do, Kiyel," his father said, incredulous as to what he'd just learned.

Jev opened his mind to Kiyel's father, sending to him his memories of the experience.

Kiyel, sensing what he was doing, added his memories

Sahl's ears pricked up with intrigue as he absorbed the memories.

"Well, Jev, you certainly are creating quite the pile of paperwork for me," he said, a thin grin tugging at the corner of his mouth.

Jev's ears dipped slightly.

"Sorry about that," he said.

"Don't be," Sahl laughed. "It's been a fascinating read so far."

"Father, we need to talk to you about some new

developments that have happened recently," Kiyel said, his tone turning serious.

The grin on Sahl's face promptly disappeared.

"Tell me," he said.

"The other day we were attacked while we were on route to the medical bay for an evaluation. Jev was subsequently injured in the attack."

"You mean by one of our people?" Sahl asked, his ears folding back against his skull in sudden anger.

"It was a member of the *Cetani's* crew," Kiyel nodded. "It seems he belongs to a group that seeks to revive the ideals of the old Chemian cult."

"Are you alright now, Jev?" Sahl asked, his tail flicking spasmodically behind him.

"Thanks to this little one," Jev answered, indicating Aiden in his arms. "He saved my life."

"How so?" Sahl asked.

"Besides being an empath, it seems that he's also a very gifted healer."

"He's one of the colonists, is he not?"

"And my adopted brother," Jev nodded.

Sahl grinned warmly at Aiden.

"Say hello to him for me, and give him my thanks," he said.

"You're welcome," Aiden said.

That Aiden understood, and even spoke, Caitaran, clearly surprised Sahl, who was definitely not expecting Aiden to respond to him.

Aiden, for his part, giggled gleefully at Sahl's reaction.

"Fascinating," Sahl said. "Has the child been tested yet?"

"Not yet, father. We wanted to wait until he had a chance to fully recover from his own injuries, which he'd received on the planet," Kiyel said.

"Not by one of our people, I hope," Sahl said.

"No, father," Kiyel assured him, but didn't elaborate.

Sahl, sensing Kiyel's hesitation, decided to let the matter drop for now.

"I am gratified, at least, to know that you have finally found someone to love, Kiyel," he said. "I know you have never been thrilled with the idea of becoming Miru's lifemate, but now that you have found Jev, it will make your bonding with her more tolerable."

"I'm sorry, father, there can be no bonding between that female and me, or any other Caitaran female for that matter," Kiyel said.

"Come on, Kiyel, be reasonable."

"I am, father. The same gestalt link that changed Jev changed me also, making me incompatible with any Caitaran female. There can be no offspring from such a union. Tiela's tests have confirmed this."

"I see," Sahl said.

Jev could plainly see that this bit of news did not please Kiyel's father at all.

"In fact," Kiyel continued, "Tiela's tests have determined that I am only compatible with Jev."

"I don't see how that's possible, Kiyel. You're both males," Sahl said, looking perplexed.

"Yes, but we've also just recently discovered that I'm what my people called intersexed, meaning that I was born with both male and female reproductive organs, and they are fully functional," Jev said.

"Kiyel, I'm really going to need to see both your medical records," Sahl said, his tail flicking in bewilderment. "Miru will not be pleased to hear this, and neither will her father. They both have been quite anxious for this union."

"I know, father, and I'm sorry," Kiyel said.

"Is there anything else I should know about?" Sahl asked.

"Actually there is," Kiyel nodded, and they both saw Sahl brace himself for more startling news. "There has been a second Enassi link established between one of our telepaths and an Alessian colonist."

"Another link you say?" Sahl asked, leaning forward in his chair, his ears pricked up with keen interest. "When did this happen?"

"Fairly recently. We just came from the medical bay where Tiela examined them."

"Has Elder Veir had a chance to see them yet?"

"Yes, but only briefly. Admiral Chuul is trying to interrogate them, since she can no longer get to us, now that she knows who I am."

Sahl nodded, his nose wrinkling in thought.

"I'll get in touch with Elder Veir myself, and discuss with him what should be done about the Admiral."

"Father, Jev and I are under the protection of the security afforded to residents on the ambassadorial level, which is where we are now. If this cult that attacked us becomes aware of this new Enassi pair, they could try to get to them instead."

"What do you suggest, Kiyel?"

"I've asked my new ajudant, Riyad, to arrange a meeting between me and the captain of the *Cetani*. It's my hope to convince him to at least provide to them the same level of protection we have."

Sahl's ears flicked in assent.

"I'll speak with the Captain as well, and stress to him the Telepath Guild's interest in seeing that this, and any other mixed-Enassi pair is given the highest protection possible."

"Thank you, father," Kiyel said, with a relieved grin. "That will certainly be helpful."

"In the meantime, be sure to send me those records."

"I will, father," Kiyel promised.

"Your mother should be arriving shortly. You'd better tell her everything you've told me when she gets there."

"I plan to," Kiyel nodded.

"Jev, it was a pleasure meeting you. You be sure to take care of that Enassi of yours," Sahl said to him.

"I promise, sir."

Sahl nodded and then closed the connection.

The image of the Caitaran Forces insignia reappeared briefly before Kiyel turned off the console.

"Everything taken care of, Kiyel?" Sam asked, coming up behind them with a couple of cups of hot k'yarri, which Jev and Kiyel both accepted gratefully.

The shuttle pilot deftly maneuvered the small craft into a holding position outside the *Cetani's* hangar bays before activating her communications board.

"*Cetani* Flight, Shuttle *Miyata*. Requesting priority clearance to dock," she said.

"Shuttle *Miyata*, *Cetani* Flight. You are cleared to land in hangar one. Level one security protocols are in effect," came the response, almost immediately, as the massive hangar bay doors began to slide open.

"*Cetani* Flight, Shuttle *Miyata*, copy that. Initiating docking procedures. Level one security protocols are in effect," she repeated, as was expected of her according to protocol.

With a skill that defied her young age, she lined the

shuttle up with the hanger bay, which was now open and ready to receive the shuttle, and gently coaxed it forward until its nose passed through the threshold. Then, with a flick of a switch, she cut the engines, allowing the shuttle's own inertia to carry it fully into the hangar bay. Only when the shuttle was safely inside, and hovering over the hanger deck, did she activate the shuttle's control thrusters, which she used to expertly maneuver the shuttle to a soft landing.

Unstrapping herself from her seat, she instructed her co-pilot to secure the vessel, and then got up and entered the passenger cabin, where she informed her lone passenger of their landing.

"Thank you, Nahla. A very smooth flight," her passenger said, addressing her by name, rather than by her rank.

"It was my pleasure, my Lady," Nahla said, ears pricking up from the complement.

While her passenger unstrapped herself from her seat, Nahla activated the controls at the rear of the shuttle, opening the hatch and lowering the ramp. As her passenger disembarked, flashing her one final smile of thanks before she left, Nahla was left in awe that she, a simple ensign in the Caitaran forces, had the incredible honour of having Pride Leader Lheiza Lhevic on board her shuttle.

At the bottom of the ramp, her passenger was approached by the Captain of the *Cetani,* his first officer, and several security personnel. There were no other personnel in the hangar bay.

"Lady Lhevic, welcome aboard the *Cetani.* I am Captain Cael and this is my first officer, Diela," he said, bowing slightly and then greeting her in the customary fashion for telepaths.

Impressed, Lheiza returned his greeting similarly.

"Thank you, Captain," she said.

"If you follow me, I'll show you to your quarters so you can get settled in," Cael said.

"Actually, Captain, if you don't mind, I would like to see my son first," Lheiza said.

"Of course, my Lady," Cael said, flicking his ears in assent. "He and his Enassi are resting in their new quarters on the ambassadorial level."

The security detail accompanying them quietly spoke into their communicators as they left the hangar bay to one of the lifts that would take them to the ambassadorial level of the ship. When the lift doors opened, the corridors beyond the lift were devoid of activity.

Cael could almost feel Lheiza's concern.

"Security protocol, my Lady," he quickly offered. "We've had some trouble on board recently related to your son and his Enassi, and didn't want to take any chances with your safety."

She nodded in grudging acceptance, determined to find out from Kiyel just what has been going on to prompt this extreme level of security.

The security detail joining them exited the lift first to ensure the way for them was clear. When they were told it was safe to do so, she left the lift with Cael and continued down the corridor to a door.

Cael depressed the panel beside the door to alert those within of their presence. A voice spoke through the intercom, requesting their identity, which Cael gave. The doors then slid open and they were greeted by an oddly-coloured Caitaran Lheiza instantly recognized.

"Riyad, what are you doing here?" she asked, automatically greeting him as she would another telepath, even though she knew the individual before her was not one.

"Lady Lhevic, it is pleasant to see you again," Riyad said, returning her greeting and bowing his head respectfully. "I have been assigned to be Kiyel's adjutant."

"I see," Lheiza said, her ears giving the briefest flick of surprise.

Riyad stepped aside to allow them entry, all of them, that is, except the security team who relieved the officers already there in the corridor and took up their position by the door.

As they were led through the narrow hallway, the sounds of a child's laughter could be heard from within. When they emerged, in the lounge a small human child was riding astride the back of Kiyel, who was running about on all fours, almost as giddily as the child himself. There were two others with them: another Caitaran, who oddly had light-coloured fur, like a female, and yet had a male's face; and an older adult human male.

Amazingly enough, it was the child who noticed them first. He ceased giggling and tapped Kiyel on the shoulder. It was then that Kiyel looked up and saw them. A look of surprise flashed across his face as he gently let the child down and stood up.

"Mother," he said.

"Hello, Kiyel," Lheiza nodded.

Kiyel quickly crossed the space between them and wrapped his arms around her in a tight hug, which she lovingly returned.

You're looking well, she sent, relieved, her tail swaying behind her. *Your father and I were concerned when we learned that you'd been injured.*

I'm alright now, mother, Kiyel assured her.

They released each other then, and Lheiza looked passed Kiyel to the Caitaran who stood with him. Instantly she could feel the strong link they shared.

And who is this? Is this your Enassi I've heard so much about? she asked.

"Mother, this is Jev," Kiyel said, speaking aloud.

Jev, seeing Riyad's reverent demeanor and deciding to play it safe, dipped his head and ears respectfully.

"It's an honour to meet you," he said.

Lheiza grinned reassuringly at his uncertainty.

"There's no need to be so formal with me, Jev," she said. "Being my son's Enassi, you're a part of our family now."

Her response surprised Kiyel, which plainly showed on his face, causing Lheiza to laugh at his confusion.

"What did you think I'd do, Kiyel, reject your Enassi?" she asked.

"Considering how adamant you were with me becoming Miru's lifemate, even though you knew I had no interest in her, I didn't know what to expect," Kiyel admitted, ears dipping apologetically.

"I still am, Kiyel," she said, her tone turning serious. "And now that you have an Enassi, whom you obviously care a great deal, you should have no objections to being bonded with her."

But Kiyel shook his head in the negative, his tail flicking, showing his distress.

"Mother, the reason for this betrothal is to ensure the continuation of our family line. I understand that. But I'm afraid that that's just not possible with me any longer, even if I wanted to."

"Don't be silly, Kiyel. Of course it is," she said, waving her hand dismissively.

"Perhaps, if I may, I could explain," Sam said, cautiously interjecting himself in the conversation.

Lheiza looked at him, her face registering the surprise she felt at Sam speaking the Caitaran language so fluently.

"Mother, this is Doctor Sam O'Riley, Jev's physician from Alessi and legal guardian," Kiyel said, introducing him to her.

"We've recently learned that your son's link with Jev has resulted in both of them undergoing some physiological changes. In Jev, it's resulted in him looking Caitaran. Even though he was born human, most of his DNA is now Caitaran. He has, however, retained some of his human traits, as you can see by the colour of his fur."

"He's a hybrid," Lheiza nodded, giving Jev a sideways glance. "I was told this on my way here."

"What you don't know is that your son also was changed, though his changes weren't as dramatic. Unfortunately, or fortunately, depending on how you look at it, these changes are sufficient to make him incompatible with a Caitaran female."

"In other words, mother, even if I were to mate with Miru, our union would be a childless one," Kiyel said.

Lheiza regarded Kiyel with astonishment, and was left momentarily speechless. At last, though, she regained her composure, though her tail continued to flick jerkily.

"Are you certain of the test results, physician O'Riley?" she asked.

"Just Sam, please," Sam said. "And yes, we're as certain as we can be. The human DNA that Kiyel has acquired makes him compatible with only one person."

"And that would be me," Jev finished.

"You?" Lheiza asked, ears pricked up sharply as she looked at Jev with bewildered disbelief.

"I'm what my people call intersexed, meaning that I have both male and female reproductive organs," Jev explained.

"I think I need to sit down," Lheiza said, overwhelmed, and took a seat on the couch.

Kiyel suggested to Riyad that he should get some k'yarri for them. While Riyad left for the galley, Kiyel invited Cael and Diela to take a seat with them.

Riyad returned a few minutes later with a full pot of steaming k'yarri and enough cups for each of them. He also had a glass of nanaya juice for Aiden, who, after climbing onto Jev's lap, happily accepted the juice.

"Phys—excuse me, Sam, would it be possible to see the results of my son's scans for myself?" Lheiza asked, correcting herself in mid-sentence. "With your permission, of course, Kiyel," she hastily added, giving Kiyel a questioning look.

"Of course, mother," Kiyel said, flicking his ears in assent. "We have already agreed to make sure father sees them."

"I will get in touch with Tiela to forward the records to you as well," Sam said.

Lheiza flicked her ears in thanks, offering him an appreciative grin. But then her expression hardened as she returned her attention to Kiyel and Jev.

"Kiyel, I have been informed by Captain Cael that there was a serious incident on this ship that necessitated the increased security I encountered when I came on board, and that this incident somehow involved the two of you. I would like to know what happened," she said.

"We were shot at on our way to the medical bay for an evaluation. Jev was hit saving my life."

"Who shot at you, one of our people?" she asked, her voice low with anger and her ears as stiff and vertical as the fur surrounding her neck and head.

"By one of our pilots," Kiyel nodded. "He belongs to a group that apparently seeks to revive the ancient Chemian cult."

"By Dahel!" Lheiza said with a startled gasp, her tail flicking with alarm. "First we learn the Chemians are still alive and well, and, in fact, are at war with the T'kri, and now you're telling me that there's a new group right here that is following in their ideals?"

"I'm afraid so," Kiyel said.

"The Caitaran Senate will need to be told of this."

"They already have been, my Lady," Diela told her. "Reports on this group have already been sent to high command, and they have forwarded them to the minister of defense."

"Commander, be certain that I receive copies of those reports. I will want to read them once this treaty is signed."

"Yes, my Lady," Diela acknowledged with a flick of her ears.

FOURTEEN

Lheiza took a sip from her k'yarri, her ears pricking up with keen interest as she glanced down at her cup.

"This is very good," she commented, looking back up at Kiyel.

"I was the one who made it, actually. Tiela showed me how," Sam said.

"Thank you," she acknowledged with an appreciative flick of her ears. "I'll have to ask her to show me as well when I see her."

Taking another sip from her k'yarri, Lheiza put the cup down on the table in front of her.

"Anyway, I suppose I need to tell you the reason I'm here. In approximately an hour's time, a delegation from Alessi will be arriving on the Cetani to finalize the details of the treaty we've been working towards for these past few days. Before that happens, however, there will be a formal reception held on the

Cetani, to allow the Alessian colonists the opportunity to get acquainted with people of the other races in the Alliance. I want you and Jev to be there, Kiyel."

It was an order, not a request.

"Yes, mother," Kiyel said dutifully, giving her a slight nod.

"I assume that Doc and Aiden are invited as well, right?" Jev asked.

"Of course they're welcome; they're a part of your family which makes them a part of ours," Lheiza gently assured him.

"What about the other delegates, when do they arrive?" Kiyel asked.

"They already have," Cael said.

"Captain, I forgot to ask, has a place been prepared for the reception?" Lheiza asked.

"Yes, my Lady. We've set up the reception in the Ambassadors Lounge."

"Excellent. Then I guess all that's required is for us to get ready," Lheiza said as she stood up to leave. The others respectfully did the same, including Aiden who had to hop off Jev's lap. "Kiyel, I've brought along some of your formal clothes from home to wear. I'm sure there's something among them that'll fit Jev as well," she added.

"Thanks," Jev acknowledged with a grateful flick of his ears.

"My Lady, I need to have a word with Kiyel and his Enassi for a moment. My first officer will be happy to show you to your quarters where you can prepare for the reception," Cael said.

"Of course, Captain," Lheiza said.

While Lheiza and Diela were escorted out by Riyad,

Captain Cael turned toward Kiyel.

"Riyad informs me that there was something urgent that you needed to discuss with me, my Lord," he said, using Kiyel's formal title.

Only the tiniest flick of his tail gave evidence of Kiyel's dislike of anyone using his title.

"I don't know if you're aware of this, but a short time ago, another mixed-enassi bond has formed between one of our telepaths and an Alessian colonist," he said.

"Yes, I was given a note stating as much, by Elder Veir," Cael said.

"Our concern is with this group that Hraka belongs to."

"I assure you, my Lord, that my security chief is making every possible effort to locate and apprehend them."

"And we do appreciate that. However, until they are in custody, they pose a very real threat. Now that Jev and I have been moved to ambassador quarters, it's unlikely they'll be able to do us any harm. But—"

"But you think they might try to go after this new Enassi pair," Cael finished for him.

"Precisely, sir," Kiyel said.

"What is it that you want me to do?" Cael asked. "Unfortunately, moving them to the ambassadorial level is not an option, not with all the delegates from the Alliance on board."

"We understand that, sir, but perhaps you could assign them a permanent security detail instead," Jev suggested.

"Once back on Caitar the Telepath Guild will make arrangements to ensure their safety," Kiyel added.

Cael slowly nodded his head in thought, the whiskers on his nose twitching slightly.

"It could be done, but I don't imagine they'd be too pleased about it," he said.

"Unless, of course, they weren't made aware of the security team's presence in the first place," Jev pointed out.

"They're telepaths, though. They're bound to sense that they're being watched," Cael said.

"Imas and Eileen are both listed as second grade telepaths. At that level, I'm sure they'd have difficulty distinguishing your security team from the rest of the crew," Kiyel said.

"And if, on the odd chance, they do figure it out, just send them to us, and we'll explain it to them," Jev said.

"It might just work," Cael said, a small grin tugging at the corners of his lips. "I'll leave instructions with Diela. In the meantime, I have to get ready for the reception. I'll see you all there."

Cael bowed respectfully, then turned and followed Riyad, who escorted him out.

A few moments later Riyad returned, carrying a large, bulky case which he set on the floor.

"This little item," he gestured toward the case, with a wry grin, "is from your mother, Kiyel."

"That's little?" Jev asked, staring at the case with disbelief.

"It is for my mother," Kiyel said, a bemused grin stretching across his face.

Through their link, Jev could hear Kiyel's laughter.

When Jev and Kiyel joined the reception a short time later, dressed splendidly in their formal robes, Jev was immediately struck by how large and diverse the crowd was that had gathered in the Ambassadors Lounge. Mingling with the many Caitarans he saw were a few Brekari as well as several humans from the delegation from Alessi. But there were also representatives from a species that he had never seen before. They were a short, insect-like species, which Kiyel told him through their link were known as the Tellari, a species that traveled about in small swarms and whose skills as engineers was unparalleled in the Alliance.

As he continued to scan the room he saw Sam and Aiden, who had arrived before them, sitting at a secluded table in an out of the way corner of the lounge. He waved to them, letting them see that he and Kiyel had arrived, and they waved back, Aiden gleefully so. There was also First Councillor Janette Pelletier, who was deep in conversation with Captain Cael and Ambassador D'lin near one of the lounge's large viewports, along with a telepath serving as their translator—as were the rest of the human delegation, he quickly noted.

One human in particular, though, suddenly captured Jev's attention, causing him to stop with a start. His tail began swaying with happy excitement as their eyes met from across the room. Unbelievably, the human he saw was his brother Mikkel, who started pushing his way through the crowd toward him. With tears of joy filling his eyes, Jev let go of Kiyel's hand, which he had been holding, and happily ran, headlong, into his brother's arms.

"I told you I'd see you again soon," Mikkel said quietly into Jev's ear.

Jev couldn't respond, except to tighten his grip on his brother further.

Reluctantly they separated, Jev looking into his brother's eyes.

"I never expected to see you here," he said.

"Well, when the First Councillor suggested that I come, I couldn't pass up the opportunity," Mikkel answered. "Besides, I heard what happened to you and Kiyel, and I just had to come. I'm glad that you're both all right."

Jev could hear the concern in his brother's voice and see it in his eyes.

"That's thanks to Doc's quick thinking, and Aiden's remarkable healing talent," he grinned.

Mikkel suddenly smiled at him in a mischievous way.

"You do know that you're supposed to duck when someone is shooting at you though, right?" he asked.

Jev's ears fell against his skull, noticeably, in embarrassment.

"It's really good to see you, Mikkel," Kiyel said from behind Jev, deciding to rescue his Enassi from further ribbing from his brother.

"And you as well, Kiyel," Mikkel said, looking up and extending his hand to Kiyel, who shook it warmly. "It seems as though my brother is making a habit of saving your life."

"He did no more for me than I would do for him," Kiyel said, matter of factly, shrugging his shoulders in a very human-like manner.

Jev was about to make a comment when Lheiza suddenly appeared at their side.

"It's nice to see that you're getting on so well with the humans, Kiyel," she said, her tail flicking with amusement.

"Actually, we already knew Mikkel, mother," Kiyel replied.

"He's my brother," Jev added, when he saw her perplexed expression.

It took her a moment, but then a wide tooth-filled grin stretched across her face.

"Yes, I forgot that you had a brother on Alessi. You certainly do have friends in high places, Jev."

This time it was Jev's turn to look perplexed.

"Didn't you know? Mikkel is a member of the Alessi council," she explained.

Jev looked at his brother with astonishment, his ears pricking up noticeably.

"Sorry, I was going to tell you," Mikkel said.

"When?" Jev asked.

"Two days ago. A special election was held. I won dad's old seat."

"I guess congratulations are in order then, Mikkel—or should I say, Councillor," Jev beamed proudly.

"Thanks," Mikkel said, blushing slightly from Jev's praise.

"Councillor, if I may, I'd like to borrow my son and your brother for a moment to introduce them to the other delegates."

"Of course, my Lady," Mikkel said, with a respectful bow. "I'll just go grab something to drink."

Each of the delegates they were introduced to offered Jev and Kiyel their enthusiastic congratulations for helping to make the treaty possible. All this praise was somewhat embarrassing to both. But they endured it diplomatically. As the heir to the Lhevic Pride, Kiyel was certainly used to such gatherings; he'd attended his share in his youth. But for Jev, who, except for a short time on Earth when he was a small child, was not used to large crowds, it was more than a little bit disconcerting. Although he smiled and nodded as required, inwardly he felt overwhelmed. He kept a hold of Kiyel's arm the whole time, glad for Kiyel's strength. Kiyel was not oblivious to his Enassi's uneasiness, and so, strove to reassure him through their link.

Eventually, after having met and engaged all the delegates in some light conversation, they finally were able to excuse themselves and retreat to the secluded table where Aiden and Sam sat, and where they could sit and continue to observe the delegates without being disturbed. No sooner had they sat down, however, when Mikkel, seeking them out, approached their table with several steaming mugs, and a tall glass of nanaya juice for Aiden, in his hands.

"Is that what I think it is?" Jev asked his brother, his nose twitching as he sniffed the air.

"Coffee," Mikkel confirmed, placing a mug down in front of each of them.

Sam stared at his mug for a moment before taking a tentative sip. He then quickly took another, much larger sip as the first washed over his tongue, and for the first time in ages he tasted real coffee.

"Where on Earth did you get coffee, lad?" Sam asked with an appreciative grin.

Jev wanted to laugh, as it almost seemed that Sam was in love with his coffee the way he was handling the mug.

"Not Earth, Alessi," Mikkel corrected. "One of my contacts in the village of Norwood owns a small greenhouse, which she uses to grow coffea plants. For a price, of course, I get enough beans from her to make a pot or two every couple months."

"What price did she ask for the beans?" Jev asked.

"I promised to look out for her son who joined the rebels a couple years back."

He gave Aiden the glass of nanaya juice, replacing the empty one in front of him, which Aiden accepted tentatively. With a little reassurance from Jev, Aiden smiled at Mikkel shyly, and then sent his thanks mentally, which startled Mikkel whose eyes opened wide with surprise.

It surprised Jev also, since Aiden had never sent to anyone except to him before, and even more surprising, since

Mikkel had never shown the slightest hint that he had a talent of any kind. Out of curiosity, Jev tried to slip into his brother's mind without him being aware of it. But, again he was surprised to find he was blocked from doing so, as a barrier suddenly sprang up—a barrier he'd never encountered before—one which pushed him forcefully from his brother's mind, leaving him slightly disoriented. There was no doubt about it now. His brother possessed a talent, but it was such a minor one that it had somehow escaped both his and Kiyel's notice. Somehow, Aiden knew, though, which enabled him to send to Mikkel as he did.

"Are you alright, Jev?" Mikkel asked, looking at his brother with concern.

Jev forced a smile.

"Yes, of course," he replied.

Should we tell him? Jev sent to Kiyel

Kiyel pondered the question for a moment.

No, I don't see the need. It could be that his mind has just become sensitive to the touch of a telepath's.

Kiyel's explanation made some sense to Jev and he allowed the matter to drop. His attention returned to the reception and to Lheiza who had gathered with Captain Cael, Ambassador D'lin and First Councillor Janette, by the bar area. It was clear to him that she was about to say something and he tuned in carefully, his ears and head turned in her direction.

"May I have everyone's attention, please," Lheiza spoke, in a booming voice that carried a note of authority, even above the din in the room.

Conversation quickly ceased as all eyes fell upon the Pride Leader.

"A little more than two months ago, the crew of the scout ship Lekur made contact with the people of the world of Alessi, which our ships now orbit. My son was among that crew.

Because of the combined efforts of him and his Enassi, his crewmates and a small group of freedom fighters from the colony, the alien race that once dominated this world has been defeated."

She paused as a wide grin stretched across her face.

"They've turned tail and are scampering away like skittish yuta."

Laughter rang out through the room, the loudest of which came from the human delegation, even though none of them knew what a yuta was. Jev knew from Kiyel's memories that yuta were a small lizard from Caitar. They were very much like the salamanders on Earth, only slightly larger. They were also the only other species on Caitar to possess a telepathic talent, although it was quite rudimentary and limited them to being able to disguise their appearance from would be predators, or their prey.

The laughter and applause soon died down, and Lheiza continued.

"From the destruction wrought upon this world by the T'kri comes the hope of a new beginning for us all. The treaty we are about to sign today between the people of Alessi and the Alliance is a testament to the desire in all of us to strive for a better future. The past informs our future, shapes it even, but doesn't control it. We do. We who are here today have decided the future that is ahead of us."

Her smile wavered then, and her tone turned somber.

"Our achievements, however, have not come without cost," she continued. "We gather on this day not only to celebrate the beginnings this new future, but also to remember those who lost their lives in the fight to free Alessi from the T'kri. I ask you, friends, to join with me now as we take a moment in silence to honour their sacrifice."

The lounge fell quiet. Everyone in the lounge had their heads bowed as each of them, in their own way, paid tribute to those who lost their lives. So many had died in the struggle to free Alessi, including Jev's father, killed by the T'kri in the fire that also destroyed their home. Tears began rolling down his face, as, for the first time since his father's death, he at last allowed himself to let go of the hold on his emotions he had bottled up inside for so long, and finally properly began to grieve the loss of his father, his quiet sobs breaking the silence in the lounge.

The wave of sadness that overtook Jev was painfully felt by Kiyel, who pulled Jev into a tight embrace, his own tears joining with Jev's. Knowing there was nothing else he could do for his Enassi, he held him close.

Mikkel, his own eyes moist with sadness over the loss of their father, reached over to put a comforting hand on his brother's shoulder. Like Kiyel, he too knew there was not much else he could do but be there for Jev.

Jev's grief did not go unnoticed by Lheiza who, thanks to her son's link with him, couldn't help but feel what Jev was feeling. She let him grieve, patiently waiting until his sobs finally began to lessen and then stop altogether before she continued.

"Thank you," she said, addressing the assembled onlookers, but still looking at Jev. He looked back at her and she offered him a sympathetic smile. She then indicated to Ambassador D'lin that she should take over.

"As there is still a lot that we need to do, I will be brief," D'lin said in her sing-song voice. "Today truly is a momentous occasion. It is a day that has seen the end of T'kri rule over Alessi, and the beginnings of a relationship that we hope will be a long and prosperous one for all our people. But before we proceed to the conference room where we will finalize the treaty, I would like to personally thank Kiyel Lhevic and Jev Bjorn, and the rest of the crew of the Lekur, without whose efforts none of us would be gathered here today. It is to them and their dedication, not to mention their determination, that has brought us to this day."

The room rang out with joyous applause which erupted from the entire assembly, including his brother and Sam who both stood from their chairs and looked down at Jev and Kiyel, smiling proudly. Jev's ears dipped in acute embarrassment as all eyes in the room fell upon them. He didn't feel as though either of them were deserving of such recognition. But, nevertheless, they accepted it in silence, not wishing to make a scene. Right at that moment Jev wanted the reception to be over so they could return to their quarters where, hopefully, they could finally have some time to themselves, and just relax.

The applause finally died down, much to Jev's and Kiyel's mutual relief, at which time Cael announced to the delegates that they should follow him to the conference room where they could begin with their deliberations. As the delegates started filing out of the room, Lheiza approached their table.

"Jev, Mikkel, I just wanted to say to you both how sorry I am for your loss. I cannot imagine how difficult it has been for you to have done all that you did while suffering such a horrible tragedy. Your father must have been a great man, one to be proud of. I just want to you to know that should you ever need me, for anything, you have only to ask. None of us can replace your father, but I hope, at least, that we can help fill that empty place in your hearts," she said to them, speaking slowly in heavily accented English, and surprising Jev and Kiyel both. Neither of them were aware that she had learned to speak in Jev's native tongue till now.

Jev nodded his thanks to her, looking up at her appreciatively.

She smiled at him before nodding to Mikkel

"I'll be waiting for you outside, councillor," she said, and then turned to follow the last of the delegates out of the lounge.

"Well, I guess this is it. After the treaty is signed it's back down to the planet for me," Mikkel said as he stood from his seat.

The rest of them at the table did the same.

"So soon?" Jev asked quietly.

"I'm afraid so," Mikkel nodded. "You take care of yourself, Jev," he said, giving Jev a final hug goodbye.

"You too. Say hello to Janice for me," Jev said. Although he felt sad that they once again had to say goodbye he was smiling with pride for him.

"I'll do that," Mikkel nodded. "And remember, we're still coming to visit you sometime once things settle down here."

Saying goodbye to Kiyel, then Sam and then finally to Aiden, who surprised them all by asking for, and receiving a hug from Mikkel, he turned and walked out of the lounge.

"What do you think, one more drink before we go back to our quarters?" Kiyel suggested.

They nodded their agreement and returned to the bar to order a fresh round of drinks.

With the reception having long since ended, and Lheiza and the other delegates now working diligently to finalize the terms of the treaty, Jev and Kiyel were relaxing alone in their quarters with Sam and Aiden, who, at that moment, was keeping himself entertained by playing with some wooden blocks of varying shapes and sizes, thoughtfully brought to him by Ardem and

Sanaa. The blocks themselves weren't actually toys, though. Instead, they were educational tools used by the Telepath Guild to help young telepaths to focus their talents. But Aiden, being only four years old, was instead using them to construct tall towers. He almost laughed with giddiness every time he placed a block which didn't cause the rest to topple.

Movement out of the corner of his eyes drew Jev's attention away from Aiden to the upper tier where he saw Riyad standing at the railing that separated the lounge from the rest of their quarters. Their eyes met and Riyad quickly made his way down to speak to him.

"What is it, Riyad?" Jev asked, sounding almost irritated at being disturbed.

If Riyad noticed Jev's displeasure, he didn't react to it, remaining as emotionless and professional as ever.

"It's a call for you, Jev, from Tiela," he said.

At that, Riyad had Jev's complete attention, any hint of displeasure quickly gone.

"Did she mention what for?"

"She just said she needed to speak with you," Riyad answered.

"Can you patch it through to our terminal, please, Riyad?" Jev asked, getting up from his seat.

"Right away."

As Riyad left to patch the call through, Jev left the lounge with Kiyel to the communications terminal where Jev sat down and waited for Tiela's call. They didn't have to wait long as the image of Tiela, sitting in her office in the medical bay, replaced the Alliance insignia on the terminal's screen.

"Hello, Tiela, what can I do for you?" Jev asked.

"Actually, I wish to talk to you about what I can do for you," she answered.

"Come again?" Jev asked, confused.

"I just wanted you to know that we're ready to perform your operation, if you still want it."

Jev's tail began to sway back and forth behind him with sudden excitement.

"Yes, I do!" he said, barely able to contain his eagerness. "When?"

"Right now, if you'd like. Physician Baskel, the one I told you about, has agreed to do the operation and can be here whenever you're ready."

Sam, overhearing the conversation, joined them and leaned over Jev, so he could be seen by Tiela.

"I will be joining you as well, Tiela, if that's alright," he said.

Tiela flicked her ears in assent.

"Do you plan to come with Aiden?" she asked Jev. "I know how close the two of you are and he might want to use his talent to help you with your recovery."

Jev thought about it for a moment, his brow furrowing slightly, but then he shook his head.

"No, I don't think so. The last time he healed me, it almost completely drained him of all his strength. I don't think it'd be safe for him to do something like that again, at least not until he's had some training," he said.

He looked at Sam who nodded his agreement.

"I'll have Riyad contact you when we're on our way, Tiela," Kiyel said. "I have to see if Ardem and Sanaa can look after Aiden while we're gone. If not, he'll just have to wait with me outside the surgery."

"I'll wait for his call, then. But in the meantime, I'll contact Physician Baskel and inform him of your decision," Tiela said.

"Thanks, Tiela," Jev said before the connection closed and the Alliance insignia returned to the screen.

He turned in his chair.

"Well, we'd better get ready then."

"Are you absolutely certain you want to do this?" Sam asked him.

Jev nodded and smiled at him.

"If nothing else, it'll stop me from having such painful cramps when my period returns," he said. "Those I won't miss.

Sam laughed.

"No, I guess you won't."

An hour later, Kiyel was sitting outside the Surgery while Jev was inside having the operation that would make it possible for them to one day have children.

After dropping Aiden off at Sanaa and Ardem's quarters, who were both very excited to have a chance to be with him again, Kiyel and Jev walked with Sam as they made their way to the medical bay. Tiela was waiting for them, as was another Caitaran, who was introduced by Tiela as Physician Baskel. By now, Jev, who before was excited about the operation, was a little nervous. He'd never before needed to have any surgery before. In fact, he'd never even been inside of a hospital before, not even for his birth. His mother had chosen a home birth, something that had become very common back on Earth.

Tiela, in her own special way, was able to assure him that he had nothing to be afraid of.

Jev turned to Kiyel, one last time, and rubbed his nose to Kiyel's affectionately.

I love you, he sent through their link. I'll be back soon.

I'll be here, Kiyel promised him.

He lovingly rubbed Jev's cheek with the back of a finger before pulling him in to give him a kiss, which Jev affectionately returned. Then Jev followed Tiela as she, Physician Baskel and Sam led him into the Surgery.

No sooner did Kiyel sit down in a chair across from the Surgery when Lheiza suddenly came running into the medical bay. Kiyel saw her harried state and jumped to his feet.

"What's wrong, Kiyel?" Lheiza asked. "What's happened to Jev?"

Kiyel put his hands on her shoulders to stop her from barging into the surgery, which she was most certainly intent on doing.

"Nothing is wrong, mother," he assured her.

"I received word that you were in the medical bay and that Jev was taken to surgery. I rushed here as soon as I could."

"I'm sorry, mother, we should have told you," Kiyel said, his ears dipping apologetically. "Jev is just having an operation so that it might be possible for us to have children some day." When Lheiza gave him a puzzled look, he elaborated further. "Jev was born without a vaginal opening," he said, letting her go.

A clearly relieved Lheiza sat down in one of the chairs across from the surgery. Kiyel sat down beside her.

"So he's here for some corrective surgery then," she said.

"Yes, when they finish, he will have properly accessible female organs. We asked Tiela before the reception to do the operation," Kiyel nodded. "She contacted us only a hour ago to tell us that they were ready to begin the surgery."

Together they sat and waited in relative silence for what seemed like an eternity. Minutes turned into hours, until, Kiyel, growing more and more restless with every passing moment, finally stood up and began pacing, much to Lheiza's amusement.

"Kiyel, can't you at least try to relax? I'm sure it'll be over soon," Lheiza said.

Kiyel was about to respond to her when the Surgery doors slid open and Sam stepped out. Sam, seeing the expectant looks on Kiyel's and Lheiza's faces, nodded while giving them a reassuring smile.

"The operation went really well," Sam said. "Jev's resting right now and we'll be moving him to recovery soon."

"Can we see him, Doc?" Kiyel asked.

"Soon. He'll be pretty groggy from the anesthetic at first, but that'll pass."

"Thank you, Doc."

"You were in there for some time, Sam. Were there any complications?" Lheiza asked.

"No, not really. It's just that since Jev is only part Caitaran, and not fully human either, his anatomy is slightly different than both our races and we had to proceed a little differently than if he was one or the other," Sam explained.

Just then Tiela and Physician Baskel emerged from the Surgery, pulling the gurney on which Jev lay with an intravenous line connected to his arm. He was still unconscious, though through their link, Kiyel could feel that he was gradually starting to come around.

"You must be Physician Tiela, the one I've heard so much about," Lheiza said with a friendly smile.

"My lady," Tiela said, stopping when she saw Lheiza and instantly recognized the Pride Leader, her ears dipping in respectful acknowledgment.

"Would it be possible to speak with you for a moment later when you are available?"

"Of course. May I ask what about?" Tiela asked, ears pricked forward with intrigue.

Lheiza's expression quickly changed to one of excited desperation.

"I really would like to know how you make such wonderful k'yarri," Lheiza blurted out, almost like an excited school girl.

Kiyel, his ears flicking with embarrassment, rolled his eyes at his mother. She was only this way when she was very excited about something, and more often than not, it was during the most inappropriate moments, like now. Although he did understand why she would be so excited. The cook his mother had hired for them couldn't make a good cup of k'yarri if her life depended on it, even despite his mother's attempts to get her to learn how.

Tiela laughed, relieved that it wasn't anything serious the Pride Leader wanted to talk to her about.

"It would be my pleasure, my Lady," she said.

FIFTEEN

The first few days after Tiela finally released Jev from the medical bay were something of a blur to him. Except for Kiyel's comforting presence, he couldn't remember the day he spent in recovery as the drugs he was on left him barely lucid. But the following day he remembered quite clearly, for it was on that day that the Explorer ship *Cetani* finally broke orbit to start its long journey back to Caitar. He had a spectacular view of the event, which he witnessed with Kiyel, Sam and Aiden from the comfort of their quarters. He remembered feeling, more than hearing, the whine of the engines as the ship left Alessi, its great bow turning away from the planet to head out into deep space. It was an odd sensation for him. For although the vibrations could be felt in the couch he lay on, there was no sensation of movement whatsoever. But the view outside from their viewport was fantastic, and he watched it with great excitement.

The only reason he was lying on the couch instead of sitting on it was because he had been given strict instructions by Tiela to stay off his feet for at least several days, to allow the wound to heal and the sutures to dissolve, and because he was still very tender, despite the anti-inflammatory and pain medications she had prescribed for him. He had absolutely no desire to try and get up and move around, although it was sometimes unavoidable when he had to visit the Personal, and needed Kiyel's, and sometimes Sam's, assistance.

His head rested on Kiyel's lap who was casually running his fingers through the fur on his head. His fur had grown quite a bit these past few weeks and he now sported a thick, prominent mane that fell from the top of his neck to just below his shoulders. At first he thought of having it cut, but Kiyel was so fascinated with it that he decided to keep it, trimming it only slightly so that it was still manageable. He had to admit, Kiyel's fascination with his new mane was somewhat amusing, but he could not ignore the pleasure he experienced when Kiyel's hands brushed through it, causing him to purr loudly. *Another reason to keep his mane,* he thought.

With Kiyel continuing to stroke his fur and also Aiden helping to distract him, mostly with his empathic talent, he was momentarily able to forget about the discomfort and the pain and enjoy the spectacular view outside the ship. The *Cetani* quickly passed the two moons that orbited Alessi, and then another of the planets in the system. The sight of another planet alone was well worth the discomfort he endured.

They were soon leaving the solar system. The sub-light engines that had carried them this far powered down, and the vibrations Jev felt died away. But then there was a new sound, a low hum that echoed throughout the ship, as the ship's FTL drives were engaged and the ship was suddenly propelled into superluminal speeds. The stars outside their viewport, which earlier had been simple pinpoints of light surrounded by the blackness of space, now streaked passed like the light from a thousand moving sparklers. Again there was no sensation of acceleration whatsoever.

A week into their journey, they learned that every one of Hraka's known associates had been located and apprehended, except for one: a flight technician named Tiimo, who was killed while attempting to flee in an escape pod. While neither of them wanted any blood shed because of them, they didn't mourn Tiimo's passing either. After all, it had been his group's intention to see both Jev and Kiyel dead. Despite this good news, however, they opted to stay in their quarters on the Ambassadorial level while the investigation of this group continued, in case there were others involved.

Security arrangements for Imas and Eileen were already in place, and as Kiyel had promised, neither was aware of the security detail's presence.

There was not much for them to do while the *Cetani* was in transit, except wait, which added to Jev's boredom. They were now almost halfway into their journey, and by now, Jev was almost completely recovered from his surgery, though he still felt somewhat stiff.

After a much-anticipated final checkup, Tiela cleared both of them for light duty, much, Jev was sure, to the consternation of Admiral Chuul, who because she was the commanding officer of the *Taigana,* was ordered to remain in orbit around Alessi to provide defense should the T'kri attempt a retaliatory strike, and never did get the opportunity to debrief him and Kiyel as she had wanted to. She was not very pleased, to say the least. Instead it was Captain Cael who debriefed them, and he had infinitely more respect for them than Chuul ever did, so it wasn't nearly as intrusive an ordeal as it had been for the rest of the surviving crew of the *Lekur*.

Their first duty after being cleared by Tiela was to report to Elder Veir's office, where their testing with the Telepath Guild would begin. They were asked to bring Aiden along with them so he could also be tested. This gave Sam the opportunity he needed, without having to worry about Aiden's care, to receive more training from Tiela on Caitaran physiology and in the use of the medical equipment.

On the *Cetani,* the Telepath Guild, which supports the telepaths on board and provided necessary training when needed, operated from a small section of the ship just down the hall from the Medical Bay. It was heavily shielded with psychic dampers for the benefit of passing crewmembers, who otherwise would be affected by the thoughts and emotions of the telepaths within. When Jev and Kiyel arrived as ordered, dressed sharply in their neatly pressed duty uniforms, Jev still limping slightly, they were immediately waved into Elder Veir's office by his aide, who greeted them at the door.

Elder Veir, seated behind his desk, stood from his chair as soon as they entered the room and came around his desk. He placed an open hand on Kiyel's chest, in greeting, then Jev's, and even did the same with Aiden, who giggled from the Elder's touch.

With the greetings taken care of, they were invited to take seats in the proffered chairs opposite the Elder's desk.

"Jev, it is good to see your recovery is progressing well," Veir said.

"Thanks, Elder," Jev replied. "Just a little stiffness, which Tiela assures me should go away soon."

Veir glanced briefly at the monitor on his desk.

"Since I see that Physician Tiela has only cleared you for light duty, we're not going to do much with you today. Instead, if you're agreeable, we'll concentrate on having Aiden tested, to see if we can find out what the limits of his talent are."

"Perhaps it would be helpful, Elder, if he begins learning to control his talent as well, so that we, and any other telepaths that might be charged with his care, will no longer have to block his talent," Kiyel suggested.

Veir nodded his agreement, his gaze turning on Aiden.

Aiden, for his part, stared back at Veir, watching him with curiosity. Jev could feel that he was a little nervous, but at the moment his curiosity overrode his nervousness. He did relax a little when Veir offered him a disarming grin.

"Are you ready to learn what you can do, little one?" Veir asked.

Aiden nodded, a grin forming on his cherubic face. He had grown quite a bit since that day when Jev and Kiyel found him being raped by his so-called father, and he'd put on quite a bit of weight, now looking very much like a normal, active four year old child.

Over the next couple of hours, Veir went through a series of standard evaluations that every new telepath was required to take, upon enrolling with the Telepath Guild. At all times, Veir was patient and friendly with Aiden, two things that made the youngster's evaluation go very smoothly, if somewhat longer than an evaluation of this sort would normally take. When Veir was at last finished, he made a few notes in his terminal before returning his attention to Jev and Kiyel.

"Well, Aiden is an interesting case, for certain," Veir began.

"What did you discover, Elder?" Jev asked, his ears pricked forward with anticipation.

"First off, we've never encountered an individual quite like Aiden, before. But then, we'd never encountered a species like his before, either," Veir said.

He paused, and glanced briefly at the terminal.

"His telepathic talent rates as a fairly minor one, not even a fifth grade. I strongly suspect he would only be able to establish a connection with people close to him, and even then they would have be at least partially telepathic themselves in order to receive his attempts to send to them. On the other hand, he scores extremely high as an empath, something we've never tested for before. Based on the results here, it seems that he's not only able to sense the moods of others, but he can affect them as well, both consciously and subconsciously. Like Caitaran telepaths, he is very sensitive to the pain of others, but unlike us, he's not repulsed by it."

He paused and looked at them in turn.

"That's a trait I understand the two of you share, also."

Kiyel nodded.

"We're both capable of fighting, if need be," he said.

"Then there is his healing factor," Veir continued, "which I believe is strongly tied to his Empathic talent. The need he exhibits, to alleviate pain and suffering that he can sense, clearly extends to physical pain as well as emotional pain."

"We pretty much knew all of this from our own observations," Jev said quietly, with an impatient flick of his ears.

"No doubt, But it's necessary to have the actual test results in his file for future reference," Veir pointed out to him.

Veir then grinned at Aiden.

"You're quite the remarkable young male, it seem, Aiden."

Aiden beamed proudly at the compliment, his skin flushing a little.

"Thanks," he squeaked shyly.

"Now, as for his training, if you'd like, we can begin that today right here. I would suggest that you both be present initially to allow him to familiarize himself with his tutor."

When Jev and Kiyel both nodded their agreement, Veir activated the intercom on his terminal.

"Uskin, will you please ask Tutor Emiri to come to my office."

"Right away, Elder," came his aide's voice over the intercom.

They sat quietly and waited when, within minutes, the door slid open. Jev turned in his seat and was greeted by the sight of a young, tan and white-pelted female entering the office. She was fairly tall, much taller than most of the Caitaran females he'd met, and wore robes similar to the Elder's, just not as magnificent. Her mind was open and friendly, which Jev was glad for. He and Kiyel rose from their seats, prompting Aiden to do the same, as the door closed behind her.

"You asked to see me, Elder?" Emiri said.

"Yes, Emiri, I'd like you to meet Kiyel and his Enassi, Jev."

"The new Enassi pair," she nodded with an almost imperceptible movement of her ears in recognition. She greeted them both in the customary manner for telepaths.

"The child standing between them is a terran empath named Aiden. He's the reason I asked you here," Veir continued.

Emiri looked down at Aiden with a friendly grin. She could feel the child's mind reaching out to her—an undisciplined mind, but a kindred one nonetheless.

"You wish me to train the child?" she asked, ears pricking with interest. Never before had she been asked to work with a telepath so young, and certainly not a telepath who was not even Caitaran.

"His talent was woken prematurely. He needs to learn to use it," Kiyel said.

Emiri nodded slowly, her nose wrinkling in thought.

"I take it he's been broadcasting then."

"We've been trying to block his talent, but we haven't been entirely successful," Jev explained.

"Our tests show he doesn't even rate as a fifth grade telepath, Emiri," Veir interjected, "but his empathic abilities are very strong. He's already become quite adept at recognizing and manipulating the emotions of others. He has also demonstrated an ability to heal physical wounds."

Emiri's eyes widened with surprise as she once again regarded Aiden. Aiden, meanwhile, continued to stare back at her with a curious fascination.

"Do you think you'll be able to work with him, Tutor?" Kiyel asked.

"If he is receptive to my teaching I don't see that there should be a problem, my Lord," Emiri replied respectfully.

Such was his concern for Aiden that Kiyel intentionally ignored her use of his title, though he couldn't stop the involuntary twitch of his tail.

"Then let's begin, shall we?" Veir suggested.

At first, Emiri had Aiden perform a series of mental exercises, to gauge for herself his level of control. Afterwards, she began working with him to develop a simple barrier that would enable him to keep his thoughts and feelings from interfering with others. It didn't take long before Jev realized their initial fear that Aiden would be reluctant to be with a stranger was completely unfounded. She was both patient and understanding with him, which he was immensely grateful for.

Aiden listened intently to the instructions given to him by Emiri. Although at times he became frustrated when he didn't get something right and they had to take a break, when he was finally successful he laughed with pride and more than just a little giddyness. He proved to be a quick learner, and Jev was already began noticing a difference as Aiden gradually began learning to put up mental barriers in his mind to prevent him from unintentionally affecting others.

When Aiden had finally gotten the hang of keeping his barriers in place, Emiri decided that he had learned enough for the day. He'd already made great progress, which surprised her and impressed the Elder. As for Jev and Kiyel, they couldn't have been more proud of Aiden, and they told him so, causing him to beam again with pride.

Before they left the Elder's office, Emiri suggested that Aiden return once every other day for a couple hours of training. Veir also suggested that if Jev was up to it, they could begin their testing and training as well, at the same time, both which Jev and Kiyel readily agreed. Before leaving they thanked the Elder and the Tutor for their help and headed back to their quarters.

Standing outside their quarters, waiting for them, were Sanaa and Ardem, who turned as soon as they saw them.

"Sanaa, Ardem, this is a surprise. What brings you here?" Sam asked.

"We came to ask if you and Aiden would be interested in a tour of the ship. We just now suddenly realized that you've been on board for two weeks and no one has offered to show you around," Sanaa said.

"Well, that's mighty generous of you," Sam said appreciatively.

He looked down at Aiden.

"What do you think, sport, want to take a look at the ship?"

The look on Aiden's suddenly excited face said it all. He looked up at Sam and nodded enthusiastically.

"Kiyel, you and Jev are welcome to join us as well if you'd like," Ardem said.

Jev shook his head though, as he was beginning to feel a little sore.

"Thanks, but I think I want to rest for a bit. I've done enough walking for the day."

"Of course, we understand," Sanaa said.

Jev watched as Sam and Aiden were led away by the two telepaths, grinning as he saw Aiden, in his excitement, practically pulling on Sam's arm to try and get him to walk faster. As soon as they disappeared down the corridor and into a lift, he pressed his hand to the panel beside the door, which then slid open for them.

They walked in to find their quarters dark and no one inside, which explained why Sanaa and Ardem had been standing outside their quarters rather than waiting for them inside. When the computer, detecting their presence, activated the lights, Kiyel noticed a note on Riyad's desk and picked it up.

"Looks like Riyad was called away by Captain Cael," Kiyel said, tossing the note in the disposal chute on the wall next to the desk.

"He didn't mention what for?"

"No, just that he would be busy for the next several hours."

Of course, Jev immediately realized what that meant. With Sam and Aiden touring the ship and Riyad off somewhere with Cael, after waiting for so long to finally be alone together, they finally had that chance. Wearing a suggestive grin he grabbed hold of Kiyel's hand and led him to the lounge where he playfully pushed Kiyel onto the long, thickly-padded couch.

Kiyel, bemused by Jev's unexpected, but not unwelcome, playfulness, pulled Jev down with him until he was lying down on his side and resting his head on Kiyel's lap. He didn't need to read Jev's mind to know what he wanted, and right away began running his fingers sensually through Jev's fur, causing Jev to begin purring with so much pleasure that his whole body vibrated. His pleasure was so intense that he couldn't move, even if he had wanted to, which, of course, he didn't.

While Kiyel continued gently stroking his fur, Jev, through the haze of pleasure, was peripherally aware that Kiyel's fingers were increasingly moving down his body; first caressing his arms, then his back, until finally, Kiyel's fingers reached the base of his spine which caused Jev's tail to jerk suddenly. A low moan of pleasure escaped Jev's lips, his body moving of its own accord to give Kiyel better access to that sensitive spot, and with a shudder, he came to the sudden realization that he was responding to Kiyel's touch. All at once he was both nervous and excited at the same time... mostly excited, though.

Kiyel felt Jev's reaction and abruptly stopped.

I'm sorry, Kiyel sent.

Glancing up at him, Jev shot him a desperate look.

What for? It feels absolutely wonderful, Jev replied. Grabbing hold of Kiyel's hand, he encouraged him to continue.

Tiela warned us that we had to be careful. You're not fully recovered yet.

I know, but it doesn't mean we can't enjoy each other's company. I know you've wanted this as much as I have.

Kiyel grinned at him.

Believe me, it's all I could do to restrain myself.

Then don't, Jev replied, as he wrapped kiyel's arm across his chest and held it tightly. *It's the first moment we've had to be alone together like this. Yes, we'll need to be careful, but this moment belongs to us, so let's enjoy it while we can.*

Kiyel, coming to a decision, disentangled himself from Jev's embrace, leaving Jev slightly confused by Kiyel's sudden movement, but then a smile stretched across his face when Kiyel bent down to carefully pick him up into his arms.

Then let's continue this in our room, Enassi, he sent as he carried Jev to their bedroom door.

A tiny knock on the door roused Kiyel from a deep slumber. Behind him, snoring softly and curled up against him with an arm draped over his chest, Jev continued to sleep soundly, oblivious to the knock Kiyel had just heard. The knock came again, somewhat more insistently this time, and Kiyel, looking over at the holographic chronometer displayed above the bedside table, saw that it was still night, ship's time. He reluctantly extricated himself from Jev's side, swinging his legs over the side of the bed, and went to open the door.

There, outside their room, dressed in his pajamas, stood Aiden, tightly clutching to his chest a plush yuta, given to him by Sanaa. The stuffed animal was almost half as big as Aiden was.

"I had a bad dream, can I sleep with you?" Aiden asked hopefully, his voice shaky.

It was then Kiyel saw that Aiden was trembling ever so slightly, his face was flushed and moist with sweat. Kiyel was alert enough now that he could easily feel the fear that caused Aiden to wake.

"Of course, little one," Kiyel said in a soft voice, as he led Aiden into the room, the door closing automatically behind them.

"Who was it, Kiyel?" Jev asked groggily from the bed, his eyes still closed.

"It was Aiden; he had a bad dream."

Jev opened his eyes and saw Aiden standing next to Kiyel at the bedside. He, too, could feel Aiden's fear, and thought, for just a moment, he managed to catch a brief glimpse of the dream that had disturbed him as well. Pushing it aside, he smiled at Aiden reassuringly as he gently patted the bed beside him, inviting Aiden to join him.

Aiden wasted no time as he scrambled up into the bed, while still holding onto the yuta, then snuggled into Jev, who quickly pulled the blankets up over him. Aiden's little body still trembled, so Jev held him close, giving him as much comfort as he could while Kiyel casually slipped back into bed, and joined them under the covers.

Soon after they were all settled, Aiden was once again fast asleep. However, neither Jev nor Kiyel went back to sleep. Instead, they lay there watching Aiden sleep, until, before they knew it, several hours had passed and night turned into day. Their room was still relatively dark, though, as the only light in the room came from the stars that zipped passed the viewport above their bed.

There was another knock on the door, startling them. Thankfully, it didn't wake Aiden, who only shifted slightly in his sleep. This time it was Jev's turn to answer the door and he found a concerned looking Sam standing outside their room, dressed in his pajamas, and with his greying hair a disheveled mess. Sam's appearance would have been amusing to Jev, had it not been for the serious expression on his face.

"Jev, I went in to check on Aiden, but he's not in his bed. Is he with the two of you?"

Jev nodded in the affirmative, which relieved Sam, who visibly relaxed.

"He had a nightmare last night and came to our room, wanting to sleep with us. He's still sleeping," Jev said quietly. "Did you want me to wake him?"

"No, let him sleep," Sam said with a shake of his head. "Since you're both up, though, I'll just go make some k'yarri if you're interested."

Jev's ears immediately perked up at the mention of k'yarri, his tail beginning to flick eagerly behind him.

"I'll take that as a yes," Sam laughed. He then shot Jev a questioning glance. "By the way, do you normally answer the door like that?" he asked.

Jev looked down at himself and suddenly remembered that he was without a stitch of clothing on. Very quickly his ears folded back against his skull in embarrassment, though he made no attempt to hide his nudity as that would have been pointless.

"Sorry, Doc, I forgot," he said softly.

Sam shook his head, a thin grin pulling back the corners of his mouth.

"Go put something on and wake Kiyel. I'll go get the k'yarri started."

"Thanks, Doc," Jev said, relieved, and closed the door. He walked over to the bed and gently shook Kiyel's shoulder.

Enassi, get up. Doc's making k'yarri, Jev sent.

Kiyel's eyes flew open and he looked up at Jev hovering over him.

K'yarri?

With a flourish, Kiyel threw off the blankets and got out of bed, but then remembered Aiden sleeping beside them, and gently replaced the blankets.

Doc suggested we get dressed before joining him, Jev sent, still a little embarrassed that he answered the door while naked.

You're starting to pick up some Caitaran habits, Kiyel replied with a wide grin, as he glanced at Jev appraisingly, his eyes seemingly taking in his entire figure. *Not that I'm complaining, mind you.*

You're incorrigible, Jev sent as he started getting dressed, eliciting a low chuckle from Kiyel.

Guilty as charged.

When they had finished dressing, they left their room quietly so as to not disturb Aiden's sleep, the door closing behind them with a soft hiss. Sam heard them leave their room, smiling as they came down to join him. He had had already set out three cups and a large pot of what smelled like some of the best k'yarri either of them could remember on the short table in the center of the lounge.

They had already finished their first cup of k'yarri, and were well into their second, when they heard and saw a very sleepy-looking Aiden wander out of the bedroom, rubbing the last remnants of sleep from his eyes. Carried tightly in his right hand was the yuta he'd been given, which dragged along the floor as he walked. After his eyes had become accustomed to the dimly lit room, Aiden saw Jev, Kiyel and Sam sitting in the lounge, and he smiled as he ran down to them, climbing up onto Sam's lap.

Jev chuckled lightly, watching Aiden trying to get comfortable while also clutching the yuta in his little hand.

"He's really grown attached to that yuta, hasn't he?"

Kiyel nodded his agreement, also smiling as Aiden snuggled up into Sam's chest. Sam put his arm around Aiden to give him a hug.

"Did you have a bad dream last night?" Sam asked softly.

Aiden nodded against Sam's chest.

"Can you tell us what it was about?"

"My daddy," Aiden answered quietly with an unsettled shiver.

"It's all right, now, though, buddy. He can't hurt you any more," Jev assured him.

A little smile appeared on Aiden's face as he turned his face to look at Jev.

"You and Kiyel saved me."

"That's right, we did. And if we can help it, no one will get a chance to hurt you ever again."

Aiden's smile grew, though Jev could tell his dream was still bothering him.

We should probably discuss with Tiela getting Aiden some counselling to help him deal with what happened, Jev suggested.

Kiyel's ears gave a flick of agreement.

I'm just surprised he hasn't had nightmares about what his father did to him, sooner.

"So what are your plans for the day?" Sam asked them, oblivious to their private conversation.

"Nothing really, except to get some breakfast into our stomachs," Jev said.

Sam chuckled knowingly.

"I should have guessed food would be the first thing on your mind," he said.

The mentioning of food appeared to get Aiden's attention as well, who looked at them with eager eyes and a suddenly vocal stomach.

"Looks like Jev isn't the only one hungry this morning," Kiyel said with a grin.

Just then the door sounded unexpectedly. Jev turned his gaze to the door, focussing his mind on it and quickly sensing the familiar presence of their adjutant out in the corridor.

"It's Riyad," Jev announced, getting up to answer the door. He returned moments later with Riyad.

"You're here early, Riyad," Kiyel observed.

"My apologies, Kiyel. I received a message this morning from Captain Kel. He asks if you, Jev, Physician Sam and Aiden would like to join him and Physician Tiela in the crew lounge on deck C for first meal."

"Why didn't he contact us directly?" Kiyel asked.

"If he went through Riyad, I'm sure he's asking us to come for something more than just breakfast," Jev said, wrinkling his nose in thought.

"Should I let him know you'll accept the invitation?" Riyad asked.

Kiyel looked at Sam quizzically.

"Sure, why not," Sam said with a shrug of his shoulders, also intrigued by the invitation.

"Go ahead, Riyad, but let him know you'll be joining us as well if that's all right with him," Jev said. "No sense in us enjoying a good meal while you're stuck here alone."

With an appreciative flick of his ears and a smile, Riyad bowed slightly, then left to contact Kel.

"Well, if we're going, we need to get this little one freshened up a bit and dressed," Sam said. He carefully stood up, still holding onto Aiden, and then set him back down. "The yuta will have to stay here though."

Aiden looked up at Sam with a frown on his face as he gripped the toy tightly to his chest, as though afraid if he let it go he'd never see it again.

"When we get back you can hold onto it for as long as you want," Sam assured him with a gentle smile.

Aiden smiled back and nodded his head, putting the yuta carefully down on the couch before he and Sam then left for his room. The way he handled the yuta made Jev smile, as he was treating the stuffed animal like a pet. Jev didn't know if Caitarans kept real yutas as pets and made a point of it to ask Kiyel about it later.

While Sam and Aiden were in their rooms getting changed, Jev and Kiyel took the opportunity to do the same, having a quick shower together before getting changed into something more appropriate. Even though they were technically still off duty for the day, they both decided they needed to put on their uniforms, since they both felt the captain had something official to discuss with them.

Sam and Aiden were already waiting for them when they left their room, but Jev was surprised to see that Aiden still had on his pajamas and was carrying a bundle of clothes. He looked quizzically at Sam who could only offer him a sad expression. Jev knew right away then what the problem was. Because of Aiden's nightmare, he was now reluctant to have Sam help him get dressed.

Nodding in understanding, Jev led Aiden into his and Kiyel's room, where he helped Aiden get his face and hands washed in their private Personal, and then helped him into his clothes. His previous injuries, Jev noted, had healed quite remarkably. He was relieved that there were no lasting scars to be found on his skin, which would have only served as a painful reminder to Aiden of what he'd been through. Moments later they re-emerged from the bedroom, a now clean and splendidly dressed Aiden beaming at them proudly in his best Alessian attire.

With all of them now ready, including Riyad who was waiting for them at the door to their quarters, they left for the lounge. Jev still, for the life of him, could not figure out what Kel had to say to them that was so important that he had to use official channels. His curiosity peaked, just like Kiyel's, he was anxious to find out and quickened his pace.

Getting to the lounge was as simple as taking the lift to Deck C, and then following the long corridor to the end where a number of Caitarans were seen entering and leaving the lounge. Once inside, they quickly saw Kel and Tiela both sitting at a large table in the center of the lounge. They were not alone, however. With them, sitting at the same table were the rest of the crew from the *Lekur:* Taaj, Jaffay and Izha. All of them stood when they saw them enter the lounge.

With confused looks on both of their faces, Jev and Kiyel made their way to the table, Sam, Aiden and Riyad following behind, also looking more than just a little curious.

"Captain, what's going on?" Kiyel asked, tail flicking nervously when they reached the table.

Kel moved from around the table until he stood before Kiyel, and smartly came to attention. Automatically, Jev and Kiyel did the same.

"Crewman Kiyel, Crewman Jev, we asked you here today because a great disservice has been done to you both that demands correcting."

From his left pants pocket he withdrew a small, black, leather bound box. Kiyel instantly recognized it for what it was and he looked at Kel in shock.

"It has come to our attention that on numerous occasions while we were stranded on the planet Alessi, you both performed tasks well above and beyond the call of duty expected of telepaths," Kel continued. "You risked your lives fighting the T'kri alongside us, and were largely responsible for making it possible for this crew to make it back home alive. Therefore, as per orders, on this date, by Caitaran High Command, as signed by Vice-Admiral Vashek, I have the distinct privilege, and honor, of promoting you both to the rank of Lieutenant, with all the rights and privileges therein."

Jev stood awestruck as Kel then placed the new rank insignia next to Kiyel's Enassi badge on his uniform shoulder, then did the same with his. With the new rank insignias added to their uniforms, Kel took two steps back, and then sharply saluted them both, which they promptly returned.

"Congratulations, you two," Kel said with a respectful bow.

Tiela and the others then stood as one and broke out into loud applause, which was joined by other crew members in the lounge who witnessed their unexpected promotions. Jev glanced down at his shoulder, thumbing his new rank insignia admiringly. A smile formed on both his and Kiyel's faces as they looked at each other and then at their former crew.

They were then invited to the table where more chairs were brought for all of them to sit down. A round of k'yarri and a tall glass of nanaya juice for Aiden was ordered by Kel, on his tab.

"There is one other thing we'd like to discuss with you two," Tiela said, looking at them. "A couple of weeks ago you made me an offer and I told you that I needed to think on it." Jev and Kiyel both nodded, knowing that she was referring to their offer to her to be their personal physician when they reached Caitar. "After much thought and consideration, and after discussing it with Kel, I've decided to accept your offer."

Jev abruptly stood up and walked over to her, bending down to give her a grateful hug.

"Thank you, Tiela, you've made the both of us so happy," he said. "Though we would have understood had you decided not to," he quickly added.

"Are you kidding? Me miss the opportunity of a lifetime? Not on your life," Tiela said, with a grin, causing the whole group to laugh.

"Since you discussed this with the captain, can we assume then—"

"That he and I are officially a couple?" Tiela interrupted. "The answer, Jev, is yes," she said, and she turned her head and rubbed her nose to Kel's, affectionately.

Jev could see the love they felt for each other in each of their eyes, and he smiled at them proudly.

"Kel has asked to be reassigned to Caitar where he plans to be a part of the team that is investigating this Chemian movement back home," Tiela said.

Kiyel's ears flicked in understanding.

"After all this time in space, and almost being stranded on another planet, I decided it's time I returned home," Kel said.

"Well, here's to the two of you, then," Sam said, raising his cup to them. "May your lives together be filled with love and joy for many years to come."

Cups of k'yarri were raised as the rest of the group around the table stood and joined in Sam's toast, all of them, that is, except Tiela and Kel, who held hands and stared lovingly into each other's eyes.

SIXTEEN

When the Explorer ship *Cetani* dropped to sub-light speed upon entering Caitaran space, it maneuvered into a synchronous orbit above the planet Caitar with a gracefulness that belied it's size. After many long months in deep space, it and its crew were finally home.

Caitar was a large world, and like Alessi, was covered mostly in oceans which separated the continents. Even from space the large, sprawling cities on the surface below could be seen clearly through the openings in the clouds. But they were small compared to the vast areas of lush forests, rolling landscapes, and mountainous terrains that covered the surface.

From their quarters, Jev and Kiyel watched as the planet loomed large in their viewport. Kiyel's arms draped across Jev's shoulders as Jev looked at the breathtaking sight with a near reverent awe. They were joined by Sam and Aiden, the latter held aloft in Sam's arms and wearing a typical child's look of curiosity and excitement.

"Welcome to Caitar, Jev," Kiyel said.

"It's beautiful, Kiyel, just like I thought it would be."

"But haven't you seen Caitar before, Jev, I mean from Kiyel's memories?" Sam asked.

Jev's head and ears swiveled to look at him.

"It's not the same, Doc," he said. "Seeing Caitar in person like this makes it feel so much more real. It's like the difference between seeing a photograph of a place and then later visiting the place where the picture was taken."

"I never thought of it like that," Sam admitted.

Just then, footsteps could be heard coming from behind them. They turned to see Riyad stepping down to join them by the viewport.

"It's time to go. The shuttle is ready for us," Riyad informed them.

"And my mother?" Kiyel asked.

"She left a message stating that she would meet us in the hangar bay."

Kiyel nodded,

As they left their quarters, they were once again joined by a security detail who escorted them through the corridors of the ship to the hangar bay. Instead of the standard class C uniforms normally worn by the ship's crew, however, the security team was dressed splendidly in their class A dress uniforms, worn only while providing security for visiting dignitaries or while attending diplomatic events. Their security detail, Jev noticed, had also doubled in size. It was plainly obvious that the captain of the *Cetani* wanted to make a statement about their importance to the rest of the crew while also ensuring there were no further problems aboard his ship because of them. Jev found it quite disconcerting and he would be glad to be rid of them once they had left the ship.

Just as Riyad had promised, Kiyel's mother was indeed waiting for them in the hangar bay when they arrived. She was standing next to a shuttle with Kel and Tiela, both of whom were dressed in civilian clothing. He could see also that the shuttle's engines were already engaged and in standby mode, the pilot obviously ready to get underway.

While Riyad stowed away their luggage, Lheiza led the group up the ramp into the shuttle where they buckled themselves into their seats. Jev sat with Kiyel opposite Sam and Aiden, while Kel and Tiela opted to sit with Lheiza across from them. Moments later, Riyad entered the shuttle and took a seat next to Lheiza.

The shuttle's engines roared to life, the ramp shut and with a slight lurch they lifted off from the deck. The pilot swung the nose of the shuttle around to the hangar bay doors and throttled up the engines. The shuttle shot out of the massive ship that Jev had called home these past few days, and headed out into open space.

"All hands, brace for re-entry," the pilot's voice announced over the intercom, just seconds before powering down the engines, which was standard procedure during atmospheric re-entry.

Because Jev didn't know what to expect, he was wholly unprepared for the violent turbulence that suddenly shook the shuttle as it began its descent into the planet's atmosphere. He gritted his teeth and held tightly on to Kiyel's hand. It felt as though the whole shuttle would shake itself apart. He dared to look outside his viewport and saw a white hot glow surrounding the shuttle. The sky was still black and he could still see the rim of the planet below. He knew the glow was caused by the heat generated from the friction of the shuttle's re-entry. But knowing this did little to settle his nerves. He averted his gaze and shut his eyes tight as the shuttle continued its descent.

Finally, after a couple of minutes, the violent shaking stopped. Jev opened his eyes and saw that they were now rapidly approaching a sparse layer of clouds. The sky was now a blue-purple-black and he could hardly see any stars as the glow of the atmosphere blotted them out. They were hurtling across the sky at incredible speeds, but they now appeared to be gliding as there was now a thin atmosphere outside. Within seconds, the shuttle entered, and then broke through, the cloud cover. The pilot angled the nose down sharply causing the shuttle to plummet quickly, pushing Jev back in his seat. He was at once glad that they had strapped themselves down in their seats.

Just as suddenly, the shuttle soon began levelling off. The engines were re-engaged, and now Jev saw the shuttle was skimming the surface of the ocean. Through his viewport, Jev could already make out the city of Ethinias, situated magnificently against the steep, heavily forested, north shore mountains, and brightly lit in the afternoon sun which shown down on it from the partially clouded sky. Just beyond the city was the beautiful, deep blue ocean. It was just how Jev remembered it, or rather, how Kiyel remembered it. But it was a comforting sight to see, nonetheless. Although he'd never before stepped foot on Caitar, he knew with certainty that he finally was truly where he belonged.

As they hurtled toward the city Jev could now make out the shuttle port, a large, metallic domed structure tucked away in a small cove to the left of the city's harbour, where watercraft of all sorts and sizes were docked. He could even make out several small craft outside the harbour below them.

Jev could feel the shuttle gradually reducing speed, the pilot throttling down the engines as they neared the cove. By the time they entered the cove, the shuttle's speed had been reduced to almost a crawl and appeared to be hovering above the water only a few hundred meters or so from the entrance to the port. Jev quickly discovered why, when a shuttle suddenly launched from within the port, flying past his viewport before angling upwards toward the sky. As soon as the other shuttle was gone, they lurched forward once again as the pilot brought their shuttle slowly into the shuttle port and over one of the landing pads within the structure. They hovered there for a moment before the pilot finally set it down, a slight bump indicating that they were once again on solid ground.

As a group, they disembarked from the shuttle, Jev and Kiyel leading the way down the ramp. They were hand in hand, and Kiyel had to hold back a chuckle as Jev was looking all around them with the fascination of a child.

It's quite the sight, isn't it? Kiyel asked through their link.

It's amazing!

Looking behind them, Kiyel saw that Sam and Aiden both wore similar expressions of awe. Like them, Sam also held onto Aiden's hand, but that was to make sure the child didn't run off to explore the many new things he was seeing. Behind Sam and Aiden walked his mother, who, as Kiyel expected, was watching them with great amusement. Tiela and Kel brought up the rear, but they were oblivious to most everything else except each other.

They all made their way to a gated area, where lines of Caitarans were forming, all of them arriving by shuttle from one ship or another.

"We have to pass through Customs up ahead, first, before proceeding into the city," Kiyel announced, looking back at Sam to make sure he heard.

Sam nodded in understanding, in response.

Passing through Customs was a fairly straightforward process. Their identities were confirmed and a security check was performed to be certain no weapons or contraband were being brought into the city. They were only slightly held up when the customs officer, a severe, imposing Caitaran male, turned his attention on Sam and Aiden. It was understandable, as no one on Caitar had ever seen a human before. But after a brief conversation with Lheiza, they were permitted to go on through.

Once past Customs, they exited into a large lobby which was crowded with travellers—both coming and going—and their friends and family. The lobby itself was quite impressive for a simple shuttle port. The walls were made of a light-coloured marble-like stone, with dark, wood pillars, which were spaced about twenty feet apart and spanned the entire length of the lobby. On each of the pillars near the top were carved amazingly life-like depictions of some of Caitar's more notable figures. Between each of the pillars, from floor to ceiling, were huge arched windows that provided a spectacular view of the city outside.

As they crossed the lobby, Jev looked back where he saw two long counters in front of which travellers were lining up, and behind the counters, ticket agents were processing travellers' tickets and securing their luggage. *It was just like the old train stations back on Earth,* he thought to himself.

They were almost to the doors leading outside, when suddenly an angry female's voice yelled out from across the lobby.

"Kiyel!"

They turned as one, and saw a young Caitaran female, roughly about Kiyel's age, with an almost pure white pelt except for a patch of grey on the left side of her face, coming towards them.

Kiyel's ears dropped noticeably, his tail swaying, as he immediately recognized her.

"What do you want, Miru?" he growled.

"What is this you wanting to break off our betrothal?" she asked, bristling with anger. "How dare you choose this alien over me!" she said, pointedly looking at Jev with undisguised loathing.

Jev stood there in shock. Not only could he feel her anger, but he realized that she was consciously projecting her anger. It was a purposeful attack on his mind.

"Miru, I told you the last time we met that I would not accept the betrothal, no matter what agreement your father and mine hatched between them," Kiyel reminded her. He was trying to keep his voice low and even so as not to create a scene. Unfortunately for them, she was doing a good enough job of that on her own, as a group began gathering around them, watching the drama unfold.

"Miru, this is neither the place or the time for this," Lheiza interjected as she stepped forward to stand with Kiyel, the set of her ears showing her displeasure.

"With all due respect, Pride Leader, this does not concern you. This is between me and Kiyel," Miru said sharply.

It was clear that Lheiza did not take kindly to being addressed in such a disrespectful manner.

"Anything that involves my son is my concern, and you would be wise to remember that," she said coldly, her tail lashing from side to side in anger, teeth bared. "Now drop this, before you disgrace yourself further."

"It is your son who has disgraced me by cavorting about with that alien whore!" Muri said with so much venom in her voice that it caused Jev to flinch. "I demand restitution for the public humiliation I have suffered."

"And just what do you mean by that?" Kiyel asked. He had always known that Miru was an ambitious female, and that she used her betrothal to him to better her status within Caitaran society, but she had never before demonstrated the level of vindictiveness that she was exhibiting now.

"If your alien whore wishes to be your lifemate, then as your betrothed, I demand the right to challenge him for that privilege."

As the confrontation with Miru was unfolding, Jev was filled with a sudden sense of dread. The whole situation was escalating fast, and quickly getting out of control. He looked at Kiyel and saw in his eyes the same fear that gripped him. He knew right then what needed to be done.

"You can't challenge a telepath, it isn't allowed!" Tiela said, alarmed.

"The laws be damned," Miru spat derisively.

"Miru, be reasonable," Lheiza tried softly in an attempt to calm the situation. "Our laws prohibit telepaths from being challenged for a good reason. We're incapable of fighting."

"I'll do it," Jev announced suddenly, interjecting himself into the conversation and causing all eyes to turn on him. "I will accept your challenge."

Kiyel whirled on him with an expression of shocked disbelief on his face.

"Jev, no, you can't!" he said, his tone desperate.

"This is the only way to ensure that we can be together," Jev said quietly.

"Jev, do you understand what this means? A challenge isn't a simple contest. It's a fight to the death," Kel told him.

Jev, shocked, became wide-eyed as soon as he realized what the consequences could be by accepting Miru's challenge.

"It's too late, the challenge has been made and accepted, and witnessed as required. As challenger I name Valael Estate as the place where the challenge will be fought, one week from today at midday," Miru announced triumphantly, her lips curling back in a wicked grin that wasn't at all friendly.

She turned and left, leaving the stunned group staring after her, but then stopped suddenly and turned her head to look back at Kiyel.

"I hope you will be ready for our ceremony once I have won," she said.

Kiyel growled at her in response, his tail twitching violently from side to side

The silence within the group as they watched Miru leave was broken by Sam suddenly whistling, almost admiringly.

"Now there's a lass who's out to cause some trouble."

Several sets of ears flicked in agreement.

"No, I don't think that's it," Jev said, his nose wrinkling in thought.

"How could you think that, Jev? You saw how she was," Tiela said.

"I know, but I don't believe she's given us the real reason for challenging me."

"Then why do you think she did it?" Sam asked.

"She's afraid."

Kiyel nodded in agreement.

"That's the sense I picked up from her as well."

"Afraid," Kel scoffed with disbelief, "of what?"

Jev turned to look back at Kel.

"That's what I need to find out if there's to be any hope of getting this challenge called off," he said.

He paused as the others looked at him with equally confused expressions.

"What, you don't honestly think I actually want to fight her do you?"

Sam, once again, was the first to break the uneasy silence. He smiled and put a hand on Jev's shoulder.

"You're certainly one with many surprises, Jev," he said.

If Jev's body hadn't been covered in fur he would visibly have shown his reaction to Sam's comment, blushing a deep red. As it was, the only indication that he'd reacted at all was a slight dip of his ears.

"Assuming, however, that Miru refuses to back down, I think some special training is in order," Kel announced.

"Reluctantly, I have to agree with you, Captain," Lheiza said.

"Jaffay has already trained me to fight," Jev reminded him with his head cocked to the side in confusion, referring to the training he received back on Alessi.

"He taught you basic self-defense and hand-to-hand combat techniques, Jev, to prepare you to fight the T'kri," Kel said. "This challenge is a different matter entirely. You need to be trained to survive it, and there isn't much time."

"Well, we're not getting anything done standing here," Lheiza said. "We should all head on home."

She turned to look at Tiela and Kel.

"The two of you are welcome to stay with us until you get yourselves settled in."

"We thank you, my Lady," Tiela said respectfully, with an appreciative flick of her ears, "however, my mother also lives in Ethinias and has already invited Kel and me to stay with her."

"Of course, then I will have Leader Lielm at the Telepath Guild get in touch with you there to make arrangements for setting up your office."

"Thank you, my Lady."

After saying goodbye, and giving Jev and Kiyel a warm hug, Tiela left the station with Kel, their luggage in hand, turning around the bend and walked out of sight.

Lheiza, deciding they had lingered long enough, led them outside where the warm breeze from the ocean whispered softly past Jev, blowing softly through his fur, and making him shiver with delight. The air was fresh and clean, much like it had been on Alessi, and a welcoming change after spending the last month on board the Cetani with its recycled air. While there was nothing wrong with the air on the ship, it was not the same as the air a planet offered. He breathed deeply, his head raised as he took in the scents of this new world. Thanks to the memories he shared with Kiyel, it was both new and familiar to him at the same time.

His enjoyment of experiencing his first few moments out in the open air, however, was suddenly interrupted by another voice yelling to them.

Turning to this new voice he smiled when he saw Kiyel's younger brother, Khelan, bounding towards them excitedly on all fours. When there were only a few feet between them, Khelan leaped up into his brother's happily outstretched arms. A tear came to Jev's eye when he saw the two brothers being reunited after so long. He was sure he could hear tiny sobs coming from Khelan, but when they eventually separated they both wore equally joyful smiles.

Khelan then managed to tear his eyes from his brother and he looked at Jev as though seeing him standing there for the first time. Without warning, Jev suddenly found himself in a tight embrace as Khelan moved to wrap his arms around him. Although it was unexpected, Jev returned the embrace, holding the youngster for several moments before letting go. Like he did with Kiyel, Khelan stared into Jev's eyes.

Welcome home, Jev, he heard Khelan say to him in his mind.

Thank you, Khelan. It's awesome to finally meet you in person, Jev sent with a wide grin.

"Awesome, huh?" Khelan said aloud, looking at Jev with a mischievous grin. "I think I like that word."

Jev laughed.

"Khelan, why aren't you at home attending to your studies?" Lheiza asked.

"When father said the *Cetani* arrived in orbit, I just had to come down to see Kiyel and his Enassi."

"You could just as easily have met them when we came home," Lheiza pointed out to him. "However, you're here now so you might as well help Aiden with his luggage."

Khelan's ears dropped as he accepted his mother's rebuke.

"Yes, mother."

Khelan went to Aiden and offered to carry the bag he was holding. Aiden smiled` and gratefully handed it to him. Although it wasn't really all that heavy—it contained only his clothes—being only four years old, his arm quickly tired. Not so with his other arm, though, under which he held his plush yuta tightly to his chest. It had quickly become his favorite possession.

"Hey, I saw you on the ship," Aiden said, recognizing Khelan.

Khelon nodded.

"You really surprised my father when you started talking to him."

Aiden giggled at the memory of Sahl's reaction when he spoke to him.

"And he picked up our language all on his own without

any help from us," Kiyel said.

"Awesome," Khelan said, using his new favorite word, and laughing with Aiden.

As they started away from the shuttle port, Khelan quickly noticed Jev limping slightly as they walked and he frowned.

"Jev, are you okay?" he asked.

Without stopping, Jev looked back to where Khelan was walking next to Aiden and Sam, and smiled at him reassuringly.

"I'm alright, Khelan. I'm just a little stiff."

"Khelan, Jev recently had to have surgery which he's still recovering from," Kiyel explained.

"It wasn't anything serious, though," Jev quickly added, sensing Khelan's concern. "They just had to fix something so that one day, if we wanted, Kiyel and I could have children."

Kiyel laughed at his brother's sudden look of bewildered confusion.

"We'll explain it to you later," he promised.

Khelan reluctantly let the matter drop, but he continued to look at Jev with a puzzled expression.

SEVENTEEN

For Jev, the trip from the shuttle port to Kiyel's home estate—and now his as well—was nothing short of breathtaking, to say the least, and one he would not soon forget. After leaving the shuttle port they hired an air car, a vehicle capable of low altitude flights and which was fully automated, much to Sam's discomfort and Aiden's delight. The ride was a mostly silent one, except for the slight humming from the car's engine beneath their feet. Not a word was spoken.

Although it was a short trip, lasting only a few minutes before the car set down just outside the main gates to the estate, the scenery that sped past below them was as Jev remembered it—or rather how Kiyel remembered it. Jev very quickly found himself anxiously wanting to get his feet on the ground and run through the rolling hills and lush forests below. His eyes immediately caught sight of some of the wildlife on the planet, running freely. Oh how he wanted to do some hunting, his mouth watering at the prospects.

He heard Kiyel's laughter in his mind through their link.

I told you you would like it here, Kiyel sent.

And you were right, Jev replied quietly, his eyes glued to the scenery below.

"Once we get settled in I'll show you around," Kiyel said aloud.

When the car had landed, and they retrieved their luggage from the trunk, Jev had to chuckle a bit as Sam stood and watched with awed fascination as the car lifted off on its own and turned to fly back to where it had come.

As they entered the wrought-iron gate that framed the front of the estate, Jev saw that the estate was moderately sized, and very old. It was, as Kiyel described it to him, built many centuries ago by the progenitor of their Pride. Its grey stone walls had been excavated from the surrounding countryside, long before the city of Ethinias was established. Carved wood framed the arched windows and front door, and although well aged, it was in remarkably good shape. The estate looked like the stately manor it was, but it still managed to retain the charm of a simple country home, despite it being situated on the edge of Ethinias.

Jev smiled as they stopped at the front entrance.

I'm really home, he thought to himself, feeling that he truly was for the first time in his life.

Yes, you are, Enassi, Kiyel sent, putting his arm around Jev's shoulder and holding him close.

With a nod and a smile from his mother, Kiyel, for the first time in over a year, opened the door to his home.

The sound of their entry into the estate brought an older Caitaran male rushing into the main foyer, who Jev instantly recognized as being Sahl, Kiyel's father. He was dressed neatly in a loose-fitting, tan tunic that crossed over his chest and was tied together with a black belt, and brown pants which ended just past his knees.

Sahl rushed to Kiyel, and, without saying a thing, pulled Kiyel into a tight, lingering embrace, completely catching Kiyel off guard. But Kiyel, enjoying this sudden display of affection from his father, something he wasn't used to, welcomed the embrace and returned it warmly.

Out of the corner of his eye, Jev thought he saw a tear of joy come to Lheiza's eye as she watched father and son reunite.

When they finally separated, Sahl looked at his son appraising.

"You're looking well."

"It's in large part thanks to my Enassi," Kiyel replied as he glanced over at Jev.

"I like to think it was a team effort, really," Jev said quietly.

"And so moddest, too," Sahl said with a hearty laugh. "It's good to finally meet you in person, Jev. Welcome to the Valael Estate." He placed his palm over Jev's chest.

"Thank you, sir," Jev said, returning the gesture. "I'd like you to meet Doctor Sam O'Riley, my guardian and physician from Alessi."

"Your Guardian?" Sahl echoed, giving Sam a questioning look.

"It's an honour to meet you," Sam said, offering his hand to Sahl, which Sahl shook after a moment's hesitation. "Jev's father was killed in a fire set by the T'kri., His mother died while our ship was in transit to Alesi. In his will, Jev's father named me his guardian."

Sahl nodded in understanding.

"You have my deepest condolences for your loss, Jev," he said quietly.

Jev could only nod his thanks as a sudden lump formed in his throat.

Just then Sahl noticed Riyad standing at the back with the luggage and he frowned, his tail flicking anxiously behind him.

"Riyad," he said, quietly acknowledging the other's presence.

Riyad simply nodded his acknowledgment, not saying a word.

Jev couldn't help but feel the tension in the room suddenly become so thick it could almost be cut with a knife, and he shivered uncomfortably. There was clearly some history between the two of them, and judging from their Sahl's sudden change in demeanor, he guessed the last time they met they probably hadn't parted on very good terms. Kiyel was just as surprised as Jev, as he didn't know how the two of them knew each other either.

The tension seemed to quickly lift, however, when a gentle tug on Sahl's pants leg suddenly broke his attention away from Riyad. He looked down to see Aiden looking up at him with a hopeful expression.

"Well hello there, little cub. You must be Aiden. Do you remember me talking to you on the ship?"

Aiden smiled and nodded, raising his hands up to Sahl and wanting to be picked up.

"He does that often," he said with a relieved grin, thankful that that bit of unpleasantness was over with.

Still smiling, Sahl lifted Aiden up into his arms, who then gave Sahl a tight hug.

"Incredible," Sahl said, sensing Aiden's feelings of gratitude flowing into him.

"He does that a lot also," Jev said, unable to resist a quiet chuckle. "I sometimes think he actually likes using his talent more to communicate with than talking."

"You must be hungry after such a long flight. Would you like something to eat?" Sahl asked Aiden.

"Uh huh," Aiden said, nodding enthusiastically.

"The bottomless pit that is a child's stomach," Sam muttered in disbelief.

Sahl, having no trouble at all hearing Sam's comment, laughed as he beckoned them to follow him into the kitchen.

They were introduced to the housekeeper, Nuria, who managed the estate for Kiyel's family. She looked at all of them with intrigue, but especially at Aiden, whose eyes lit up as the enticing aroma of freshly baked bread reached his nose. Jev could sense a sadness quickly welling up inside her, though, as her gaze remained on Aiden.

Nuria lost a cub about Aiden's age two summers ago in an accident, Kiyel explained to him over their link.

Jev could feel Kiyel's own sorrow over the loss and he realized that the two of them must have been close. He was about to respond when out of the corner of his eye he saw Aiden wriggling his way out of Sahl's arms, and then make his way over to Nuria, his eyes catching hers. At first she was surprised by this, as was Jev and Kiyel, but then tears began to form in her eyes when Aiden looked up at her and raised his arms to her in the same fashion, Jev believed, her own cub must have when he was alive. She was a little hesitant at first as she lifted him into her arms. Very shortly, however, she was cradling him tightly to her chest as tears freely fell from her eyes. Aiden, hugged her as tightly as he could.

Jev could feel that Aiden was once again working his magic on her, helping Nuria to let go of the pain that she must have been carrying with her every day since losing her cub. He smiled as he looked on, certain that the two of them would be almost inseparable from that moment on. And that's when Jev suddenly realized that this was what Aiden had been searching for all along, and what he really needed: a mother.

What struck Jev as being particularly odd, though, as he looked at the others in the room, was how intently Sam was staring at Nuria. It was obvious to Jev that Sam was clearly quite taken with her, and Jev couldn't blame him one bit. She was, in his opinion, quite an attractive female. She was not quite middle-aged yet. Her soft fur, which was as white as snow but with some patches of light brown and grey, shined brilliantly in the sun's light streaming in through the kitchen window. But never before had he seen Sam so captivated by a female before, much less one of a different species.

Wonders will never cease, Kiyel chuckled in his mind.

I guess not, Jev replied. I wonder if she notices.

I'm sure she does. She may be terrible at making k'yarri, but there's very little else that escapes her notice. It's why mother trusts her so much with the estate's upkeep.

The sound of Sahl gently clearing his throat broke the silence that had befallen the group.

Nuria, quickly composing herself as she suddenly remembered where she was, looked at Sahl, her ears folding back against her skull in acute embarrassment.

"My lord, I'm sorry," she said with a slight bow. "Second meal will be ready shortly."

"That's fine, Nuria," Sahl said with a reassuring smile. He nevertheless was astonished that Aiden was somehow able to accomplish what no one else on Caitar had been able to.

He's something else isn't he? Kiyel sent to his father.

I've never seen anything like it, Sahl replied as Nuria, with Aiden's eager help, started to prepare the table.

Neither have I. I never would have thought it possible that a child so young could possess the strong talents he does.

That's an empath for you, Jev sent proudly.

"If you boys are finished gawking, perhaps you could lend a hand?" Lheiza interjected admonishingly as she held out a stack of plates to them.

After finishing a very satisfying mid-afternoon meal, consisting of the freshly baked bread they smelled coming into the kitchen, sliced meat, a variety of vegetables that Jev couldn't hope to identify—but enjoyed immensely—and some speckled blue cheese, which surprisingly tasted a lot like old cheddar, Kiyel wanted to show Jev to their room. They excused themselves from the table.

Lheiza watched them leave and then turned to Sahl, her mood quickly becoming serious.

"We need to talk."

Sahl, sensing the urgency in his lifemate's voice, flicked his ears in assent. They excused themselves, leaving Sam and Aiden alone with Nuria and Riyad, who, it seemed, were all completely oblivious to their presence. Except for Riyad, that is, who politely stood with them and sat back down when they left.

Sahl and Lheiza entered her office, closing the door behind them.

"Alright, Lheiza, what's this all about?"

"It's about that female you chose for Kiyel."

Sahl's ears pricked up with interest, cocking his head to the side.

"What about her?"

"She was at the shuttle port when we arrived."

"How did she know when you would be returning?" Sahl asked.

"Dahel only knows!" she said, throwing her hands up in

exasperation. "But she immediately confronted Kiyel about his being Enassi-linked with Jev and issued a challenge."

"She did what?!" Sahl roared in sudden fury, ears folding back against his skull and tail flicking violently behind him. His voice was so loud it echoed beyond the door into the main foyer.

"What's more, Jev accepted."

This time Sahl's eyes widened with alarm.

"But the laws—"

"He knows them as well as Kiyel, thanks to their link. But he chose to accept it nonetheless."

"By Dahel," Sahl whispered, dropping himself heavily into the long couch that was by the door, wrinkling his nose in thought as he tried to absorb this new information.

"For some reason, however, Jev is of the impression that Muri isn't doing this out of anger," Lheiza continued.

Sahl looked up at her with surprise.

"And Kiyel agrees," she finished.

"I must contact Muri's father right away to put an end to this," Sahl said.

Getting up from the couch and moving swiftly to Lheiza's desk, he activated the terminal. He was so upset that he didn't balk when Riyad's image appeared on the screen.

"Yes, my Lord?" Riyad said respectfully, ears flicking in acknowledgment.

"Riyad, get me Cherin at Ielasi estate, right away."

"Right away, my Lord," Riyad answered without hesitation, bowing slightly before closing the connection.

Looks like father has learned of Muri's challenge, Kiyel commented as Riyad left the kitchen to answer the terminal in the foyer.

Jev, still concerned with what he'd gotten himself into, simply nodded in response.

"Well, I think it is time to show you all to your rooms," Nuria said as she stood from her chair, Aiden hopping off her lap but still holding her hand.

"Yes, that would be wonderful, thanks," Sam said softly, nodding in agreement.

They left the table and headed out of the kitchen to go up the stairs. They were as grand as any Jev had seen in those old holo-movies he used to watch with his brother and father before they'd left Earth. But in real life they were even more impressive. His hands slid over the soft, dark wood rails as they ascended to the second floor, marveling at the impressive craftsmanship. At the top of the main stairs were two smaller sets of stairs, each on opposite sides, and both leading to the second floor landing.

Nuria led them to the first door at the top of the stairs, which she opened.

"Master O'Riley, this will be your room."

She touched a panel next to the door and the room lit up from, surprisingly, a fairly modern looking ceiling lamp.

"Please, just Sam," Sam said.

He peered into the room to find his luggage already sitting at the foot of a large, very comfortable looking bed. Opposite the bed was a large dresser with a mirror above it, set in oval-shaped wood frame. On either side of the bed were two small night tables on top of which were a pair of lamps. The window in the room was open slightly, and the curtains drawn, to allow the warm breeze to enter the room.

"Thank you, lass," Sam said, smiling at her appreciatively. "It's perfect."

Although she didn't show it, Jev could tell she welcomed

Sam's compliment. He looked at Kiyel who barely was able to contain a knowing grin.

They continued on to the next room, which Khelan suddenly opened as he scooted past a surprised Nuria.

"This is my room," he said proudly, grinning at Aiden. "You can share it with me if you'd like," he added hopefully.

Aiden looked up at Sam as though asking if it was alright. Sam nodded his approval, and Khelan, wasting no time, pulled Aiden into the room by his arm, the both of them laughing with glee.

Jev glanced inside and saw that the room was similarly arranged as the room Sam would be occupying, however it was clearly the room of a young boy. Posters of Caitarans Jev didn't recognize hung from the walls, though they clearly were musicians if those things in their hands were instruments. He made it a point to ask Kiyel about Caitaran music at some point. On shelves near the opened window, were an assortment of trophies and awards that Khelan had won. Just like a young boy, however, not all was organized. The bed, which was just as comfortable looking as Sam's, was not made, there were clothes strewn about on the floor, and on the dresser, Jev thought he saw a used, empty plate. He smiled, as it reminded him of all the times his mother used to scold him about the mess in his room when they were back on Earth. It was definitely a little boy's room, no doubt.

"Kehlan, you straighten out this mess right away before your mother sees it," Nuria admonished him.

Predictably this made Kehlan laugh a little harder as he promised her he would. But with the excitement of sharing a room with Aiden, Jev had no doubt it wouldn't get done.

"Khelan, just be careful with him. He's not Caitaran and doesn't have your natural defenses, lad," Sam cautioned him.

Sobering up slightly, Khelan looked at Sam and nodded his understanding.

Shaking her head, Nuria led them to the next room, which Jev could immediately feel belonged to Kiyel.

And now you as well, Kiyel sent to him as he opened the door.

Inside it was dark, except for the moonlight coming in from the open window. But Jev could easily make out the partially drawn curtains billowing in the gentle evening breeze, the neatly made bed, the large dresser opposite it, and to his shocked amazement a painted picture on the wall next to the window of a rolling landscape that looked eerily familiar. He gasped when he saw that the painting depicted the hillside surrounding Hillsford back on Alessi.

He turned and looked at Kiyel in disbelief.

"For many months before I left home, I'd had dreams about that very place," Kiyel said. He touched the panel by the door to activate the lights so that everyone could see the picture. "I rarely ever painted anything, since I was never really any good at it, but for some reason, after the dreams I was having, I just had to paint this."

"But that looks like Hillsford!" Sam exclaimed, also recognizing it immediately. He pointed to the painting. "You can see the stream."

And indeed it was the very same stream that Jev had often taken Kiyel to when Kiyel was still recovering from the wounds he'd suffered from the crash of the Lekur.

I never recognized the importance of this image that I kept seeing in my mind until that day you took me to our spot by the stream. I realized then that somehow, for whatever reason, we were meant to discover each other.

I never knew, Jev replied quietly. With a smile he

reached up to touch the side of Kiyel's face.

"All right, you two," Nuria said, rolling her eyes at them, but with a wry grin on her face. "Time enough for that later."

It was then, without warning, that Jev suddenly felt the urgent need to visit the personal.

Kiyel could feel Jev's distress, and pointed him to the room at the far end of the landing.

Jev apologized and hurried from the group, covering his mouth just as he felt he was about to be sick to his stomach.

After a few minutes, he re-emerged from the Personal, definitely not looking well. His fur above his brow was matted slightly with sweat. Sam, seeing the state Jev was in, hurried to him and felt his forehead while also looking into his eyes. He then turned to Kiyel.

"Kiyel, get a hold of Tiela," he said.

Kiyel didn't hesitate as he raced back down the stairs to the terminal.

At that moment, Lheiza and Sahl started up the stairs and saw everyone hovering around Jev, who, in his weakened condition, had to lean up against the wall to stand.

"What's going on, Nuria?" Lheiza asked, looking concerned.

"I'm not quite certain, my Lady," Nuria said, turning to meet her and bowing respectfully. "I was showing them to their rooms when Master Jev suddenly took ill."

The sound of footsteps climbing the stairs altered them to Kiyel's presence. He rushed to Jev's side and put Jev's arm around his shoulders to help him to stand.

"Oh god!"

Another wave of nausea just then hit Jev, and Kiyel quickly led him back to the Personal. When they re-emerged a few moments later, Jev appeared so weak that Kiyel was practically carrying him. With Sam's help, Kiyel led Jev to their bedroom and carefully lay him down on the bed.

"Tiela says she'll be here as soon as she can," Kiyel told Sam who nodded in silent acknowledgment.

Aiden just then appeared in the doorway with Khelan. After both sensing and hearing Jev's distress he had come out of his and Khelan's room to see what was going on. As soon as he saw Jev, spread out on Kiyel's bed and sweating profusely, he quickly went to him and put his hand on Jev's.

Kiyel knew immediately what Aiden was attempting to do, and indeed his presence did appear to help restore some of Jev's strength. But even Aiden's empathic talent, curiously, did little to relieve Jev's upset stomach.

They waited for Tiela like that for what seemed like hours. But when they finally heard the door sound, and then the unmistakable sound of Tiela's voice downstairs, there was an audible collective sigh of relief in the room from everyone.

They all heard Tiela hurrying up the stairs with Riyad, who'd let her in, and then she entered the bedroom. She took one look at Jev and rushed to his bedside. At her gentle urging, Aiden reluctantly moved out of the wait to give her room, but he stayed close to Jev, refusing to leave his side. Jev tried weakly to sit up for her, but she gently coaxed him to remain as he was, which he was only too glad to do as his stomach suddenly threatened to heave again. He swallowed hard in an effort to fight back the urge to throw up. Luckily, it worked... this time.

"When did this start?" she asked, looking at Kiyel.

"Shortly after second meal."

"It can't be food poisoning then," Tiela said, almost to herself, as she withdrew from her medical kit a scanner.

She activated it and began running it slowly over Jev's midsection. At first she found nothing, but then she suddenly stopped, her eyes opening wide with shocked amazement.

"What-what's wrong, Tiela?" Kiyel demanded, his tail lashing violently from side to side, showing his growing distress.

Tiela deactivated the scanner, setting it aside, and took out a pillbox from which she shook two oval pills into her palm. She ordered Khelan to get a glass of water for Jev as she replaced the pillbox and the scanner in her kit. A few seconds later Khelan returned with the glass of water, handing it to her.

"Clearly, you and Jev didn't listen to me back on the ship," she said, looking at Kiyel sternly as she helped Jev sit up.

Jev gratefully took the pills and the water and swallowed both down. Almost immediately he felt his nausea beginning to subside, much to his relief, and Kiyel's.

"I don't understand," Kiyel said, ears dropping slightly under her glare.

Tiela sighed audibly.

"Kiyel, there's no other way to say this, but congratulations, you're going to be a father."

All eyes suddenly fell on Jev as everyone in the room looked at him with bewildered expressions on their faces. None of them was more surprised and shocked, however, than Jev, who looked at Tiela in disbelief. He was momentarily struck speechless, his mouth opening and closing several times as though to say something, but no words came out.

It was Kiyel who broke the stunned silence.

"He's pregnant?"

"Morning sickness," Sam nodded, understanding now the cause of Jev's nausea.

"I will need to see Jev at the guild first thing tomorrow morning to determine how far along he is and to check on the condition of the fetus," Tiela said.

"But, Tiela, I can't be pregnant," Jev said quietly, finally finding his voice, his tail flicking nervously beneath him.

"You knew that getting pregnant was a possibility after the operation, Jev," Tiela said reprovingly as she stood up from the bed. "I just wish you and Kiyel had waited until after you'd had a chance to heal from your surgery. You could have injured yourself quite severely."

"Except, Tiela, we haven't mated yet. Yes we have shared some intimate moments on the rare occasions when we had a chance to be alone together, but you should know by now that I would never do anything to potentially hurt Jev. Our link wouldn't allow it," Kiyel said.

Tiela frowned, looking back at Jev who nodded in confirmation. Her ears flattened backward in apology.

"You're right, Kiyel. I'm sorry, I shouldn't have jumped to conclusions like I did," she said, her tone softening noticeably.

"It's perfectly understandable," Kiyel said, giving her a reassuring smile. "Quite frankly I'm at a loss to explain how Jev could have become pregnant myself."

"It's definitely something we need to discuss when you come to see me at the guild tomorrow," Tiela said.

Kiyel and Jev both nodded in unison.

"Does this mean Jev's going to have a baby?" Aiden asked, looking up at Sam.

"It certainly looks like it, buddy," Sam replied.

"Cool!" Aiden exclaimed excitedly, causing everyone in the room to laugh, including Jev.

Seeing that Jev was no longer in any distress, one by one they began filing out of the room until only Kiyel and Sam remained with him.

"Are you sure you're ready for this, Jev?" Sam asked, his tone serious.

"I don't know," Jev answered honestly in a quiet voice. He looked up at Kiyel who offered him a weak smile of assurance. "But I do know that I want this child." And he meant it.

Sam nodded in understanding.

"If there's anything you need from me, you have only to ask," Sam offered.

"Thanks, Doc. That means a lot, to the both of us," Kiyel said, giving him an appreciative flick of his ears.

Sam turned, as if to leave, but then from the doorway looked back at Jev.

"And, Jev. I'm sure your father would have been just as proud of you as I am."

The mere mention of his father made Jev's eyes begin to water. He could only nod his head in appreciation as Sam then left the room.

Kiyel sat down on the bed to hold Jev comfortingly as great heaves of grief and slow tears began to course from him.

I miss him, Kiyel. I miss him so much! Jev sent as he cried into Kiyel's chest.

I know, Enassi. I think Doc is right, though. Your father would be proud of you. And so am I.

After a few minutes Jev's sobs slowly subsides.

"Come have a shower with me?" Kiyel quietly suggested in Jev's ear.

Jev looked up at him, the fur on the sides of his face wet with his tears. Slowly he nodded, a faint smile tugging at the corner of his lips. He let himself be pulled up off the bed and led by the hand into the personal by Kiyel. The shower stall was easily large enough to accommodate the two of them, and after disrobing and starting the shower, making sure the temperature of the water was just right, they climbed in, sliding the semi-transparent, glass stall door closed as they did.

Immediately Jev was bathed in the spray of the hot water from above which washed over and through his fur. He closed his eyes as its warmth penetrated deep into his skin providing a gentle massage that quickly began relieving the tension in his muscles. And then there was the magical feeling of Kiyel's hands as he began washing his fur, further relaxing him and now causing him to begin purring audibly with pleasure. At Kiyel's urging Jev turned his back to him. There was no way he could hold back the deep, pleasurable growl that echoed from deep within his throat when Kiyel deftly, and sensually, started running his fingers along Jev's spine from the nape of his neck to the base of his tail, nor was he able to resist responding to his Enassi's ministrations when he felt Kiyel lean close and began tracing the edges of his ear with his tongue. Jev's excitement quickly grew until he was overwhelmed by a sudden explosion of pleasure that was so strong his knees threatened to give out under him. Had Kiyel not been there to hold him steady, he likely would have collapsed in a heap.

Jev breathed hard in Kiyel's loving embrace, utterly exhausted and spent, his whole body tingling from the aftereffects.

Now it's your turn, he sent, a wide, playful smile on his face.

EIGHTEEN

torm clouds dragged across the dark sky early the next morning, bringing thunder and rain while Jev and Kiyel slept. A sudden flash of lightning outside briefly lit up their bedroom in a bright blinding light, waking Jev from an already restless sleep.

He felt Kiyel stir beside him.

Can't sleep? Kiyel asked through their link.

Jev turned to see Kiyel staring up at him from his pillow.

Worried about tomorrow's appointment with Tiela I guess, Jev admitted.

You're afraid our cub won't be viable, Kiyel sent. It wasn't a question.

Jev nodded sadly, fearful tears filling his eyes.

I want so much to have this cub with you, Kiyel, but I'm afraid that we might be just too different.

Kiyel put his hand over Jev's, comfortingly.

Don't worry. You heard what Tiela said, we're only

biologically compatible with each other. If her readings had indicated that there was a problem with the cub, she would have told us right away.

Jev knew Kiyel was right. He tried to smile reassuringly at Kiyel, but it was difficult to be sincere when he still felt so uneasy.

Maybe what's causing you to be so upset is all that food you ate last night, Kiyel suggested wryly.

This time Jev did smile, seeing the humour in Kiyel's suggestion, and even chuckled lightly.

Before retiring early for the night, and shortly after their shower, they had both joined the rest of the household for a very hearty third meal. Thanks to the pills Tiela had given him before, he finally felt like himself again. His appetite returning with a vengeance; he wound up eating not one, but two, full servings, even dessert, much to the amusement of everyone else at the table. Even Aiden and Khelan had giggled as they watched Jev wipe his plate clean with his third slice of bread.

Shortly after finishing dinner, Jev felt suddenly tired, so he and Kiyel headed off to bed. But once they got settled in, sleep did not come easily to Jev. What little sleep he did manage to get was interrupted by frightening dreams, filled with the misshapen face of a grotesquely formed Caitaran cub's face.

Jev visibly shook himself of the memory of that dream, pushing it as far back in his mind as he could.

"You're probably right, Kiyel," Jev said quietly.

He snuggled back into Kiyel's warm embrace as Kiyel lay back down, eventually closing his eyes and falling back to sleep. This time, however, his dreams were far more pleasant. All he had needed, it seemed, were the assurances that only Kiyel could give him.

* * *

The new day brought with it clear skies and singing birds. The storm that had washed across the land the night before had passed, leaving behind the scent of fresh, clean air mingled with wet vegetation. The enticing smell roused Jev. He breathed the deeply taking in the fresh air which was being blown gently into the room through the partially open window by the breeze from outside.

Yawning deeply, he stretched and felt Kiyel lying beside him, still fast assleep and snoring softly. His Enassi looked so restful—not to mention cute, the way he lay with his arm partially draped over his face, covering his eyes—that Jev was perfectly content to continue to lay in bed all morning with him. But then he felt that all too annoying and suddenly intense pressure in his bladder, strongly indicating his need to visit the Personal.

Slipping carefully out of bed so as to avoid waking Kiyel, Jev quietly put on his robe and crept out into the hallway, partially closing the bedroom door behind him.

When he returned from the Personal, he found Kiyel wide awake and sitting up in bed.

"Good morning," Jev said, walking up to the bed and rubbing his nose affectionately into Kiyel's.

"Good morning to you," Kiyel replied. "I'm glad you're feeling much better."

"How could I not with such a cute guy holding me the way you did last night?"

Kiyel pricked his ears and grinned wryly at Jev.

"Do I know this guy?" he asked with mock suspicion.

"Oh you!" Jev exclaimed, laughing as he grabbed a pillow and playfully lobbed it at Kiyel.

Just as Kiyel lazily got out of bed to put on his robe, the unmistakable aroma of freshly brewed k'yarri began wafting up from down stairs and through their partially open door. It was enough to cause both their mouths to water with anticipation. Without another word spoken between them, they quickly left their room and headed downstairs where they were greeted in the kitchen by Nuria and Sam, who were busy preparing First Meal for the household.

Jev, who by now was used to seeing Sam awake so early, had to suppress an amused grin when he saw him this morning so readily, and even happily, he thought, taking directions from Nuria. Jev was easily able to sense from her a growing attraction for Sam and there was no doubt in his mind that given time those two could eventually become a couple. He didn't want to spoil it for them, though, by embarrassing them, so he said nothing.

Nuria was the first to spot their entrance and invited them to take a seat at the table, which they did, while she went to prepare some k'yarri for them.

"Good morning, you two. How did you sleep?" Sam asked with a cheerful grin.

Jev shook his head, his ears dipping slightly.

"Not too well at first," he admitted quietly. "I kept worrying about whether Tiela's tests would tell us that the fetus is developing normally because I'm only part Caitaran. And when I did get to sleep, I mostly had nightmares." He shivered involuntarily from the memory of his dreams.

"I'm sure there's no need to worry and that your cub will be just fine," Nuria said with a reassuring smile as she placed two steaming mugs of k'yarri on the table before him and Kiyel.

Just then Aiden entered the kitchen with Khelan, weary-eyed and dressed in their pajamas. He saw Jev and ran up to him, giving him a hug which Jev lovingly returned. Jev could feel

Aiden using his talent to ease his worries so that he was once again at peace. It still amazed him how easily Aiden was able to do that.

Sam directed Aiden and Khelan to sit at the table while Nuria poured a couple of glasses of nanaya juice for them.

Riyad followed soon after, looking as alert as ever. He was a strange one, Jev felt—and not for the first time. For although he could sense Riyad's presence, his mind was oddly quiet. Jev couldn't even sense a stray thought or emotion from him. It was a little disconcerting, but intriguing at the same time as well.

"My lord," Riyad said, his ears giving a little flick of acknowledgment to both Kiyel and Jev before he then proceeded to the counter to help himself to some of the k'yarri.

Right after Riyad joined Jev and Kiyel at the table, and as Nuria and Sam started serving their meals, Lheiza and Sahl entered the kitchen. When they did, Riyad quickly stood back up, bowing respectfully.

With a slight frown, Sahl waved Riyad back down, still clearly uneasy with Riyad's presence in his home, though acknowledging him with a flick of his ears.

"Is there enough for two more, Nuria?" he asked.

"And some of that wonderful smelling k'yarri as well?" Lheiza asked, who had caught the unmistakable, and enticing, scent of freshly brewed k'yarri in the air. "Sam, did you make it?"

"No, Nuria did, with my help," Sam replied.

This earned Nuria a curious glance from Lheiza, causing Nuria's ears to dip noticeably with embarrassment.

"I'm sorry, my Lady, that I was not able to make k'yarri as well as you'd have liked in the past. I hope you enjoy this brew. To think that I'd need to learn to make k'yarri from a non-

Caitaran."

"Well, as I told her, I have Tiela to thank for teaching me how to make it," Sam said quietly, blushing noticeably from Nuria's compliment.

With everyone in the household now present, either sitting at the table or standing up against the counter, the conversation quickly turned to Jev's imminent appointment with Tiela and the cub that he and Kiyel were going to have. Aiden, not wanting to be left out, suddenly announced that he wanted to go with Jev and Kiyel. But Sam said no, telling him that he was later going to school with Khelan.

"But I don't want to go to school," Aiden said, beginning to pout, which resulted in everyone else in the room beginning to laugh.

Eventually, Aiden was able to see how silly his reaction had been, and he laughed with them. The truth be known, he was actually excited to be getting to go to school with Khelan. It was clear to anyone watching the two of them that they had grown very close to each other in such a short period of time. If it were not for the fact that they were of two different species they could easily be mistaken for brothers.

"I can arrange for transport to take you and Jev to the Guild if you wish, my Lord," Riyad offered.

"Thank you, Riyad. But I believe we'll travel there on foot instead," Kiyel said, shaking his head.

"After being cooped up on the ship for so long, there's no way we'd pass up this opportunity to get out and stretch our legs," Jev added.

Riyad smiled knowingly.

"Of course," he said.

"Speaking of which, we should really be getting ready to go now," Kiyel suggested. "Knowing Tiela, I bet she's probably already waiting for us at the guild."

Jev nodded in agreement. They finished their meal quickly, then quietly excused themselves from the table and headed back up to their room where they changed into clothing more suitable for travel. Their excitement was tempered only by Jev's lingering concern over what Tiela's scan would reveal about their cub. Jev pushed his worries aside, though, as they returned to the others to say their goodbyes before heading out.

Outside, and well past the gates of the estate, Jev bounded up the grassy hill, running on all fours with Kiyel racing alongside him, and feeling the most exhilarated he had felt in a long time as they followed the trail that would take them to the Guild. Not since he went hunting with Kiyel on Alessi did he feel as free as he did now, especially as he leapt over a rock and scared some of the nearby wildlife, which quickly scattered into the woods. While they ran they played like the two mountain cats from Alessi they so closely resembled, grabbing each others tails as first one and then the other would take the lead, all the while laughing joyously.

When finally they crested the hill, They came to a stop to catch their breaths. Jev sat down in the tall grass and looked behind him, where, below, and some distance away, he could see the estate, and beyond that the city of Ethinias. He could even make out the shuttle port and the cove it sat in, where tiny specs that were shuttles were arriving and leaving at regular intervals.

I don't have to ask how you're feeling, Kiyel sent through their link as he sat down next to Jev.

All of this makes me wish I had been born Caitaran, Kiyel, Jev sent wistfully. *I have a lot of catching up to do.*

Kiyel laughed.

Just wait until I take you hunting.

Jev looked at him eagerly, his eyes lighting up with

anticipation.

I can't wait!

"And look up there," Kiyel said aloud, turning to look up at a magnificent doughnut-shaped steel and glass building surrounded by trees and a well manicured lawn. "That's the Telepath Guild, where we're going."

Deciding they had rested enough, they stood and began once again heading toward the Guild, Jev's tongue protruding slightly, as he marveled at the building's intricate design.

They entered through the glass sliding doors, which slid open automatically for them with a slight hiss, and approached the receptionist seated behind an ornately carved desk positioned directly in front of them in the main lobby.

Jev slowly gazed around as he took in the magnificent decor. A huge domed skylight lit up the wood paneled walls and marble floor of the lobby in the brilliant light of the morning sun. Of particular interest to him, though, was the large aquarium set into the wall behind the receptionist, and surrounded by book shelves that reached up from the floor to the tall ceiling. In the aquarium were some of the most beautifully coloured fish he had ever seen swimming about some very exotic looking aquatic plants.

Reaching the desk, Jev was immediately taken aback, for he was unexpectedly unable to sense the receptionist behind the counter like he could other telepaths. And that meant only one thing.

"You're not a telepath!" He exclaimed, his voice inadvertently loud enough that it echoed in the almost empty room.

His ears dipped noticeably with embarrassment as he saw a few Caitarans staring at him.

"Sorry," he said quietly.

The receptionist smiled at him reassuringly.

"It's all right. My family has been a part of the Telepath Guild for generations."

"We're here to see Tiela. She's expecting us," Kiyel said, quickly changing the subject to spare Jev from any more embarrassment.

She checked her terminal and nodded, tapping a few commands into the terminal.

"Someone will be right with you, my Lord," she said.

Sure enough, only a few short moments later, a younger Caitaran male dressed in the loose flowing robes of a medic approached them. Jev guessed from his attire that he was an orderly. He certainly looked much too young to be a physician.

"Hello, my Lord Kiyel, Jev," the Caitaran said with a respectful bow. "Tiela is waiting for you both. If you'll come this way?" he said.

They were led down a long winding corridor that was framed on one side by huge arched windows that offered a tranquil view of the gardens and courtyard outside. The sunlight the struck the wall basked the corridor in a white-orange glow. They stopped at a pair of sliding doors made of a thick transparent material with a large white insignia that marked the entrance to the infirmary.

The doors slid open for them and they stepped inside. Tiela, who had been in an adjacent office with similarly transparent walls that encircled it, saw them enter and hurried out of her office to meet them.

"How are your feeling this morning, Jev?" she immediately asked without even so much as a simple hello to either of them, or even acknowledging the orderly who had brought them there.

"Fine I guess. A little queasy though. But thanks to those

pills you gave me yesterday I don't feel like I have to throw up," Jev answered.

Tiela smiled and nodded. She then invited them through an open doorway opposite her office and into a large windowless and dimly-lit room. It was mostly empty except for a number of beds, similar to the ones he had seen in the medical bay on the *Cetani,* along the far wall. On the long wall, above each of the beds, was a monitor. Most were not active, except for one, which Tiela guided them toward.

"Alright, Jev. Hop on up," Tiela instructed as she picked up a pad from a tray beside the bed.

No sooner did Jev get up onto the bed when a pair of bright lights above the him flickered to life. He had to squint against their brightness for a moment until his eyes managed to get accustomed to the light. Tiela pressed a few commands into her pad, and he watched with curiosity as two arched metal arms extended from either side of the bed to encircle his torso and lower abdomen, clicking together when they met in the middle.

"It's a diagnostic imaging scanner," Tiela explained, seeing his curious look. "It'll help me determine how far along your are and how your cub is doing."

Jev gave her a little flick of his ears in understanding. The device gave no indication that it was working, but from Tiela's expression, and the way that she manipulated the controls on the scanner he knew that it must be.

For several impossibly long minutes he lay there on the table, waiting anxiously and wondering why it was taking Tiela so long. But wisely he kept his mouth shut. He knew she would not take kindly to being interrupted when she was working and his impatience would only serve to slow her down.

Finally, at last, the device separated and retracted back into the sides of the bed. Kiyel helped him to sit up.

"So what are the results, Tiela?" Kiyel asked, his tail swaying impatiently. He was just as anxious as Jev to find out how their cub was doing.

Tiela looked up at them from the pad she was holding, a wide smile stretching across her face.

"It would appear your cub is doing just fine," she answered. "It's a normal Caitaran gestation and I would say from these scans that you are about one week along in your pregnancy, Jev."

Jev let out an audible sigh of relief, releasing the breath he wasn't even aware he had been holding.

"Would you like to see your cub?" Tiela asked.

"You can do that already?" Jev asked, surprised, as he hopped off the bed, his ears pricked up with definite interest.

"The computer is able to project a three dimensional holographic representation of your cub from the DNA data it collected," Tiela nodded.

Jev looked at Kiyel excitedly, his tail flicking anxiously.

Kiyel almost laughed at his Enassi's excitement. And the truth was, he was just as curious to know what their cub would look like as he was. He smiled and nodded to Tiela.

"Show us, Tiela," he said.

They walked with Tiela to a work station off to the side of the Infirmary, where Tiela then punched a few commands into her pad. and once the computer signaled its readiness, she activated the holo-emitters. A few feet from them, suspended in mid air was a semi-transparent image of a very young Caitaran cub. A soft downy coat of fur covered its tightly curled up body, featuring colours never seen on a Caitaran before. The fur was predominantly white, but there were areas that were orange and dark brown as well. The fur on its head was especially long, and almost looked more like human hair.

Kiyel noticed something else as well.

"It's a girl," he said quietly.

"You're right, Kiyel, she is," Tiela said.

"She's beautiful," Jev said, his eyes moistening.

Kiyel put an arm around Jev.

She is that, Enassi, he sent.

I want to name her Nica,

Kiyel pulled away suddenly and looked at Jev with startlement.

How did you know that name? he asked.

Jev shrugged.

I don't know, the name just came to me.

Nica was the name of my younger sister, Kiyel sent softly.

Now it was Jev's turn to give Kiyel a startled look.

I didn't know you had a sister.

She would be three now. But she arrived stillborn. She was buried out in the gardens.

Jev could clearly feel the anguish in his Enassi's mind and he held his hand.

Do you think your mother would mind if we gave our cub your sister's name?

Kiyel smiled.

No, I think she would be happy.

"So, do you have any idea how Jev wound up getting pregnant in the first place, Tiela?" Kiyel asked aloud.

"Sam discussed a possibility with me yesterday. He suggested that some of your … seed … could have seeped inside Jev when the two of you were being intimate."

Kiyel nodded as though in understanding, but his expression was still confused.

"He indicated that human females have been known to

get pregnant even if penetration didn't occur. Her body would naturally draw the seed into her," she quickly added.

"But Jev's not human, Tiela," Kiyel said.

"Nor am I fully Caitaran, either," Jev reminded him quietly.

Kiyel conceded Jev's point with an embarrassed flick of his ears.

Changing the subject to avoid causing Kiyel further embarrassment, Tiela quickly went over with Jev a few of the details that he would need to know as his pregnancy progressed. She also supplied him with more of the pills should he again begin to experience nausea.

After they had thanked her and left the infirmary to return to the estate, smiles beaming on both of their proud faces, Tiela returned to her office and called up the image of their cub on her terminal's monitor. Her brow furrowed and her tail began to flick with apprehension as a sudden fear took a hold of her.

A new species is going to be born, she thought. *But will she be accepted by the Prides?*

Despite all the advances in Caitaran society, one undeniable fact remained: there still existed within the Prides a strong desire to protect the integrity of their bloodlines. While feelings were not as extreme as those that had existed within the radical Chemian movement all those years ago, Tiela nevertheless knew there was bound to be a backlash toward Jev and Kiyel once it was discovered that their unborn cub would not be fully Caitaran.

A jubilant Jev and Kiyel returned to the estate and immediately sought out Kiyel's mother, who was at that moment seated at her desk working on some of the paperwork that had been accumulating during her absence. So excited were they, in fact, that they didn't even bother knocking on her office door, or waiting for her to tell them to come in. They simply rushed into her office, startling her and almost causing her to drop the pad she held in her hand.

"Kiyel, you know better than to come barging in on me like that," she admonished him, ears flicking in annoyance. But then she noticed their excitement. "What is it?" she asked, her tone softening.

"We're going to have a daughter!" Kiyel blurted out, unable to contain his joy.

Lheiza, her displeasure immediately forgotten, hurried from behind her desk to gather him in an especially tight embrace. The suddenness of her embrace, though welcome, surprised him, for telepaths as a rule, after all, avoided physical contact with others, even within families.

"Congratulations!" she exclaimed, gushing with happiness for them.

She released Kiyel and hugged Jev similarly, though he thought she held him just a little more tightly than she did Kiyel. Had Jev been human, he would have been blushing. As it was, though, he allowed himself to be held by Kiyel's mother.

"We decided we're going to name her Nica," Kiyel added.

Lheiza abruptly let Jev go and stared at Kiyel, her eyes wide and ears flicking in startlement.

"You named her Nica?" she echoed quietly, almost in a whisper.

Jev could sense the flood of emotions that flashed across Lheiza's face—sorrow, anger, regret, self-recrimination—even as tears began welling up in her eyes.

"It was my suggestion actually," Jev said quietly. "Kiyel

told me that you had lost a daughter in childbirth. I don't know how I came up with the name, but Kiyel and I would like to name our daughter Nica in memory of the daughter you lost."

Lheiza smiled at Jev and drew him into another embrace. Jev could feel her gratitude and he hugged her back.

Oh thank you, Jev. That is the most thoughtful thing anyone has ever done for me, she sent as her tears fell upon Jev's tunic.

When they separated, although tears still filled her eyes, she was smiling.

"Come on, my son, we must tell your father," she said to Kiyel.

NINETEEN

Their excitement waned a little, though, the moment they stepped into Sahl's office to deliver the news, when they saw that Sahl wasn't alone. Instead they were curious to see Riyad present as well, but not as they had ever seen him before. He was now wearing what Jev could only describe as a type of dark, ceremonial, hooded robe with large embroidered Caitaran script, of a type he didn't recognize, on the cuffs. Attached to a black belt around his waist, which he wore over a dark leather formed tunic, hung a long knife nestled inside a brown scabbard, emblazoned with an intricate gold weaved pattern.

"We've been waiting for you, Jev," Sahl said.

"Father, what's going on?" Kiyel asked, for the first time feeling uneasy in Riyad's presence and instinctively stepping between Jev and Riyad as though ready to protect his Enassi.

"It's time for Jev to come with me to the Warrior's Guild to begin his training for the challenge," Riyad answered.

"You're going to train me?" Jev asked, with a note of incredulity in his voice. He had, in fact, expected it would be either Kel or Jaffay who would offer to train him.

"Riyad belongs to a quasi-religious order called the Order of Dahel that is closely associated with both the Warrior's Guild and the Telepath Guild, but belongs to neither. From time to time the Order is hired by the Telepath Guild to evaluate telepaths with potentially wild talents to see if they can be taught to control their talents." Sahl explained.

"Unfortunately, sometimes they cannot and it becomes necessary for us to make sure they can never pose a threat," Riyad added.

The implications of Riyad's revelation sent chills up and down Jev's spine. He was now beginning to understand Sahl's earlier reluctance to have Riyad in his home, and he didn't like it any more than Sahl did. That Riyad actually hunted down and killed telepaths whose talents were deemed dangerous was unfathomable to him, and quite alarming. Kiyel, he felt, was just as disturbed as he was. His tail had begun flicking in agitation.

"Is that what you were doing on the Cetani, evaluating us to see if we had a wild talent?" Kiyel asked, eyes narrowing at Riyad.

"In part, my Lord," Riyad said evenly, his ears dipping apologetically. "But mostly I was, and still am, tasked with ensuring the safety of you and your Enassi." A barely perceptible grin tugged at the corner of his lips. "I figured the easiest way to accomplish that was to become your aide."

"So who hired you?" Kiyel asked.

Riyad shook his head as a slight frown creased his lips.

"I'm sorry, my Lord, my contract prevents me from revealing my employer to you or to any one else."

"There is one thing I am curious about," Jev interjected,

hoping to reduce the growing tension in the room. "Who is this 'Dahel' I keep hearing about?" he asked.

By the surprised stares he received, he thought maybe it was a foolish question.

But then Sahl began to chuckle lightly.

"I'd forgotten that while you have Kiyel's memories thanks to your link with him, you're not aware of the knowledge until it is shown to you," he said.

"Dahel is the founder of our society," Riyad began to explain. He had a reverent tone in his voice. "Several millenia ago our world was fractured by conflict between the Prides as they fought over land and power. Dahel was a simple, yet charismatic, farmer who managed to gather together a coalition of telepaths and warriors, who, like him, saw the inevitable destructive conclusion should the constant fighting continue. Under his leadership, they were able to bring together the leaders of the Prides in the hopes of ending the conflict. As a result of those negotiations, the guilds were eventually established. And except for the short period where our entire world was threatened by the Chemian dissident group, we have lived together in peace."

"This estate was built by a descendent of one of those telepaths, our family's ancestor. It was named after him and has been in our family ever since," Sahl finished.

Jev's ears flicked in appreciation as he thanked them with an acknowledging nod.

"Father, I take it since Riyad is here to begin Jev's training that you haven't had any luck getting Muri's father to convince Muri to withdraw the challenge," Kiyel said.

"I'm afraid so," Sahl answered with a tired sigh. "Muri is being as obstinate as ever. She is adamant that the challenge will not be withdrawn."

"Sahl, Jev and Kiyel are going to have a girl. They've chosen to name her Nica, after our daughter," Lheiza told him.

Surprised by this news, Sahl looked at Jev, his ears pricking up. Jev could see the sadness in his eyes and knew he still grieved the loss of his daughter, even as a tiny smile tugged at the corner of his lips. But then Sahl shook his head and frowned deeply.

"I'm sorry, Jev. I wish there was something more I could do to end this damned challenge."

It was the first time Jev had heard Sahl swear and he was taken aback slightly by it. His ears folded back against his skull, showing his distress, for he was, after all, in part responsible for the predicament he now found himself in. Now, more than ever, he wished he'd never accepted Muri's challenge in the first place.

"I guess I'm just going to have to be resigned to the fact that I will be fighting Muri, whether I want to or not," he said quietly, lowering his gaze.

"So it would seem," Sahl reluctantly agreed.

Over the course of the next couple of weeks, Jev was made to endure a grueling training regimen with Riyad, learning various advanced hand-to-hand combat techniques. Never before in his young life had his muscles complained as much as they did the first few days of intense training, which began at the crack of dawn and didn't finish until near sundown. His training, in fact, was so rigorous that by the end of each day he didn't even have the strength to remove his clothing before collapsing in bed from exhaustion.

It was only thanks to Kiyel, who had accompanied him to the Warriors Guild and even took part in some of the training, that Jev was able to make it past the first week at all. At the end of each day Kiyel was always there to help soothe his aching muscles by giving him a firm, but relaxing, massage that wound up putting Jev to sleep.

Although Jev's training almost always resulted in him being covered in cuts and bruises, Riyad was constantly mindful of the fact that Jev was with child and made allowances for his condition, insisting that Jev take a break whenever he seemed to tire to the point that he could barely move, much less fight. During those breaks, Jev was given plenty of k'yarri to help recover his strength, but not food, which he was only permitted two times a day.

By the beginning of the second week, though, Jev found he had developed muscles he did not even know existed. As a result, he found the training getting easier with every passing day, though it had actually become more intense as Jev became more proficient in the techniques Riyad was teaching him.

Combined with his training with Riyad, Jev was also required to attend testing and training at the Telepath Guild, where they sought to determine the strength of his seemingly endless talents. Although he had demonstrated a substantial telekinetic ability—as evidenced by his dramatic change back on Alessi—numerous subsequent attempts to test this talent failed, and it was eventually determined that Jev's telekinetic talent may, in fact, only have been the result of the extreme stress he was under while on Alessi. They concluded, though, that, like Kiyel, he was indeed a first class telepath, which was certainly no surprise to either him or Kiyel as they both were discovering that with every passing day their combined talent was significantly stronger than the most proficient Caitaran tested thus far.

When the day of the challenge finally arrived, Jev was

feeling quite confident in his ability to hold his own against Muri, whom he had no doubt had also been training for their challenge. But he had doubts as well. He felt torn between being ready to fight for all he was worth, and regretting the fact that he would have to inflict serious bodily harm to someone he barely even knew, except in passing as they confronted one another back at the shuttle port on the day he and Kiyel arrived.

He knew what the rules of engagement were, though. Riyad had, after all, drilled it into him enough times during the past two weeks. It was a winner take all fight. Only two outcomes were possible: either he would be dead or Muri would. He just didn't know if he really could go through with the final blow, should it come to that, and he wanted desperately to find an alternative conclusion to this challenge, one that did not result in either Muri or him getting killed.

Both families, along with their supporters—Tiela and Sam among them, who, besides supporting Jev, were also present to render medical aid which would likely be required— gathered out of range of the combat area proper, but near the small clearing in the gardens of the estate, where it had been designated the challenge would be fought. Not a single word was spoken amongst them as they began arranging themselves along opposite sides of the of the clearing. The tension on the field was rapidly growing until it had become so thick, it could almost be cut with a dull blade.

After much fussing about, the two combatants finally entered the field, staring down at each other. There was no arbitrator telling them to begin. They just did. Neither one taking their eyes off the other as they circled the perimeter of the field.

Jev could feel Kiyel's fear, but he pushed it out of his mind. He couldn't afford any distractions, not when his life, and that of their cub, was at risk. As they continued to circle, Jev felt the adrenaline pumping into his system, increasing his anxiety, but also filling him with the energy he knew he'd need for this fight.

The first move was made by Muri, who came straight at him, her front claws extended as she let out a massive blood curdling battle cry. Naked, unbridled fury filled her eyes, making her initial attack sloppy, and Jev was easily able to dodge as he deftly leaped out of the way.

"Is that the best you can do, coward?" she taunted him as they began circling once again.

Jev knew she was trying to goad him into lashing out in anger, which, thanks to his training with Riyad, he knew would be a mistake. He somehow kept his emotions in check as he continued to watch her. He noticed that she tended to dance on her feet, as though trying to keep him guessing from where she'd attack. But he knew also that her constant moving about was costing her her strength. All he had to do was remain patient.

Again, she struck, lashing out at him in the same manner as before. Again he dodged, but suddenly she shifted, dropping low and striking out with her left foot which landed a solid hit on his leg.

He grunted in pain as a long gash on his leg began bleeding. For a second, he almost faltered, but through sheer force of will, he remained standing. She laughed with glee as she backed away, easily evading his weak attempt to strike back at her.

The pain in his leg was agonizing. He knew without looking that the wound was bad, but he concentrated and pushed the pain aside, instead, focusing all his attention on Muri. She still danced, this time more confidently than before, as though she believed the fight was already won.

He suddenly saw an opening and struck out at her, just

barely grazing her arm with his claws. She was no longer laughing. A vicious snarl came from her throat as she launched into another attack of her own, taking Jev by surprise and knocking him down. Suddenly she was upon him, reigning blow after blow upon his face and chest, most of which he was able to deflect or stop entirely. Some of her blows, however, landed, creating long cuts from her claws.

Somehow, he was able to get his foot under her and with a tremendous heave, he kicked her off him, and just barely managed to scramble to his feet before she was on him again. This time the advantage was his. She had grown overconfident and let her guard down just enough for him to land a powerful blow to her belly, creating four deep slashing cuts across her skin.

She howled with pain, gripping her stomach, and looking at him with disbelief. Anger had taken hold of her and she launched into a sudden ferocious attack and Jev once again found himself on the ground defending against her attacks.

The gash in his leg was deep enough that he was bleeding profusely from it, as well as from the numerous wounds that covered his arms, chest and face. Already, he was growing weak from the loss of blood and he knew he had to act quickly to end this. With the last of his remaining strength, he pulled her down to him unexpectedly and clamped his jaws shut on her throat, pressing down on it hard enough to draw blood, the bitter taste of it filling his mouth. Then, when she was distracted by his sudden attack, he pushed off with his leg to roll them over, reversing their positions so that he was now on top. His jaws were still firmly clamped around her throat, and before she had a chance to recover, he quickly positioned himself so that her arms were restrained and she was unable to move her feet, preventing her from using them to rake his exposed belly.

She stared up at him, fear in her eyes, as she found herself held in a death grip. What's more, she suddenly realized that escaping from his grip was impossible, as every muscle in her body was frozen stiff, as though her body was in the throes of an immobilizing seizure. There was no doubt in her mind that Jev was somehow responsible, but by the way he continued to hold her down, she also didn't think that he was even conscious that he was doing it.

Submit, she heard his voice in her head.

Never, she answered, defiantly, even as his jaws tightened on her throat even further, making it difficult for her to breath.

I do not wish to kill you, Muri, but I will if I must, to protect my child, he sent.

She reacted to that, her eyes opening wide with shock at Jev's revelation.

Yes, I am pregnant with Kiyel's child.

When her father had come to her to deliver the news that Jev was with child, and urging her to withdraw her challenge, she quickly dismissed it as preposterous. After all, it was impossible for a male to become pregnant. But now somehow, she suddenly knew it was really true. She didn't know how, but somehow she could feel that it was. Yet despite this, she still could not let go of her hatred for him.

You do not hate me, Miru, Jev sent, as though he had heard her thoughts. *It is fear that you feel—the fear of being alone. Your whole life you have felt that no one paid any attention to you other than because of your connection to Kiyel. You are afraid that I am now taking him away from you. You have to live your own life, and let yourself discover your own strengths, and most importantly, you must be honest with yourself about your true worth. You have a talent, Muri. It is a very important talent; one that could be used for good, if you are willing. But you have to let go of your resentment of me. For the sake of the future you could have, and for the life of my child, I implore you to submit.*

I don't want to be alone, she sent back, suddenly afraid, not for her own life, but for facing the world alone.

You will not be alone. You have both your family and ours.

You would welcome me, despite what I've done to you both?

Yes.

This time the voice was not Jev's, but Kiyel's. She felt Jev's grip on her loosening, and she drew in a deep breath, but he did not release her entirely. She was still trapped, unable to move.

Muri, I have always cared for you, but I deeply resented our fathers' desires to see us become lifemates. I had to leave to find my own way. It's time that you find yours, Kiyel sent.

After several long seconds, she closed her eyes, and opened them again, coming to a decision.

I submit, she sent.

Almost immediately, she was released, both from Jev's grip and from the mysterious force that held her motionless. She watched as Jev climbed off her and slowly backed away cautiously, still keeping a wary eye on her.

Slowly she rose to her feet. Her ears folded against her skull and her tail dropped as she lowered her face in submission.

"I submit," she said in a clear voice, so as to be clearly heard by everyone around them.

A collective sigh of relief could be heard as her father rushed out from the crowd to embrace her. She welcomed his embrace, holding him tightly as she sobbed into his shoulder.

Over and over again she told him she was sorry, and he just held onto her like he did when she was just a little cub.

She opened her eyes to look at Jev, just as he suddenly dropped to his knees. He'd lost too much blood and was close to losing consciousness.

"Jev!" she screamed, and letting go of her father she rushed to Jev's side.

He smiled up at her, reassuringly while Tiela, Kiyel, and Sam hurried to his side also.

"I'm so sorry, Jev," she whispered, while they gently lay Jev down.

Suddenly, from the crowd, the small child that she had seen accompanying them at the shuttle port twist free of the Caitaran who'd caught him as he charged across the field, and hurried to Jev's side. She watched, with shocked awe as he lay his hands on Jev's wounds and saw them miraculously being healed. Jev's breathing, which had become laboured, was once again strong and steady, and she could see his strength already returning to him, albeit slowly.

Jev's eyes opened slowly, gazing up at Aiden. He wasn't in the least bit surprised that Aiden had somehow found his way to him. He smiled up at Aiden appreciatively, but by then Aiden was already beginning to slump forward as he lost consciousness. Muri caught him before he hit the ground, and held him delicately like she would a precious package. Sam, seeing Aiden slip into unconsciousness, quickly checked on him, sighing with relief when he discovered that he had only just fallen asleep.

Tears filled Muri's eyes as she looked down at the small child in her arms. She did not know why, but all of a sudden, she felt as though a tremendous weight had been lifted from her shoulders. She felt a tingling sensation all over and for reasons she couldn't explain, she thought it came from Aiden, despite the fact he was unconscious.

She looked up at Sam, who smiled reassuringly at her.

"Aiden is Jev's brother. He's an empath and a healer. He just needs to sleep now to recover his strength."

"I feel him doing something to me," Muri said softly.

"He does that to everyone."

Jev sat up with the help of Kiyel. His wounds were completely healed, although the clothes he was wearing were shredded beyond recognition from their fight. Jev and Kiyel looked at Muri, cradling Aiden in her arms.

"This is your talent, Muri," Kiyel said.

"What is?" Muri asked, not understanding.

"You're an empath, just like Aiden," Kiyel explained. "We both sensed that back at the shuttle port. Only, Jev was able to pick up on it first."

"An empath?" Muri echoed quietly, her nose wrinkling in thought as she considered the unexpected revelation. In fact, until Sam spoke it, she had never heard that word before.

"I think I should put Aiden to bed no," Sam said.

But as he moved to take Aiden from Muri, she stood and held him more tightly to her chest, shaking her head at Sam.

"No, if it's alright with you, I'd like to do it," she said.

At first Sam was hesitant, but after receiving reassuring nods from both Jev and Kiyel, he agreed to let her.

After moving back into the estate, both families gathered in the library, where Nuria immediately set about getting refreshments for everyone, while Muri and Sam went upstairs to put Aiden into his bed to get some much needed rest.

Khelan, having followed Muri and Sam with Aiden into his and Aiden's room, offered to stay with him and watch over him while he slept.

Though surprised, Sam was grateful that Khelan would do this when instead he could be downstairs with his family and their guests. He thanked Khelan, playfully ruffling the fur on his head, which had begun to grow long, much like Jev's, he noticed. Khelan, of course, protested and tried to put his fur right again, but he was giggling happily at the same time.

Jev, meanwhile, also had gone up the stairs, heading for his and Kiyel's room so he could get out of his torn and muddied clothing and into something more comfortable. He had to be helped up the stairs by Kiyel, however. For although his injuries were fully healed, thanks to Aiden, Jev still felt drained from the ordeal and was a little unsteady on his feet. Rather than putting his discarded clothes into the hamper like he normally did, he quickly tossed them out into the garbage chute in the hallway. He did this not only because they were no longer useful to him—they were beyond repair—but also because he did not want to keep them as they would only serve as an ugly reminder of his fight with Muri and how close he had come to losing Kiyel forever, as well as their unborn cub.

Upon joining the others back downstairs, they could both sense the tension that had permeated the field during the challenge had lessened significantly, but not entirely. The conversation around the room was light, consisting mainly of small talk, with everyone being careful to avoid anything having to do with the challenge, much to Jev's appreciation.

While scanning the room, Jev found Muri sitting alone on a couch tucked away in the corner, far from everyone else, including her own family, and looking quite miserable. During the fight, Muri's clothing hadn't fared any better than his, so he was a little surprised to see that she had in fact changed into some of Kiyel's mother's clothes, who had graciously lent to her. The wounds she had sustained during the challenge had also been treated.

As soon as they entered the library, she looked up, but then quickly averted her gaze from them when she saw them.

Jev at once felt sorry for her. All her life she had held certain dreams. As time went on, those dreams had, somehow, become expectations. She had become trapped by a system that never gave her the chance to live her own life, just as Kiyel had, before he found a way to escape. And now she was feeling both lost and ashamed of herself.

With a nod from Kiyel, who also could sense Muri's inner turmoil, they made their way to her and sat down with her. She tried to get up, still refusing to look at either of them, but they gently coaxed her back down.

You don't have to leave, Muri, Jev sent reassuringly. He wanted to keep this conversation between them so he did not speak aloud. Kiyel and I have forgiven you. We don't blame you for what happened.

This time she did look up at him, but with a surprised expression, the tip of her tail flicking nervously on her lap.

After what I did, what I almost did, I don't understand how you can say that, she sent, slightly unnerved that although she was not a full telepath, she could so easily talk with Jev this way.

Because you were as much a victim of a system that denied you your freedom as it did me, Kiyel sent. *Neither of us was given the chance to have our own dreams. Every moment was dictated to us by tradition, from the moment we were born.*

Muri slowly nodded in understanding, recognizing the truth Kiyel was telling her, and seeing it now for the first time in her life. It made her angry.

I was promised a fairy tale life by my parents. And I eventually came to expect it. Then when that life appeared to be slipping away from me, for the first time in my life, my future was uncertain, and I became afraid.

You don't have to be afraid any longer, Jev sent, offering her a reassuring grin.

She smiled back.

"May I?" she asked, her hand hovering over Jev's stomach.

Jev knew right away what she wanted and he nodded.

"She's only a week old, so there's nothing to feel yet," Kiyel said.

"No, there is," she said, her ears pricking up with surprise. "I don't know how, but I can actually feel her, in my mind."

Jev was about to respond when all of a sudden, he heard the unmistakable sound of tiny footsteps coming down the stairs, even through the din of the library. He looked over to the library doors and saw Khelan and a very sleepy-looking Aiden appear.

Well, that was a quick nap, Kiyel observed through their link.

Jev nodded in agreement. He was just as surprised as Kiyel was that Aiden had woken already. Clearly his talent was growing stronger.

Lheiza, who had been engaged in a quiet conversation with Tiela and Sam, apparently also noticed the two boys standing there and turned her attention to them.

"What is it, Khelan?" she asked.

"It's Aiden."

"Is there something wrong?" Sam quickly asked, standing up abruptly from his seat.

"I'm thirsty," Aiden said quietly.

Sam smiled as he visibly relaxed and made his way to them.

"Then let's go get you something to drink," he said.

Nuria, who had been sitting alone near the door in case one of the guests needed more refreshments, stood to help. But he quickly let her know he would take care of it, by waving her back down.

"Me, too?" Khelan asked.

Receiving a nod from Lheiza, Sam laughed.

"You, too," Sam said as he then led them from the Library.

Before they disappeared, though, Jev was shocked to see Sam lean over and suddenly give Nuria a quick peck on the cheek. Although he couldn't see it underneath all her fur, Jev knew she was blushing and a knowing smile crept over his lips.

TWENTY

With the challenge now resolved, there was no longer any reason for Sahl's continued objection to Jev and Kiyel formalizing their relationship. In the short time that Jev had been with them, Sahl had grown quite fond of him as Lheiza had, and readily gave his blessing to Kiyel for them to become lifemates.

Preparations for the Bonding Ceremony began almost immediately the next day after the last of Muri's family had left the estate. Lheiza wasted no time insisting on taking charge of organizing everything herself, which Jev and Kiyel didn't object to. Very quickly they discovered how daunting a task organizing such an event would be, and the both welcomed her intervention gladly.

It was quickly, and unanimously, agreed that the gardens behind the estate house would be the perfect venue for the ceremony as they could easily accommodate all the guests. Jev also thought it appropriate considering the last time he was in the gardens it was to fight Muri's challenge. The last thing he wanted was for the gardens, as beautiful as they were, to be a constant reminder of the ugliness of that experience, a sentiment, he was sure, was shared by everyone else as well.

The only drawback to ceding control to Lheiza was that although Jev and Kiyel were deeply involved in deciding many of the details—it was their ceremony, after all—they were nevertheless forbidden by Lheiza from seeing it all come together.

On the other hand, it afforded them the unique opportunity to do the one thing Jev had been itching to do since they first arrived in Ethineas, and that was to tour the city.

They were just getting to leave when a disturbing thought suddenly occurred to Jev.

"Kiyel, how am I to pay for anything?"

"You don't have to worry about that. Ever since we were joined as Enassi you've been a part of the Caitaran military, so I suspect there is a sizable amount in your bank account already," Kiyel said.

Confused, Jev looked at Kiyel incredulously.

"How can I have a bank account? I've never set one up. In fact, I haven't even been to one of your banks before."

"It would have been set up for you by the forces, and your pay retroactively issued to you when we were rescued," Kiyel explained. His ears then dipped apologetically. "I'm sorry, Ensasi. I did not realize that this had not been explained to you on the *Cetani*."

A wide grin then stretched across Jev's face.

"Well, what are we waiting for? Let's go do some shopping," he said, eagerly, causing Kiyel to laugh.

Once again they opted to travel on foot rather than hire an air car, which Riyad again offered them. They declined, but

Riyad still insisted that he accompany them into the city.

Kiyel frowned at this, for he was hoping to spend the time alone with Jev. He relented only when Riyad promised to remain largely out of their sight, but where he could still watch over them. Jev thought it was a reasonable compromise. Still, he thought it ridiculous that Riyad thought there could be any further threat to them. After all, they had long ago been told that every one of Hraka's associates had either been arrested or killed while attempting to flee, and as far as anyone knew, there were no other members of that group still unaccounted for.

True to his word, Riyad hung back, allowing Jev and Kiyel the time alone that they both needed and wanted, as they traveled the road that would lead them into the inner city.

No sooner had they reached the downtown core when Jev's nose was assailed by the mouthwatering smells of freshly baked breads and pastries, newly caught fish and prepared foods of all sorts. Despite having eaten a rather large first meal before heading out that morning, Jev's stomach noisily growled. It was loud enough that Kiyel easily heard it.

Jev's ears dipped slightly in embarrassment.

"I guess I'm still a little hungry," he said sheepishly.

"A little?" Kiyel echoed, shaking his head incredulously, with a wide grin on his face.

"Well, I am eating for two now," Jev reminded him, gently rubbing his abdomen.

Kiyel led Jev down the familiar streets of his old stomping grounds, which were empty save for the row of trees running down the center and a number of Caitarans going about their business, to a small restaurant, which coincidently was the same one he had frequented often during his many trips into the city.

The moment they entered the establishment Jev heard

someone excitedly calling out Kiyel's name. They turned and saw a group of young Caitarans, about Kiyel's age, sitting at a table by the front window. Jev immediately recognized them as Kiyel's friends from when he was a student at the Guild Academy.

They all appeared to be quite happy and excited to see Kiyel. But none more so than one of them, a small female with an almost completely white coat of fur, except for a small patch of grey above her brow, who leaped out of her chair and rushed toward them.

"Kiyel!" she screamed excitedly, in a shrill voice that was so piercing that it caused Jev to wince and instinctively fold his ears back against his skull to protect them.

The suddenness of her rushing embrace caught Kiyel slightly off guard for a moment, but he quickly recovered, returning her embrace affectionately as he was reunited with an old friend.

"It's good to see you, too, Kiera," he said.

Jev smiled as the rest of the small group got up to welcome Kiyel back, each one just as excited as Kiera, though their greetings were far less painful, much to Jev's thankful relief.

Still smiling, and even giggling with glee, Kiera grabbed both of their arms and began leading them back to their table, where two more chairs were brought over for them to sit in.

No sooner had they sat down when Kiyel was inundated with a barrage of questions.

"What happened to you?" one asked.

"Where did you go?" another one asked.

Kiyel patiently answered all of their questions as best he could. Some he had to decline answering, however, as it was still considered classified information by the Caitaran Forces. It was not until they turned their attention to Jev that Kiyel was finally able to introduce him to them.

"This is Jev, my Enassi," he said.

All eyes turned on Jev, looks of surprise and wonder on each of their faces.

Kiera looked Jev up and down appraisingly, as they all did.

"He almost looks female," she said quietly.

"Kiera!" one of the other females in the group admonished, elbowing Kiera sharply in the ribs.

"You'll have to forgive my sister. She can sometimes be a bit insensitive. My name is Elori," she said.

Jev knew from the feel of her mind that she had no talent, so he was surprised to see her greeting him as a telepath would. As he returned her greeting gratefully, he could sense that she had, in fact, spent a lot of time amongst telepaths, explaining why she would be greeting him in this manner.

"Thank you, Elori. I wasn't offended, though," he assured her. "She is, in fact, partially correct. I'm actually a bit of both."

"We've recently discovered that Jev was born with both male and female reproductive organs," Kiyel explained when he saw their confused faces.

"Kiyel, how is that possible?" the lone male in the group asked.

"Well, Dezik, when I first met Jev he was not as he appears now. He was actually human, and it's how on rare occasions some of them are born."

Jev had to contain an amused grin when he saw the shocked reactions on each of their faces, their mouths hanging wide open, at the revelation.

Show them, Kiyel sent.

A collective gasp rang out around the table as Jev concentrated, focusing his mind on those around him, until with a little effort he once again looked like the human he once was to the assembled group.

Kiera, sitting closest to him, tentatively reached out to touch his arm, jerking her hand away with surprise when her fingers touched fur instead of the pale, naked skin she saw.

Jev found that he was only able to maintain the illusion for a short time, though. A sudden wave of dizziness overcame him, forcing him to grip the edge of the table for support, and very quickly the illusion faded away.

Kiyel both seeing and feeling his sudden weakness, frowned and hurried from the table to the counter where refreshments and food were being served.

"Are you alright, Jev?" Elori asked, looking as concerned as the others with his sudden discomfort.

Jev nodded weakly and smiled at her reassuringly.

Kiyel returned with two cups of k'yarri which he placed in front of Jev.

"Well, I don't think I'll be doing that again anytime soon," Jev said, with some embarrassment, drinking the first cup quickly and already beginning to feel the k'yarri's effects and his strength returning.

"What just happened?" the last female of the group asked, who introduced herself as Alisa.

"I forgot that I've got other demands on my strength these days," Jev said, looking down at himself. "You see, I'm pregnant."

They were met with a stunned silence that, to Jev, seemed to last for an eternity. It was Keira who ultimately broke the silence, doing so by rushing from her chair and throwing her arms around Jev in a lingering embrace.

"I'm so happy for you!" she said excitedly. Still holding Jev she looked back at Kiyel. "For the both of you!"

"Thanks, Kiera," Jev said quietly, somewhat bewildered by her sudden display of affection, especially for someone she had just met.

"Jev and I are to be bonded as lifemates also."

"Wait a minute, what about that Muri character, the one your father had you betrothed to?" Elori asked, her tone turning sour as she practically spat Muri's name.

"She's the reason you left, isn't it?" Dezik added.

"She never seemed the sort to let something like that go so easily," Dezik snorted derisively.

"No, she wasn't," Kiyel conceded in a sullen voice. "She, in fact, issued a challenge."

"But that's against the law!" Kiera said with alarm. It was a reaction that could be seen on each of their faces as they looked at Kiyel. "Telepaths can't be challenged."

"Nevertheless, a challenge was issued, accepted and ultimately fought."

"You actually fought her, Kiyel?" Dezik asked, unable to believe what he was hearing.

"Actually, I did," Jev admitted.

"So, does that mean she's dead then? Challenges are generally to the death, after all," Kiera said.

Jev shook his head.

"I didn't want to kill her; I had no reason to. So I convinced her to submit instead."

"But how were you able to fight in the first place? Telepaths are incapable of fighting," Elori pointed out.

Jev smiled weekly.

"That's a limitation that human telepaths don't suffer from," he explained. "We're perfectly capable of fighting if necessary, although we don't like doing it. And now, because Kiyel and I are linked, he's acquired that trait as well."

"So there's more than one human telepath then?" Dezik asked.

"There's one other that we're aware of," Kiyel said. "And we know that Jev's adopted younger brother is a very strong empath."

"So then, when's this ceremony to take place?" Kiera asked, clearly wanting to change the subject to something more pleasant.

Kiera's infectious smile and gentle demeanor made it impossible for Jev not to like her. His father would have said that she was blessed with a sunny disposition. Jev couldn't resist smiling at her enthusiasm.

"It hasn't been decided yet. My mother is currently making all the arrangements," Kiyel answered.

"Which is why we came here, because she's forbidden us from seeing everything come together," Jev added.

Just then his stomach rumbled again, more noisily this time than before, he was sure.

"And to feed this one's insatiable appetite," Kiyel added.

This caused laughter from everyone at the table, including Jev, who, although a little embarrassed that his hungry stomach could draw so much attention to him, couldn't help himself.

"Remember, I am eating for two now, Kiyel," Jev again reminded him, which caused another round of laughter.

As Kiyel got up from the table to order the food they came in to eat, Jev turned to the others.

"Kiyel just suggested that we invite you all to come celebrate our bonding ceremony with us," he said.

"You're linked that closely that you can read each other

330 | JASON FINIGAN

like that?" Dezik asked, clearly surprised.

"Even more so," Jev nodded with a wry grin.

"Jev, I think I speak for all of us here when I say you and Kiyel needn't have had to ask. Just tell us the place and time of the ceremony and we'll be there," Elori said.

There were nods of agreement all around the table, and Jev couldn't have been more happy.

As the anticipated day of the Bonding Ceremony finally came upon them, guests slowly began to arrive at the estate. Among them was the entire crew from the Lekur, which Jev and Kiyel were overjoyed to see. There were embraces all around, even from the normally stoic Jaffay, who couldn't hold back the grin of happiness for them that appeared to be permanently pasted to his face. With him were his wife, Awyn, and their young daughter, Jisa. As expected, because of his infectious smile and playful demeanor, she and Aiden became quick friends and were almost inseparable. They played together with Khelan out in the gardens and generally getting in the way of everyone else who were trying to get everything ready for the ceremony.

Of course Kiera and the rest of Kiyel's friends came, just as they said they would, and were quickly introduced to Kel and Tiela—who arrived together, arm in arm—and the rest of the crew.

From the very beginning Jev knew that he wanted Sam to give him away to Kiyel. When asked, Sam immediately drew him into a long, loving embrace, and he even thought he felt a tear or two fall onto his shoulder. Sam, of course, readily agreed to be the one to walk him down the aisle.

He was just finishing helping to put plates out on the table set up in the library, when he all of a sudden heard a familiar, but unexpected voice coming from the main foyer. He turned slowly, not daring to believe his ears, when he caught sight of the one person he didn't expect to see coming into the room. With tears of joy welling up in his eyes, he put down the plates he was holding, almost dropping them, and rushed headlong into his brother's arms. Crying openly, he held tightly onto Mikkel, as though afraid of losing him if he let go. He didn't notice Sam and Kiyel coming up behind him, or Janice standing beside Mikkel with a happy smile on her face. All he cared about was that his brother had come to be with him, just as he promised he would.

"I knew Jev would really like it if his brother could be here for this," Sam said quietly to Kiyel.

Kiyel had tears in his own eyes, being so overwhelmed with Jev's happiness.

"How in Dahel's name did you manage to arrange for them to be here?" he asked in awe.

"While Jev was still training for the challenge, I asked your mother to make a call to D'lin on Alessi for me and request that Mikkel be sent here as soon as possible. I knew that if Jev wound up losing the challenge his brother would want to be here to say goodbye. But I hoped that Jev would win, and Mikkel would be able to be here to see the two of you get married ... I mean, life-bonded."

"Thank you, Doc. You were right. It's just what Jev needed as well."

Sam nodded as the two brothers finally separated. Both of their cheeks were streaked with tears, but both of them wore equally wide smiles on both their faces.

Their reunion was short lived, however, as Riyad came to collect Jev to get ready, for it was almost time to begin the ceremony. Jev gave one final hug to his brother before following

Riyad out of the library and up to his and Kiyel's room.

Stepping out onto the covered veranda overlooking the gardens roughly an hour later, Jev thought, was like walking straight into a scene from a fairy tale book.

Lining either side of the garden, in neatly arranged semi-circular rows, were magnificent white arches with elegantly designed woven frames. Growing up the structure of the arches were beautiful vine-like plants with brilliant red blooms, that to Jev almost resembled the red roses that had once grown in his father's garden, only more beautiful.

Within the arches were rows upon rows of similarly white chairs, crafted with care and love and as ornate as the arches. The rows of chairs were broken in the middle, forming a long aisle which ran from the edge of the veranda to the far end where the most magnificent-looking gazebo Jev had ever seen stood. It also was white with elegantly designed woven frame, but Jev could see also thin strands of gold that weaved in and out of the structure like vines. The gazebo reflected the sunlight shining behind it, bathing the whole garden in a stunning display of gold and silver.

Standing under the gazebo, dressed in an elegant white ceremonial robe, stood the Priestess of Dahel, and to her right, dressed splendidly in a cream-coloured, flowing gown, with brilliant gold embroidery and a splash of purple, was Kiyel. Under the gown he wore a tunic of light purple, the colour of the Telepath Guild.

Jev's heart was struck still by the sight of his, having never before seen anything so beautiful in all his life. With a proud grin, and guided by an equally proud Sam, who held his hand, he slowly started down the wide stairs of the veranda, down the aisle and past the many assembled guests who watched him, all the while unable to take his eyes off his Enassi.

Just before Jev and Sam reached the gazebo, Kiyel's father, who was sitting at the front with Lheiza, and where Khelan, Aiden, Mikkel and Janice sat, unexpectedly rose from his seat and stood in Jev's path, forcing him and Sam to come to an abrupt, and confused, halt. Jev frowned, uncertain as to what Sahl was doing.

Sahl offered him a warm smile as he stood before him. Jev was surprised to see that, for the first time, Sahl was offering him a fatherly one. Tears welled up in his eyes when he saw this, for it was the smile he expected his father would have been giving him had he been here to see him become Kiyel's lifemate.

"Jev, I know how saddened you are that your father is not here to see this day," Sahl said, his tone both solemn and comforting. "I know that he would have been proud of you, and would have wanted to be a part of this. I am not your father, but in the honour of his memory, I ask that you allow me to walk with you also, just as your father would if he was here."

Sahl's offer caught Jev completely off guard for he had not expected this from him. As tears of immense joy and gratitude rolled down his cheeks, he threw himself into Sahl's arms, feeling for the first time in such a long while, the embrace of a father.

Eventually they separated, and smiling at Sahl, Jev allowed him to take a hold of his other hand and to lead him to gazebo until they at last were standing at a smiling Kiyel's side.

In a clear, loud voice, so as to be heard by everyone assembled, the priestess began.

"Welcome, friends, as we gather on this blessed evening to celebrate the union of Jev Bjorn, son of Lars, and Kiyel Lhevic, son of Sahl. Dahel, we ask you to bless this couple, their love, and their joining as lifemates as long as they shall live in love together. May they each enjoy a healthy life filled with joy, love, stability and fertility."

With a warm smile, she lowered her gaze to Jev and Kiyel.

"Jev and Kiyel, as you stand before us today to join together as life-mates, may you be blessed with communication, intellectual growth, and wisdom. May you be blessed with harmony, vitality, creativity, and passion. May you be blessed with friendship, intuition, caring, understanding, and love. And may you be blessed with tenderness, happiness, compassion, and sensuality."

Jev and Kiyel looked fondly at each other. The love they felt for each other shone brightly in their eyes.

"Who has the honor of presenting these two to become lifemates?" the Priestess asked.

"I do," Sam and Sahl answered in unison.

She nodded, and Sahl placed Jev's hand in Kiyel's, smiling at them both as he held their hands together for a lingering moment, before retreating back to his seat beside Lheiza, and accompanied by Sam.

"In all the eons, the long slow climb of evolution has no greater culmination than the union of two people in love," the priestess continued. "From the time the first amoeba fissioned into two, there has been the possibility of companionship—and the possibility of loneliness. From the time sexual reproduction was possible, love has been a quickening. In Caitarans, as self-aware beings, sexuality provided a way that our love can conjoin the bodies, hearts, minds and souls of those who love. Sadly, we have largely turned away from that harmony. Where there once was peace, now stands conflict, loneliness and desolation, and our world mourns. So when there are those of us who love enough to make a commitment such as this one this evening between Jev and Kiyel, the very stars rejoice at the rediscovery of love, joy and bounty.

"Love has its seasons the same as does our world. In the spring of love is the discovery of each other, the getting to know the mind and heart of the other. In the summer of love comes the strength, the commitment to each other, the most active part of life, the sharing of joys and sorrows and the learning to be Caitarans who are each complete and whole but who can merge with the other. In the fall of love is the contentment of love that knows the other completely. Passion remains, and ease of companionship. In the winter of love, there is parting and sorrow. Love remains, however, ready for renewal in the spring as life and love begin anew.

"Now is the time of summer. Jev and Kiyel have gathered here this evening before Dahel and their friends and family to make a statement of their commitment to each other, to their love."

She had them face one another, still holding hands.

"Jev and Kiyel, do you now commit to each other to love, honour, respect each other, to communicate with each other, to look to your own emotional health so that you can relate in a healthy way, and provide a healthy home for your children; to be a support and comfort for your partner in times of sickness and health, as long as your love shall last?"

"I do," Jev and Kiyel said in unison.

"Then recite the vows you have written for each other," she nodded.

Looking at Jev, the love he felt for him shining brightly in his eyes, Kiyel recited the vows he had prepared.

"I, Kiyel Lhevic, son of Sahl, take you Jev, to be my lifemate, best friend, partner and lover. I will honour and respect our bond and love you more each day. I will trust you, laugh with you and share your tears with you. Always by your side in good times and bad, regardless of challenges we may meet. I give you my heart, my love, my hand in all our days together. In the presence of Dahel and our families and friends I promise to be a loving and faithful partner for as long as we both shall live."

Tears stung Jev's eyes as Kiyel finished his vows. Not only had the words Kiyel spoke affected him, filling him with so much joy and love, but also the love behind those words. A love that at that moment seemed the strongest he had ever felt.

"I, Jev Bjorn, son of Lars, take you Kiyel, to be my lover and my friend, the father of my children and my beloved partner in life. During times of plenty and times of want, times of sickness and times of health, I will be by your side. When we are blessed with sorrow as with joy, we will face and share those experiences together. I vow to respect and cherish you. I will care for you and protect you. I will comfort and encourage you. I will be to you faithful and always true for all eternity to come."

With their vows said, the priestess then beckoned them to follow her to a table with a red cloth draped over it and three white candles, each held in identically ornate, gold holders.

"These two candles are yourselves, as whole and complete individuals," she said, indicating the two outermost candles. "Each of you please light one."

She waited while Jev, and then Kiyel, using the two wood lighting sticks that rested beside another, shorter burning candle, lit the two candles as asked.

"Now together, light the third candle, but do not extinguish the first two. For as lifemates, you do not lose your individual selves; you add something new, a relationship, and the capacity to merge into one another without losing sight of your own self."

When they had done as instructed, she smiled at both of them.

"We Caitarans are born of stardust and deepest oceans, of erupting volcanoes and the bones of Caitar. In celebrating love you celebrate a heritage of all these things, and of the love of all our people from the dawn of time. In making a commitment to loving each other, you share that which is best in us and give a moment of light to the world. I am pleased, then, to now pronounce you lifemates! May you each and together be blessed with health, happiness, harmony, and love."

ABOUT THE AUTHOR

Jason Finigan was born in Bracebridge, Ontario in 1973 and was raised in Burlington, Ontario by his adoptive parents. At the age of seventeen, he graduated from Lord Elgin High School. As an avid science-fiction fan growing up, Jason immersed himself fully in the genre, watching series such as Doctor Who and Star Trek on TV as often as he could, as well as collecting and reading as many science-fiction novels as he could get his hands on—many of which he still has to this day. He was in fact so fascinated with the genre that he began writing his own science-fiction short stories while in elementary school, many of which earned him high praise from his teachers. In March of 2007, Jason began work on his first science-fiction novel, Destiny's Edge. He currently lives in Hamilton, Ontario

www.ingramcontent.com/pod-product-compliance
Lightning Source LLC
Chambersburg PA
CBHW031104030726
47496CB00002BA/377